FALL *of* POPPIES

FALL *of* POPPIES

STORIES OF LOVE AND
THE GREAT WAR

JESSICA BROCKMOLE ✦ HAZEL GAYNOR
EVANGELINE HOLLAND ✦ MARCI JEFFERSON
KATE KERRIGAN ✦ JENNIFER ROBSON
HEATHER WEBB ✦ BEATRIZ WILLIAMS
LAUREN WILLIG

wm

WILLIAM MORROW
An Imprint of HarperCollinsPublishers

FALL OF POPPIES. Individual pieces copyright © by their respective author as noted on page 358, which constitutes a continuation of this copyright notice. All rights reserved. Printed in the United States of America. No part of this book may be used or reproduced in any manner whatsoever without written permission except in the case of brief quotations embodied in critical articles and reviews. For information address HarperCollins Publishers, 195 Broadway, New York, NY 10007.

HarperCollins books may be purchased for educational, business, or sales promotional use. For information, please e-mail the Special Markets Department at SPSales@harpercollins.com.

FIRST EDITION

Designed by Diahann Sturge

Library of Congress Cataloging-in-Publication Data has been applied for.

ISBN 978-0-06-241854-8

16 17 18 19 20   OV/RRD   10 9 8 7 6 5 4 3 2 1

Contents

FALL *of* POPPIES

The Daughter of Belgium

Marci Jefferson

November 7, 1918
Brussels, Belgium

SISTER WILKINS CAUGHT MY EYE FROM ACROSS THE NURSE'S
parlor of Institut Cavell. The day I'd been dreading had arrived.
The British nurse had lost much during this war, though she knew
better than anyone that I'd lost more. She also knew my secret,
and that I'd do anything to protect it.

"You're leaving," I said.

"The new hospital is finally finished." Sister Wilkins spoke in
French, like all the nurses here. "If I don't move the nurses and
patients in soon, the governor general will claim it for German
wounded. I can't let them have what Matron Cavell worked so
hard to build."

Matron Cavell had designed the new hospital, then watched
construction stall when the Germans marched into Belgium on
their way to conquer the world. The German occupation had

changed everything here in Brussels. Those who dared defy them, as Matron Cavell had done, paid with their lives.

I tried not to panic. "She wouldn't want me turned out on the street. She saved my life."

Memories flooded unbidden, and I saw the group of drunken soldiers coming to claim my family's tea shop as their new lodgings that first year of the war. The shop was also our home, so Papa tried to defend it. Fists flew, rendering Papa and Maman unconscious. That's when the Germans held me down. They violated me, then used liquor from their flasks to light the shop on fire before fleeing. It took neighbors an hour to put it out.

Maman's head wounds put her into a sleep from which she never woke. Her slow death weakened Papa. That, and the knowledge of what the Germans had done to *me*, eventually killed *him*. I'd tried to hide my disgrace, to ignore the pain between my legs. I never cried in front of him, but the walls between our upstairs bedrooms were damaged. For a month I ran back and forth from Matron Cavell's clinic for medical supplies and advice on how to care for Papa. He often experienced pains in his chest. One day, they simply overtook him.

That was the day I realized I'd missed my monthly bleeding. It was the day I used Papa's penknife to open my wrists.

Now, three years later, safe at the clinic, Sister Wilkins put her hands on my shoulders. "Is that what you think, Amélie? That I'd turn you out on the street after all you've done to help this clinic?"

My tension eased a little. "No amount of dishwashing and cooking can repay you for housing me and my—"

She put a finger over my lips. "I must prepare for tomorrow's move, so listen to my proposal." She trailed from the parlor and started upstairs, crisp skirts and white nurse's apron rustling. "There is one case whose condition is so delicate we must leave him behind."

I followed her, stunned. "You're leaving a *case*? An actual medical patient?"

She looked over her shoulder. "Give yourself some credit. You've heard all of my nursing lectures. If you'd had time to practice your knowledge on the wards, you'd be a nurse by now."

I gasped. "You intend me to *nurse* this case?"

For years I'd been building the courage to step outside of the protective clinic, hoping Sister Wilkins would let me move to the new hospital with her.

Matron Cavell had found me that terrible day. She'd stitched my wrists and held me while I cried. My belly swelled, and Matron Cavell tried to convince me a strong woman could transform shame to hope. She'd put a hand on my belly and repeated, "Hope." I'd refused to believe her. Instead I'd walked to the tea shop, burned a stack of articles I'd drafted in the fireplace, then nailed boards over every window and door. I'd sealed memories and one valuable treasure inside. It was the last time I'd shown myself in public.

I'd become part of the clinic, helping Matron Cavell forge documents and cook for the fugitive Allied soldiers, her fellow Englishmen, whom she covertly helped escape to neutral Holland. I'd hidden in the attic when German police came to arrest Matron Cavell for those treasons. Sister Wilkins had allowed me to remain living there, belly shielded from the war outside. There my daughter was born. And there my daughter stayed, for the possibility of encountering the soldiers from the shop terrified me. If they discovered my daughter—well—I would kill anyone who tried to touch her.

Sister Wilkins reached the third floor. "I know why you never leave this clinic, and I don't blame you. With us gone, little Hope will have room to roam."

Matron Cavell would've been pleased I'd named my daughter Hope. I washed dishes and laundry in the early mornings before Hope woke, and cooked or listened to nursing lectures in the classrooms during naps. I carried her out to the walled-in garden behind the clinic every morning in good weather; otherwise we remained on the deserted attic floor, out of the way. Now that Hope was nearing her third birthday, she could use more space.

"You'll be safe here. Besides," Sister Wilkins went on, "this case requires little nursing care."

Most of our cases were ill Belgians. Germans only brought their wounded when there were no other open hospital beds in Brussels. My one remaining underground source informed me Matron Cavell's execution had caused international uproar. Under Allied pressure, the German governor general not only cracked down on soldiers seizing houses, he kept his men away from Institut Cavell.

"Who is this case?" I asked.

Wilkins pointed to a door. "A gunshot victim transported here months ago by his commander. If he overheard talk of war, he shook with tremors. They call it shell shock. He seems better now, sitting and staring most of the time."

"So," I said, concealing my fear, "he is a German soldier?"

"Yes, but the commander who brought him was arrested by the governor general. I believe they've forgotten about this man."

I turned for the attic. "No. I will return to my tea shop."

She grabbed my arm. "I didn't want to tell you, but a group of Germans have staked out the tea shop."

Sister Wilkins had been Matron Cavell's right hand, aware of her treasonous activity, even guiding some Allied soldiers to Holland herself. Like me, she was still in contact with hidden members of the underground network.

"The ones who killed my mother?"

"I only know they watch it."

I would recognize them. The whole thing was my fault for wearing prohibited Belgian tricolors and circulating copies of *La Libre Belgique*. The patriotic newssheet protested the German occupation. The governor general had banned it, and I'd done more than just circulate copies. The soldiers had followed me to the tea shop, threatening to arrest me for treason against the occupying government. One soldier in particular with a cigarette and a strong, square jaw kept eyeing the painting by Anthony van Dyck displayed behind our counter. When Papa asked him to leave, he'd blown smoke in my face. He and his comrades returned a week later. That night was a blur of fists, smoke, and a torrent of shameful tears. I didn't see which man raped me because of the blindfold. Now I imagined my rapist in every German face.

"Sister, don't ask me to care for a German."

Wilkins wore the neutral expression Matron Cavell had always worn; never upset or excited, always calm. "A nurse cares for a person, not a nationality."

"I am no nurse."

"You have what it takes. You embraced an infant that some women in your situation would have abandoned."

"My daughter's origins are not her fault."

She tipped her head toward the door. "This man's nationality was not his choice. He followed orders, and now he cannot even speak. All I'm asking you to do is ensure he doesn't starve."

"If that's all he needs, why not take him with you?"

She hesitated. "When we move to the hospital, the Germans will demand an account of patients. This man's commander told me to get him well enough to *defend his actions*. Some Germans realize this war can't go on. They're angry. There are riots in Berlin, mutinies in Kiel, and surrenders on the Western Front."

"You suspect this German is a traitor against his own country?"

"If so, he should stay here where he won't be discovered."

I fought a wave of nausea. "You want me to *protect* him?"

"Germans avoid this place, so *you* will be protected, too."

From my attic window, I'd watched German patrols thin as they shipped available men to the Western Front. If I could just survive until the Germans were beaten, I might return to my shop, sell the valuable van Dyck painting that had passed through my mother's French family for generations, and use the money to build a new life.

Sister Wilkins handed me a stack of papers, the nursing reports for the shell shock case. "The Allies are pushing through the Western Front. Germany is about to lose. They will retaliate by seizing goods as they retreat. Brussels could become more dangerous."

It occurred to me that the soldier with the strong jaw might have realized he'd been studying the portrait of an English royal by van Dyck behind our shop counter. I hoped he wasn't one of the men staking out the tea shop now. If he stole that painting, Hope and I had no future.

I took the nursing reports reluctantly and headed toward the attic.

Sister Wilkins's tone betrayed a hint of relief. "You'll stay away from the shop? You'll care for this man?"

I called over my shoulder. "I'll never care a thing for him. But I'll see to it he doesn't starve."

November 8, 1918

THE NEXT DAY I DID SOMETHING I'D NOT DONE IN THREE YEARS. I stepped out of the clinic's front door. Loading baskets and barrels onto a stream of carts and wagons, and supporting patients as they limped into ambulances, I helped Sister Wilkins and other nurses empty the clinic. "There are rations in the larder," Wilkins said as she embraced me. "Remember your promises."

I didn't bother pointing out that I'd made no promises, simply waved as they departed. Then I hurried back inside.

Hope looked up from her bench by the front window.

"Come down to the kitchen," I said, gesturing to her. "I'll show you how to make turnip soup."

She closed her little hand around one of my fingers, like a tiny grip on my heart. "Tou-nips?" she asked, blue eyes wide.

I nodded. "If you're good, we'll fry an apple and sprinkle it with cinnamon."

"Cin-on-am-an?"

I laughed, scooping her up and carrying her down the basement steps to the kitchen. We made a pleasant mess cooking our meager feast, and I put her to bed with a smudge of rye flour still on the tip of her nose.

After Hope fell asleep, I returned to the kitchen. I lined a tray with a white napkin and ladled the last of our soup into a bowl. I added half an apple and a flagon of water, then carried the tray upstairs. Outside the soldier's door, I paused.

His nursing reports had revealed little. Lars Ludwig's episodes of rocking and trembling had abated in his months at the clinic. He'd arrived with a healing gunshot wound to the right shoulder that no longer required dressing changes. He ate breakfast and supper. He used the chamber pot regularly. Nurses walked him to the water closet at the end of the hall twice weekly; there he bathed himself. Otherwise he sat by the window or slept. He never left a mess. He never uttered a word.

Now he was in my care and, not only did I *not* care about his well-being, I hated him. I pushed open the door. Sitting by the window with his back to me, he didn't stir. When I set the tray on the table beside him, he didn't budge. I moved to jot the contents of his supper on the report hanging from the bedstead, but it contained no papers. So I grabbed the chamber pot. I'd emptied plenty in my years at the clinic, a task made simpler by modern plumbing at the end of the hall. When I returned with the pot clean and sparkling, he still hadn't moved. "I wish all Germans were so little trouble as you."

He said nothing, and I regretted my harsh tone. I left, pulling the door closed behind me.

I sped downstairs and out to the back garden as the moon rose above the roofline. Beyond the far wall, Marie waited for me. I stepped upon a stack of bricks and reached across, handing her the other half of the apple I'd served to my German. "Is it true German sailors mutinied in Kiel?"

Marie took a bite of the precious apple, so rare in these times of scarcity and confiscation. "Better," she said with her mouth full. "Sailors from Kiel traveled throughout Germany spreading outright revolution." Marie had assisted Matron Cavell by sharing updates she received from her son, a lawyer working for our Belgian King Albert's advisors beyond the Western Front. She now shared information with me, and I shared Red Cross food rations. "They're taking over military and civil offices, forcing aristocratic leaders of German states to abdicate. Amélie, it's spreading all the way to Munich!"

My breath caught. "The Kaiser will be forced to abdicate! The war will be over."

"I shudder at the thought of all those German companies marching through Brussels again, this time full of the bitterness of defeat. Lock yourself in."

Hope and I could hide in the attic with rations for days. If I placed rations in my German's room, he could make out for himself.

It was as if thinking of him made me sense him. I glanced at his window. A face quickly backed into shadow. His window was open!

"I'll see you tomorrow night," I whispered to Marie. I hastened inside, vowing to be more careful during our next conversation. My German might be silent, but he apparently had no trouble *listening*.

November 9, 1918

THE NEXT MORNING HOPE WATCHED ME STOKE COALS IN THE range then boil oats for our breakfast. I gave her my ration of ham. As I kneaded rye dough into *boules* and put them in *bannetons* to rise, she wrapped herself in an apron and banged pots with a spoon. Watching her made me wish for the old days when sugar and eggs and white flour were available. I longed to grill up a waffle and smother it in chocolate and serve it to her with a glass of fresh milk.

Soon.

I'd tossed and turned all night wondering about the end of the war. Would the Germans take us as prisoners as they retreated from the Western Front? Or would they merely take everything we had left? I'd made the decision to prepare. Regardless of Sister Wilkins's warnings, I would make a trip to the tea shop.

Out in the garden, I gave Hope her favorite basket of blocks to sort and stack while I took my German his breakfast.

He'd made his bed. He sat in his chair wearing the same long nightshirt. I placed a tray of oats and ham on the table and picked up the remnants of his supper, empty flagon and bowl rattling against the tray. Then I noticed a pair of boots between his bed and the window. Not the grubby marching boots of an average soldier; these shone as if just polished. I flung open his cabinet. A pair of standard German gray trousers hung from a peg, laundered but threadbare. The matching jacket had permanent bloodstains around bullet holes in one shoulder. No other boots. *The shiny ones must be his.*

I turned to find him watching me. I wanted to upbraid him

for eavesdropping the night before. But there was no malice in his stare. His features had a softness that made him look almost kind. I reminded myself to avoid a harsh tone. *What would Sister Wilkins say?* "Do you need anything?"

He stared without answering. There was no confusion, no trace of shell shock as he studied me. I knew in my bones he had regained his ability to speak.

Why wouldn't he?

I pulled a chunk of lye soap from my pocket and a linen towel from the waistband of my apron and set both on the bed. "Today is bath day, but you likely know that, don't you?" Still no response. "You're fully recovered, aren't you?" I ignored his chamber pot and walked out saying, "I'll bring supper at the usual time." I closed the door too firmly.

HOPE TOOK HER MORNING NAP, AND I MEASURED RATIONS. I left enough in the larder for one person for a week. I sealed rye flour in tins, wrapped root vegetables in baskets, and gathered apples and pears in a sack and hauled them upstairs.

My attic level extended the length of the townhouse, but it was inhabitable only in the middle, where the roof peaked. The wall with the stairway overlooked the alley with a little window. The opposite wall housed an armoire and the bed I shared with Hope. Matron Cavell had covered the walls and ceiling in mismatched scrap panels, not only for insulation, but to distract from one panel, on the other side of the armoire.

I pushed it. The secret door opened with a gentle creak. A hidden attic extended over the top floors of the clinic's other three townhouses. I ducked to enter.

During all those unannounced German inspections leading to Matron Cavell's arrest, they'd disregarded my attic level after they saw the sparse furnishings. Tearing downstairs through the other interconnected townhouses of the clinic, they'd never thought to look for more attics. Matron Cavell had hidden Allied soldiers here, a hundred at a time. Her hoard of counterfeit documents was still concealed under the floorboards. Soon I would hide here with Hope.

I stowed food rations in trunks. I lugged in cans of lamp oil, a down mattress, linens, chamber pots, coal, a cook pot, and a brazier. As I set a barrel of water down heavily, my daughter woke.

"Maman!" She toddled from the bed into the secret attic. I'd never shown it to her, and now she claimed it as her own. She ran up and down the long room, then made a game of sweeping dust into little piles.

I felt too knotted up with tension to play. Even if the Germans didn't find us or my painting, even if I rebuilt the tea shop and managed to abide with the violent memories within, customers would scoff at a single mother to a half-breed war child. I wouldn't expose Hope to derision. We needed to leave Brussels.

To fund such a move I must retrieve the van Dyck from its hiding place at the tea shop. I could not risk leaving it there with troops of looting Germans on the way.

Maman had told me the painting's history. Centuries earlier, the English king Charles II fell in love with our ancestor and gave her the painting along with other precious gifts. During the next reign, she gave it to her sister, a Jacobite fleeing to France, with instructions to sell it if ever faced with hunger. Successive generations passed it to their daughters with the same instructions: *sell it if ever faced with hunger.*

Maman would want me to sell it now. As soon as King Albert returned with ministers and statesmen who might have money, I would. The painting would fetch enough to move us to Holland, England, or America. I could become a nurse. We could start fresh.

"Come, Hope." I coaxed her away from her dust piles. "Let's go down to the kitchen to bake for the days to come."

"An sup-per?" she asked.

"Tonight we'll use one carrot to make a soup for three."

THAT EVENING I TOOK RYE BREAD AND A BOWL OF WATERY carrot soup to my German and traded it for his empty breakfast tray. As usual he sat by the window, but I whiffed a trace of lye soap on him. I checked the chamber pot. He'd cleaned it himself! *He has indeed recovered.* I glanced at the empty report board. *I must look around for his nursing reports to document his intake.*

"I will bring a clean gown and linens tomorrow and do laundry in the afternoon," I said. *If my morning goes according to plan.*

He didn't respond.

"Go to bed now," I said, uneasily. "Get away from that window."

He turned. His gaze, ever silent, betrayed no emotion.

It unnerved me. "I don't want you listening to my conversations. My business isn't yours. So go to bed."

I closed the door too firm again. *How can I become a nurse if I allow this one case to upset me?* My hands shook so badly, the bowl and flagon rattled on the tray.

OUTSIDE I GLANCED UP AT MY GERMAN'S WINDOW BEFORE climbing the bricks to greet Marie. His window was closed. No shadowed face peered down. I turned to my friend and handed her a loaf of rye bread.

Normally she would eat on the spot. Instead she grabbed my wrist. "The Social Democratic Party in Germany demanded the Kaiser's abdication. They will declare Germany a republic. A delegation is on the way to sign an armistice!"

"Already?" My thoughts raced to what I must do.

"Keep this bread for your daughter and hide. The Germans will be in retreat any moment."

I pressed the bread into her hands. "Do something for me. Keep an eye on the clinic from your house in the morning. If you do not see a white kerchief hanging from my attic window in the alley at ten thirty, go in and take care of my daughter. She'll be waking from a nap."

Marie seemed confused, clinging to the bread. "But—you never go out."

"There is something I must do. I don't want her to be frightened if I'm detained." I didn't share all the reasons I was asking this of her. Her family had money and generous hearts. She knew our story, that we had no living family. If the worst happened to me tomorrow, Marie would care for Hope as her own.

She frowned. "Even some Germans here in Brussels are joining the revolution. There will be trouble."

In that moment I cursed myself for hiding the van Dyck in the tea shop all those years ago. I cursed the paralyzing fear that kept me from going to retrieve it sooner. What if it had already been looted? I looked down, feeling defeated.

Then, beside the stack of bricks I stood upon, I spotted a white napkin from the clinic's kitchen. *How did that get here?*

"Amélie, are you unwell?"

I glanced up to my German's dark window. Had he come outside without my knowledge? Suddenly I remembered the trays I'd retrieved from his rooms; the dishes had rattled because the napkins had disappeared! I grabbed the napkin and sniffed—a faint trace of ham. Either my German had ventured beyond the water closet at the end of his hall, or he'd been giving food to someone who used my bricks to get in this garden. Chills ran down my spine.

Hope.

I ran.

"Amélie!" called Marie.

"Look for my kerchief tomorrow!" I called, rushing inside. I mounted the steps two at a time up the four flights of stairs to the attic and didn't draw breath until I saw her.

Safe, there she slept, just as I'd left her.

I panted, seething, wondering what my German was up to. I raced down to his room and threw open the door.

In the dim light filtering through the curtain, I saw him sit up in bed. I'd startled him. Good.

I hid the napkin in my apron pocket. "Stay away from me, do you hear?"

No response.

"Stay away from my daughter."

Sheets rustled, but he didn't speak.

In the years since my attempted suicide, I'd formed the habit of keeping my father's penknife with me always. I reached into my apron pocket now and felt its cool heft. "Cross me, and I'll kill you." I backed out, closing the door, shaking with rage.

I did not sleep that night.

November 10, 1918

BY MORNING I'D DISCOVERED RAGE WAS THE PERFECT ANTI-dote to fear.

At the start of this war, Germany swept into Belgium and stripped her of dignity. Belgium had been broken, but not defeated. Deep within still stirred the will to survive, and a hope for better days.

I'd been brave once, before I started cowering in this clinic. For the first time, Hope was under real threat. The mist of fear had evaporated. I was ready to fight again.

I took the German a tray of porridge. He didn't speak and, this time, I didn't speak to him. I dumped fresh linen on his bed and slammed his door.

In the hallway, I leaned against the wall, heart thudding. Who was I kidding, thinking I could become a nurse? I would support Hope another way. At one time I'd written articles. Dangerously truthful articles that had brought German wrath upon my family. I didn't have what it took to be a nurse, but could I find the courage to write again?

Down in the garden, Hope convinced me to play hide-and-seek until it was time to go in. Then, instead of carrying her to the attic where I had no view, we went to a back room. She quietly dressed her dollies in tiny nurse's uniforms while I watched the garden from a window.

He came over the wall.

He used my stack of bricks to ease himself to the ground. He crept to the clinic and climbed up the drainpipe to the German's window.

I recognized him but could not believe my eyes. A middle-aged Belgian with a hollow scar where one eye should be, Charles Vanderlinden hadn't qualified to join our army. He'd come to work for Matron Cavell's underground network. He'd been in love with her, and she'd called him Vander. He'd guided countless soldiers to Holland for her, retrieved the most impossible supplies, doing any dangerous thing she ever asked, all in the name of patriotism. After the Germans shot her, he came to the clinic vowing revenge against the Germans and liberty for Belgium. He'd buried his face in my lap beside my pregnant belly and cried more from his one good eye than I'd ever cried from two. I hadn't seen him since.

Now Vander spoke to my German shell shock case, words too muffled to make out through the window. Moments later he shimmied down holding a bundled napkin. He ran back to the stack of bricks chewing a mouthful of rye bread and bounded over the wall.

Sister Wilkins had suspected my German of treason against his homeland. Vander's appearance proved Wilkins was right. Lars Ludwig was in hiding! Whatever Vander was doing for him in exchange for food, it would be for the good of Belgium.

Relief flooded through me. With Vander involved, I had no reason to worry for Hope's safety. I could go to the tea shop as planned. "Hope, I must prepare Mr. Ludwig double rations from now on."

She looked up and yawned.

"But first, I have work to do." I took her up, sang lullabies, and, when her breathing was regular, I crept downstairs.

I opened the front door and glanced both ways. Besides an old woman carrying a basket, the street was deserted.

Taking a deep breath, I stepped out and locked the door behind me. I walked briskly, face down. In one apron pocket I gripped my father's penknife. In the other I gripped the key to the clinic. The tea shop was a few blocks and one military checkpoint away. Hope would sleep only an hour and a half. I quickened my pace.

I reached the intersection. Where the military checkpoint should have been stood an unmanned gun. I paused, glanced around. Where were the military police? Had the German rebellion already taken hold of Brussels?

Confused, I crossed the street and walked faster. As I rounded a corner, I ran smack into a German officer.

He put one hand on the gun in his holster. "Ach!" he exclaimed.

I held out my hands in an apologetic gesture. "I'm sorry! Sorry!"

"Go home," he said in German. "You stupid Belgian." He rushed onward.

I ran toward the shop. When I reached it, I hurried past it to the next corner and turned. *Oh no!* The front of the shop was not as I'd left it! One window's boards had been broken and nailed over with extra boards. At some point, someone had gone inside.

I reached the gate to my former neighbor's back garden. They'd deserted Brussels at the start of the war, and their garden looked clear. I went through the gate to the wall of my own garden. I removed a loose brick from atop the wall and propped it on the ground. Gathering my skirts, I stepped on it to give myself enough leverage to scale the wall. We had no gate, and I didn't dare make a display of prying boards from the front of the shop. Would the van Dyck still be inside?

I gazed up. Here every board remained intact—even over my old bedroom. I'd boarded it differently, nailing vertical boards up the sides, and sliding horizontal boards down behind them. I'd done it this way on impulse so I could return and easily slide the boards out to get in. It was the one smart thing I'd done in the aftermath of disaster. Now the pressure to return to Hope drove me.

I darted to the corner of our garden and dug into a pile of leaves. I kicked, tossed, and pushed them until my hands closed on the ladder I'd hidden there. In three years, the leaves had rotted and turned to mold. My hands felt grimy. My heart raced. I dragged the ladder to the wall, propping it under my window. I smiled for the first time that day, put both hands on the ladder, and put my foot on the first rung.

My foot went straight through it.

The rung fell apart into shards of dry-rotted wood. I put my foot on the next rung and tried to step up. That rung shattered. I inspected the third rung carefully. I put my hand around it and squeezed. The wood disintegrated in my hand. Struggling to remain calm, I eased the ladder down. Even missing a few rungs, I might still be able to reach my window. I tested others with my hands, but each gave way. "No," I uttered, fighting tears. I tried to shimmy up the side of the ladder. Rot had ruined it. It bent under my weight until it broke, and I fell to the ground.

I pulled out Papa's penknife and started prying at the boards over a downstairs window. This wood, undamaged by rotting leaves, held secure. I grabbed a rock and pounded the boards. Nothing gave way. I squeezed my fingers through a tiny slit, scraping my cuticles until they bled. I pulled the boards with all my might, but I didn't have the strength. I tugged my fingers free, embedding splinters in my knuckles. *I need a crowbar.*

I would have to go back empty-handed. I cleaned my hands on the underside of my skirt, dried my tears with my apron, and hurried back to the clinic.

But the clinic was not as I'd left it.

An automobile sat parked on the street in front of the clinic, tiny German flags fluttering from the corners of the grille. A clutch of German officers stood at the front door with a handheld battering ram. The door itself gaped open, shattered at the latch. The officers turned to stare as I approached.

I tried to summon the courageous woman I'd once been. *Rage conquers fear.*

I walked past them into the front hall determined to check on Hope. *Please, God, let her still be asleep.* One man stood in the hall, an older German in high-ranking dress with deep frown lines. With a shock, I realized this was no mere officer, this was the German governor general of Brussels.

I decided I should appear surprised but respectful. "Sir, what is the meaning of this?" I asked in broken German.

He turned to me. "Who are you?"

I hid my bloodied cuticles under my apron. "I am the housekeeper here."

"Nurses and patients vacated this building, yes?"

Would he stake claim so close to the end? Force me and my daughter out at such a critical moment? *Not if I can help it.* "They will return. When Brussels flourishes once again."

I might as well have waved victory flags in front of his face.

He gaped as if I'd slapped him. He started barking commands in German, and the officers from the street rushed in. I deciphered "search the rooms" and "find him" in the torrent of orders.

I couldn't let them discover Hope. "No," I cried. "This building operates under the Red Cross. You have no right!"

They ignored me. They pulled pistols from holsters, barging through the lower level, kicking open doors and searching closets. I followed, struggling to keep up with what they were yelling. They divided, each taking different levels and spreading throughout the different townhouses. I followed the governor general upstairs as he made his way to Lars Ludwig's hall.

His door stood open. I rushed past the governor general into the room. Lars wasn't there.

The governor general entered, eyeing the linens on the bed and the empty breakfast tray. "This is a patient's room?"

"Patients moved to the new hospital," I said stripping the sheets from the bed. "I just haven't finished cleaning all the rooms yet." Such blatant lies to this man were grounds for arrest. As I crumpled the sheets into a wad, I spotted the shiny boots. *Lars must be hiding within the building.*

The governor general grunted. Officers tramped through the other rooms, shouting. If they found Lars, they would arrest me for lying. The governor general marched toward the attic stairs.

I followed, trying to distract him. "Sir, why are you here? Tell me what you want. Leave me in peace!"

He ignored me and went up. He would scare poor Hope. *Lord, please don't let them take her!*

Our bed was empty. The hidden attic door was sealed. There was no sign of her. My vision blackened. I gripped the stair rail.

"This is your room?" the governor general asked me.

"Y-yes."

Just then an officer called from downstairs, "There's no one here. But there's ham in the kitchen!"

The governor general pushed past me and went down calling, "Take it. Take whatever food you find."

Dazed, I realized a failure to follow and protest would look suspicious. "You can't! Those are Red Cross rations."

The men gathered in the front hall holding bread, potatoes, and apples. "Watch us take them!" one of them cried. They filed out, snickering, forgetting their battering ram in the front hall. Not bothering to fix the door, they drove off.

I used the battering ram to wedge the door closed, then I ran upstairs. "Hope!" I stopped on every floor crying, "Hope! Lars! Are you here?"

As I reached the attic I heard, "Maman, I here!"

My room was the same, except the secret panel door now stood ajar.

"I here!" She peeked from the secret room with a lollipop in one hand. She held it out. "Loll-lley!"

Behind her, Lars Ludwig appeared.

The last words I'd spoken to him had been "I'll kill you." I put my hand in my apron pocket and gripped Papa's penknife. "Hope, darling, come here to me."

Lars put out his hands. "Don't be angry," he said in perfect French. "I knew you wouldn't want them to find her. I thought this would be the safest place."

Hope didn't move. "Lars loll-lley!"

I addressed him. "You mean it would be safest for *you!*"

"I don't think they'd recognize me, and I destroyed the nursing reports listing my name."

Hope pointed to her lollipop. Colorful and thick, it was the kind that came only from England or America. I hadn't seen one in years. "You speak without a German accent, and you fraternize with a Belgian patriot." I pulled out the penknife and opened it, slowly walking to Hope. I pulled her away.

Lars kept his hands up. "I'm a linguistics expert. I speak several languages with accurate accent variations. English, Irish English, American English, French, Belgian French, Dutch, Russian. The Germans used to send me into other countries to—to blend in and get information."

I couldn't hide my shock. "You're a German spy! Why hide from the governor general? What have you done?"

"I work for a secret branch of the German army that specializes in destabilizing foreign governments. I disguise myself and infiltrate dissatisfied communities to encourage rebellion. But I've switched sides."

"How did you know about this room?"

He shrugged. "A friend of yours named Vander told me about it. He's told me a lot of things."

I thought of the missing nursing reports. "So Lars is your real name?"

He grinned. "Yes, my commander shouldn't have written it down, but he's inexperienced when it comes to espionage."

I frowned.

"Listen," he pleaded. "I'll explain. Just . . . put away the knife."

"Hope," I said, handing her my kerchief, never taking my gaze off Lars. "Help me hang this from the window." I put my knife back in my pocket and said to him, "Fill your hands with food from the attic and walk down to the kitchen in front of me. You better start talking."

Lars sat at the table so I could watch him while I chopped potatoes. Hope sat on the floor, engrossed in her lollipop.

"Is that lollipop from England?" I asked Lars.

"America."

I shot him a skeptical look.

"My commander, the man who brought me here, met Vander and sent him to the clinic to find me. Vander is now my intermediary. He obtained the lollipop through my English connections."

"Why did your commander not come for you himself?"

"Because he is in prison. But let me start at the beginning." He repositioned himself. "I spent most of the war at a desk deciphering British military codes. Until the beginning of last year, when my branch sent me to Russia."

I considered what he'd already told me. "Isn't that about the time Czar Nicholas was overthrown?"

He nodded. "Russians were angry, starving while factions battled each other to form a new government. My branch sent Vladimir Lenin in to seize power, knowing he would be sympathetic with Germany. They sent me to help."

"You were part of the Bolshevik Revolution?"

He shrugged. "Lenin and Trotsky orchestrated that. I infiltrated workhouses, factories, and garrisons speaking out against oppression, garnering support for the revolution. There were strikes, riots, and Lenin won control by the end of the year. I was sent to the Eastern Front."

"Now Russia is ravaged by a civil war."

Lars put his head in his hands. "They killed the Czar and his children in cold blood. Thousands of Russians are dying." His voice broke.

My heart ached, not only for Russia. Guilt was a familiar feeling, and it was palpable in his tone. I tried to redirect him. "What did you do on the Eastern Front?"

"Lenin couldn't end the fighting on the Eastern Front fast enough for Germany. They sent me to incite Russian soldiers to surrender."

I knew from Marie that many Russians *had* surrendered at that time. "And when the peace treaty was signed between Germany and Russia?"

His hands balled into fists. "That is when I learned of my mother's death in Berlin. Officials said she died of old age, but letters from friends say she gave her rations to a sector of orphans. *Starvation* killed my mother. My *father* was shot by the police in a workers' strike." He paused to compose himself.

"Where did you go?" I draped my shawl across a crate for Hope. She curled up on it, rubbing her eyes. It was nearing time for her afternoon nap.

"To our naval station in Kiel to interpret more codes. But I kept thinking of how desperate my parents must have become to resist before they died in Berlin. I decided the deprivations, the slaughter, the futile fighting, all of it must end. So I turned the tables. I started sowing discontent among German sailors."

"In Kiel?" I asked, piecing it together.

"The admiral started to suspect me. But the sailors wouldn't rat me out. He could prove nothing to warrant my arrest, so in March he sent me to fight on the Western Front—a death sentence."

"Those sailors in Kiel started the German revolt that is bringing this war to an end!"

Lars shrugged again. "All revolutions begin with seeds of discord. I told every company of soldiers I met on the Western Front that their lives were worth more than Kaiser Wilhelm's whims. My commander in the trenches even joined my cause. But we lived under constant shelling, day and night, amid unceasing terror and death without a chance to make our move. After the advance to Amiens, the Allies decimated our ranks over three days of bombardment. That's when our efforts took hold. Tens of thousands of my comrades laid down their weapons and surrendered. I was shot. I woke up in the Brussels hospital and couldn't stop shaking and twitching. My commander brought me here to recover. And to hide me from the generals."

"Between the soldiers' mutiny in Kiel and the surrenders at Amiens, they've figured out what you've done."

He gave me a pointed look. "If they find me, they'll execute me for treason, armistice or not. But they'll never catch me. I'm leaving as soon as the revolt takes hold in Brussels."

Before I could question where he'd go and what he meant about Brussels, we heard gunfire outside.

I RAN TO HOPE, COVERING HER BODY WITH MY OWN. SHE RE-mained fast asleep.

"Stay here," said Lars. He crept upstairs, still in his long night shirt and socks. He moved and spoke with such self-possession, I'd forgotten about his undignified apparel. The sounds of men yelling and the distant rumble of cannon blasts filtered down to the base-ment. Lars returned within moments.

He wasn't alone.

Vander followed Lars into the basement kitchen, clutching his hat. "Been a long time, Amélie."

"Still serving the Belgian cause, I see." I couldn't resist smiling.

Lars nodded to me. "It has begun."

"What's happening?" I stood.

Vander peeked at Hope, then spoke softly. "The Kaiser ab-dicated. Much of the German military police in Brussels joined the revolt this morning. Officials throughout the city are ignoring commands. But a strong force of loyalists are tracking down and killing revolutionaries. It's anarchy in the streets." He sounded de-lighted. His one eye sparkled.

"And the garrison?" Lars asked.

Vander turned to him. "The guards your commander targeted did as you predicted. They mutinied against their officers. Allied prisoners are being set free as we speak."

"Lars." I suddenly understood. "You and your commander have continued to push a revolution all this time!" The depth of his trea-sonous efforts awed me, and my respect for Vander soared.

Lars looked relieved. "The city's stronghold belongs to the revo-lutionaries. The German delegation will have no choice but to sign the armistice tomorrow."

Vander reached for the stair rail. "Our plans are all in order," he said firmly to Lars. Then he glanced at me. "As soon as they sign that armistice, King Albert and what's left of our army will return from the coast hot on the Germans' heels. Until he arrives, Brussels will be dangerous. Take care of yourself and the little one." He rushed upstairs.

I felt torn between his warning and the broken boards over the tea shop window. *I must take Hope to Marie's and go get that painting!* "If you'll excuse me, I must tend to some personal matters before it's too late." I moved to wake Hope.

Lars grasped my arm. "Listen to what's happening up there." The air still shook with occasional gunfire and shouts. "The situation in the city has changed. You cannot leave."

"I appreciate the work you've done to stop this war and set Belgium free, but I must retrieve my belongings from my old home before the Germans start raiding or I'll have no means to support my daughter."

"You cannot go out."

"You don't understand."

He leaned closer. "Don't I? You wear your tension in the way you move. Hatred and pain are in your voice when you talk to your neighbor in the evenings about what you've lost."

My face flamed with both shame and anger. "You know nothing about me."

"I know you were once a fighter and now you hide. I know how you think because I've read the articles you wrote in old copies of *La Libre Belgique*."

I gasped. So few knew I'd been writing articles for *La Libre*

Belgique. But those soldiers had come to the tea shop that night because they'd figured it out. I carried that guilt in my soul.

"You've forgotten your own strength, mired yourself in your own remorse, and now you're letting anger cloud your judgment. I know how it feels to lose those you love. I don't intend to let your little girl lose her mother this night. You will wait until the early morning hours."

I shook free from his grasp, reeling more than I let him see.

Hope stirred, and I went to her. "Hello, sleepyhead."

"Maman, bake time?"

I forced myself to smile. "Yes it is. Help me mix the dough, then you can knead it."

She helped me measure the ingredients Lars had carried down earlier, and I was grateful for the distraction. Lars returned to the table, a quiet force, a silent conviction.

At last I broke the silence. "What will you do now?"

He studied his hands as he spoke. "People think the world simply went mad and went to war. But world leaders were grasping up territory, building empires and battleships, and daring other kingdoms to check their power for years. War hasn't solved the world's problems. Germany will retreat and pretend they are heroes for protecting the fatherland. They have been stopped, not beaten. There will be another war. Next time, I won't be on Germany's side."

I watched Hope attempt to knead dough. "Your knowledge goes deeper than what is reported in smuggled newspapers. You have contacts willing to exchange state secrets and share American lollipops."

He nodded. "Vander obtained a German officer's uniform for me to use in my escape. When the armistice begins, I make for Holland. I only lack the proper documents to show at German checkpoints. Once peace is secured, I'll go to my contacts in England or America."

"To stop the next war?"

"If possible."

Hope dumped misshapen dough into a *banneton*, and I realized I admired Lars. Like him, I'd believed in freedom and justice and moved in subversive circles and risked everything for liberty. The Germans had broken me because of it. *Broken, but not defeated.* "It will not be easy," I said.

"In one of your articles you wrote, 'The right thing to do is never easy.'" He chuckled. "Your articles have been an inspiration while I've been closed up in this clinic."

I blushed. Then I felt a strange shyness and turned away. Evening approached, and I needed to meet Marie at the wall to secure her assistance for the early morning hours. "Come, Hope, let's set this aside to rise and go fetch a pear upstairs for your dinner. Soon you shall have a bath and go to bed."

"You should both sleep in the secret room come nightfall," said Lars, standing as we climbed the stairs.

"We will," I said softly. I paused to look down. "And . . . thank you."

He nodded, and I ushered Hope to the secret room.

AT DUSK, I TOOK A PEAR TO THE GARDEN WALL.

Marie ignored it. "It is nearly over!" she cried. "But it isn't safe yet. Germans lurk on every street corner aiming to kill each other."

"Have you ever noticed a one-eyed man sneaking over our wall?"

"Who, Vander? Oh, he's always about. He shares news and keeps a fierce watch over you."

All this time, and I'd been too bogged down by my own guilt and fear to notice. "I need your help."

Marie looked worried. "I saw your kerchief in the window and assumed all was well."

"There's something I must do. Will you come over the wall tomorrow morning an hour before dawn to sit with Hope?"

"I thought you took care of everything today," she said, dismayed.

"Please," I begged. "I'll give you a day's rations."

"I'll do it for free, but it isn't safe for you."

"It will be safer in the early morning hours. Will you promise?"

She agreed and we said farewell. On my way back into the clinic, I spotted Lars looking down. I stopped at the garden shed long enough to find a crowbar and pluck a few withered flowers from the neglected window box. Then I hurried in, for the night would be brief.

November 11, 1918
Armistice Day

THE NOISE OUTDOORS QUIETED DURING THE NIGHT, AND I woke long before dawn to study my daughter, wondering if all children slept so peacefully. Perhaps she slept well because I made her feel secure. I would continue doing so for as long as I had breath.

I opened the door to the secret room and lifted the floorboards. I grabbed the box containing Matron Cavell's supplies. Lightly kissing my daughter's curls, I went down to Lars Ludwig's room.

He sat at the table with a lit oil lamp and papers before him. He smiled.

"I brought you these." I set the box on the table and slid it toward him.

He studied the scars on my wrists without a touch of surprise in his expression, only concern. With a gentle finger, he traced the raised white lines, then he held my hands.

Lars knew things about me that I had concealed even from myself. He'd reminded me of my own strength. I wanted nothing more than to let him continue caressing my hands.

Instead, I hid them under my apron. "The box contains hazy identification photographs and stamps and documents with official watermarks. They belonged to a woman who was like us; she fought for what she believed in. You might find what you need in here."

He stood. "Thank you, truly."

I nodded. "My neighbor is coming to watch Hope while I take care of something. I imagine you'll be gone by the time I return." *I must show him how he's touched my heart.* "I wanted to say . . . that is . . . do keep fighting. Be our battles large or small, we must never give up on what is just."

"You have my word," he said tenderly.

I rushed downstairs, and I let a sleepy-looking Marie in the back door.

I CONCEALED MY CROWBAR UNDER MY APRON AND RAN, AWK-wardly, toward the tea shop. At the military checkpoint, a clutch of uniformed Germans stood around the gun. Were they revolutionaries or loyalists? I pressed myself into the recess of a doorway and prayed they would leave. I prayed again that they weren't the men Sister Wilkins said were staking out the shop or the ones who'd broken those front boards. It took an age, but they finally walked down the road. I ran again, passing through the neighbor's gate and scaling the wall. Without pause I attacked the window to the back parlor.

I panted. Sweat beaded on my forehead and grew cold in the crisp November air. My scabbed cuticles throbbed, and I grunted, thrusting all my weight against the crowbar to ply off the boards, one at a time. Finally I hoisted the window open. I dropped the crowbar and climbed inside.

It was dark. This time I'd come better prepared. I pulled a candle and matches from my apron pocket and fumbled with them until a soft glow blossomed. I held the candle aloft and looked around. *What a mess.*

This was my home, where I'd been born and raised. I pictured my mother playing parlor songs at the piano, which now stood covered in ashes and dust. The chair where my father had smoked a pipe every evening was now torn and stained, with a quiet family of mice nesting in the seat. What I'd come for was toward the front, in the tearoom itself. I fished the poppies I'd plucked the night before out of my pocket and placed one on the piano stool and the other on my father's chair. I walked out of the parlor before waves of nostalgia overtook me.

I passed the table the Germans had bent me across to rape me. I passed the spot where Maman's head wound left a stain on the floor. I passed the place where Papa had fallen after they'd hit him. I passed charred piles where the ceiling had caved in. I leaned into the fireplace, glancing at the ashes of the articles I'd burned years earlier in an attempt to eliminate feelings of guilt.

I reached up into the fireplace, felt around, and grabbed the carefully rolled and wrapped painting. A great sigh of relief rushed out of me.

When I was little, Maman had confessed she'd nearly sold it once, when she still lived in Paris and her own parents had died. But she soon met Papa, fell in love, and moved to Brussels to be with him. She used to say his house became hers, but my arrival made it a real home. Now I would do as she'd done. I would take this gift she'd given me and make a new home for my sweet daughter. I would even do as Lars and fight for the things I believed in. I'd take up my pen again.

Suddenly, I heard the strike of a match behind me. "Clever," said a voice in German.

I spun around, holding the painting behind me and the candle in front of me. It was him. The German with the strong jaw, sucking on a cigarette.

"With the flue closed the painting would never get damaged. I regretted not taking it before my comrades lit that fire, and I tore this place apart looking for it after you disappeared. Never thought to look there."

"Stay away from me."

He huffed. Smoke swirled around him. "I don't want you, I want that painting."

"You—can't have it." Wax dripped from the candle and burned my fingers. A hot hate took hold of me. "You raping, pillaging bastard."

He merely shook his head. "You think I was the one who pulled up your skirts? You filthy Belgians killed my father in the Franco-Prussian War. I wouldn't soil myself with the likes of you. But my comrade ached to slake his lust." He took a long drag. "You should be thankful. That rape *saved* you. If it were up to me, I'd have *killed* you. In fact"—he threw down his cigarette—"this time, I will."

He lunged for me. I threw the candle at him and thrust my hand into my apron pocket. The candle hit his shoulder. He cursed, swatting the flame, pausing long enough for me to whip open Papa's penknife.

I flew toward him. He grabbed at me, but in the darkness he merely bumped me. I slashed, and my blade ripped down the side of his face.

He howled, leapt back. "Give me that painting!"

I tried to run past him to the back parlor, but he collided with me again. I fell and the painting flew from my hands, landing somewhere among the ashes. That's when I heard the click of his pistol being cocked.

"Light that candle, woman, and find that painting."

I couldn't let him shoot me. I had to live for Hope. "I'll do it," I lied, grasping around for something to strike him with. "I will. You can take it."

I watched his form, a shadow in the darkness. He clutched the side of his face. "You stupid little—" He raised his pistol in my direction. I dashed behind the counter. A shot rang out. He stomped after me and kicked around behind the bar until he found me. He grabbed me by the hair and pulled me up, jamming the end of his pistol under my chin.

A terrible crash sounded. The soldier and I froze. Light filled the space. There was another crash and the front door of the tea shop splintered open, wood flying everywhere.

I blinked in the brightness. The soldier gripped my hair harder. In walked two German officers with a battering ram. *No, not German officers. Lars and Vander dressed as German officers, shiny boots and all!*

Lars strolled over to the rolled painting and picked it up. "Ah, I've heard rumors about this painting," he said in polished, high German. He really was an expert linguist.

The soldier dragged me out from behind the counter, lowering his gun to aim at the floor. "That's mine."

Lars studied him. "Says who?"

The soldier stammered.

"That's what I thought," said Lars, keeping up the act. "You can't admit who you are to your superior officer because you're a revolutionary traitor."

The soldier looked upset. The gash in his cheek oozed blood. "Germany's cause is lost."

Lars shook his head. "I still outrank you. Shall I arrest you and have you court-martialed? Or," he said, putting his hand on the butt of the pistol in his holster, "should I take justice into my own hands right now?"

The soldier tensed, glanced at the painting first, then at Vander and the battering ram. He slowly put his gun down on the counter. "Take the painting. Call it even?"

Lars pretended to consider it, then tipped his head. "Get out of here."

Just like that, the soldier ran past Vander and down the street in the glow of dawn.

Lars turned to me, switching back to Belgian French. "Are you harmed?"

"I—no."

He handed me the painting.

Vander walked out and climbed into the driver's seat of an old ambulance from the clinic. Sister Wilkins must have loaned it to him. It was then I realized Vander must have been the one who told her of the men staking out the shop.

Lars held out a packet of papers. "I threw together a few extra documents this morning for you and Hope, just in case you want to get out of town."

I took them. They looked stamped and official, complete with hazy identification photographs. "How did you know about the painting? That the soldier was a revolutionary?"

"A woman Vander once loved asked him to watch over you and this place. He's been doing it a long time. I guessed about the soldier. And I'm also guessing when I say . . . come with us."

I hesitated. "With you?"

"Today is Armistice Day. There will be a cease-fire at eleven, and the retreat will begin. You can hole up in that hidden room and pray they don't find you and take your painting, or you can come with us." He pointed to the ambulance. "Marie brought Hope and she packed some things for you."

I looked inside the ambulance. Marie held Hope on her lap in the backseat, and Hope held another lollipop.

Lars took a deep breath. "It's either the longing in your eyes or the name you gave your daughter, but something tells me you want to start a new life as much as I do. You can sell your painting or not, let Marie's son sell this tea shop for you or not, just give England or America a try. Vander and I have enough money to keep us afloat for a while. You can come back here if you don't like it. There are possibilities."

"With you?" I asked again.

He ducked his head, almost sheepish. "*With* me, or just *along* with me, whatever you want. We can see about that part." He looked up, leaned in. "I just know I can't bear to leave you here."

Marie hugged Hope and got out of the ambulance. She gave me an encouraging smile. Vander must have told her everything.

I studied Lars. "*Possibilities*, you say. *We can see about that part*, you say."

He put a light hand on my shoulder and kissed my cheek.

I thought about sea voyages, about museums that might wish to acquire a van Dyck, about writing honest articles, and about finding a house that Lars and Hope and I might turn into a home. I glanced at the sun's rays peeking over the roofline. Armistice Day. A fresh start. "There *are* possibilities," I said, feeling joy.

I started walking toward the ambulance.

Lars put his arm around me. "And there is hope for a future."

The Record Set Right

Lauren Willig

Kenya, 1980

A<small>T FIRST, I THINK THAT IT MUST BE A JOKE.</small>

The letter is slipped in among all the others, bills and circulars, an invitation to a friend's child's third marriage (on cheaper card stock, this time, than marriages one and two), the chance to claim my prize if only I call the number on the top of the page. The usual debris of the post box fans out across the pale wood of the breakfast table. And there, nestled in the middle, this, this unexpected whisper from a world away.

I would have known the device, if not the handwriting, uncertain now with age, blurred with distance.

I fumble for the glasses that hang on a chain around my neck. The curse of age; my eyes and my mind play tricks on me these days, conjuring ghosts in odd corners, shadows and memories. My glasses confirm what my heart already knew. The letter is from Carrington Cross. Edward's writing has changed over the course of time—haven't we all?—but it is still unmistakably his, with those crooked As, and the swoop on the d. It was, at one point, nearly as familiar to me as my own. I saw it on copybooks, on envelopes, on checks, and then, nothing, nothing at all, for the longest time. If we communicated, it was through the mutual weapon of the press, which turns the simplest statements into accusations, speculation into truth.

Even that, even that last, feeble link, had died out long ago; who cared for a scandal of sixty years ago when there were so many new and more interesting ones in the making? The world had changed. The doings of debutantes were no longer front-page news; the old families had ceded place to activists and visionaries—more worthy, if less attractive.

One knows one is truly old when the importunities of the press, clamoring for details, are succeeded by cautious letters from historians. I received those every so often, guarded inquiries into the events of sixty years ago, fumblingly prefaced, in some cases, by "would you be so kind," in others making demands in the interest of Truth and the Historical Record. Some pretended to an interest in the larger context, the Bright Young Things, the Lost Generation, whatever it is they're calling us these days. I was never particularly bright, nor particularly lost, but Nicholas was both, extravagantly so, and it is for Nicholas's sake that they sidle around me, pecking and pawing, ever so cautiously working up to what they truly want to know.

My secretary generally sends a form letter, refusing. When I die, they may have my papers. That is enough—and should occupy at least one graduate student for some time.

Yes, the Old World still comes calling from time to time. But never so directly. Never from Carrington.

I fumble with the letter opener, shaped like a dagger, made of wood. I once had a proper metal one, but my granddaughter Annabelle thinks I am less likely to hurt myself this way.

Sensible Annabelle. They say these things skip a generation, or perhaps there is something to the argument that nurture matters more than nature. In that case, though, why did we all turn out so differently? We were, all four of us, raised in the same nursery at Carrington Cross: Daphne, Edward, and I. And, of course, Nicholas. And, yet, of the four of us, no two came out the same.

There we all are, preserved in perpetuity on the lid of the piano that no one ever plays. Children, grandchildren, weddings, engagements, debutantes, and dotages, it's all there, all lined up on display.

There's something comforting about caging memory, encasing it in silver frames and setting it out to fade, as if, with that, all the dissensions and scandals, the mistrust and misuse might fade, too, blurring away until only the happy outlines remain.

I even have a picture of Edward on the piano, not Edward as he is now, but Edward as he was then, in 1909. We're all there, the entire nursery, herded into place to be recorded for posterity. There's Daphne, age eleven, bouncing with enthusiasm, one curl blown across her face, blurring her features; Edward, seventeen, sturdy in the middle, hair cut short for summer, looking sunburnt and bored. And Nicholas. Just the same age as I, but so very different in every other way. Thirteen, with a radiance even the boxy fashions of the day couldn't hide.

There I am, too, off to one side, part but not quite part of the group, always a little bit on the outside, even four years in.

"An unpromising thing," Cousin Violet liked to say, "all hair and eyes." I believe she does me an injustice. I have seen the photo-graphs of my younger self, the one or two that survived from those pre-Carrington days, and I can attest the fact that I had no more or less hair than any other girl my age, pulled back at the sides and tied in the back with a ribbon. I wear high black boots and a white pinny over a dress whose color might have been anything from yellow to blue; in the photograph, it comes out as gray, as does my hair. Gray to gray, gray in sepia then, gray in reality now. I look, in black-and-white, like any other girl of a similar era, a little shy, perhaps, head ducked, one foot tucked behind the other, but hardly the Caliban of Cousin Violet's imaginings.

Although, given how it all turned out, one can't entirely fault Cousin Violet. I can hear her now, voice low and serious as she told her eldest son, "I tell you, Edward, no good will come of it."

Edward was only thirteen when I came to Carrington in 1905, but he was already the man of the house.

The envelope tears as I attempt to sever it. The Carrington writing paper is frail with age, as yellowed as my skin. I imagine Edward, alone at Carrington, sitting at the writing desk in the library, taking this page from that pile of writing paper, com-missioned in his parents' time and not replaced since. This paper in itself is history, part of my history as well as his. It looks in-congruous on the light wood of my breakfast table, here, in a sunny room on a sunny day half a world away. The bright light brings out the stain on the paper, the faded green of the crest. It looks like a museum piece, something one would see on velvet in a museum. Correspondence of Sir Edward Frobisher, Bart, 1892–?

The paper is old but the ink is fresh and new.

"Dear Camilla," Edward writes, and it makes my heart hurt, that, after all this time, he can't bring himself to treat me with anything but formality.

He built a cage for my pet mouse once, a fantastical thing, with a mouse castle and a mouse moat, which took the better part of the summer half; he danced with me at ball after ball, when we all knew how much he hated it, to keep me from the dreaded company of the wall; he even chased after me to that nightclub in Chelsea, that time when I got in above my head, but he cannot now bring himself to call me Millie.

It had never occurred to me, back in those early days, to consider those small gestures of affection a luxury, or to think that they might someday end.

I lift my coffee to hide the trembling in my hands. They don't brew it strong enough for me, not anymore. I know the truth of it, that the doctor told them I must cut down, that the stronger stuff isn't good for my heart, that it makes it race, as it is racing now. But this is my coffee, from my fields, and I'll drink it as I like. Surely age has accorded me that much privilege. I am not the little girl I was. I am no longer the charity girl in the nursery.

I am no longer the charity girl in the nursery, but seeing Edward's writing brings it all back: the ragged cutouts on the fire screen, the tattered mane of Whisper, the rocking horse, the smell of barley water and milk pudding, the fall of light across the floorboards on a summer afternoon.

"Dear Camilla," Edward writes, and I try to picture him as he must be now, an old man, older than I am, his fingers seamed with veins, his hair thinning on his scalp, his eyes blurred.

I can't do it. To me, he will be forever frozen as he last was, that day at Carrington, his face flushed despite the November cold, his hair still blond then, not yet beginning to gray, rumpled around his face.

It's you, Millie. It's always been you.

I toss the letter down and turn to the television. They thought it might divert me, my children, this talking box, people piped into one's home in miniature, as garishly colored and strangely exaggerated as the puppet shows we used to put on in the nursery at Carrington, although I like to think our humble productions were better scripted than the effusions one sees on the television.

The screen flickers to life. It is a local news anchor, speaking of the capture of a gangster in Bulla Kartasi, a successful raid by the government. I have heard whispers of other things, other stories; misplaced force, rape. The anchor's smile never wavers. Will this be the official version? Truth is written by the first to get around to it, but it never quite stays as one might want it to. Rumors do their work, leaving us in the end with a mesh of half-truths, harder to untangle than fishing line.

In the end, what are we left with? Supposition, conjecture, and a dose of wishful thinking.

I silence the grinning anchor with a click of my finger. Amazing things, these remote controls. But memory isn't as easily tamed. There is no push-button solution.

"Dear Camilla," Edward writes, and I force my eyes to follow the line of his writing, less sure now than it once was. "They tell me I haven't much time left."

Sixty years gone like a song, like a record on a gramophone, with the needle left to bump against the edge, around and around, the music gone. Edward would be eighty-eight now, four years older than I. It is not so very surprising. The passage of years works as well on one side of the world as another. And, yet, I feel my eyes misting, for the boy in a sailor suit, the boy I remember. We were fond of one another once. We trusted one another. Loved one another.

"I write to ask you to come to Carrington. I would like"—and here, a space, as though the writer himself couldn't quite put his thoughts into words—"to see you before I go."

He can't really expect that I'll leave, just like that, pick up and fly around the world on a whim. I have responsibilities here, a company, even if it's largely Henry's these days. All right, entirely Henry's. They trot me out for the odd meeting and for publicity purposes, in the mistaken belief that I add a touch of what the ad people call "class." To them, it doesn't matter that I was the poor cousin; they don't care that I was the cuckoo in the nursery nest, tainted, or so it was seen, by my mother's disastrous marriage.

"Old World charm," say the marketing department, and I wince, but I perform. My voice and my bearing win us sales and sales are what we seek. The world has changed and we with it.

Yes, Henry can manage without me.

But does Edward really believe that I'll just pick up and go? After all these years? As if I were still the one running behind, following them in their games, grateful to be included, knowing that I stood one rung down in the complicated hierarchy of the nursery, another rung down in the eyes of the world, making my curtsy in Daphne's shadow.

I am about to toss the letter aside—surely, even the meanderings of politicians on the talking box is preferable to this—when the last line catches my eye.

"I know," he writes, "that it is a great deal to ask. But we are the only ones left."

The only ones left. Cousin Violet, Daphne.

Nicholas.

Would Edward have sent this letter if Nicholas were still alive? I can't be certain, but I think not.

Whether they're eighteen or eighty-eight, men are all the same.

Or perhaps not. I'm being unfair, I know. Old resentments, old hurts. Nicholas and Edward were always as different as chalk and cheese. No, not chalk and cheese. Champagne and stout, one all bubbles, the other with a hint of bitter.

There is still something left in the envelope. It's been folded, poorly. It makes a lump against the card stock. I draw it out and unfold it, pressing down on both sides. A crease runs down the middle, but the print on it is still legible enough. It's an airline ticket. Nairobi to London.

Should I be alarmed that Edward didn't think to provide a return trip?

No, it's all very like Edward. Economical where Nicholas was extravagant, parsing and paring to try to keep Carrington going in an age in which it has become, increasingly, an anachronism. Rather like us. It's no matter. I can afford my own airline ticket.

But can I afford the rest of it?

It's a very long way back. Back all the way to Carrington Cross. To Carrington, in another world, another time. You can see the date in the history books. November 11, 1918. The day the world changed. Armistice. Peace, at long last.

But it didn't bring us peace, did it, Edward?

Somewhere over Africa, 1980

T HE SMELL OF STALE SMOKE HAS SEEPED INTO THE NUBBY SEATS of the chairs on the plane. There is pink chewing gum in the ashtray, congealed until it has become immovable, part of the decoration, a bright splash of color against the dulled metal.

My family has prevailed upon me to take the trip. Annabelle has stocked my bag with bottles of water and custard crèmes, her concession to the exigencies of travel; Pamela contributed a pile of glossy fashion magazines that recount the scandals of persons of whom I have no knowledge and offer advice on the application of paint and powder I would never wear. But she means well, so I flip through them all the same, wondering at the tendency of the young to find the most unflattering garments possible and refer to it as style.

Henry provided me my return ticket, with a date set two weeks hence. He didn't quite meet my eyes as he murmured, "Once you've gone all that way . . ."

What he means is that he wants me out of the way for the next meeting of the board.

But I didn't argue. Tickets can be changed. And there's a benefit to the element of surprise. I learned that during my marriage.

Nicholas was always best managed on a long leash.

I lean my head back against the seat rest and try to ignore the movie on the screen in the front, little airplanes whizzing about an improbable futuristic world, up in the stars and all built of reinforced concrete. I used to enjoy Jules Verne and H. G. Wells, back in the time before the war, when the future was something rich and strange, but their futures—and mine—never looked quite like that.

The little airplanes in which they whiz about remind me

of Nicholas's. That Moth he treasured so, until it came to grief near Dagoretti field. He took me up in it once, but I was too busy clutching the sides to enjoy the view.

"You have your feet on the ground," he told me, with resignation. "You and . . ."

He didn't say the name. He didn't need to.

After that, I stayed home and saw to the seedlings while Nicholas managed the charter business, flying rich industrialists and bored heiresses around Africa.

The Aviator in the Iron Mask, the papers called him.

It wasn't iron, of course. That would have been impossible. Instead, it was tin, the very finest of its kind, hiding the ruin of the left side of his face. The way he wore it, though, gave him a certain dash and panache; his unwillingness to remove it, even in bed, made the papers in two continents.

"Are you married, or do you live in Kenya?" That was the way the saying went, in those years after the war.

We'd been like so many flocking out to British East Africa in 1919, Nicholas and I. Find peace in an untainted paradise, they'd told us. Plant coffee and make your fortune. Endless opportunities. That was the rhetoric of it, but, like so many others, we weren't running toward; we were running away.

His talisman, Nicholas called me. His lucky charm. He credited me with saving him, and perhaps I had, in a topsy-turvy way, if only by taking him away. Away from Carrington, away from England. In Kenya, it didn't matter that he had only half a face; no one had known him as he had once been. The Aviator in the Iron Mask rose phoenixlike from the ashes of the Nicholas Frobisher that had been.

Every now and again, I would torture myself with wondering. Wondering how it might have been different if I had stayed in England. I find myself rewriting the script, changing the words, erasing the last sixty years and replacing them with—what?

Where do I stop the reel and start it playing again?

Carrington, 1915

G OOD-BYE, MOUSE."
The train station was crowded with other women seeing their men off, their faces obscured by coal smoke and tears. A band was playing. Not a very good one. The horn was tinny and the drum was out of tune. As a send-off, it left something to be desired, but it was no matter. They would be home by Christmas, everyone knew that. Or if not Christmas, certainly by Easter.

In my imaginings, this was the moment when Nicholas, glorious Nicholas, would sweep me up in his arms, kiss me with the sort of fervor reserved for the books that Daphne hid beneath the sheets in the airing cupboard, and vow that he was coming home to me, only me.

In reality, I received a chuck under the chin and a rumple of my carefully pinned hair. "Don't sniffle, mouse. I'll be home before you've had a chance to miss me."

"I'm not sniffling," I protested, although perhaps I was, just a bit, although whether at the prospect of Nicholas going off to war or that casual, hurtful "mouse," I wasn't quite sure.

I'd been in love with Nicholas from the day I'd walked through the door of Carrington House as a nine-year-old orphan; I'd been in love from the moment he'd grabbed my hand and pulled me out to play. I'd loved him through tumbling out of trees and into brooks; I'd loved him through scoldings from Nanny and bed without supper. I loved him without reason and without hope and never more than now, as I saw him before me in uniform, the epitome of every brave soldier who had ever sought that bubble reputation in the cannon's mouth—or however it was that the bard put it.

Why had I thought today would be any different? *'Twere all one / That I should love a bright particular star / And think to wed it, he is so above me.*

Shakespeare might well have written that line for me.

"You—you look very dashing," I ventured.

Nicholas's teeth flashed in a grin. "That's the point of it, you know. Well, that, and to give the Hun a jolly good thrashing. What do you say, Ned?"

I hadn't realized that Edward was standing there until Nicholas addressed him, just over my left shoulder. Twisting, I saw Edward grimace, rubbing his forehead as though the band of his cap pained him. "I would rather stay here."

"And miss all the fun?" Nicholas winked at Ivy, the upstairs maid, dressed in her best and lurking in the general vicinity. I studiously looked the other way. I'd seen them kissing in the gazebo the previous summer.

From the way Edward's brow darkened, he'd seen them, too. "Someone needs to mind the farm."

"You have the turnips, I'll have the glory. What do you say, mouse?"

That I wished he wouldn't call me mouse. "I'll make you parcels."

"Cakes from Fuller's and hampers from Fortnum," said Nicholas. "And tea what is tea as Mrs. Potter likes to say. Ah, don't cry now, Mrs. P."

"He thinks it's a picnic," said Edward in a low voice.

It was impossible that anything bad might ever touch Nicholas. He was the prince from a fairy tale, impervious to swords and spells alike. "You'll be there to keep him safe." With an effort, I tore my attention from Nicholas and looked up at Edward. "Shouldn't you be saying your farewells to Pansy?"

They weren't officially engaged, not yet, but we all knew it was a matter of time. Pansy's family had made their fortune in banking and were determined to prove their country bona fides by being duller than anyone else. Their tweeds were always just a bit baggier, their hats a bit more like porkpies. It was a love match, as such matches are: Pansy loved the idea of being Lady Frobisher and Edward loved the idea of being able to finally repair the roof, which was sagging ominously over the unused rooms of the East Wing. As a farm, Carrington Cross paid its way, but only just. There wasn't much left over for leading. Or, for that matter, for Fortnum's hampers.

I could see Pansy at the other end of the platform, taking a proper lady-of-the-manor interest in the departing tenantry, her lilac frock blending nicely with the coal smoke.

Edward glanced over at her and away again. He looked down at me, two deep furrows between his eyes. They were rather nice eyes, somewhere between gray and blue. Not the sort of color the poets would write sonnets about, but comfortable, like time-faded drapes. "You'll see to Carrington for me?"

"I thought you had Keeley for that." Keeley had been at Carrington forever, a gamekeeper turned general factotum.

"I do, but . . . he's getting on. And he's never been much for accounts."

I gave Edward's hand a quick squeeze. "I'll make sure the numbers tally." I could hear Nicholas's laugh down the platform, but I couldn't see who he was speaking to. "Don't fret."

"Thank you." It was the fact that Edward was still holding my hand that caught my attention. I looked up at him and found him looking at me, his face serious. "You're the only one I trust to see to it properly."

From Edward, that meant a great deal. "Thank you," I said, around a lump in my throat that had nothing to do with the coal smoke. "I'll do my best."

"You always do," he said, and leaned down and brushed his lips—not across my lips, but against my cheek. Only my cheek.

Why, then, did it feel like something more?

The whistle was blowing, the boys were jumping on board, the train was leaving. I could see Edward taking a formal leave of Pansy, Nicholas pinching Ivy's cheek, babies wailing, women waving, the band playing on.

And I stood there, one gloved hand against my cheek, and watched them as they went until—

"Come along," said Pansy briskly, "I'll drop you at Carrington," and she led me back to her father's motorcar.

London, 1980

THERE IS A YOUNG WOMAN WITH A SIGN WAITING FOR ME AT Heathrow.

I hadn't expected that. I am even more surprised when she greets me, in transatlantic tones, "Aunt Camilla?"

Not a paid driver, then. But I would have known that anyway, from the hair. Frobisher hair, inherited from one of the long-ago Saxon ancestors who dug in their tent posts on a particular plot in Hampshire and refused to budge from it. Dynasties might rise and fall, civil wars might be fought, but fair-haired Frobishers clung close to their own. On Nicholas and Daphne it had shone golden; on Edward it had been tow. This girl wore her long blond hair twisted into a casual bun with something thrust through it, but it had that same straw-colored quality as Edward's.

His granddaughter?

I feel it like a sharp pain. I shouldn't. But I do.

I hobble forward painfully. My limbs are stiff from the long flight, that's all. I'm not usually so infirm. I want to tell her that, but it would seem to protest too much, so I say, formally, "I am afraid you have the advantage of me."

The girl sticks out a hand, American-style. "Amanda Merrill."

"And you are . . ."

"Emma's daughter." That means nothing to me. I have deliberately kept myself from Carrington and all it contains. Edward might have a dozen daughters, each named Emma or Esmerelda. But I nod as though I know and follow her through the terminal, past a confusion of shops hawking magazines and scarves, duty-free gin and scarlet lipsticks. I have time enough to examine all of it; the pace my grand-niece sets would shame an industrious snail.

There is nothing more humiliating than the solicitousness of youth.

"You needn't fuss over me," I tell her, as she helps me into the car, earnestly inquiring into the state of my creaky limbs.

Don't fuss over me.

It's Edward's voice in my ear, an echo from sixty-odd years ago.

Don't fuss over me, he snapped, as I rushed forward to help him up the steps, my hair pulled back untidily beneath a kerchief, my breeches tucked into my boots. My nails were brown with dirt; they were always brown, no matter how I scrubbed at them. The soil left a stain. *What's a leg more or less?*

They'd fitted Edward with a prosthesis in France, but he hadn't got the knack of it yet; he lurched dangerously as he tried to climb the three stairs to the entrance of Carrington. There were a pair of crutches, but he'd left them in the trap, an ancient governess cart I'd used to pick him up at the station. I could see from the sweat on his brow how much it was costing him to ignore those crutches.

He had lost his leg at Cambrai; had lain in a wagon with a field dressing clumsily wrapped around the bloody stump, shaking with shock, while the bells rang in the church in Carrington village and we had all celebrated, happy for any victory, however small, not knowing yet that that small victory would be lost and the casualty lists come in with the names of our own. It wasn't until two weeks later that we'd heard, and it was only now, in April, that we were getting Edward home, after a long convalescence in a hospital somewhere in France.

He hadn't told us how close he'd come to dying, but it was easy enough to read through the lines.

I had always thought of Edward as solid, the English countryside personified, but he'd grown thin, so painfully thin, and his whole body trembled with the effort as he lurched into the familiar hall, with the wood paneling that was meant to be saved from rot by Pansy's money—if Pansy would still have a man with one leg.

Pansy hadn't come to the station, but she had a good excuse for that; she had taken a course in nursing and volunteered at the local hospital.

I didn't ask Edward where matters stood between them.

Catching himself on the high back of a Jacobean chair, he said, with difficulty, *Where's Daphne?*

London. In all our letters, I hadn't told him, hadn't wanted to tell him. Edward didn't need more worries. *She wanted to train as a nurse.*

Edward glanced out the window at the lawn, plowed up to make room for carrots and cabbages. It was a piecemeal affair. There were so few of us, just the women, left at home. How could I ask the wives of Edward's tenant farmers for help, when they had work enough maintaining their own? So I did the best I could, digging, planting, harvesting. I'd been banned from the kitchen end of things by Mrs. Potter after a spectacular explosion that heralded the destruction of most of the following autumn's jelly.

You mean she wanted a holiday in London, he said grimly.

It's hardly a holiday. I couldn't dispute Edward's assessment of his sister's motives—Daphne had always yearned after London— but she had stuck the course. Blood and bandages suited her. *She's working hard.*

So are you. I could see Edward looking at my hands, at my ragged nails, the calluses on my palms, and quickly stuck them behind my back, wishing I'd thought to put on gloves. *You shouldn't have to do it all on your own.*

Maybe it was his haggard appearance, but there was an intensity that hadn't been there before. Or maybe it always had, and I had never noticed. Never noticed because there was always Nicholas, stealing the sunshine.

Hastily, breathlessly, I said, *Have you—have you heard anything of Nicholas?*

And I watched the light fade from Edward's face as he gave a slight shrug, which nearly unbalanced him, and said, *All right, I think. Is that the gong for lunch?*

It wasn't the gong, of course. We'd abandoned the gong, with so much else. A phantom sound from the past, like the phantom limb that I could tell, over the following months, still pained Edward. There was no question of his going back to the front. He'd dug in, pushing himself further than he ought, overseeing planting, taking his turn at the plow, staying up late trying to make the numbers in the ledgers tally.

His leg wasn't the only phantom presence among us. There was Nicholas, whose letters had grown longer, which ought to have been satisfying, but was instead disconcerting. He'd begun to fantasize about what he might do after the war, and those fantasies became ever stranger. Open a nightclub in London, find the fabled Mountains of the Moon, set off to sea in a pea-green boat.

What is Nicholas writing you? Edward would ask, half-glancing over my shoulder, but I could no more tell him than he would tell me what he found to say to Pansy every week, when her parents' motor would pick him up and carry him to Belleview, their unimaginatively named manor, for supper.

Dreams, I told him. *Fancies and dreams.*

"Did you know that the family were originally recusants?"

"What?" I've been woken from a half doze. Dreams. Fancies and dreams. I hadn't been aware that I was sleeping. I was merely—how does it go?—resting my eyes. That's the danger of resting one's eyes. It takes so little to drift back into a past that is, increasingly, more real than the present.

"That's why it's called Carrington Cross," says Amanda confidingly, as I try to remember what she's talking about. Oh, yes. Recusants. The word comes out of long-ago lessons. Secret Catholics in the reign of Elizabeth I. "For Carrying the Cross. At least, that's what some of the sources say."

Carrington had certainly been Edward's cross to bear. Mine, too, during that last year of the war. We'd worked together, the two of us, trying to keep it going.

Was that when I'd fallen in love with him?

Amanda is still talking, something about her M.Phil. "—that's how we saved the house. By converting. James I gave us a baronetcy and confirmed our ownership of the land. After that, the Frobishers became model Calvinists."

It's you, Millie. It was always you.

But in the end, it hadn't been.

"Oh, yes," I say drily. "The Frobishers always do what they need to do to save Carrington."

We've reached the gates, which were one of Cousin Violet's additions. She always did like the idea of keeping people out. Like my mother, she came from a thoroughly respectable middle-class professional family. My mother was a vicar's daughter; Cousin Violet was the child of a doctor. My mother ran off with an actor. Cousin Violet married a baronet and spent the rest of her life turning herself into the lady of the manor.

I wonder what she would make of her American great-granddaughter, so casually speaking of "we" and "us." Or, for that matter, of me. I've worn a Chanel suit and the diamond brooch that Nicholas inherited from Cousin Violet. Just because.

I may have left in disgrace, but I'm not going to return that way.

The trees look just as I remember, an alley of oaks, their branches now bare, just as they were that November long ago. It was a cold, wet November—or maybe it's just the recollection of how it all turned out that makes me remember it as cold and wet. Maybe it wasn't cold and wet at all. Maybe I'm a butterfly dreaming of being a philosopher. Memory plays tricks. Sometimes I suspect myself of remembering things as they ought to have been, rather than as they were.

Not that I would ever admit that to Henry. He already suspects me of being a little less than compos mentis.

A turn in the alley, and there it is: Carrington. It's no Blenheim or Hatfield House, no Castle Howard or whatever else the filmmakers are using as backdrop for their costume dramas. It's merely a modest Elizabethan manor house, with a pseudo-Palladian addition built along the back in a time of relative prosperity in the mid-eighteenth century. Mercifully, straitened funds in the nineteenth century kept the Victorians from improving it out of existence.

The funds don't seem to be so straitened now. The lawn is well kept, the gravel has been swept; there are even some rather fanciful topiary in stone urns posing on either side of the front door.

Does Edward know that I could buy and sell him ten times over?

Maybe not ten. But five, at least. I get an unworthy satisfaction out of that. Once, Carrington was the height of my desiring. I could imagine nothing grander and better. But I've seen more now, done more now. No Grinling Gibbons or Inigo Jones had a hand in Carrington's construction; Adam never squinted at those ceilings, nor did Capability Brown ever wander through the modest park. For all Cousin Violet's fierce pride and Edward's dogged determination, it's just a house, like a hundred others. I recognize it now for what it is, a relatively uninspired example of its kind, not particularly significant or unique.

Except to the Frobishers. Except to Edward.

So long ago, and yet, the closer we come to Carrington, the more I find that I'm angry still.

"We're here!" says Amanda unnecessarily.

"I know," I say, and pull my wool skirt down over my knees. "I have been here before."

Once, I had thought to be mistress of it. I almost laugh at myself for the thought. It seems, against Amanda's cheerfully modern attire, almost painfully outdated, something straight out of Brontë or du Maurier.

Last night, I dreamt I went to Carrington. . . .

There is no one waiting for us at the door, no dowager in black with keys at her waist. No Edward. Amanda lets us in, prosaically enough, with a modern key that seems at odds with the great oak door.

And there is Nicholas, waiting for me.

His portrait rather. It's where it always was, pride of place in the hall, Cousin Violet's last splurge.

It takes me aback, rather.

Amanda nearly runs into me. "Oh! I should have realized. Is that"—her voice drops—"Uncle Nicholas?"

Her voice is appropriately hushed, as befits, it seems, speaking of the deceased to the bereaved.

Never mind that I've been a widow for thirty-odd years now or that ours was hardly a love that transcends time. The mythology is always more attractive than the reality.

"Yes," I say. The portrait was painted before the war. There is Nicholas in all his glory, incorrigible even in oil paint. I'd grown so used to seeing him as he'd become, always in the mask, first of painted tin, later, as he grew older, a simpler affair of black silk, that it comes as a shock to see him whole again, to remember him as he was, in those long-ago days when I sighed over him from my maidenly bower.

It's always hard to admit you've fallen out of love with someone; it's that much harder when they return home without a face.

In my own defense, I would like to think that I had fallen out of love with Nicholas already, or, in truth, that I had never been in love with him at all. He was my impossible dream, my lady in a tower. Such loves are never meant to be requited; like a falling star, they fade before they hit the earth, leaving only a faint memory of brightness lost.

In my case, I caught my star as it was falling and burnt my fingers in the process.

Go and catch a falling star, tell me where all past years are....

"Er, that's John Donne, right?" says Amanda, and I realize I've been speaking the words aloud. "Get with child a mandrake root? We did him in English 125."

England and America, divided by a common language. "Yes."

We're spared further attempts at conversation by a rustle-thump, rustle-thump that stops just shy of the door.

And there he is. Edward.

The entrance to the hall is in shadow. For a moment, I could swear it is the Edward of sixty years ago, still too thin, even after six months home from the front. There is a blaze of red on his chest. A poppy.

I realize, belatedly, what day it is. Armistice Day. The day the world healed and we fell to pieces.

The familiar smells of the hall engulf me: old upholstery, lemon oil, decaying wood, beeswax. The light falls just as it did then. I could swear I hear the faint sound of a gramophone playing, tinnily, from Nicholas's room upstairs.

November upon November falls away. But we're standing in the wrong places. That much I remember. It was Edward in the hall and I on the stairs. . . .

Carrington Cross, 1918

Edward?" Blinking a little, I leaned over the stair rail. The hall wasn't particularly well lighted, but it was bright in comparison with the deliberate gloom of Nicholas's room, blinds drawn, mirrors gone.

Nicholas had been home for nearly three months now, since August, but it didn't seem to be doing him much good. He had, I suspected, been easier in the hospital in France, surrounded by other men more maimed than he. Here, at Carrington, he was reminded at every turn of what he had been. Ivy, who had once giggled and flirted with him, brought his tray to his room with averted eyes, hurrying away as quickly as she could.

We'd had a mask made for Nicholas, a beautiful thing, designed at Anna Ladd's studio in Paris. It was a work of art and it cost the earth. But he wouldn't go near it. Instead he lounged half-clothed in his darkened room on the rumpled sheets of his bed, half-dozing, picking up books only to fling them across the room again, pacing in short bursts and napping in even shorter bursts. He had never been one to find his own entertainment; his pursuits had always been of the vigorous sort. But he refused to go out, refused to ride, refused to take any interest in the management of the estate.

"What, do you want me to scare off the peasantry?" he'd said, bitingly, when I had suggested a ride—a sacrifice on my part. I had never been much of a rider. Another mark against me in Cousin Violet's eyes. "They can set me up as a bogeyman to scare wayward children."

"Only if you behave like one," I snapped, driven beyond endurance. I was tired, more tired than I could ever recall.

"Wait—Millie." Nicholas grabbed my hand, stopping me as I rose. "Don't. Don't go."

"I'm just going downstairs," I said, freeing myself. "Ivy ought to have been up with your tray an hour ago."

It was an excuse. I wanted out, away. The funk of the sickroom was in my nostrils; my head ached with the half-light. As I left the room, I could hear the mournful shrill of the gramophone, playing, endlessly, Caruso and Gluck performing the banquet scene from *La Traviata*. Always that one record, over and over.

"Edward?" I'd heard his steps downstairs, but I couldn't see him. There was an odd quiet about the hall. No Ivy dusting, no sound of pots banging in the kitchen. Just quiet. Utter quiet.

"Here." He was beneath the overhang of the stair, in a little nook where he had put in a telephone. His voice sounded strange and flat.

I hurried down, nearly tripping over my own feet. "Is something wrong?"

He was holding the edge of the telephone table with both hands, his shoulders bowed. He looked up and I could see his face contort with the effort of speech. "It's over. It's done."

"What's done?" Upstairs, Anna Gluck was belting out *Enjoy the hour, for rapidly / The joys of life are flying*. . . .

"The war." The words came out like an accusation. "The war."

Enjoy then the wine-cup with songs of pleasure, sang the chorus.

I stared at Edward, thick and slow as mud.

"Done." I couldn't make it come together in my head. "The war."

We'd prayed for it for so long, prayed for peace, prayed for it to be over. Done, Edward said. Done. What did that mean, now?

Upstairs, the record bumped to an end, began again.

There were holes in my stockings that needed to be darned, holes in the lawn where we'd dug vegetable patches, a hole in Nicholas's face where his left eye should have been. And Edward, Edward balancing on his false leg, his entire body shaking.

I ran forward to steady him before he could fall, but he didn't, which is just as well. He was a head taller than I, and, even without much flesh on him, solidly built. I put my arms around him all the same as his body trembled.

"What good is it?" His voice seemed to be torn from his chest. I felt moisture on my hands and realized that Edward, unflappable Edward, was crying, in great, shuddering sobs. "It's too bloody late. Oh, God!"

"Please." I wasn't even sure what I was saying please for. I lifted a hand to Edward's cheek. His hair was too fine and fair to leave stubble. I cradled his cheek in my hand, felt the moisture of his tears against my palm. "Edward, don't."

"It's all lost." His eyes were red, bloodshot. "I couldn't keep them safe, any of them."

I had no idea what them he was talking about. His regiment presumably. "You did the best you could."

Edward gave a bitter bark of a laugh, rocking on his good leg. "My brother lost his bloody face! I wasn't there. I left him. I left him and he lost his face."

I wrapped my arms as tightly around him as I could, trying to stop the shaking, trying to make him warm again. "You'd lost a leg. What were you meant to do? Hobble after him?"

I could feel Edward's head shake, his chin brushing against my forehead. His voice was a whisper against my hair. "There's so much lost and I don't know how to put it right again."

I tilted my head back, looking up at him. "It's not all on you, you know." Even as I said it, I knew it wasn't entirely true. It was all on Edward. Nicholas had been trained to be decorative, not useful. And Daphne had fallen in love with a Yank. She meant to go away with him somewhere once the war was over. Over. It seemed impossible that it could be over. I felt like a man marooned on an island must, at the too long-awaited sight of a sail, more apprehensive than eager. I couldn't even imagine how Edward must feel. "You have me."

"Do I?" Edward's eyes were brilliant, like a sky after rain. I couldn't look away from them. "I don't know what I would do without you, Millie. You've been the only bright spot in all this."

The words themselves were mundane, prosaic, but something about the way he said them made me feel as though I'd just been given a bouquet of red roses, had champagne drunk from my shoe; I might have been garbed in satins and velvets instead of old tweed and a saggy jumper.

"Anything," I said hoarsely. "Anything you need."

Was this what love really was, wanting to give instead of take? All I knew was that whatever Edward needed, I would be there to provide it. He'd carried so much alone; I wanted to carry it for him.

The joys of life are flying—like summer flow-rets dying, sang the gramophone. *Improve them while you may!*

Edward's fingers were in my hair, moving the heavy locks back from my brow. "Just you. Just you." And then, as his arms closed around me, as his lips descended toward mine. "It's you, Millie. It's always been you."

Carrington Cross, 1980

I SELF-CONSCIOUSLY RAISE A HAND TO MY HAIR AND MAKE myself stop. "Well," I say, a little too loudly. "This is a proper wrinklies' reunion."

Edward is leaning on a stick, a concession to age, I imagine, rather than his missing leg. His current prosthesis is sophisticated enough that had I not known of its presence, I would never have guessed.

"Camilla," Edward says formally.

A far cry from *It's you, Millie.* But, then, why should I be surprised? We had parted that afternoon with soft touches and murmurs of love.

The next morning, he had greeted me at breakfast with the news that he had proposed to Pansy and been accepted.

I touch my fingers lightly to Cousin Violet's diamond brooch. "Should I call you Sir Edward? I would curtsy but my knees are a bit stiff."

Edward's face relaxes into something slightly less Victorian. "Don't be absurd."

"Is it? When I received your summons, I wasn't sure if it was to be fatted calf or humble pie."

Amanda looks from one of us to the other. "I'll go make some coffee," she says, and flees.

"Wise child," I say, watching her go. "Your granddaughter?"

"Daphne's." Edward moves painfully across the room to the sofa. Not, I note, the same one on which we spent that memorable afternoon so long ago, lost to propriety, to fear of discovery, to anything. Clothing half-unbuttoned, flesh to flesh, *La Traviata* urging us on to enjoy the wine cup with songs of pleasure. "Pansy and I were not blessed with children."

"Ah." I sit down carefully on a chintz-covered chair, folding my hands in my lap so that my engagement ring, Nicholas's ring, is on top. "Is that why you asked me here? Because of Henry?"

I should have known. Not, in the end, unrequited love. Not loss and regrets. But always, inevitably, Carrington.

That's the great irony of life, isn't it? After all that, my son, my Henry, will take Edward's place.

The Fates have a nasty sense of humor.

"No." There's that wrinkle between Edward's brows, and part

of me still, even now, wants to reach up and smooth it out. It was easier to hate him from a distance. That, perhaps, was part of why I had stayed away so long. Nicholas's weapon was charm; Edward's earnestness. "I wanted to see you again. Is that so strange?"

From the man who had left my bed—so to speak—to propose to another woman? "I hadn't noticed the urge overtake you before."

"Are you surprised?" he says quietly, and that's something I had forgotten about him, how sensible, how reasonable he always sounded.

"No." I cross my legs at the ankle. "I imagine it would be awkward to present your wife with your lover. If one can even call me such. After all, it was only the once. Just a bit of Armistice exuberance."

"For you, perhaps. Not for me." Edward sounds so sincere I might have believed him, but for the fact that he'd proposed to another woman the following day. His eyes slide sideways, to the portrait of Nicholas, Nicholas grinning his victor's grin. "I should have remembered it always was Nicholas for you."

Was that the fairy tale he told himself to assuage his conscience?

"I only eloped with Nicholas because you proposed to Pansy," I say sharply. It's important to have the record straight. "I wasn't going to stay in the house with your new wife."

I can still remember the pain of it, staring at Edward as he made his announcement. Nicholas, down for breakfast for the first time since he'd come home, putting his arm around my shoulders, declaring a little too loudly that we had an announcement, too.

I was so grateful to Nicholas for saving me, for saving my pride. Cousin Violet had always wanted the match with Pansy. I suppose I had known, deep down, that Edward would never choose me, that Cousin Violet still reigned from beyond the grave.

"No," says Edward, his voice surprisingly strong. "That's not how it happened."

What does he mean that's not what happened? I was there. I know what happened.

At least, I think I know what happened. The story has been told and retold so many times that it's become something flat and bright like a fairy tale, more ritual than reality.

Edward is still speaking. "Do you think I blame you? I always knew it was Nicholas for you. Ever since we were children. But I had hoped, just for that once— Well, never mind. It was my foolishness, not yours."

Henry tells me my mind is going, but I had never believed him until now. In exasperation I say, "What are you on about?"

Edward tugs at the poppy in his buttonhole. "I saw you, Camilla. I saw you together, in Nicholas's room. On his bed."

In the resulting silence, crockery rattles on a tray. "Coffee, anyone?" says Amanda brightly.

Carrington Cross, 1918

THE CUPS CLATTERED ON THE TRAY AS I CARRIED IT UP TO Nicholas's room. Ivy was still missing—celebrating, undoubtedly.

I paused outside the door, making sure my blouse was buttoned all the way up, before opening the door with one hip. For once, I was grateful for the gloom of Nicholas's room, grateful that it hid my crumpled skirt, my flushed cheeks. I was exhilarated; I was terrified. Nice girls didn't do what I had just done.

But it was Edward.

It's you, Millie. It's always been you. The tray was heavy, but I didn't feel it. The world was moondust and thistledown; the long war was finally over, and I was in love with Edward, always Edward.

In the back of my head, I knew, I suppose, that there was Pansy to be dealt with, and years of grinding work making the farm pay again; worries about the roof and arguments with the bank. But that was for later, not now.

Now there was only the giddy euphoria that came of vows made and received, of surrendering oneself, entirely and foolishly.

My euphoria received a slight check as the smell of Nicholas's room hit me, the smell of unwashed sheets, smuggled brandy, and despair. Nicholas lay on the bed, not reading, not sleeping, just lying there, staring at a crack in the ceiling, one of the cracks that was meant, before today, to have been repaired with Pansy's money.

The record was stuck in a groove. *The joys of life are flying. . . . The joys of life are flying. . . .*

I set down the tray before taking the needle off the record. "The war is over. Mrs. Dean from the post office rang. The announcement was made at eleven this morning."

They said that in London there was cheering and celebrating, bonfires and dancing in the streets, but in Nicholas's room there was only a horrible stillness. He turned his face to the wall, so I could see only the good side. "Am I expected to be happy?"

I sat tentatively on the edge of the bed. "Relieved, perhaps?"

"Why?" The savagery in his voice took me aback. When he turned, it was almost a shock to see the ridged flesh, the empty socket where his left eye had been. "I'm done for."

I thought of all the men who were truly done for, the men who hadn't come home. "You're alive."

"I'm a monster." He looked at me straight on, giving me the full effect of his distorted face. "What am I meant to do? Set myself up as a sideshow freak? I might as well be in the grave as rot here in Carrington."

"No one's holding you here."

"This is." Nicholas waved a hand in the direction of his face. "No one will want me now."

I took his hand and squeezed. "Don't be absurd."

"You wouldn't think of marrying me, would you, Millie?" I couldn't tell if he was joking or not. "You loved me once."

"I love you now." I wasn't lying, not really. I did love him. He was in my blood, part of my childhood.

But it wasn't the sort of love he meant and Nicholas was canny enough to know it.

"Not the same way." His face contorted with self-loathing. "How could you? I'm a monster."

"No more than you ever were." I scooted closer, putting an arm around his shoulders. "Nicholas, don't. I mean it, truly. You are everything you were before. You just need . . . a new interest. Something to do with yourself. Other than kissing the housemaids."

"You saw that?" For a moment, Nicholas sounded almost pleased with himself. But then he flopped back against the pillows. "She won't kiss me now, you know. She won't even look at me. No one will."

"Stop it," I said, and kissed him.

I could say I kissed him because I felt sorry for him, and it was true, I did. But I would be lying if I claimed that was all there was to it. I kissed him because I had spent years daydreaming of being kissed by Nicholas, because there was a part of me that would always remember what he had been, and what he had been to me.

His mouth hadn't been affected by the shell that had gutted his face. It was a perfectly serviceable kiss, practiced even.

But it wasn't love, and I knew it.

I kissed Nicholas and I kissed him good-bye. In the midst of it, I fancied I could hear a metaphorical door clicking shut, closing off that old infatuation.

Carrington Cross, 1980

BEHIND AMANDA, THE DOOR SWINGS SHUT WITH AN AUDIBLE click that makes Edward start and his cane clatter to the floor.

I can hear the echo of it, the sound of a door closing.

"Are there any biscuits?" I ask Amanda.

There are biscuits on the tray. I can see her almost start to say so, but she's bright enough to know when she's being asked to go.

"Sure," she says, and turns away.

I wonder if she'll listen at the door. I would.

To Edward, I say quietly, "Whatever you saw, it wasn't what you thought."

"Wasn't it? You don't need to lie to me," he adds, and there's the bitter tang of wounded pride in his voice. "I knew I was second choice."

Hoist by my own petard. How can I blame him for saying that, when I'd gone to considerable lengths to make Edward think it?

The papers had been full of our romantic elopement. We'd gone to Paris first, and from Paris to Kenya, courting flashbulbs all the way. Nicholas had been sufficiently decorated during the war—and sufficiently public before it—to generate news. Perhaps it was a craving for scandal in the wake of so much seriousness. In any event, there we were: baronet's brother elopes with cousin, with much hemming and hawing and pointing at my waistline, or what was left of it. It was scandalous, it was romantic, it was uplifting.

Tin Face, Warm Heart!

Who doesn't want to believe that he can still be loved despite his scars, despite his deformities? We performed a public service, Nicholas and I, even if it was half by accident, even if it was all based on a lie. But it was what people wanted to hear, what they needed to believe.

And I had needed it, too. Let Edward believe it was a love match. *Let him,* I had thought vengefully, *enjoy his cold bed and his new roof.*

Let him believe I had the choice of brothers and hadn't chosen him.

"It was just a kiss," I say now. "That was all. We never— It felt too much like incest."

For me, at least. As for Nicholas, he'd never really desired me, not that way. We were partners, not lovers.

Edward shakes his head, stubborn to the last. "Nicholas told me—that you were lovers. That you had been lovers."

I sit up straighter in my chair. "When?"

"That night." He doesn't need to specify which night. November 11 will always be that night. Edward looks down, shamefaced. "After I saw you—well, I confronted him about it. He told me you'd been lovers for weeks, practically since he'd come home."

I ought to have known. That's all I can think. *I ought to have known.*

I knew Nicholas. I knew Edward. I knew them both, through and through. Why hadn't I seen it? Why hadn't I guessed?

My lips feel numb. "Nicholas lied," I say. "He was scared. He was afraid of being left alone."

We'd been his pillars, Edward and I. If we'd married—Nicholas would have been the odd man out. He hadn't wanted me for himself, not really, but he certainly hadn't wanted me for Edward.

Edward gives his head a little shake, like a horse swatting off flies. I know how he feels. It's rather hard to believe one thing for more than half a century and then discover it's another. It's enough to make one doubt one's judgment.

I make light of it, but my hands are shaking in my lap. What scares me isn't that I was wrong, it's that I didn't have the sense to know I was wrong.

We knew Nicholas. We both knew Nicholas. Why didn't we see it at the time?

Was it because we didn't want to?

Love is one thing, the reality of a life together another. Particularly when there are bills to be paid.

"Millie," says Edward. And that's all. But it's enough. There's a lifetime of apology in that one word.

"Cookie?" It's the ubiquitous Amanda, with a plate of digestives. I ought to have known she was one of Daphne's. Daphne was like that, too, as insistent as a pointer with a fallen grouse.

For a moment, it feels like we're all there again: Daphne, trying to manage people. Edward, steady and sensible. Nicholas, his portrait looming over us, always the joker in the pack.

I don't know whether to curse him or thank him.

"Thank you." I take a biscuit from the tray. To Edward, I say, as casually as I can, "It is what it is. Although it does seem appropriate that Henry will follow you."

It takes him a moment. He can't ask right out, not with Amanda there. "Do you mean—?"

"Oh, yes." I raise a brow, rather enjoying myself now. It's amazing what a difference it makes, being the one who got away, rather than the woman scorned. "Henry was born in August of '19. He has two grown girls, Annabelle and Pamela. And a little boy, Nicky."

It was the old story. Pass the midcentury mark, lose your hair, start shagging the secretary. Annabelle and Pamela were both out of university before Nicky was out of nappies. Whatever the biology of it, Henry had always been more Nicholas's son than Edward's.

I decide not to mention that to Edward. There's really no need to further muddy the waters. They're muddy enough already.

"A little boy." Edward looks dazed and well he might. It's not every day that one inherits a slew of descendants. I can see the family tree scrolling out in front of him. Sir Henry Frobisher, Bart. Sir Nicholas Frobisher, Bart.

The family we might have had, together.

If. And that's the rub, isn't it? We can blame Nicholas all we like. But deep down, I'm still not entirely sure that Edward would have married me. I might have been his only bright spot, his light in a dark world and so on, but Pansy had the money to save Carrington.

It would be nice to believe that love conquers all, but when it comes down to love or money, money has a way of winning.

Cynical? Perhaps. But I've had sixty-odd years to whet my sharp edges. Sixty-two years to be precise. Sixty-two years of believing that the man I loved had thrown me over to save his house.

I take a big bite out of my biscuit. "The line will go on. Henry will have Carrington. So you see, it's all come out right in the end."

"Except for all the time between," says Edward quietly.

I almost ask it then. *Would you have married me?* But Amanda is sitting there. And the truth of it is, I would rather not know. Better to bask in the assurance of it, to know that I was loved, that—but for a misplaced moment of pity, a foolish kiss—it would have been a different ring on my finger.

When I try to think of what my life would have been with Edward, all I can see is my farm in Kenya. Which was not, for the record, at the foot of the Ngong Hills. I remember going to parties with Nicholas, feeling that thrill at knowing that I was married to the most sought-after man in the room. I'd enjoyed being the wife of the Aviator in the Iron Mask. I'd enjoyed the fuss and notoriety.

I'd enjoyed my own discreet affairs.

It wasn't the life I would have chosen at twenty-two, but having had it, the alternative seems curiously colorless.

I love Edward, I do. But would I have loved him after a lifetime at Carrington, of worrying about the roof and the rates and a dozen kinds of rot?

My mind flits back again, to the day after the Armistice, when I might have stayed and fought—and hadn't.

But none of that matters. We write history for our own ends. This is my chosen history now: the one in which Nicholas tricked us both, in which we have found each other again after all these years, the record set right.

"We're here now." I straighten the poppy in my onetime lover's buttonhole. "Peace, at last."

All for the Love of You

Jennifer Robson

PART ONE

Paris, France
March 1925

Her father was dying. Dr. Sorel didn't trouble to mince his words.

"Your father has pneumonia, Miss Fields, and there is no effective treatment."

"I don't understand. It was only a cold. Surely it can't be that serious."

"His lungs are weak, as you know, and now the infection has set in. He is dying. One day, perhaps two. It will not be long now. I am very sorry."

Dr. Sorel's diagnosis was shocking, of course, but it wasn't precisely a surprise. She had seen her father diminishing over the past months, his coughing fits becoming more frequent, more severe, and though he'd insisted it was simply the damp Paris winter disagreeing with him, she hadn't been convinced. Yet she had never quite imagined *this*.

Daisy sat at his bedside all that night, and for the day and night that followed. He slept nearly the entire time, rousing only when the medicine wore off and his cough stirred to life again. And then, in the wee hours near dawn, when light had begun to tug at the charcoaled fringes of night, he awoke.

His gaze was clear, unfogged by the morphia Dr. Sorel had administered, and he motioned for her to draw even closer, though her head was only inches away from his. He looked ghastly, his skin paper-thin and almost gray, and his features, in the thin light of dawn, resembled a death mask more than living human flesh.

She kissed his brow and grasped his near hand in hers, wishing it were enough to tether him to life.

"Forgive me," he whispered. "Did it . . . out of love. Didn't think . . . not worthy . . ."

"I don't understand, Daddy—you did what?"

"Forgive me . . ."

"Of course I will. I love you, Daddy."

He smiled feebly, and then he was asleep again, his expression slackening into something that almost resembled peace. Minutes passed, the space between his exhalations growing longer and longer, and though she longed for him to wake again, to see that she was there, to know that she loved him, he slipped further away with each rasping sigh.

A long-drawn whisper of escaping breath, and then . . . nothing. He was gone.

She stood, her limbs protesting after the hours she'd spent hunched at his side, and painstakingly straightened the sheets and coverlet over his still form. There was a fleck of spittle at the corner of his mouth, and she wiped it away with the same handkerchief she'd been using to blot the perspiration from his brow.

Somehow she made it across the bedchamber to the bathroom, its white tiles and gleaming chrome shockingly bright once she switched on the electric lights overhead. Standing before the sink, she splashed cold water on her face and wrists, watching with a calm sort of detachment at the funny way her hands were shaking. She smoothed back her hair, half of which had fallen out of its pins, but was too tired to do anything more.

At that moment she wanted nothing more than to crawl into bed and cry herself to sleep, but she had to take charge. For the first time in her life, she had no one to look up to for advice and support. She would have to manage on her own.

Knowing that her father wouldn't wish anyone else to see him struggling, she had kept the servants out of his bedchamber, only occasionally opening the door to admit supplies of fresh towels and lemon water. Their butler was waiting in the hall, as she'd expected he would do, and for all she knew the poor man had been there all night. He probably hadn't sat down the entire time.

"My father has passed away, Mr. Bishop. It was very peaceful," she added, seeing how he struggled to contain his shock. "Could I trouble you to send a note to Dr. Sorel? I shall need his help in sorting out the formalities."

"Yes, of course. May I fetch you anything, Miss Daisy? You haven't eaten anything in hours."

"No, thank you. I need to go through some papers in my father's office now, and I'd prefer not to be disturbed."

"Of course. I am so very sorry, Miss Daisy."

She tried to smile, and when that failed she set a comforting arm on the butler's sleeve, just to show him that she appreciated his kind words. Then she went downstairs to her father's office.

It smelled rather musty inside, for it had been shut up since that first awful chest infection had laid her father low at the beginning of the winter. After switching on the lights, which only managed to enhance the layer of dust over everything, she crossed to the windows beyond his desk, folded back the interior shutters, and opened the casements.

She'd been in this room only half a dozen times before, if that, for her father hadn't liked to be disturbed when he was working, and she'd never been brave enough to venture beyond its threshold when he was away from the house. Even now, his presence was still so strong she almost expected to blink her eyes and see him sitting at the huge double-pedestal desk, his degrees and citations adorning the wall behind him.

At length she found his will in a half-empty filing cabinet. Its terms were just as she'd expected, with her inheriting the entirety of his estate, apart from a few token bequests to colleagues, distant relatives, and servants. In a codicil, executed the same time as the will, he had expressed his wish to be buried in Green-Wood Cemetery in Brooklyn, New York, next to her mother. Daisy had no idea if it was practicable or even possible to transport her father's body such a long distance, but perhaps Dr. Sorel would be able to arrange something.

Setting aside the will, she resolved to make a list of everything that needed to be done. Lists always helped. She pulled out the desk drawer to her left, hoping to unearth some paper, but found only a sad collection of pen nibs and blotters, used-up pencils, bits of string, and, at the very back, an old envelope. That would have to do.

She took up one of the pencil ends, set the envelope on the desk before her, and was about to start writing when something, some half-felt frisson of curiosity, impelled her to take a second look. The envelope might hold a keepsake, or even an important document. It wouldn't do to deface it for nothing.

The front of the envelope bore her father's name and their address in Paris, but there was no return address. She pulled out the single sheet of paper inside; it was soft and worn, as if it had been read and refolded a hundred times.

November 27th, 1918

Dear Dr. Fields,

I hope you will forgive my boldness in writing to you directly, but I was so shocked by the sad news you imparted during our brief meeting today that I fear I left without properly expressing my sincere condolences on the untimely death of your daughter. I came only because I had been told that Miss Fields was ill and I was concerned for her well-being, and I apologize sincerely if my intrusion caused you any further distress.

I only knew your daughter for a short time, but in that period I came to consider her a true friend. I was a client of the Studio for Portrait Masks, and she was at my side

for every moment of my visits to the studio while my mask
was being fashioned. She was kindness and understanding
personified. She looked upon my ruined face without pity or
disgust. I shall mourn her for the rest of my life.

    Yours faithfully,

    Cpt. G. D. Mancuso

    Company C

    1st U.S. Engineers

Captain Mancuso. Daniel. The only man she had ever loved.

She had last seen him on Armistice Day, when bells had rung across Paris and people had danced and wept and embraced in the streets, and she had thought, then, that perhaps he might feel the same about her. She had gone home that night dizzy with delight and feverish with excitement—only it hadn't been happiness that had provoked such sensations, but rather the Spanish flu.

The following month had been an achy, shivering blur, and the only voice she could recall from that entire period was her father's, who had insisted on caring for her personally. As soon as she was able to sit up in bed, she'd written to Mrs. Ladd, who ran the studio, saying she was on the mend and asking after Captain Mancuso. Mrs. Ladd had answered promptly with the disappointing news that he had returned to America, and that she sadly had no notion of where to find him.

In desperation Daisy had turned to her father, saying only that she was concerned for the welfare of one of the studio's clients, and wished to assure herself that he was well. But her father had been adamant that it would be next to impossible to find Captain Mancuso, and had refused to discuss the matter any further. Why risk her heart and reputation, he had asked, for a man who had left France without even bothering to say good-bye?

She had spent the intervening years convinced that Daniel was indifferent, while Daniel had been told she was dead. Why on earth would her father have perpetuated such a lie? And what had prompted him to hide the letter rather than simply destroy it?

She read Daniel's letter again and again, and soon she had memorized its simple words. He had cared for her; she was sure of it. And yet . . . he had thought her dead for almost seven years. He might easily have married since then, and had a family. He might have forgotten about her entirely.

All true, but simply to *know* was better than anything else—better, certainly, than always wondering and wishing and hoping against hope.

She had to return to America in any case, for she had to deal with her father's estate, and she had his funeral and interment to arrange. She would have to leave things as they were here, and return later on to pack up the house and make arrangements for the staff.

"Mr. Bishop!" she called.

He was at the door in an instant. "Yes, Miss Daisy?"

"Would you mind coming in for a moment? Thank you. I'm not sure how to ask this, but hear me out. Back at the end of 1918, when I was ill with the flu, do you recall an American officer coming to the door and asking for me? You'd remember him because he was wearing a mask over one eye—the sort I helped to make at the studio."

"I do, Miss Daisy. I didn't notice the mask at first, but then I realized only one eye was blinking. It was rather, ah, disconcerting."

"I guess it can be. Well, I've found a letter in my father's desk, and it's from that officer. It seems my father may have told him I was dead. Do you remember anything about that?"

"I do recall his visit. He came to the house one day when you were sick. Your father spoke to him," Mr. Bishop said, swallowing reflexively. "I didn't listen to their conversation. I cannot abide an eavesdropper."

"Of course," she said soothingly.

"Your father took me aside after the officer had left. He told me the man was a cad and a bounder, and a danger to you. He made me swear not to speak of it. I do apologize, Miss Daisy. I thought I was helping to protect you."

"As did he," she whispered.

And then, because the time for talking was over, she opened another of the desk's drawers, found some paper and a decent pencil, and began to write out her list.

PART TWO

The American Red Cross Studio for Portrait Masks
Paris, France
October 20, 1918

As Daisy hurried along the boulevard du Montparnasse, she reflected on the anniversary she was celebrating, for it was exactly six months to the day—very nearly to the minute—since she'd first begun her work at the studio.

It wasn't the sort of thing she'd ever imagined she would end up doing, not least because she'd never imagined that such a place as the studio could even exist. The notion that a man might have his face blown apart and yet *live*, and then be expected to spend the rest of his life exposed to the horror and fear his appearance provoked, was something few people had thought of before the war and its chillingly modern apparatus of death.

Six months ago, however, she had met Anna Coleman Ladd at a dinner party. Mrs. Ladd's husband was a doctor, brought to France to aid in pediatric care, while Daisy's father was doing similar work at the American hospitals in Paris. Mrs. Ladd was a sculptor of some renown in Boston, and she'd seemed pretty intimidating to Daisy, who was only just eighteen and not accustomed to being included in the conversations of grown-ups.

But there had been something compelling about Mrs. Ladd, too, something that had encouraged Daisy to admit she was bored and restless, and badly in need of something to occupy her days. Mrs. Ladd had told her about the studio she had set up, the sort of work she and her assistants were doing, and had asked if Daisy might be interested in coming to help out with mundane tasks such as making tea and keeping the studio's clients company during their visits.

The position was unpaid, of course, for Daisy's father was wealthy and the studio operated on an exceedingly modest budget, with most of its funding coming from the American Red Cross and the French government. But she hadn't minded, for the work had promised to be interesting as well as fulfilling.

At first she'd only been allowed to make tea and tidy the studio and hold the hand of clients who were feeling anxious while casts of their features were being made, for it was a long and uncomfortable process. She had longed to do more, though, and at home, in the evenings, she had taught herself how to paint the iris of a human eye in an entirely realistic fashion.

Daisy had always enjoyed painting, and had benefited from the tutelage of some enlightened governesses over the years; what she lacked in technique she made up for in attention to detail. She couldn't block out a landscape or portrait to save her soul, but she could copy almost anything she was shown, down to the last brushstroke. If only forgery were considered a noble career.

She turned onto the rue de la Grande Chaumière, and then, almost straightaway, onto the rue Notre-Dame des Champs. Crossing through the high gates and across a courtyard strewn with statuary, none of it the work of Mrs. Ladd, she ran up the five flights to the studio itself.

"Hello, everyone! *Bonjour!*" she called out.

Mrs. Ladd had four proper assistants, all of them trained sculptors, and though sometimes they tended to be serious and even a bit stuffy about Art and Beauty, Daisy liked all of them well enough. Miss Blair was American, with some sort of connection to Harvard University that Daisy hadn't been brave enough to ask about, while Mr. Vlerick and Miss Brent were English. There was one Frenchwoman, too, Mademoiselle Poupelet, and she was awfully chic, with a severe, geometric haircut that put Daisy in mind of Cleopatra.

She exchanged hellos with everyone except Mrs. Ladd, who was at her desk attending to some correspondence, and went straight to work on preparing everyone's tea and coffee. Once that was done and everyone had been furnished with the morning's first round of refreshments, she set to work on arranging the bunches of marguerites and chrysanthemums she'd bought at the market on rue Cler, clipping the flowers' stems short and clustering them in old jam jars.

The day before they'd had a final fitting for a shy and very young Frenchman, perhaps only a few months older than Daisy herself. His injuries had healed months before, but he hadn't dared to return home, afraid of his mother's reaction if she were to see his missing jaw and contorted palate.

The mask had fitted him perfectly, with only the narrowest line showing where it ended and his face began, and she had been at his side for the final test: a walk along the boulevard du Montparnasse. They had walked arm in arm to the boulevard St.-Michel and back, and all that way no one had given him a second look. He had been shaking, the poor dear, and when they'd returned to the studio he had gone over to Mrs. Ladd and wept in her arms.

Today they had a new client coming in at half-past nine. Mrs. Ladd hadn't said much about him at all, only that his mask would be a straightforward commission, and that she might consider allowing Daisy to paint the eye.

Over the past six months, she had become a master at controlling her facial expressions. Before she had begun work at the studio, Mrs. Ladd had given her an envelope of photographs, and had instructed her to sit in front of a mirror and watch her reflection as she looked at the men they depicted. Only once she was able to entirely master her response could she begin.

It had taken her a week, and many tears shed for the men whose suffering she beheld, but she had done it. She wasn't indifferent, for no matter how many times she met a man with a ruined face she was horrified, and she likely always would be. It wasn't his appearance that upset her, though, but his pain.

By the time men came to the studio they were often beyond despair. They had seen their faces, and they were usually convinced their lives were over, although they still lived. She had grown to dread the look of weary acceptance in their eyes, but she had also discovered the joy of walking along the boulevards with a man who had learned how to hope again.

That initial flicker of hope—that was the first step for the men who came to the studio. It was a place where they might sit and talk and feel safe, and when they left for good they did so with a mask that protected them from the worst of strangers' reactions.

As for the response of those who loved them best? There was nothing any of them could do about that. She and Mrs. Ladd and the others could only hope that their clients' families would welcome them with open arms, and one day look upon their injured faces with placidity, understanding, and some degree of acceptance.

A few minutes after nine o'clock she heard it: the sound of careful, measured steps on the stairs. Sometimes those steps betrayed evidence of other injuries. Sometimes they simply marked a man's dread of exposing the stark truth of his injuries to complete strangers.

Daisy and the others always kept at their work when the client arrived. It was for Mrs. Ladd alone to go forward and greet him, and her warmth and unflinching gaze set the bar high for everyone else. Once their director had shown the man around the studio, Daisy was expected to greet him, make him tea if his injuries allowed him to drink comfortably from a cup, and then remain at his side throughout the entire process, especially at uncomfortable or emotionally difficult moments.

The footsteps were louder now; the new client would be at the door in a moment. Daisy continued with her task for the morning: trimming paper-thin sheets of tin into narrow, ruffled strips. These would then be painted to match a client's hair and used as eyelashes for his mask, for Mrs. Ladd thought the metal was more durable than actual hair.

The door to the studio was ajar, like always, but the man stopped and knocked at it tentatively. He took a step inside, and then another.

"Hello?"

Nearly all their clients were French, so his greeting was unusual enough for Daisy to pop her head up quickly, only long enough to see that he was wearing the uniform of an American infantry officer.

"Captain Mancuso. How very good to meet you. I'm Mrs. Ladd."

"Pleased to meet you, ma'am."

"Do come in, Captain, and allow me to show you around the studio. I'll introduce you to my colleagues, and then we'll get started.

A pause. "Sure thing, ma'am."

Daisy couldn't quite make out his accent, but his voice was strong and clear; without looking up she could tell his palate and jaw were uninjured. She longed to get a decent look at him, just to get a better sense of where he was from, but Mrs. Ladd would not approve. So she kept on snip, snip, snipping, and as she worked she listened carefully as Captain Mancuso was introduced to the other assistants, one after the other. And then their footsteps turned in her direction.

She wiped her hands on a cloth, for she didn't want any of the grease from her tin snips to get on his hands, and waited until she was certain Mrs. Ladd and Captain Mancuso were standing in front of her worktable. She looked up and met his gaze, and kept her face perfectly neutral for a count of three. Only then did she smile and extend her hand for him to shake.

"Captain Mancuso, this is Miss Fields," Mrs. Ladd explained. "She helps us out here at the studio. If you need anything during your visits—refreshments, for instance—she is at your disposal."

The man's injuries were far less severe than some she'd seen, and before the war he must have been accounted a handsome man. He would still be considered as such if he stood in profile with only the left side of his face showing, for he had a straight, high-bridged nose; dark, wavy hair that was cut very short; and his left eye was a clear, bright green, the exact color of new grass in the spring.

But his right eye was missing, the occipital bones around it shattered, as was his cheekbone. There were scars around the perimeter of his injuries, too, the skin there a livid red. Perhaps he had been burned as well.

He tried to return her smile, but it wasn't reflected in his gaze. That was to be expected, of course, for she hadn't yet earned his trust. She had to show him that she regarded him as a man, first and foremost, and not as an object of pity or derision. It wouldn't happen right away, but she was nearly always able to win over their clients, and she felt certain that she could persuade him to be her friend.

"It's a pleasure to make your acquaintance, Captain Mancuso. What part of the States do you call home?"

"New York City. I grew up in Manhattan, just north of Delancey."

She widened her smile. "I know exactly where that is. I grew up in the city, too."

"Now that you've met everyone," Mrs. Ladd began, "we'll get down to the work of creating your mask. If I could trouble you to come over and sit in the chair by the window? I need to examine your face in the best possible light. We'll take some measurements and make some observations, and then make a plaster impression of your face."

"Just the bad parts?" he asked, and it was hard to tell if he was fearful or simply curious.

"Although your injuries are confined to a small area, we like to take the mask of your entire face. That helps to ensure your mask is symmetrical. It is a rather uncomfortable process, I'm afraid, but Miss Fields will remain at your side. Some clients find it helpful to have a hand to hold, you see."

By way of answer he nodded, and when Mrs. Ladd and Miss Blair measured points on his face with a pair of calipers and a cloth tape he sat perfectly still, his back ramrod straight, his only movement the steady blink of his remaining eye. If he noticed or was distressed by their discussion of his wounds, he gave no sign of it.

"I think we are ready to begin the next step," Mrs. Ladd announced at last. "Mr. Vlerick will mix up the plaster and take an impression. If you'll excuse me for the moment."

Daisy had been standing just off to the side, but now she took up a stool and pulled it close to Captain Mancuso. "May I fetch you a cup of tea? Or a coffee?"

"A coffee would be nice. Black, no sugar. Thanks."

When she returned with the coffee, he gave her another smile, this one much less tentative, and she decided to see if he felt like talking.

He winced, just a little, at his first swallow of coffee.

"Is something wrong?" she asked.

"No," he said, smiling a little. "It's hot, that's all."

"It's a good thing you weren't here for my first efforts at making it. I didn't use nearly enough coffee grounds, and the results looked a lot like, well, dishwater. Mademoiselle Poupelet was the only person brave enough to tell me, you know. 'Miss Fields, this café is—'ow do you say?—exécrable.' And I said I was sorry, and next time I would make it stronger, only I was worried that I might accidentally make it too strong, and d'you know what she said? 'My dear Miss Fields, it is impossible to make the coffee that is too strong.' So next time I just filled the basket right up with coffee grounds—you know, the little thing inside the percolator?—and everyone loved it."

This provoked an even wider smile. "How did an American girl like yourself end up here in Paris during a war?"

"My father oversees the American hospitals here. He's good at that kind of thing—he's a doctor by training, you see—and so he agreed to come over and help when the army came calling. That was about a year ago. We have a house near the Champs de Mars, which is close enough for me to walk to the studio."

"He's fine with you coming here to work?"

"I'm not working, not really. I don't get paid—that wouldn't be right. I just come and help out, and it helps me pass the time. Daddy approves . . . I suppose. He knows Mrs. Ladd, you see, and he knows she has a studio here. I didn't . . . well, he may not be *entirely* aware of what Mrs. Ladd does here. And I'm not about to tell him, just in case he decides to get all old-fashioned about it."

He'd finished his coffee, so she took his cup to the sink and rinsed it out, and when she returned she decided to ask him a few questions. Nothing pressing or invasive, and she certainly wouldn't ask about the cause of his injuries.

"How long have you been in France?" she began.

"Just about as long as you, I guess. I signed up with the First U.S. Engineers, and we shipped out last summer. We spend most of our time clearing barbed wire, repairing trenches and dugouts, that kind of thing."

"I see," she said carefully.

"It happened about five months ago. We were getting ready for a big push on Soissons, and a German plane dropped a shell right in front of my dugout. A piece of casing spun off it. Bounced off an iron joist and hit me in the face. You know how some people say they didn't see it coming? Well, I did. It was the last thing I saw out of my right eye. There was a flash as the metal hit the joist, and I knew it was coming for me. I just knew it. And then it hit, and it was like someone had emptied a bucket of white paint over me. Everything went white. I woke up in hospital about a week later, but they didn't tell me about my face for a while after that."

"Is it still painful?" She wasn't supposed to ask such questions, but she needed to say something, and the usual platitudes were useless when talking about such a thing.

"Nah," he said, shaking his head. "The skin pulls a bit around the edges, right where they stitched me up, but mostly it's numb. The hard thing is seeing so little. I'm hoping I'll be able to work once I'm out."

"What did you do before the war?"

"I was a civil engineer. Not in the city, though. I worked in a little town upstate. Helping to plan new neighborhoods, deciding where to put the roads and water mains and sewers. That kind of thing. No idea if they'll want me back, or if . . . if they'll want me in the office. Hard to get used to a busted-up face like mine."

She squeezed his hand, for there was nothing she might say to take away the sting of truth in his words. His face wasn't hideous, not by a long stretch, but his injuries were arresting enough that others were likely to feel uncomfortable.

"Is your family still in the city?" she asked, hoping to lighten the mood.

"Yes. Both my ma and da are still alive. I've got two little sisters—not so little now. Both are married, with kids of their own. Haven't met my youngest niece yet. But it won't be long. Hoping they'll ship me home before the end of the year. Not much more I can do for the army now."

"It won't take forever to make your mask," she reassured him. "The longest stage is the painting. Mrs. Ladd is a perfectionist. She won't let you leave until it really is perfect."

"I know. I've heard about her. That's why I asked the colonel to get me in here."

"She is the best," Daisy agreed. "And your mask is the easiest one to make and fit, since not much of your face is affected."

"If you say so."

"She may suggest we attach the mask to a pair of spectacles. They help to hold it in place, but I find they also divert people's attention. They notice the spectacles, but that's all."

Mr. Vlerick approached them now. "We're nearly ready to get started, Captain Mancuso. Perhaps you might wish to visit the lavatory first. It's a rather long wait for the plaster to dry."

"Oh, sure. Good point."

When he returned Daisy was waiting for him at the casting chair, which was actually an old dentist's chair that Mrs. Ladd had found somewhere. He sat in it, a little gingerly, and looked at her expectantly.

"I'll be next to you the entire time, I promise. Your eye will be covered, and your mouth, so we need to settle on a signal for you to use if you really cannot bear it. Perhaps three short squeezes of my hand? I've a notebook, too, and a pencil. You can scribble notes to me—I know you won't be able to see as you write, but if I can read my father's handwriting I can read yours."

She took Captain Mancuso's left hand in hers, grasping it lightly as Mr. Vlerick began to work. He was very gentle as he covered their client with a draped sheet, and tucked his hair under a cotton cap. At each step, Daisy explained what was to occur.

"Mr. Vlerick is spreading petroleum jelly over your face, which will help to protect your skin from the plaster—it won't hurt you, but it can be a bit itchy. The plaster, that is. Now he's going to cover your face with some gauze strips that have been soaked in liquid plaster. Did you ever make papier-mâché in school? It's a bit like this."

Soon his good eye had vanished beneath the gauze, along with the rest of his face. Mr. Vlerick left small holes in front of his nostrils, and another, larger hole in the center of the captain's mouth, but that was all. It took a strong man indeed to withstand the sense of suffocation the drying plaster often provoked.

As soon as the gauze had been set in place, Mr. Vlerick applied a thicker layer of plaster, smoothing on layer after layer with a palette knife. All the while she stayed at Captain Mancuso's side, and when his grip on her hand tightened, she responded by wrapping her other hand around his wrist. He needed to know that she would not let go.

"We have to wait until the plaster is good and set," she explained once Mr. Vlerick had finished applying the final layer. "It might be as long as forty-five minutes. Would you like me to sing to you? Squeeze my hand if you do." His hand tightened decisively around hers.

"Oh, good. So . . . let me see. Why don't I try this one—my mother used to sing it to me.

> I'd choose to be a daisy
> If I might be a flower
> Closing my petals softly
> At twilight's quiet hour.

She sang the whole song through, and then embarked on "I Do Like to Be Beside the Seaside," another childhood favorite. And then she remembered a song she hadn't sung for ages.

"How about 'A Bicycle Built for Two'? At least, I think that's the name of the song. I like it because my name is Daisy. I was christened Dorothy, but no one calls me that." He squeezed her hand. "Yes, yes. Daisy Fields. Ha, ha. Someone ought to have told my parents that eighteen years ago. Let me see, now—how much of it do I remember?

> *Daisy, Daisy, give me your answer, do*
> *I'm half crazy, all for the love of you*
> *It won't be a stylish marriage*
> *I can't afford the carriage*
> *But you'd look sweet*
> *On the seat*
> *Of a bicycle built for two.*

She had nearly exhausted her repertoire of cheerful songs when Mr. Vlerick returned. "We're going to take off the plaster cast now," she explained.

As the cast was loosened, Captain Mancuso sat perfectly still, not even flinching when it pulled at his hair. The instant it was carried away, though, he took several deep breaths, as if he'd been starved for air when the plaster was covering his face.

"You stay here," she ordered. "I'll fetch a basin of soapy water, and we'll wash off the petroleum jelly and get you straightened away. While I do that, I'll tell you what's next."

He allowed her to wash his face, and if she lingered over the task, taking special care with the sensitive skin around his missing eye, it was only because he seemed to take comfort in her gentle touch, his rigid posture softening fractionally with every stroke of the washcloth across his skin.

"From here on in, it's quite nice," she told him. "The only unpleasant part of the process is the casting, and you're done with that."

"When am I supposed to come back?"

"One week from today. In the meantime Mrs. Ladd and her assistants will make two positive impressions using the cast. The first will show your face as it is now, and the second will become the base for the sculpture Mrs. Ladd will make of your restored face. We'll use that for the mask."

"So there will be one mask that shows me as I am, and another as I used to be?"

"As close as we can make it. Mrs. Ladd will want you to look at her sculpture, just so we know we've got it right. Once you're happy, we'll make the mask itself."

"You said it won't be big. I was worried . . . I thought I might have to wear something that covered my entire face."

"Oh, heavens, no. Hardly any of our clients needs more than a partial mask. Yours won't be large at all—just the area around your eye. We'll fit it to your face exactly, and since the copper is only one-thirty-second of an inch thick, there's barely any gap between it and your own skin."

"Can a piece of metal really look like skin?"

"In the hands of an artist like Mrs. Ladd it can. You'll wear the mask while she's painting it, and that way it will match perfectly. She won't let you go until it's perfect."

"Honestly?"

"It will be good enough for you to walk along the boulevard du Montparnasse in broad daylight and no one will take a second look at your face. And if they do, it will only be to remark on what a handsome young man you are."

"No," he said, disbelief shading his voice. "I don't believe it."

"I know it's hard to believe, but it is possible. I wouldn't say so if it weren't."

"It's just . . . I've got so used to it. The look in their eyes when they see me. No one means to be cruel, but . . ."

"People are shocked by anyone who is different, and very few are able to hide that shock. It's rather feeble of them, to be honest, but it won't be something you have to worry about for much longer. There—all clean. Here's a towel."

"Thanks."

"How are you getting home?" she asked once he had dried his face.

"I'll walk. I'm staying in barracks at the American hospital in Clignancourt. I have a kind of patch that I wear. See?"

He pulled a wide strip of khaki cloth from the breast pocket of his uniform jacket and tied it diagonally across his face. "How's this?"

"Very dashing. You look like a buccaneer. All you need is a parrot for your shoulder and a gold hoop in your ear."

They both stood, and he shook her hand, and then she went to check the date and time of his return visit with Mrs. Ladd. He remained next to his chair as she did this, absolutely motionless, and she wondered if he'd always had the gift of stillness. Perhaps it was something he'd only learned in the wake of his injury, for many of the studio's clients were equally good at blending into the woodwork.

"Mrs. Ladd says next Wednesday is fine. Does half-past nine still suit you?"

"It does."

"Then I'll see you next week."

"Thanks, Miss Fields. Thanks for everything."

DAISY WAS RARELY MORE THAN AN ARM'S LENGTH AWAY FROM Captain Mancuso on his subsequent visits. He talked about his childhood on Orchard Street, where he'd grown up in a three-room cold-water flat on the fourth floor of a crumbling tenement building. He told her how he'd worked two jobs after school, even when he was a boy, to help out his parents and save up for college. He explained how structures like the Statue of Liberty and the Brooklyn Bridge had been built with the help of engineers. He described some of the work he had done since graduating from college, and the things he wanted to do with his life once he returned to America.

Daisy responded with gentle tales of her childhood—summers in Narragansett, outings to Central Park with her governess, a tour of Continental spa towns the year before her mother died. It was impossible to hide the difference in their upbringings, and it would have been insulting to Captain Mancuso even to try. Besides, they were both Americans in Paris now, with more to unite than divide them.

One afternoon they happened to leave the studio at the same time, and he was kind enough to escort her home. Afterward she could recall nothing of their conversation, for her thoughts had been entirely consumed by the man who walked beside her. His height. The breadth of his shoulders. His strong, capable hands. The rumble of his laugh. Just thinking about the way he laughed made her smile.

She had to conceal such sentiments, for Mrs. Ladd would

surely have disapproved, and yet she couldn't bring herself to affect complete disinterest in him. That would have served only to crush his confidence, or whatever shreds still remained of it. Instead she took pains to be her normal, friendly self, treating Captain Mancuso just as she would any other client who came to the studio, and if her heart began to beat a little fast when he arrived at the studio—well, no one ever needed to know.

Soon he was at the studio every other day, for his mask had been cast and silvered, and Mrs. Ladd had begun to paint it to match his complexion. Slowly but surely, the gray of the metal vanished beneath layers of enamel paint, and the mask itself seemed to disappear.

When all was complete but the iris of the mask's single eye, Mrs. Ladd handed her brushes over to Daisy. "Miss Fields will paint your eye, Captain Mancuso. She has a fine eye for color, and your eye is a most unusual shade of green. I hope you don't mind."

"Not at all, Mrs. Ladd."

Daisy had been hoping for weeks now that Mrs. Ladd would allow her to contribute to Captain Mancuso's mask, and with that goal in mind she had spent many hours practicing in the early morning, before leaving for the studio, on scraps of silvered copper that she'd fished out of the wastebin at the studio. It had taken some experimentation to get the striations of his iris just right, but eventually she'd discovered the trick of including minute streaks of brown to the brighter green and gold that one noticed so readily.

It took two long sessions for her to paint the iris, and as she worked she had to stare into his existing eye to ensure the two exactly matched. For the most part they didn't talk, for he needed to stay perfectly still as she worked, and there were times she longed to set down her brush and ask him what he was thinking, for the expressions that traveled across his face had a nearly mesmerizing effect on her.

At last, and with a certain amount of regret, she set down her brush. The eye she had fashioned was perfect. The mask was perfect.

"May I see?" he asked.

"Not until Mr. Vlerick has added the spectacles. Then Mrs. Ladd will inspect it—and if she approves I will bring you a mirror. But I will tell you right now that it is perfect."

"When should I come back?"

"Anytime tomorrow is fine. The last layer of paint needs to cure overnight, but it will be ready by the morning."

"I'll come around ten. Perhaps we'll have had some news from Compiègne by then."

"We can only hope. Until then, Captain Mancuso."

As Daisy walked to the studio the next morning, everyone she passed was speaking of an armistice, though no one was entirely certain of the details. Maréchal Foch and the other Allied leaders had been meeting with the Germans and Austrians at a secret location near Compiègne, and the Kaiser had abdicated two days earlier. Yet nothing seemed certain, not yet, and Daisy couldn't quite bring herself to hope.

When she arrived at work, no one there was any more certain, and without any definitive news one way or the other it seemed best to simply carry on and see what the day would bring. Captain Mancuso arrived at ten on the dot, and everyone gathered around as he sat for the final fitting of his mask, which had been attached to a pair of spectacles with clear lenses. Mrs. Ladd adjusted it minutely, and then, after a long, final look, nodded her head in approval. That was Daisy's signal to bring forward the hand mirror, which was kept hidden at other times.

She stood before Captain Mancuso and held it so he might see his new face, and the look of wonder and delight that crept across his features was enough to bring tears to her eyes. He smiled, and nodded, and everyone burst into applause.

"Thank you, Mrs. Ladd. I think you and your colleagues may have given me my life back."

"I earnestly hope so. Now it is time for your final test. Miss Fields will—what is that sound? Is that church bells?"

They stood there and listened to the sound of bells and car horns and cheering in the street, and presently Mr. Vlerick ran down the stairs to investigate. He was back, tears streaming down his face, only a minute or two later.

"It's over!" he shouted. "The war is over! The Armistice began at eleven o'clock."

Suddenly they were all embracing one another, laughing and crying at once, and without thinking she threw her arms around Captain Mancuso and hugged him tight. She drew back a moment later, alarmed by her effrontery, and more than a little concerned that she might have dislodged his mask. But it was still in place, was still perfectly unobtrusive, and it was time for his final test.

"I think we should go down to the boulevard now," she told him. "May we, Mrs. Ladd?"

"I can't imagine a finer way to celebrate. Off you go."

They ran down the stairs together, arm in arm, and were quickly swept up in the growing crowds along the boulevard du Montparnasse. Someone had brought an accordion, and as its opening drone expanded into the familiar chords of the "Marseillaise" everyone around began to sing, and Daisy thought she had never before heard such a glorious choir. The accordionist played "God Save the King," and then "The Star-Spangled Banner," and she and Captain Mancuso held their hands over their hearts and sang at the top of their lungs.

The final notes of the anthem died away, replaced by faster, jauntier music, and all around them couples began to dance. Captain Mancuso swept her into his arms and down the street, and after she had digested her first reaction—that he was an astonishingly good dancer—she realized that she was happy, deliriously so. Although some of her joy was certainly wrapped up in the news of the Armistice, much of it was attached to the man who held her, a man she had come to know so well, but about whom she knew so little. She didn't even know his first name.

At last they swirled to a halt, and rather than continue to be pushed along the street by the ever-growing crowds, Captain Mancuso directed them toward one of the side streets, where it was quieter and calmer.

"Thank you, Miss Fields. You don't know how long it's been since I danced. That was just great."

"Won't you call me Daisy?" she asked.

"I will, but only if you'll call me Daniel."

Daniel. Such a lovely name for a man. "I suppose we ought to go back to the studio. I don't want Mrs. Ladd to worry."

"You're right. I guess I passed the test."

"That you did. I don't think anyone so much as blinked. I'm so happy for you, Daniel."

They walked arm in arm, back through the side streets, the

gaiety of the boulevards a half-heard echo. Before long they were at the gate to the courtyard, and then they were at the bottom of the stairs, where the light was clear and pure, and it seemed to her that he was the handsomest man she had ever known, mask or no mask.

Daniel Mancuso was the nicest man she had ever met, too, and he was funny and intelligent and well-read, and she knew it wasn't kindness on her part to a man who had suffered so much—it was simply the truth. He only had to turn his head toward her and everyone else in the room faded away.

It tore at her heart, the knowledge that he would soon be leaving for America. Perhaps he might give her an address in America where she might send him letters. Perhaps, one day, she might see him again.

She opened her mouth to suggest just this, but then Daniel was bending his head and his lips were on hers, and he was kissing her so fiercely, so passionately, that she forgot to breathe. When he did pull away they were both gasping.

"I'm sorry," he said. "I shouldn't—"

"Don't apologize. I'm glad you kissed me. It was my first kiss, and it was wonderful."

If only they might stay where they were a little longer. Not forever, not long enough for their absence to be noticed and remarked upon. Only long enough for another kiss or three, and the chance to bask in the comfort of his embrace. But they had been gone far too long already, even taking into account the celebrations outside.

"We had better go upstairs."

"I know," he said, and he took her arm and they walked upstairs to the studio.

"Success?" asked Mrs. Ladd when she saw them.

"Success," Daniel agreed. "Thank you so much. I'm . . . I wish I could tell you what this means to me."

"You are most welcome, Captain Mancuso. I should like you to return in one week, if you can spare the time, just to ensure your mask requires no further adjustments."

"I'd be happy to return," he said, and Daisy knew, without his saying, that he would be counting the hours until his appointment.

"Good-bye, then," he said, and they all said good-bye, and then he was gone.

Daisy floated home not long after, for Daniel had been the studio's only client of the day. Her father was at the house when she arrived, and was uncharacteristically ebullient.

"We shall hold a party. Next week, I think, and we'll have all my colleagues to dinner. What do you say, my dear?"

"That sounds wonderful, Daddy. I wonder . . . I'm feeling a little tired. I think I ought to go to bed."

"Too much excitement, I'll bet. Well, off you go to bed, and I'll see you in the morning."

As she got ready for bed, Daisy let her thoughts drift to the future. Daddy would wish to return to New York before long, and Daniel would be there, too, and she would introduce him to her father. Daddy would be sure to like him, for Daniel was an officer and an educated man, and after that who knew what might happen?

She slept badly, waking in the middle of the night with a fever that seemed intent on consuming her, and a terrible tightness in her chest that made every breath a painful ordeal. If only she could get to her father. He would know what to do.

She toppled out of bed, only catching hold of the bedstead at the last moment, and by force of will alone propelled herself across the bedchamber. The door was so hard to open, for her palm was slick with sweat, but finally she was in the hall, running in search of her father, calling his name.

"Daisy—oh, God! Daisy, my girl!"

But before her could reach her, the world turned on end, the floor rushed up to meet her, and she knew no more.

It was broad daylight when she woke, the fever gone, and with it every particle of her strength. She was so weak she couldn't even lift her head from the pillow, and it was another fifteen days—on top of the three she'd been out of her mind with fever dreams—before she was able to sit up for more than a few minutes.

She begged her father for permission to visit the studio, for Mrs. Ladd must surely need her there, but he wouldn't even consider it.

"You're not well enough, and I doubt you will feel like yourself for some time."

"But Daddy—you know what it means to me. I loved my days at the studio."

"It's simply too taxing. Besides, Mrs. Ladd is returning to America. The Red Cross has cut its funding now that the war is over."

So she wrote to Mrs. Ladd, thanking her for everything, wishing her well, and only at the end, in a postscript, did she dare to ask after Captain Mancuso. A reply was delivered the next morning.

December 2, 1918

My dear Miss Fields,

Such a relief to receive your note—I have shared the news of your recovery with everyone at the Studio, and they all extend their warmest regards. I return to Boston in several weeks, which is a great disappointment as I had so hoped to continue my work here, but with our funding reduced so dramatically I cannot bear to go on.

If you do return to America I should be very happy to see you again. You have the makings of a fine artist in you and I do encourage you to develop your talents so far as your interest allows.

I'm afraid I have no information on Captain Mancuso's current whereabouts, for those details are kept by military officials and were never freely shared with me. He did ask after you when he came for his last visit, and was visibly unsettled by the news of your illness. I do hope you are able to find him again.

With my fond regards,
Anna Coleman Ladd

All she had was his name, the knowledge that he was an engineer, and a neighborhood in New York that was one of the most populous in the world. Besides, he didn't even live there anymore—he had moved to a town outside the city, and as he'd never told her its name she had no notion of where to even begin.

After another two days, she worked up the courage to ask her father if he might help her locate Captain Mancuso. Though normally an even-tempered man, her father refused her request before she'd even finished explaining herself.

"This illness has made you soft in the head, Daisy. There's no way of knowing where he's gone, or who he truly is. How do you know that's even his real name? I cannot use my connections to find him, and you ought to know better than to ask."

"I'm sorry, Daddy, I only—"

"If he had any real interest in seeing you again, surely he would have left a note with Mrs. Ladd. Take my advice and forget him. You'll be happier for it—I know you will."

PART THREE

New York City
October 20, 1925

EXACTLY SEVEN YEARS AGO, AROUND ABOUT THIS TIME OF day, she had met Daniel for the first time. Seven years, and they had been parted for nearly all that time.

She had been searching for him for months, ever since her return to America that spring. She'd arranged her father's funeral, sorted out the muddle of his finances and properties, and even taken part in the wedding of her best friend in June. All the while, her search for Daniel had occupied her every waking hour, and had been the cause of many sleepless nights, besides.

She had begun with the veterans' offices in New York, all of them, but none had been especially forthcoming, citing privacy concerns as a deterrent. She then turned to a private investigator, which seemed sensible as he might simply furnish her with a list of potential names and other pertinent details. Instead he made off with her money before placing a single telephone call.

Almost as disheartening was her realization, once the mess of her father's estate had been untangled, that he had been living well beyond his means for years, if not decades. Once his debts were settled there was little left, apart from the windfall of a small insurance policy. So she moved out of the Plaza hotel, where she had been wallowing in luxury for some months, found a modest ladies' hotel on the Upper East Side, and set about tracking down every Mancuso in the state of New York.

There were hundreds of them, she soon discovered, and while many lived in Daniel's old neighborhood off Delancey Street, hundreds more were scattered across the five boroughs of the city and farther afield.

She spent a few precious dollars on classified advertisements in the English- and Italian-language newspapers, with no success. She wrote to every engineering firm in the state, also to no avail. She even considered drawing a portrait of Daniel and walking door-to-door with it through the streets of the Lower East Side, but quickly abandoned that scheme as unrealistic. It had been years since she'd seen him, after all, and her memories might play her false.

For so long she had refused to admit it, but now the reality of her failure was staring her in the face: Captain Daniel Mancuso had disappeared off the face of the earth, and she was unlikely to ever see him again.

It was depressing, but then a lot about her life had turned upside down in the past six months. Feeling badly about it would only make everything seem worse. She needed to get out of her room at the hotel and walk through the park for an hour. Central Park was lovely in the autumn, and once she'd had her fill of crisp, clean air and copper-bright leaves, she would think seriously about what she ought to do next.

When she returned home, the morning mail had been delivered. There were a few envelopes that looked interesting, so she fished them out of her pigeonhole and went upstairs to her room. From Columbia University: a brief letter stating that no Daniel Mancuso had ever been enrolled in their Department of Civil Engineering. From Manhattan College: the same. From the City College School of Technology: the same, followed by the qualification that a Giovanni Daniele Mancuso had been a graduate of the class of 1914.

With trembling hands she opened Daniel's letter from 1918 and scanned it again. He had signed it G. D. Mancuso.

She had to focus: he had once worked as an engineer at a growing town in upstate New York. She would write to the public works department for every possible town, and this time ask if a G. D. Mancuso were in their employ. It might take months, even years, for there had to be hundreds of towns large enough to merit such a department. But what else did she have but time?

ASTONISHINGLY, SHE FOUND HIM A WEEK LATER. HE WAS LIVING in Rome, New York, not far from Syracuse, and was the manager of their public works department. Her letter, which she dashed off in a matter of minutes, went into the post that same day.

October 27, 1925

My dearest Daniel,

>*I am alive.*
>
>*I am alive, and I am so sorry that you were led to believe otherwise by my father, whose motivation for deceiving you escapes reason. He died earlier this year, and only then did I learn what he had done to you, and to me.*
>
>*I am well, and I have been happy enough over these intervening years, but I have never forgotten you, and I have hoped, always, that I might one day see you again.*
>
>*I am living in Manhattan, at Mrs. Young's Hotel for Ladies on Lexington Avenue, and expect to remain at this address for some time. If you can bear to renew our friendship I should be very glad of it, but at the same time I promise that I will understand if you prefer not to hear from me again.*
>
>*All I wish for you is happiness, and I pray that you have found it.*
>
>*With my fond regards,*
>
>*Daisy*

A week went by, then another, and she received no reply. It was just possible, of course, that there were two men named G. D. Mancuso working as civil engineers in the state of New York, and that one of them was currently puzzling over a love letter he had received from a complete stranger.

It was also possible that the right G. D. Mancuso had received her letter but had decided not to answer, or was afraid to do so. He might be married, or otherwise attached.

These worries and questions carried her through the first part of November, and then she woke up one morning and realized it was Armistice Day. There was a memorial in Central Park to the fallen soldiers of the 107th Infantry, she recalled, and likely there would be some kind of remembrance ceremony at eleven o'clock. She had nothing else to do, and nowhere else to go; and there was a great deal she wished to remember, besides, as well as a great many men who deserved her prayers of thanksgiving.

She was at the front door of her hotel, about to leave for the ceremony, when she remembered that she would definitely need a handkerchief. Had she tucked one into her handbag? Best to make sure, first, before setting off for the—

"Hello, Daisy."

She looked up, or rather down, at the man who was standing at the foot of the steps outside her hotel.

It was Daniel, and he was exactly as she remembered him. He hadn't changed a bit, not in all those years, although he now wore a patch over his missing eye rather than the mask she had helped to create. It was Daniel, and he was every bit as handsome as her memories had insisted.

She walked down the steps, her legs trembling so much that she had to clutch at the handrail. And then she was standing on the sidewalk, looking up at him, and for a moment they simply stood and stared at one another.

"I got your letter last week. I wrote back right away. I mean, I wrote a letter to you, and it took me forever. I must have gone through a forest's worth of paper."

"That's all right. I'm sure you had a lot to say."

"I finished it yesterday, but when I went out to mail it I walked right past the post office and ended up on the train to Manhattan. It took me until now to work up the courage to come here."

"I'm glad you did," she said.

"Now that I'm here, though, I'm not sure what to say. I . . ."

"What are you holding?" she asked, noticing the envelope in his hands. "Is that the letter I sent you?"

"No. It's my letter to you. The one I didn't mail. Would you . . . would you read it for me now?"

Her hands were trembling, so it took her a few tries to tear open the envelope and unfold the single sheet of paper within.

November 10, 1918

My dearest Daisy,

It's not a romantic thing to say, but my life has been fine in the years since we parted. I have a good job, I live in a nice town with people who don't seem to notice or care how I look, and I have enough friends and family to keep me busy on Saturdays and give me company on the holidays. It has been a fine life so far, but something has always been missing—you.

I think of you in the morning, when I first wake and I'm still sleepy enough to imagine I might see you again, and I think of you during the day, sometimes at the strangest moments. I think of you whenever I see daisies growing in a garden, or I drink a cup of crummy coffee, or I hear someone singing that song about the bicycle built for two. I think of you in the evening, as I sit alone in my little house, with only my dog for company—he's a fine dog, by the way, and I think you'd like him. I think of you as I fall asleep, and pray that I'll see you in my dreams.

I don't wear the mask you made me, for it's chipped and bent and it doesn't really fit me anymore. Yet I keep it still, sitting on my bedside table, for it's all I have of you. All your kindness and loveliness and grace is wrapped up in that piece of copper and paint, and if my house were burning down that mask and my dog would be the only things I'd save.

I wish I could hate your father for separating us, but I don't, for you loved him and he loved you, and I guess he was just trying to do what he thought was best.

I wish I could tell you how I felt when I opened your letter, and realized that you were alive. Alive. I'm not ashamed to say I cried, and I might have cursed your father once or twice. But that's all in the past.

I want to see you as soon as you're ready, and I want to try to make up for lost time. I won't push you for anything more than you want to give—I'm happy just to know that you are happy.

I know we need to begin again, for seven years is a long time, and I'm sure we've both changed a lot. So that is all I ask—if we might begin again.

Yours faithfully,
Daniel

She read the letter through a second time, just to make sure, and as she did so the last of her fear melted away, replaced by a calm and wonderfully steady sort of certainty.

"Do you remember the song I used to sing for you?" she asked.

"Yes," he said, and he began to sing, right there in front of her hotel, on Lexington Avenue, as bemused pedestrians wandered by. "*'Daisy, Daisy, give me your answer, do. I'm half-crazy, all for the love of you'*—"

"Yes, Daniel," she interrupted. "Yes. I want to begin again."

For Claudio

After You've Gone

Evangeline Holland

Paris—Late November 1918

FUTURE GENERATIONS WILL LOOK BACK AND WONDER WHAT it was like to be alive in the last days of the war. Of the moment when the earth, churned beneath the armies of Allied forces and Central Powers, heaved one last gasp of victorious violence before settling into a silence weighted with exhaustion and death. At the moment, the task of finding my way back home was of greater concern—wherever and whatever home was—and I could not share the elation bubbling forth across the Western Front and in Allied capitals. The end had come too late for me.

But I've never been the type to peek at endings, and as Armistice celebrations carried on across Paris, I was in my little garret room packing my meager possessions in the cracked leather kit bag Charles had bequeathed me upon his death, preparing to fling myself blindly into whatever future lay ahead of me. I had little regrets about abandoning this room. It was dank and dark, with a ceiling of slanted, smoke-scarred beams and two small windows that were stingy with light even on the brightest of days, and prone to attracting quizzical, brave mice.

Into the bag went my shirtwaists and skirts, my soft-brimmed hats, my wooden brush and comb set, and the silver picture frame of myself, Charles, Addie, and Louis in our last act—a valuable I hadn't the heart to pawn. Foolish, they would have called me, for I dearly needed the money. Soppy, I often told myself, because the war had steadily leeched every ounce of sentiment from my body. I paused in packing, my dancing slippers clutched to my chest. Perhaps that was why I had been turned away by more than one director in Paris's numerous variety theaters.

Not that I would have had much success otherwise. The Folies Bergère, where I'd managed to obtain a sporadic part dancing in the chorus of one of their many revues, hadn't needed me after the matinée two months ago. It was time to celebrate Vive La France and *la patrie*, and I, a distinctly colored Scot—no matter how fluent my French—would take a position rightly given to a more deserving French girl.

My fingers curled around the satin shoes, rubbing fabric pilled with age and wear. Charles and I had moved so well together, our steps as one, as we danced the maxixe or the tango across the floors of the best European nightclubs and theaters. I had even set a minor fashion with my draped hobble skirt, which made the fluid, leggy movements so much easier to execute. It had also made running easier, which we had done much of when war swept across the Continent, almost stranding our four-piece dancing troupe in Budapest. I had run again, tripping down the railway platform, pushing through the crowds, in order to keep my hand linked with Charles's, as he and Louis were shipped off to the Front after joining the French army.

I jumped in shock, the shoes thudding on the floor from nerveless fingers, when a blurry shape pounced onto the kitbag. The gray and brown tabby that had followed me to my garret one night and refused to leave, now sat on my clothing and stared at me with accusing green eyes.

"Go away." I flicked my hands at the cat, who predictably declined to obey my order.

I had learned a painful lesson during the one and only time I attempted to handle this intractable cat, and so I turned back to my open clothespress to gather the rest of my belongings. I pressed my lips together at the sight of Charles's uniform, folded neatly at the bottom of the drawer. In the dim light cast by the tallow candles on my nightstand, the faded, ashen blue twill of the French poilu's uniform appeared a deep, vivid navy. Only closer inspection revealed the shadowy patches to be the dark spread of Charles's blood after he'd been killed by shrapnel. There hadn't been enough of Louis to send back to Addie.

Part of me wanted to leave the uniform where it lay, to shed any and all tangible memories of the war when I departed. I knew he was dead, and how he'd been killed, and that he wasn't ever coming back. A bloodstained uniform wasn't a necessary aide-mémoire. Still, I reached for it, stiff and heavy with age, to place inside my suitcase (the cat had abandoned it once I showed no interest in it, and was now washing his face with his paw). The dancing shoes I'd dropped were the last items left unpacked, and once these had been stuffed between my shirtwaists, I could now tug the kitbag closed and fasten the leather straps.

I sat for a moment on the bed to lace my sturdy boots and then grabbed the bag and hat.

The cat was at my feet in a trice, nearly causing me to stumble over his sinewy body as I moved toward the door.

He glared up at me, mouth opened wide on a terrifying whine of defiance.

"No, you can't come," I scolded.

The cat let out a series of chirps, his furry head cocked, as though to demand I explain why I wouldn't take him with me.

"You just can't," I said tautly, feeling ten times a fool for trying to reason with this cat.

A cat whom I hadn't had the heart to name though he had slept on my bed for the past six months, and had been the only one waiting eagerly for me when I trudged home, footsore and weary, after a late show.

The door slammed open, causing the cat to flee through whatever hidey-hole he burrowed into whenever someone entered my garret. I looked up to see Françoise Daudet lounging in my open door. A Gauloises cigarette dangled between two fingers and the other hand clutched the lapels of a short dressing gown stretched over her ample breasts, as she surveyed me through kohl-rimmed eyes between the haze of her cigarette smoke.

"So you're leaving, are you?" said Françoise in her rapid, Lyonnais-accented French. "Not without what you owe me."

"I've paid my share of the rent through next week," I replied coldly, moving past her indolent form.

"You've forgotten about the doctor's fees when you were sick for a fortnight, and the medicine I sent Marie to fetch during an air raid," she said, stepping into my path. "There's also the matter of your excessive use of candles."

She fidgeted nervously beneath my flat stare, her rouged lips pulling into a clownlike grimace.

I set my bag on the floor and opened it to retrieve my small handbag. The short stack of francs were cold and heavy, and I plonked them one by one into her waiting palm. Avarice gleamed in Françoise's pale eyes as she glanced around the neat garret room, undoubtedly hoping to discover another infraction. She gave a little Gallic shrug, her mouth pursed into a moue of disappointment as she brought the cigarette to her lips.

"I would have regretted calling a gendarme on you after your wretched experience." She pocketed what were the last bits of my savings and stepped aside.

I owed her far more than this, she'd reminded me countless times over the last three years. Five hundred francs she'd spent to collect me from the jail where I'd been sent after a gendarmerie picked me up on the streets of Montmartre—and to pay for documents that allowed me to remain in France. My gratefulness was grudging; since her rescue was based on so many conditions I had often wondered if I wouldn't have been better off in a French prison. At least I would have had my dignity—no, I paused mentally. I had my dignity. It was my excessive pride that had been trampled and bruised by what I'd had to do in order to survive.

I didn't look back after picking up my bag to pass Françoise and descend the narrow, creaking staircase of the equally narrow house of ill repute.

MORE THAN A LITTLE TREMOR OF TREPIDATION PASSED THROUGH me as I squinted beneath the early afternoon sun from where I stood on the Pont de la Concorde. This was the very bridge from which Addie had thrown herself not quite four years ago, to be fished out hours later by sympathetic *Bateau-Omnibus* passengers not yet inured to the sight of death. At the time I had mourned her as a coward; I now thought her brave.

And now I was the coward, intimidated by the long, unknown vistas of life just as I was by the long, unknown vistas of the war.

Try as I might, I couldn't ignore the truth: I had very little money, I knew very few people in Paris (well, who would acknowledge me outside the cover of night), and very little claim to anything resembling a home. Memory of a letter I'd hoped to be my salvation suddenly sprang into my mind, like a blast of artillery. It broke me to pieces like artillery, too, and I tightened my grip on my kitbag as I crossed the bridge to the Right Bank, where the remnants of last night's orgy of celebration littered the Place de la Concorde. French flags, American flags, British flags, and striped bunting fluttered from windows and balconies of the Hôtel de Crillon. Wreaths of flowers now encircled the Strasbourg statue at its center, and multicolored confetti blanketed the pavement, shushing beneath the wheels of the motorbuses and automobiles crossing the square.

The gurgling waters of the Fontaines de la Concorde were a balm, however. They reminded me of the first time I saw Paris; a dazzling, beguiling Paris that seemed to offer endless oppor-

tunities. Charles had often discussed settling here on a permanent basis, perhaps in one of the bucolic suburbs, as the French
had been the most welcoming and enthusiastic over our colored
dance troupe. That was why we hadn't left Paris during the mad
rush during the war. By the time Louis had been killed at Artois,
six months after he and Charles joined the French army, it was
far too late for me and Addie to leave the country, even had we
desired it.

My arms began to tire of holding the heavy leather bag, and I
started for the Jardin des Tuileries, at the right of the square, also
ignoring the nascent ache of hunger in my belly. I had to remain
vigilant about the expenditure of my last francs. The cost of living
had risen tremendously over the past four years, and rationing had
made the traditional French breakfast of rich, buttery brioche and
piping-hot cup of coffee a thing of the past. Still, my mouth filled
with a taste memory of such *petits déjeuners*, and in my gastronomic
distraction, I failed to notice the knot of idlers standing in the pas-
sageway to the Orangerie until one of them backed directly into
me. I went sprawling on the grass, my bag flying from my grasp to
land above my head.

A press of people immediately surrounded me. I looked up, my
brows slanted in irritation, and one of the group peered at me over
the cover of their English-French dictionary in surprise.

"Why, you're a colored girl!" the woman exclaimed in American-
accented English. "Help her up, Lionel, since you were the one to
knock her over."

"Allow me."

I closed my eyes at the sound of the rich, molasses-tinged drawl
of the man extending his hand to me. What memories it evoked,

for Charles had sounded just like this; its foreignness had delighted and stymied me upon our first meeting, so accustomed was I to the clipped accents nearly everyone in the British theater circuit took on—unless the broad regional accents were part of their skits. But there was something a little more substantial in this man's voice, a bold purposefulness that was absent from Charles's easygoing tenor.

His hand was still waiting when I opened my eyes, and despite the barrier of our gloves, something strange ran through me when I placed mine in his.

I handily identified the emotion that bathed my face in heat when I glanced up the length of his sleeve to meet his eyes. Shy! There I was, at twenty-eight, with reams of ill-begotten experience, and was unexpectedly, absurdly bashful at looking a man in the face. And it was the most beautiful face I'd ever seen. Tawny tanned skin stretched over features both sharp and strong, with cheekbones so high it was as though a sculptor had scooped a tad too much clay while forming his appearance. The fullness of his bottom lip and the faint crease of dimples—dimples I knew would be deep enough to pillow my forefingers when he smiled—softened the severity of his face.

It was a crime for a man to be this handsome, and as he helped me to my feet, I was reminded of how worn and tired I must have appeared. Too thin beneath my heavy coat, the bruises of fatigue shadowing my eyes, and my unruly hair just reaching my jawline after the doctor had cut it when I came down with a virulent strain of influenza. His intense scrutiny exacerbated my sudden feelings of inadequacy. Those who had collected my cigarette cards, or saved my clippings from theater periodicals, would find little trace of the vivacious, curvaceous music hall performer I'd been before the war.

"I recognize you," he said suddenly, his grip tightening around my hand. "Didn't you play in—"

"You must be mistaken." I pulled my hand from his and bent to grasp my bag, almost hugging it to myself as a shield.

"Are you sure?" He moved to block my path. "Miss Morven Williams?"

"Now why don't you let her alone, Sidney?" one of the older women, in blue-green khaki uniform and cap, scolded. "Are you all right, honey? Do you need some assistance?"

"No, I'm all right," I replied, backing away from their curious gazes. "I was on my way to the British consul."

The woman's deep-set brown eyes softened with sympathy. "On your way back home now that the war is over, I'll bet. Your folks will be mighty glad to see you."

"Yes." I forced my mouth into a smile.

The smile wobbled at the corners and then threatened to collapse when my eyes met his—Sidney, the woman had called him. The narrowing of his eyes and the rigid line of his jaw as he stared at my face made my stomach churn, as though he knew something about me that I didn't . . . or feared to know. There was something disturbing in his insistence that he recognized me. I had never toured in America, especially after marrying Charles. It was possible that he had caught one of my shows, but our colored community was quite small enough that we all bumped into one another eventually. I'd never laid eyes on him in my life, and it further disturbed me that I didn't want to stop once I had.

"Well," I said brightly, turning back to the older woman, "I must be off. There's bound to be a queue."

"If you're sure . . ." Her brow puckered beneath her fringe.

"I'm sure," I said and turned to leave.

A hand on my arm stopped me as I made my way toward the Quai des Tuileries. I knew it was him before I glanced at his hand and back to his face. I frowned.

"I beg your pardon—"

He smiled, a thoroughly disarming, dimpled smile I was sure he had long ago learned to use to its full effect. It lit his dark eyes and raised his eyebrows, giving him a mischievous look that must have gotten him out of an outlandish number of scrapes. I pressed my lips firmly to fight its infectiousness.

"I beg yours, Miss Williams." His eyebrows rose again, as though impressing upon me his assurance that I was who he said I was. "Now that we've met, it would be most convenient of you to lead our group on a guided tour of Paris."

A rush of heat—irritation—swept across my throat and forehead. Here was a man accustomed to getting what he wanted no matter whom he trampled over.

"Perhaps you've forgotten that I am British, therefore not obligated to provide entertainment to American troops—"

"Why, that's a wonderful idea!" The older woman's voice swallowed my retort.

The murmurs of agreement and the exchange of joyful smiles lapped over my anger like a tidal wave.

"We're mostly YMCA, with a sprinkling of doughboys," explained the older woman, pointing at the other six with her. "I'm Annette Rochon, and these are my assistants Mrs. Tanner Craigwell and Netta Mosswell. YMCA secretary Lionel Richardson and Reverend Bullock of the 369th. You've already been acquainted with Lieutenant Sidney Mercer here."

I could feel Lieutenant Mercer's gaze sharpen as I reluctantly gave my name, and the air, charged with a peculiar sensation of triumph, made me glance in his direction. I met his eyes with an unwavering stare. Yes, I was Morven Williams, though the woman who'd earnestly borne that name had died in Flanders field. My breath released on a gust of air I hadn't been aware I was holding when he lowered his gaze and released my arm. Miss Rochon was speaking again.

"Lionel here hasn't a lick of direction. He's liable to lead us into the catacombs."

"I'm not that bad!" Lionel exclaimed as he folded the map of Paris into his red leather-bound Baedeker. "We managed to get to this garden."

"After getting turned around on the Metro," Mrs. Craigwell retorted.

I was still clutching my bag to my side, my fingers clamped so tightly around the handle they tingled with numbness. Their easy warmth, their camaraderie, disturbed and frightened me. The bitter chill of detachment, which I'd so successfully retreated into, threatened to thaw, and I wanted no part of it.

"We'll compensate you for your time, if that's a concern," said Miss Rochon. Her hand on my arm, in the same place as Lieutenant Mercer's, was gentle and considerate where his was insistent and assertive. "Please say yes. It's a blessing to see a familiar face where one least expects it."

There was Addie—that was what she'd said the moment we met in a provincial theater in the middle of Yorkshire, she an elocutionist on the marquee, and me a lowly eleventh-billed act. What was it about these colored Americans—Negroes, as they were called and called themselves—that made them open their hearts and their arms to people of their shared skin, no matter if they were born and raised in the heart of Edinburgh? My curiosity and longing pulled me in their direction, though my instincts recoiled away from what their proximity would crack open within me.

What my proximity to Lieutenant Mercer would crack open within me, if I so chose.

SHE DIDN'T APPEAR TO BE A FLIMFLAM ARTIST.

Lieutenant Sidney Mercer hung back behind the YMCA group making its way through the Louvre as the woman who called herself Mrs. Charles Williams paused to study a painting of a woman with a chubby baby between kneeling saints. Filippo Lippi, *La Vierge et L'Enfant Entourés d'Anges*, said the label. Morven Williams's pinched, drawn expression relaxed for the first time, revealing traces of the soft, sparkling woman he'd seen in Julia's scrapbook. He uncrossed and then recrossed his arms again, unsettled by the reality of her in the flesh. The weariness in her eyes hadn't dimmed their vivid green color, nor had her photograph prepared him for the texture of her skin or the curl of her hair against the vulnerable column of her throat.

She was supposed to be blowsy, garish even, with a mean, greedy look in her eyes. Morven Williams wasn't supposed to be this slender woman of medium height, whose clothes nearly swallowed her frame, and who had hell in her eyes.

Sidney forced himself to look away from the flat curve of her lips as she listened to something Lionel and Netta were saying. It was as though she'd forgotten how to smile. In one pocket of his tunic, a letter from his aunt, and in the other, a cashier's check he'd drawn from Bordeaux's American Express branch even before he'd joined his company at the Front.

The decision he'd thought so easy to make when marking his journey to France had blossomed into a new set of complications.

LEADING MY YMCA CONTINGENT ACROSS PARIS FORCED ME TO look at my adopted city through new eyes. Sights I'd taken for granted, and then ignored as the days grew grimmer and darker, and the nights darker still, dazzled anew. Miss Rochon and her group were thrilled to see everything: Napoleon's tomb, the Grands Boulevards and the Champs-Élysées, the surprisingly noisy markets at Les Halles, even the graves and headstones of the infamous dead buried in the Père Lachaise. And their enthusiasm was shared by other sightseeing members of the American Expeditionary Forces and their connected organizations we often came across—Americans, it seemed, had an insatiable appetite for cultural consumption.

We found ourselves among the throngs of Parisians and sightseers walking up the steps to the basilica of the Sacré-Cœur, a grand, white stone edifice at the crest of the butte Montmartre. As the others passed through its ornate doors, a wave of lightheadedness swept through me, so intense I pushed through the line of people behind me until I found an empty, quiet space. I sank onto my sturdy bag, my head in my hands as I struggled to contain the emotions threatening to erupt and spill over. It was because the opulent Catholic basilica outraged my Presbyterian sensibilities. I was quite famished, having eaten nothing since leaving Françoise's. I grasped for any excuse but the truth—that I was bitterly angry at God for taking so much from me.

A shadow fell over me as a pair of booted toes came into my line of vision. My shoulders tensed; I was too much on edge to accept Sidney Mercer's harassment. I lifted my head with a defiant and shockingly rude, "What?"

An inscrutable expression crossed his face as he stared down at me. "When was the last time you've eaten?"

The unexpectedness of his query wrenched an honest reply from me before I could help myself.

"I don't know," I said wearily, brushing a stray hank of hair behind my ear. "Last night, perhaps."

"Get up," he said, grasping my arm. "We're going to have some supper."

I was on my feet and my suitcase in his hand before I could protest.

"The others—" I twisted to look back at the basilica.

"They'll be fine. I'm sure Annette will find a cause to rally up while we eat."

His stride was long and quick, eating up the distance between the Sacré-Cœur, its innumerable number of steps, and the bottom of the butte, and forcing me into a skip-run to keep up.

"I thought you knew nothing of Paris," I said breathlessly, not even allowed to catch my breath as he whipped us down the rue de St.-Pierre.

"I know it well enough—or rather, my stomach does." The corner of his mouth curled, a dimple creasing his cheek, as he cast a droll, sidelong glance my way. "I was in Paris years before the war, and I—"

He seemed to check himself with an almost imperceptible shake of his head.

"And you what?" I pressed. He hadn't allowed me to retain my secrets, so what was sauce for the goose was sauce for the gander.

He stilled abruptly on the pavement (the French, ever so blasé, merely swerved around us) and my bag banged against his leg.

"And I had dreams of being a musician," he finally answered. "There's a café up ahead, if I'm recalling it correctly."

He had. The café was covered with the tricolor swags of bunting and the remnants of Armistice celebrations, as was usual these days. A waiter swept at the clutter around the chairs and tables in front of his door, successfully ignoring the patrons lounging in the chairs, as they did his efforts. We took an empty table and as I was seated, my stomach put up an embarrassingly loud protest against its emptiness. Lieutenant Mercer looked astonished, and then he laughed.

Thankfully, a waiter brought us large cups of hot, inky black French coffee and plates of steaming rolls topped with pats of yellow butter. I eyed Lieutenant Mercer as I buttered my third roll. There was something about him—something I couldn't quite place my finger on—that stoked my curiosity to an usually high degree.

"What happened to those dreams?"

He stared into his coffee cup, the dark, fathomless liquid rather like his eyes when he finally turned them to me.

"I . . . my daddy is a preacher in Mississippi. The fire-and-brimstone sort, you know? And he expected me to follow in his footsteps."

"And you didn't."

"I tried," he said pensively. "How hard I tried. He even sent me away to seminary—a preacher's school—to be formally trained when *he* hadn't anything more than a fifth-grade education. It was there that I discovered ragtime."

A warmth had crept into his voice with the last sentence. He didn't need to explain—ragtime had gripped me from the moment I heard the tunes wafting into my mum's dressing room backstage in a provincial music hall.

"They kicked me out when they discovered I was playing in local brothels, and I assumed my daddy wouldn't want me back." His mouth twisted wryly. "Music swept me up from Jackson to Memphis, and then to St. Louis and Chicago, before I thought to try Europe, where a few associates had struck it rich. I was green as unripened tomatoes, for all my arrogance, and my failed auditions showed me the error of my ways."

My head spun with the names of cities I'd only known from a map, or from Charles's and Louis's reminiscences of their growing up in America. I closed my eyes, soaking in the colorful descriptions of his life, feeling the hot sun on his back and the packed dirt roads beneath his feet, hearing the cacophony of sounds as he attempted to play over the thumping bedsprings and wails in his Mississippi brothels; the energy of music and performing. I opened my eyes; I hadn't realized how much I missed all of it now that there was only me.

"My husband was from Mississippi," I found myself saying. "Pelahatchie."

Those black eyes were fixed on my face, and his unasked questions filled the air.

"He's dead," I said quietly. "He was killed in the retreat from the Marne."

"I wondered." His voice was stiff, not with disdain, but with emotion. "So you're alone in France. Like me."

"Not at all like you," I exclaimed. "You have a family in the United States. Something to go home to."

My face flushed with anger and chagrin. How had he induced me to voice my unspoken fears?

"Morven," he said urgently. "What of your husband's family?"

"No!" I wrenched back in my chair, almost dropping my butter knife. "No."

That letter, with its short message in black-and-white, said everything necessary. I understood it quite clearly—I was not welcome.

There was a peculiar tightness in his expression, and his hand brushed against one of his tunic pockets before he raised it to summon the waiter. His French was rough and rudimentary, but fluent enough to order a meal. Minutes later, there was a bottle of *vin rouge* and two glasses on the white tablecloth. Sidney's movements were relaxed as he poured the wine into both glasses, and I breathed deeply of its rich, yet ordinary bouquet. Memories exploded with my first sip—of nights spent counting our meager francs on the table with Addie and Louis, of times where Charles would surprise me with a bottle of champagne, of the bitter cold where we had only one another's bodies, soft and entwined, to keep us warm . . . to keep me safe. My hand trembled as I set the glass down with a plonk.

Sidney's eyes were waiting for mine when I glanced at him. He finished his wine and set his empty glass beside mine, his fingers nudging against my own.

"This husband you mentioned . . . he was an actor as well?"

My gaze fell to that tiny brush of connection where our hands met, brown against the whiteness of the linen, and I wanted to tell him.

"Of a sort. Along with Louis and Addie Dismond. We were a dancing quartet, sometimes with a skit or two to pad our act in the music halls." I smiled. "We never blacked up, though at first I didn't see the harm. If you could only see the way Charles exploded when I brought black and red greasepaint from the theatrical shop. I'd never seen him so angry in my life, not even when we were triple-booked in our disastrous, short-lived attempt to use a manager."

"He—that's understandable, if you'd grown up in the States." Sidney moved his hand away to pour another glass of wine. "It's quite different."

"They never discussed it—Charles and Louis," I said pensively. "News of those terrible lynchings reached some of the British papers, of course, and I remember when Mr. Washington of Tuskegee attended the Duchess of Sutherland's ball, but they didn't like to talk about things of that nature with me and Addie."

Our conversation paused when the waiter returned and set two bowls of a clear, fragrant soup and thin slices of brown bread at our places. I spooned a little of the thin garnishes—scallions and carrots—into my mouth; delicate flavors burst on my tongue in spite of the soup's wartime austerity. The bread was equally surprising in flavor, with the slightest hint of sweetness.

"And Addie?"

My spoon stuck against my palate and I slowly swallowed my soup. How to describe Addie, whom I considered closer than the sister I'd always longed to have? Her honking laugh and rib-creaking embraces? Of the way she'd climbed into my hospital bed, ignoring the nurses' squawks of outrage, when Charles was too distraught to bear my miscarriage? That she peeked between her fingers, half-frightened and half-allured by the flickering melodramas, when at the cinema?

And who'd chosen to leave me. At least Charles and Louis hadn't chosen to die. I gripped my spoon bitterly, suddenly awash with the blinding anger that had stricken me at the basilica.

"She drowned herself in the Seine after Louis was killed at Artois."

Sidney flinched.

I didn't want or need his pity. I had survived on my own feet— literally—since I was fourteen, orphaned and penniless after my mother's death from fever. The losses of Charles, Louis, and Addie had bent but not broken me, and neither would Lieutenant Sidney Mercer.

HIS CHOICES LAY HEAVILY ON HIS MIND WHEN THEY REJOINED Annette and the others. Sidney stared at Morven's profile, her skin now smoothed of that pinched look after a few cups of coffee and a nourishing supper. The sunlight caught the gold flecks in her green eyes, wide and sparkling as she studied the map of Paris that Lionel had unfolded from his guidebook. There was that woman again, gay and beguiling, mighty like a rose.

"Careful now, they might fall out."

He smiled tightly at Reverend Henry Bullock, a chaplain in his regiment. The reverend grinned broadly.

"I wasn't—"

"A body can't help but stare at a pretty girl," Bullock interrupted, raising his graying eyebrows sardonically. "Now if I was you, I would snap her up quick before any of these other fellows about to descend upon Paris lay eyes on her."

"I'm not—"

"Oh yes you are," the reverend interrupted again. "You boys fight and fight it, but the Lord knows. He always places the right girl in your path."

Sidney wanted to laugh. He supposed his daddy would consider himself well served on his chosen path to hellfire by marrying an unscrupulous adventuress.

Something tightened in his chest and he looked away from Morven, unwilling to just give up his assertion that she had been up to no good. He didn't want to touch the burgeoning truth that Chas, the eldest cousin he'd idolized even after he'd left the family in Mississippi to follow his dreams, had recklessly and selfishly hurt two women. The cold snake of jealousy twined itself around all of that somewhere in his gut; jealousy that Chas had Morven at her most vibrant and alive. But then he'd died and left her to whatever had put such suffering in her eyes.

Something thumped against his leg, drawing his attention

away from Morven. It was only her battered kitbag, which he'd been carrying. It bulged strangely at the sides, but he supposed she had packed each and every one of her possessions. A sharp pain stabbed his heart at the thought that all she owned could be tucked inside of this one suitcase, rather like a soldier always ready to march. Always prepared to escape should the enemy attack.

He supposed he could be classified as that enemy.

"Sidney?"

Annette was calling his name.

"We should all fit in an automobile, right?"

"Miss Rochon wants to go on a tour of the battlefields," Morven said, her tone as neutral as her gaze. "There are motors for hire, though I'm not certain of what's available these days."

He shifted her bag to his other hand, his shoulders tightening with tension. Only those who hadn't seen the trenches firsthand, beneath the terror of artillery and hand-to-hand combat, could view the Front as a mere tourist's site.

"If there's no room, I'll stay behind," he replied evenly.

But there was, unfortunately. The garage they found after riding the Metro back to the Grands Boulevards supplied them with a massive, three seat gray Panhard touring car. Lionel took the wheel and Annette sat at his side, while the remainder of the group stacked inside the other two seats. His mouth twitched with faint humor when he saw Reverend Bullock, Mrs. Craigwell, and Netta squeeze into the middle seat, leaving the rear for him and Morven. He settled into the squeaky leather seat, her bag placed at his feet between them, careful to keep his distance.

The winding, narrow streets of Paris as Lionel drove across one of the bridges to the Left Bank, and through southern Paris, defied his attempts. With every turn, he slid neatly against her, until the last time, when she raised her eyebrows and placed a hand on his arm, holding him still beside her.

I COULDN'T BELIEVE MY BOLDNESS IN THE MOTORCAR, BUT HOLD-ing on to Sidney Mercer served me well when we reached the outskirts of the Western Front. His hand caught and held mine when our feet sank into the loamy, churned soil of the French line. My fingers gripped his so tightly my arm shook as I stared at the desolate landscape that had swallowed most of civilization whole. Other sightseers dotted the now abandoned trench lines, and grubby children even darted in and out of them, already play-ing at French versus Huns on a battlefield that had only ceased its violence not quite two weeks ago.

Was it forgetfulness, or resilience? Or the naïveté of children?

My courage failed me when I saw dirt-begrimed, uniformed men shoveling dirt. Or, what I took to be dirt at first; further in-spection revealed the mounds to be the unburied dead. I turned my face into Sidney's sleeve. His other hand skimmed up my spine and over my shoulder to rest against my nape.

"Have you ever seen where your husband was buried?"

"It isn't necessary to do so."

He was quiet, for which I was grateful, and I gathered myself before lifting my head. His hand dropped away from my skin after a moment, and for a brief second, I regretted leaving his solid, comforting warmth. We stood at the edge of the Front while the others gawked and climbed over the wretched earth; we hadn't any need to see proof of what had happened. It was there in our minds, imprinted on our skin.

NIGHTTIME HAD FALLEN WHEN WE RETURNED TO PARIS. THE Armistice celebrations had started up again, and Sidney was staring up at the darkened sky through the window as colorful fireworks pierced the glossy-smooth clear night and burst entrancingly above our heads. I stared a moment, too, wondering when this orgy of celebration would reach its bitter end. For where there was great joy, there was also deep pain, and even with peace there remained a festering wound that the war's end wouldn't heal.

"Sometimes, I can't quite believe it—those could just as easily be the explosion of artillery over No Man's Land." His voice was low enough to force me to draw closer.

"Was it so bad? At the Front?"

"It was unspeakable."

My hand found his again, and our fingers twined together. It was mad. Perhaps he caught my mood, this erratic mixture of highs and lows, of fear and courage, all wrought by the war. His grip tightened as the motorcar made its way through the busy Parisian streets, where motorcars and taxicabs attempted to inch their way through the scores of people stepping from the pavement at any point along the way. We were a wounded people—walking wounded—with some of us more scarred inside than our exteriors revealed. Who and what was going to glue us together again?

Love.

That word, devastation in one syllable, snuck into my heart as I stared at Lieutenant Sidney Mercer. I hardly knew him and had only met him not one hour ago. This was mad—I was mad. How did I dare to snatch at happiness when so much had been snatched away from me? When the world had yet to shake itself free of the blood and agony of the past four years?

But dare I did, gripping the tiny shards of courage and fear that had kept me alive when everyone else had fallen.

THE OTHERS CLAIMED FATIGUE, YAWNING AND STRETCHING EX-aggeratedly. I hid my skeptical smile as they exited the motorcar and walked up the path to the colored YMCA hostel in Marais. Now I was alone with Sidney, who drummed his fingers on the steering wheel. His gaze was intent, his brow wrinkled in a frown, and he eventually spoke.

"Why did you remain here when you had nothing left? Surely your husband's family—"

"His family!" I wanted to spit. "I wrote to them immediately after he was killed and received a stiff but polite letter stating there was no knowledge of my existence."

He frowned harshly. "There must be some mistake."

"There was no mistake, Lieutenant Mercer." My fingers trembled when I linked them in my lap. "Charles wasn't the kind to look back, and I assume that meant whatever he did prior to our marriage ceased to exist for him and for his family. And he chose that I didn't exist to them either."

"But, Morven—"

"Besides," I continued caustically. "I have my career—"

"Where? Doing what? What have you been doing since he died?"

A dull, angry flush of shame rose against my skin at the in-sinuation in his tone. It pricked that small, hidden part of me that knew Charles's family would have rejected me anyway, once they'd discovered what I had done to survive.

"I am a performer; there are still plenty of ways in which I can support myself. I could even return to England, where my career began."

He stared at me, his dark eyes so intense, and then he turned away to start the motorcar.

"There's something I want to show you."

The something Sidney wanted to show me was the Casino de Paris. Its art nouveau edifice was familiar to me, since I had danced there once, after my mother's death prompted me to risk moving to Paris with my very poor French and rudimentary experience on-stage. However, to my surprise, Sidney took me around the corner to the backstage entrance, where I was immediately assaulted by memory. The smell of greasepaint and—to be frank—sweat, the flash of sequins, the chalky sawdust coating the floor, and the general bedlam of mounting a performance fired my blood.

This bedlam was also how we managed to maneuver through backstage with little question, and when the curtain separated us from the actual stage, Sidney stopped to push it aside. I peeped at glimpses of whatever revue had captured Paris's attention until Sidney's finger drew my attention to the band in the pit. My eyebrows rose in surprise: a colored band. And—my ear fairly jumped in delight—they were playing that jangling new type of ragtime a few were calling jazz. Another surprise was the drummer, who dominated the band. His drumsticks moved rapidly across the drums, almost faster than my eyes could see.

"Louis Mitchell," Sidney murmured.

We watched Louis Mitchell and his band for another quarter of an hour until Sidney touched my arm, gesturing for me to follow. This time he led me to a tiny dressing room, where the discarded sheet music and half-smoked cigarettes denoted that this space was designated for the Mitchell band.

"Are we permitted to be here?" I said as I sat on the chair he pushed in my direction.

"Louis won't mind," Sidney said, lighting one of the abandoned cigarettes. "In fact, he'll probably be delighted to see me. Has been after me to join him here after I'm demobilized."

"Shall you?"

Sidney made a face, examining the cigarette in his hand. "It's possible, but I'd prefer . . ." He gave me an embarrassed, abashed sort of smile that made me sit on my hands to quell my initial urge to touch his dimples. "I'd prefer to own a nightclub of my own, or at least part ownership. I've had my fill of playing gigs where the wind takes me—I want something settled. Permanent."

I glanced at him, almost afraid to wonder if he had stressed the word *permanent*.

"I thought you might like to join me—well, not me, but the club," he stammered. "Since you're an experienced performer. I'm sure you'd prefer something permanent as well."

A corner of my mouth lifted in bemusement. "You're awfully certain of yourself, Lieutenant Mercer."

"That's one lesson learned at my daddy's knee that stuck—sublime faith," he said with a laugh. "You've just got to leap and feel in your bones that you'll be caught."

"Even despite the war?" My bemusement faded. "Its unspeakableness."

He gazed at his cigarette for a moment, where a curlicue of smoke twisted into the air like one of the Egyptian dancers I'd once seen at the Alhambra.

"What we saw out there wasn't unspeakable in its horror, but in its hope. Not even sunrise was a thing to cling to—that made it easier for the Huns to pick you off. And so you sometimes hoped for death. A quick and painless one, of course, because you watched and heard the suffering of the wounded trapped in No Man's Land, their dying pains echoing in the air long after they'd expired—"

"Stop it!" I gripped the seat of my chair until my arms quivered. Suddenly, death, which I had blamed for so much of my unhappiness, didn't seem like something to embrace as an end to suffering.

I wanted to live. Like Sidney, like the other men who'd made it to Armistice Day, I wanted to live.

And I wanted Sidney Mercer. I wanted him so badly I trembled.

My hand trembled in his as he urged me to my feet. I hadn't danced since—oh God—since that night in Strasbourg's train station, when the four of us had been merry with assurance that the railway delays created by the start of the war weren't too serious. We'd foxtrotted and sung the melody on the railway platform beside the idling cars of the Orient Express, laughing as other passengers waiting to enter France joined in our lighthearted gaiety. Our foolish, naïve, stupid gaiety.

Here Sidney and I had meant to enter into a foxtrot or a tango, but somehow found ourselves standing still in the middle of the dressing room, arms tight around one another.

I suppose I must have moved first, but he was the one to touch me, his fingers sinking into my hair as he swept me into a kiss from the ages. The kind of kiss Cleopatra must have given Caesar *and*

Mark Antony. One that had toppled kingdoms and moved mountains. A kiss that shattered and healed in equal measure. I turned away, entirely overwhelmed by his touch.

"I shouldn't have done that." He sighed into my hair.

"Is it so wrong?" I asked quietly, an entire host of fears taking room in my mind. "Any man would despise someone like me."

"No, don't say that." He held me slightly away with a frown. "You survived. No one can fault you for that."

"How magnanimous of you." I couldn't help the faint asperity in my tone. "I don't suppose your father would agree."

"Considering my father considers laughter on the Sabbath a black mark that could damn one's soul for eternity, there aren't many he considers untainted."

The laughter in his eyes made me snort.

"But he would like you—Daddy always had an eye for a pretty girl."

Pretty Girl. I had the unshakable memory of my father holding me up high to see my mum performing onstage, my arms wrapped around his neck and my chubby cheek pressed against his. "*Look at mum, Pretty Girl.*"

And later, Charles pushing his way through the greenroom after a Christmas panto, in which I'd played a Lost Boy and him a member of Captain Hook's crew, declaring his intention to kiss the prettiest girl beneath the mistletoe.

My focus drew back to Sidney when he touched my face, his finger tracing the faded scar from the corner of my left eyebrow down to my jaw. The product of my own skirmish to survive. I hadn't been Pretty Girl for a long while.

"And just what do you want, Morven? Now that the war is over?"

"Home," I said softly. "I just want to go home."

A stricken look crossed his face, and his fingers tightened around my waist. All traces of humor vanished from his expression, leaving his sharp and strong features stark with emotion. "There's something I must—"

He released me to reach into his tunic pocket. His expression tightened as he began to place it into my hand.

"Wrong envelope." He snatched it away, but not before I'd glimpsed the American Express emblem.

The envelope he pulled from his other pocket was plain and small, with my name written in neat lettering across its surface.

I bowed my head to read the restrained copperplate script of Charles's mother, Mrs. Rose Williams.

My eyes stung with hot, unshed tears. I was wanted. I had a home.

Sidney swallowed, his expression uncertain and almost hopeful. He held the other envelope loosely, and I snatched it back and tore it open. A cashier's cheque for two hundred American dollars. That was forty pounds. One thousand French francs. He had certainly assumed I had a price for silence and disappearance.

"Morven—"

"When—" I paused to wet lips dry with disbelief. "When were you going tell me? And which of the envelopes had you intended to give me?"

My voice cracked with bitterness.

"I was going to tell you when we met—"

"When? After you'd paid me off, like . . . like a thieving whore?"

"No! I wasn't sure who you were, and I thought it would help. I wanted to help you."

I looked away from the entreaty in his eyes, wanting to deny what else was written all over his face.

"Tell me who you are. You must be connected with Charles since you also come from Mississippi."

"His cousin. Years younger." Sidney's laugh was short and airless.

I wanted to laugh as well. At my stupidity. Charles was there—not as beautiful, but there in the shape of Sidney's eyes and the timber of his voice.

"Charles was . . . he was already married when you married him. Julia Hammond was her name. They'd wed young, possibly because their son was on the way."

I sank onto my abandoned chair as a pleasant numbness spread from my heart to my limbs. Sidney made a gesture, possibly to touch me, and I flinched, not that benumbed. He tucked his hands behind him and continued.

"Julia died last year. After she passed she willed my aunt Rose, Charles's mama, her papers, including a scrapbook of newspaper clippings she'd kept since Charles ran away to become an actor, and I saw you." His swallow was audible in the silence. "I saw you and realized that if Charles had been killed, you were somewhere in France, possibly without resources—"

"And you came to find me."

"My aunt wanted you to come home. It didn't matter that Charles hadn't been free to legally wed you—you were his wife and you belonged with your family."

"She—Julia—was the one who . . ."

"I'm certain," he replied flatly. "If she weren't already dead, I'd strangle her. Morven, you aren't alone. You were wanted. I . . . well, I want you."

I closed my eyes rather than allow myself to be swayed by the longing in his voice. He had lied to me. They had both lied to me. My skin flushed with the humiliation of where Sidney found me. He knew without a doubt what I'd done to survive and fully intended to treat me in kind.

"I will go," I said finally. "But I never want to speak to you again."

"Morven, please—"

I ignored him and grabbed my kitbag in a blind sort of panic, only for it to pop open, spilling its contents all over the floor. Spilling a yowling, very angry cat onto the floor.

I didn't know whether to laugh or to cry as I stared down at this persistent feline.

"What—who is this?" Sidney bent to reach for the cat, who, to my surprise, went contentedly into his arms.

"He's yours," I said spikily, stuffing my belongings back into my bag. "Even animals believe they can do as they please, not caring about what someone else wants. Or needs."

"Morven, forgive me, please." He looked so young and appealing, and sweetly absurd holding that bloody cat, and my heart quivered. "What can I say to make this up to you? I'm sorry. I lo—"

"Don't."

That stiffened my resolve and I tightened my grip around the handles of my bag. Sidney stared at me, his mouth set in a mutinous line, but he made no move to stop me from leaving. For which I was grateful, because when I passed him, the brief flash of his warmth threatened to thaw my chill. I walked alone into the night, but now the promise of home, of family, beckoned—what I'd hoped for and—yes, reluctantly prayed for—to the very marrow of my bones.

Paris—June 1919

"COME ON, MERCER, YOU'RE OFF BEAT AGAIN!"
Sidney twirled his drumstick between his damp left-hand fingers. They sweated less from the sweltering early summer heat than from the anxiety that had plagued him since returning to France after his discharge from the army. He had done Morven wrong by not telling her that she was wanted, that her rejection had been the response of a bitter, abandoned wife. Damn Chas. He wished he could strangle his dead cousin to (a second) death for the mess he'd made of their family.

If it wasn't for Chas—no, if it wasn't for Julia—

Sidney set the sticks to the drums again. He was to blame for further muddying the waters. Aunt Rose hadn't sent him to France to find Chas's "wife" and pay her off. That had been his own arrogant solution to tidying away the sin of bigamy; he was more like his sanctimonious daddy than he liked to admit.

The five-piece jazz band he'd recruited to play at the club he opened with the Comte de Fontaine Delibes's backing was in top form—when he wasn't missing his cues, that was. Sidney tempered the pride that wanted to burst forth at the thought of his very own nightclub. It wasn't open yet, and though he wanted to hurry its debut to beat the other jazz nightclubs he'd heard were opening soon, he wanted everything to be perfect.

Perfect for Morven.

Would she come? His brow furrowed as his drum strokes slowed, his mind wandering to when he'd last seen her. She hadn't responded to any of his letters, either.

"Mercer! If you don't stop your nonsense!" His bandleader, Gene Cheatham, tugged his conk until it stood up on end.

"Sorry, Cheath." He dropped his sticks onto the taut skin of his snare drum. "I just need a break, some time to cool my head."

Cheath muttered something he was certain was obscene, but he told them all to take it easy.

Sidney got up from his drum set and went to the bar. It wasn't stocked, mostly because they were still waiting for their liquor license, but there was half a bottle of Scotch the last owner of this joint had left behind. Sidney poured a glass and leaned against the counter, sipping the smooth liquor as he examined the nightclub. Antoine—the comte, who'd been the officer over his battalion once the AEF had booted the colored infantries to the French army—had given him carte blanche with his checkbook. Who was he to turn that down?

The décor was swank, all done up in greens and golds, with a large floor for dancing and shows, a stand for the band and a feature singer, and dozens of small tables for the revelers.

He thought the cat motif was a nice touch. The nightclub's namesake lay behind the bar, curled atop a makeshift bed of linen scraps. He rose from his nap and stretched his furry spine before twining himself around his ankles with an earsplitting meow. Sidney picked him up and sank his fingers into the cat's nape as he purred.

"She's sure to be missing us both by now," he murmured.

The cat gave him a skeptical look with green eyes uncannily like Morven's, and then squirmed out of his hold to stalk off into the club. Damned cat.

He finished off his Scotch and rummaged behind the bar for pen and paper. She would come, even if he had to use Antoine's largesse to fund the sending of a letter a day until she arrived.

Mississippi—August 1919

THE STEAMSHIP TICKET ARRIVED BY POST WITH AN INVITA- tion to the opening of a nightclub on the rue Pigalle. LE CHAT OR was emblazoned across the header, and beneath, the promise of the hottest jazz band, authentic southern cuisine, and a glittering cabaret show. I couldn't suppress the smile tugging at my mouth, as the name and logo of his nightclub quelled my anger as thoroughly as tossing a bucket of water onto flames. I used the invitation and ticket as a fan, flapping away the sultry, sluggish heat of the Mississippi Delta. There were times where I couldn't feel more British, accustomed as I was to the milder, often wetter climate of the isle of my birth.

It was midday, the sun high in the sky, and I shielded my eyes to see the figures moving slowly across the cotton fields toward the Big House in anticipation of luncheon. I still couldn't quite wrap my head around the fact that cotton actually grew from the earth. The Williamses' fields stretched for acres, from what I could see out of my window each morning; row after row of this magnificent plant. When I first arrived, I attempted to go out and help, flush with gratitude and guilt over my indolence, but Mother Rose—Charles's mother—Sidney's aunt—gently shooed me back inside.

My fingers, blistered and cracked the next day, spoke loudly of my unsuitability. I had, according to Mother Rose, more than given to my new family, having tirelessly nursed Charles's sisters and his son back to health after the Spanish flu swept through this tiny, fertile corner of the South.

I could also help in the kitchen, where I was welcomed after shattering the skepticism of Charles's female relations by preparing the popovers—biscuits, I had to remember to call them—for breakfast. Granted, I'd had a few mishaps trying to come to grips with an American range, but the biscuits emerged from the oven light and golden-brown, each bite drenched in melting butter. I could smell them now, just in time to feed the hungry men in the fields, and made my way through the parlor to the swinging white door that led to the kitchen.

The tongue-teasingly delicious scents of well-seasoned meat and sweet yams swirled through the air, now familiar and comforting after the past six months residing with the Williams. Oh how they'd laughed at my bewilderment over such dishes as collard greens and hog maw—though the latter was somewhat similar to the haggis my mum used to search for in the nearest greengrocer's each year for Rabbie Burns Day.

I found my mother-in-law and a few other relatives busily preparing heaping trays of food.

"Butter the corn bread for me, Morven," Mother Rose tossed over her shoulder. "Then tell that daughter of mine to pull her nose from her books to set the table."

"I can do that, Mother Rose," I said, rolling up my sleeves to slather the fresh butter over the tins of corn bread laid out on the counter. "Cynthia requires time for studying if she's to attend Fisk."

"She's already told you her plans." My mother-in-law rolled her eyes a little. "Now what's that poking out of your pocket?"

I smiled wryly, knowing nothing escaped her detection.

"It's from Sidney."

All conversation stopped, and my cheeks flamed at the knowing glances exchanged and then tossed my way.

"Well?" Mother Rose gestured with her serving fork.

"He's sent me a steamship ticket to France," I said, turning back to my corn bread. "A nightclub where he performs."

Any response was interrupted by the noisy arrival of Charles's youngest brother, Isaiah, who was promptly chased from the kitchen after he attempted to steal a taste of the golden-battered fried chicken piled high on a plate.

I dutifully trooped behind the line of women bearing trays of mouthwatering dishes with my tins of cornbread to the large dining room, where Cynthia was slowly setting the table with one hand—the other was holding her textbook in front of her face. It was snatched from her hand, and the sixteen-year-old's mutinous expression smoothed beneath one raised eyebrow from her mother. We set the trays and tins in the center of the table just as the men tramped in, sweaty and obviously hungry.

My hands tightened around the back of the dining room chair when Sidney's father entered behind them, carrying his Bible beneath his arm. He removed his wide-brimmed black hat to reveal features startling like his son's, though there was a stern, officious quality to the set of his mouth and the way he looked at the world from his dark eyes. He greeted me stiffly, still, after six months, unable to know what to make of me. Or of Sidney, I suppose, since he was the one to fetch Charles's bigamous wife from France.

We sat for luncheon after the men washed up and changed their shirts. Reverend Mercer cleared his throat to signal his imminent prayer over the food. His eye fell on me once again and I hurriedly bowed my head. There had been a mild contretemps over this until Reverend Mercer worked out that my vaguely Presbyterian upbringing wasn't entirely antithetical with the African Methodist Episcopal Church.

The initial hungry silence of eating soon gave way to the Williamses' rousing, intense conversation. The laughter, the finishing one another's sentences, the talking over one another, the family jokes—they all reminded me of my life on the stage, whether it was with my mother, or later, with Charles. That give-and-take, that trust, the knowledge that you were with people who understood you and accepted you. Who liked you. Even when they quarreled, there was a coating of love beneath the anger—such as the fiery argument between Charles's other brother, Ephraim, and two other men.

"Self-determination for everyone but the colored man," exclaimed Ephraim. "Trotter should have known Wilson wouldn't press for a fifteenth point."

"You've been reading the *Guardian* again," his mother scolded.

"And why not? I wish I had been old enough to fight, and been able to see their faces when I told them why I wasn't enlisting." Ephraim threw down his napkin. "Charles died for nothing at all."

I could feel the eyes on me in the brief silence. "It's all right," I said quietly.

"Now you just hush, Ephraim Williams," Mother Rose replied sternly. "This isn't proper dinner conversation. Tell us what you've been studying, Cynthia."

I smiled my thanks at Mother Rose, though the pain over Charles's death and betrayal had long since healed.

It was Sidney Mercer who caused me more pain these days.

THE ONLY PLACE ONE COULD FIND SOME SOLITUDE AFTER luncheon—the men loosened their belts in the dining room and the back parlor after the women departed; anyone was liable to barge into my bedroom—was the small room where Mother Rose did her accounts. What a marvelous woman, I thought, examining the spines of her ledger books and the stacks of correspondence on her desk.

I sat on the low-backed leather chair near the window, rather contented by the warm breeze sweeping through the room. How easy it would be to remain here. The days would pass smoothly, save for the sometimes challenging ups and downs of this region of America, and I would be content.

Or would I?

I turned away from contemplating the window when Charles's mother entered the accounts room.

"Don't think I've forgotten, young lady." She sat, the wheeled chair squeaking beneath her weight.

"I didn't believe you did, Mother Rose," I said drily.

Mother Rose tilted her head, eyes narrowed as she thoroughly scrutinized me. She found something there that pleased her, and she nodded her head. "Do you love him, baby? That is the only question you ought to be asking yourself."

She had Charles's eyes—bright and warm like sherry—and I no longer wanted to add more lies on top of the ones that drew us together.

Yes, I did love Sidney Mercer, and I would go to France.

I DECLINED THE ASSISTANCE OF THE RAILWAY PORTER AND CARried my suitcase down the platform myself. It was bittersweet to walk down the same platform where, five years before, I watched the train that took Charles away from me grow smaller and smaller.

Only the faintest traces of the war lingered—a few empty sleeves or trouser legs, the tattered remnants of bunting from the peace conference celebrations last month, much stricter customs and passport bureaus. But instead of poilus and officers in the distinctive blue khaki of the French army rushing down the platforms and spilling into trains, it was children and their nurses, red-faced businessmen, midinettes in their gray frocks, all on their way to the beaches along the Normandy coast to escape the summer heat.

Paris had seen it through, and so, I realized with surprise, had I.

I shifted my baggage into my other hand, my fingers damp and sticky beneath my cotton gloves, and stepped inside the railway station proper. It was then that I saw him, peering about the station, turning this way and that, walking backward through the crowd, and anxiously scanning the faces of passing women. My eyes fell on the wicker carrier he carried and the restless cat inside and I stopped, my heart in my throat, suddenly swept by anxiety.

He was leaner, less imposing perhaps, though his loose summer jacket couldn't hide the military bearing that held his broad shoulders erect. Those elegant, piano-playing fingers tapped a syncopated beat against the boater crushed in his other hand, and I laughed.

He turned then, somehow hearing my joy in spite of the bustle of the station and the yards between us. When our eyes met, it was as though we'd never parted in anger. I began to walk toward him, one foot in front of the other, and sternly reminded myself to breathe.

I now saw the end of my story, and I wasn't afraid.

To the torchbearers of democracy
and
the sisters of a certain soldier

Something Worth Landing For

Jessica Brockmole

I FIRST MET HER, CRYING, OUTSIDE OF THE MEDICAL DEPART-
ment at Romorantin.

She'd been there, hunched on the bench in the hall, when I
arrived for my appointment and was still there when I stepped
from the doctor's office. She wore the same bland coveralls and
white armband as the other women who worked in the Assembly
Building and I might have walked straight past. I always managed to make a fool of myself in front of women—on one memorable evening with an untied shoe and a bowl of chowder—and
was sure today would be no different. After all, I'd just been
standing stark naked in front of another man and was still a little
red in the face.

But she chose that exact moment to blow her nose, with such
an unladylike trumpet that I couldn't help but turn and stare.

I'd never heard such an unabashed sound from a woman. She

didn't even seem to care that she sounded like an elephant. She just kept her head down and her face buried in an excessively crumpled handkerchief.

She looked as healthy as a horse to be sitting outside the medical department. Not as scrawny as the other French girls around here. She had dark hair parted on the side and pinned up in waves, but her neck was flushed pink. I wondered what kind of bug she'd caught to leave her so stuffy.

"Hello. Are you waiting for the doc?" I asked. The army doc wasn't much—despite the file in his hand, he'd insisted on calling me "Weaselly" instead of the "Wesley" on my paperwork—but he could probably give her some silver salts or, at the very least, a replacement handkerchief.

She lifted her head and blinked red, wet eyes. I could have smacked myself. I was a dope. She wasn't sick. She was miserable and sobbing and I had no idea what to do.

If I'd had a sister or a girlfriend or a mother with a heart made out of something softer than granite, I might have known how to handle a teary woman. I'd never gotten as far as breaking a girl's heart.

Regardless, a clean handkerchief would be a start, and I dug in my pockets until I found a slightly wrinkled one. I held it out, but between two fingers, like feeding a squirrel.

She looked surprised at my offer, though I wasn't sure why. A nice-looking girl like that, surely she was used to kindness. She stared at me, then the square of cotton, then me again, considering.

I thought to add a few words of eloquence to my offer. "Go on," I said instead. "I have dozens."

It wasn't Shakespeare, but it worked. She swallowed and took it with a watery "*Merci*."

That probably wasn't enough. Chaplains and grandmothers always had a reassuring word or two. I wondered if I should take a cue from the padre and go with a pious *Trust in God* or an old-fashioned *There, there*. I realized, belatedly, that I knew how to say neither in French.

She saved me from having to make a decision. "I am fine, really," she said in quite excellent English. Tears welled up fresh in her blue eyes, but she nodded, almost too vigorously. "Yes, never better." She crushed the handkerchief to her eyes.

I didn't believe her. People who were fine didn't cry uncontrollably in the hallway. "Bad diagnosis?" She looked healthy enough, with those pink cheeks and bright eyes, but I was no expert. Maybe she had just found out she had a week to live.

She blew her nose again, thunderously. "Bad, good, maybe both."

This was mystifying, but I suppose that was the way of women. "I'm sure the doc can give you something. Aspirin usually does the trick for me."

"If only aspirin were enough." She daubed at her nose. "The doctor's price is too high."

I had nothing else in my pockets but a pencil stub and a harmonica, but I asked, "Do you need money?" I wasn't sure how much the women working in the Assembly Building earned. They gossiped in French, met evenings in Pruniers for coffee, and largely ignored the squadrons of American men in uniform working all over Romorantin. I'd never seen her out with the other women, but, then again, I hadn't been looking. "I can help you."

"Help?" She straightened and lifted her chin. Suddenly she didn't look so damp and weepy. "Do I seem like someone who needs help?"

Suddenly "yes" seemed like exactly the wrong answer. She sat spine-straight on the edge of the bench. On the front of her dark coveralls, a button had been sewn back on with Alice-blue thread. She raised two neat eyebrows, as though daring me to utter it.

"Well . . ." I said, and left it dangling unfinished.

"Well." Apart from her pins and combs, her only adornment was a slim gold crucifix. "I am a woman working in an airplane assembly plant full of men. I can take care of myself." She might be small and soggy, but she was no sponge. With a dismissive wave of cloth, she held out my handkerchief.

Clearly I was no better with French women than American. This was a new record for me. Two and a half minutes from hello to sodden handkerchief. I nodded down at the well-used bit of cloth in her hand. "Keep it." When I looked back over my shoulder, I swore, for a moment, she was smiling.

I was halfway down the hall when I heard the door squeak open behind me and the doctor's nasally voice say, "Why, hello. You're still here?"

I turned, but the doc wasn't talking to me. He crossed his arms and looked down at the girl. That quick smile had disappeared and she was back to staring steadfastly at the crumpled handkerchief on her lap. I wondered what had happened to the starch in her spine from a moment ago. I wondered why she clutched the crucifix around her neck.

The doc didn't seem to notice or care. Though his back was to me, I could see him eyeing her up and down, like she was a roast hanging in a butcher's window. "Well, well," he said. "Have you reconsidered my offer, mamselle?"

Even from down the hall, I saw a tear drip from the end of her nose. She shook her head.

"Don't cry." He reached down and lifted her chin with a finger. "It's a small price to pay for taking care of your problem."

I didn't know what her problem was or what he'd offered to fix it, but I did know that she was looking even more miserable than before and that the crucifix was probably wearing an indentation into her palm.

"Leave me alone," she said, shrinking away from his finger. I could scarcely hear her. "Please."

I wasn't as intrepid as my older brother Val. He would've marched down the hall like Tom Mix with a pair of six-shooters and an "Unhand her, you villain." Rank be damned. Val would've managed it without a court-martial.

I couldn't be Tom Mix, riding in with guns a-blazing. I was more Charlie Chaplin—clumsy, even a little embarrassing, but always with good intentions. Superior officer or not, I couldn't leave the French girl crying on the bench.

Taking a deep breath, I stepped into view. "Well, you know me," I said. I let myself trip over my own feet a step. "I walked straight out of the office and down the hall before I remembered you. Sorry! I forgot we were both walking to the Assembly Building."

The doctor turned. "This isn't your problem, Airman."

I saluted. "You're absolutely right, sir." I nodded down at her. "It's ours."

She blinked and sniffled, but didn't argue and she let go of that crucifix.

I offered her a hand. "Are you ready to go ..." And then stopped. I didn't know her name. We hadn't exchanged more than a hand-kerchief. The doctor stared. " ... my dear?"

She hesitated, then took my hand and stood.

"Oh," he said, glancing between us. "*Oh*." The doctor gave me a long appraising look. "Well, then, *dad*, you'd better get her straightened out before I make my report. Because now, you'll be on it."

Her name, I learned, was Victoire.

We met that night in the smallest of the taverns in Pruniers. I combed my hair and put on a fresh shirt. When I arrived, she already had a mug waiting for me. It wasn't hot and was suspiciously maroon.

"I know you soldiers are not allowed to drink wine." She shrugged. "'Coffee,' though, is acceptable."

I glanced around, but saw nobody I recognized apart from the somewhat tipsy padre of the squadron. He was an earnest young man, as fluent in French wine as its language. He wouldn't peach on me.

"Thank you."

She'd changed, too, into a shabby gray dress. She'd added a spotted blue scarf and, with that one little touch, somehow made the plain dress nicer and very French. "You are probably wonder-ing," she said, cradling her own mug.

"I'm wondering about a bunch of things." I took a big gulp, wishing it were a beer. "Like why you didn't just tell me straight-away."

"That I am *enceinte*?" She put a hand to her lap. "Pregnant?"

She shook her head. "It isn't exactly a conversation for introductions."

"Introductions. Forgot." I wiped my mouth and held out my hand. "John Wesley Ward. Wes."

"Victoire." She declined my offered hand. "Victoire Donadieu."

"How did you . . ." Asking how she came to be in a family way, it seemed indelicate. "How did you come to speak such good English?"

She sat for a moment, quietly, then said, "I was an ambitious student and the man who raised me an exceptional teacher."

"The only things my father taught me were how to be unhappily married and miserably employed."

"It does not sound like much of an inheritance."

"He never saw me as much of an heir." Father's favorite had always been Val, smart, valiant, everything-I-touch-turns-to-gold Val. Even I was half in love with him.

"Surely you're mistaken." She looked almost stricken.

"About my old man? Ha!" I shook my head. "I've always been a disappointment to him. I can't even grow a proper mustache."

"Fathers love their children," she insisted.

I nodded down in the direction of her stomach. "And that little one's father?"

She sat quietly for a minute or two. In the corner, the padre was enthusiastically telling the parable of the ten virgins to a sleeping pair of drunks. A woman in a dark apron and scarf came by with a carafe and topped off my mug.

"He's already done enough," she finally said. "The rest is up to me."

I drank and didn't say anything right away. "And me."

She straightened. "You?" She didn't need to sound so scornful. "What do you have to do with anything?"

"Well, you heard the doc. I'm being reported."

"For 'fraternizing with the local women'?" This was said with the air of a recitation. She'd heard it before. "You'll have a slap on the hand . . ."

"On the wrist."

" . . . but I'll be dismissed. Monsieur, our problems are not the same."

I realized how little I knew about this woman, about what it would mean to her to lose her job and her income. I wondered what she'd miss more.

"You could go home," I said. "To see your father? If you're dismissed, I mean."

"My father?" She froze.

"You said he's a teacher. You said he is . . ." But I caught myself. With four years of war in France, *is* had so often become *was*.

The waitress came by with a bowl of mussels, garlicky and hot, and Victoire was saved from having to answer right away. I didn't remember her ordering them and wondered if I was expected to pay.

She leaned in to inhale the garlic and herbs. "I would be welcome at home, that I know. But not with a bastard child."

"Times are different," I said.

"Not different enough to shatter expectations." She offered me the bowl. "I would much rather prove people wrong than prove them right."

"Well, I understand expectations. My brother was a pilot. He was over here years before the U.S., in the Lafayette Flying Corps.

Father was so proud he could've burst and Mother never stopped reminding me how much more useful Val was being. I was at college, but Val was at war." I took a mussel with my fork. "When he went west, everyone just waited for me to go take his place."

She took my discarded shell and used it to pluck up a mussel of her own. "Went west?"

I dug the tines of the fork into the scratched wood of the table. "Fell. Crashed. Flew himself into an early grave."

Two years later and it still stung. Despite everything else, he was my brother. And here at Romorantin, with the roar of airplanes coming in for repairs and out for delivery, with the uniforms, with the swagger of the ferry pilots in the barracks, it stung even more. The most unexpected things made me think of Val.

As if I didn't have enough of that with the rare letters from back home. Father never wrote, just Mother. Brief, perfumed notes that reminded me I'd never live up to the memory of Val. I'd never fly as high as he had.

Victoire pushed the bowl of mussels to the side. "Monsieur Ward, I am sorry."

"Isn't the war full of things to be sorry about?" I shrugged. "Anyway, I always do what's expected of me."

"You became a pilot."

"Halfway." We'd arrived in France to find more cadets than airplanes. So the air service put its excess men building more planes and overhauling the old things the RFC and Aéronautique Militaire didn't want any longer. My squadron had been at Romorantin on fatigue. "But the doc called me in today. I'm finally being sent up."

She watched me carefully. "You must be happy."

Maybe it was the wine, maybe the loneliness, maybe the strange intimacy of this shared bowl of mussels and conversation. Maybe it was because I'd seen her cry. I took a deep breath. "Truth be told, I'm scared to death."

Victoire reached across the table, not quite meeting my hand, but laying her fingers close. "Perhaps, then, our problems are not so different."

"What do you have to be scared of? You're not flying straight into combat."

"Sometimes," she said, "we carry the battles right along with us." With her other hand, she brushed her stomach. "I am afraid to go home. I am afraid to stay here." For the first time since that morning, she blinked away tears. "I do not know where I . . . where we . . . belong."

I knew she was talking about the baby, but, if I listened sideways, I could pretend she was talking about me. I'd never felt like I belonged, not at college, not in the army, not in my own family. But, for a half hour over a bowl of mussels, I had found someone who understood.

"What if you had a husband?" I blurted out.

It wasn't what I intended to say, and I peered down into my mug of wine.

But, intended or not, her eyes stopped filling with tears. "*Pardon?*"

I had spoken without thinking, swept up in the moment and in her blue eyes. Was I really suggesting what it sounded like I was suggesting?

"Well . . ." I fumbled. "I meant . . ."

It was a completely crazy idea. Wasn't it? Kindness and understanding did not a marriage make. Though, thinking of my parents, relationships had been built on less.

"It isn't much, but will you marry me?" It was quick and breathless, the boldest thing I'd probably ever said in my life. "And not just because you're the first girl who's ever been nice to me."

She could've laughed and sent me on my way. For a split second I thought she would. I was used to it. But instead she inhaled and said, "You'd . . . do that?"

I took this as an encouraging sign. "I'm probably going the way of Val. Pilots don't last more than a few weeks. But you'd have my name and a ring to take back home. Widows' pay after I go." I spoke in a rush, not wanting to give her a chance to say no. "It isn't much," I said again. "But maybe I can help."

She thought about it as she finished the mussels. I watched her face, wondering if that crease in her brow was concern or indigestion. Maybe both. I thought I should offer her a glass of water and an apology. Nothing said that the indigestion wasn't due to my proposal.

Only after she'd drunk the broth and wiped the bowl with a crust of bread did she speak. "And what do you gain, John Wesley Ward?"

It was a fair question. I hadn't thought through my end of the arrangement. Certainly not a kiss good-bye. I already knew I wouldn't ask that of her. And *a warm glow at helping someone* sounded obnoxious and somehow more Val than me.

Tomorrow I'd be flying out. Loneliness stretched like a horizon. "Knowing that someone is thinking of me," I said simply.

She looked up at me from under her lashes.

"If you were my wife, would you write to me? Every day. Every week, if I last as long as that." I twisted fingers around my mug. "Somehow tonight, I don't feel so alone."

I counted thirty seconds as she thought, thirty seconds of the waitress complaining to the barkeep, of the piano playing, of the padre proselytizing.

"I agree," she finally said. "Thank you. I will marry you."

GETTING MARRIED, IT TURNED OUT, WAS QUITE EASY IF YOU had a tipsy priest.

The padre was delighted at being asked to officiate. "I've done more last rites than marriages. And the confessions that I hear . . ." He shuddered. "Anyway, a marriage! How marvelous!"

By my side, Victoire looked as nervous as a cat. If I knew her better, I'd have tried to take her hand. As it was, I nodded at the padre. I was just as nervous.

"So when is the happy day?" The padre picked up his tumbler of wine. "Spring weddings are full of hope."

"Well, we were thinking of maybe, uh, right now?"

He coughed on the wine. Victoire jumped and I clapped him on the back.

"Right now?"

"If it's not too much trouble." I tried to sound polite.

"Trouble?" He coughed again and washed it down with a swallow. "To marry with no preparation or prayer, that's trouble. My son, I am happy to officiate, but these things must be done with a clear conscience and a pure heart."

"You'll never find a purer heart than Victoire's," I said, hoping I wasn't mangling her name too badly.

She tugged at my sleeve. "Monsieur."

"Wes."

"Wes, this won't work," she whispered. "It was a terrible idea."

Given that it was *my* terrible idea, her words stung. "It can work. We just need to be more convincing."

She shook her head. "Never mind." She shrugged. "My problems are small in the middle of such a war. I shouldn't think that my fears are bigger than anyone else's."

She turned to go, but I caught her arm. If there's one thing I knew, it was that fears were exactly as big as they wanted to be. "Wait another minute. Please?"

She hesitated, but stopped. I let go of her arm and went up to the bar to retrieve the carafe.

"More wine?" I didn't wait for the padre's answer before filling up his glass. "See," I said, sliding into the chair across from him, "I'm leaving tomorrow. Moving from building airplanes to flying them. It's risky business, I know, and Victoire here has enough to worry about without adding me to the list. But it gives me a comfort to know there's someone thinking of me down here on the ground." I looked over at her, still standing in the doorway, listening. "And I hope she thinks the same thing. With all her worrying, I hope she takes comfort knowing that there's someone trying to make the skies safe for her and hers."

Maybe it was the dim light of the tavern, but I almost thought she might cry again. The padre, that sentimental goat, was un-ashamedly misty-eyed. He emptied his glass and smacked it down on the table. "I'll do it."

"You mean it?" Victoire came over to the table, fists clenched tight against her sides. "You'll marry us? Tonight?"

"Oh, why not." He peered into his now-empty glass. "It's been a good night."

She exhaled. Her "never mind" had come with a held breath.

The padre plucked the carafe from my hand. "Tonight, a wed-ding. Tomorrow, a marriage!"

An hour later, a missal in one hand and a glass of wine in the other, the padre married Victoire and me at the bar of the little Pruniers tavern. I slipped my class ring onto her thumb and, for the first time that evening, she smiled.

WE HAD WHAT WAS LIKELY THE SHORTEST AND LEAST INDELI-cate honeymoon in the history of time. It lasted, from "I do" to farewell, about an hour and a half.

After our quick little ceremony, there were many rounds of drinks, paid for, I think, by me. The padre offered an excessively long toast that managed to reference Jesus, Abraham Lincoln, and *Tarzan of the Apes.* It was quite a feat. I played "Grand Old Flag" on my harmonica. The waitress took off her apron and sang in French. From the roars of laughter and the padre's red cheeks, I was sure it was bawdy.

As the song was followed by a second, and then a third and fourth that had the waitress crying with laughter, Victoire got qui-eter and quieter. I could guess what she was thinking. Businesslike marriage or not, it was technically our wedding night and my increasing drunkenness probably didn't inspire much confidence. We hadn't so much as held hands during the wedding ceremony, and the padre, who forgot half of the words despite the missal in his hands, never quite got to the "kiss the bride" part. Of course an insistent part of me had very high hopes for the rest of the evening, but my pickled brain remembered, somewhat regretfully, that I was a nicer guy than that.

"Don't worry," I said to her, leaning in. She had, I noticed, exceptional eyebrows. "All I ask is for a handshake to seal the deal."

"Really?" she asked, with such a note of relief that I felt like a clod for my thoughts only seconds ago.

I swallowed. "Really."

The padre came up behind us and slung an arm companionably over my shoulders. "May your marriage last longer than the wedding."

"It happened so quickly it hardly seems real," Victoire murmured.

"Oh, it isn't," the padre reassured her. Which, come to think of it, wasn't reassuring at all.

"What?" I blinked and slid out from under his arm. "Wait, you *are* a real priest, aren't you?"

He swayed on his feet, but he nodded.

"Then why did you say it isn't real?"

He hiccupped. "Well, in the eyes of that guy up there"—he pointed a wavering finger up at the ceiling—"you're as married as two geese."

Victoire frowned. "But geese don't get married."

"Shh! Don't interrupt." He licked his lips. "Where was I?"

"*Not really married*," I reminded, somewhat more forcefully than necessary.

"Ah, yes. Eyes of God . . . married as geese . . . but, you see, the French government has a very different opinion." He helped himself to more wine. "God may have more commandments, but the French, they have more paperwork."

Victoire steadied herself on the edge of the table.

"Well, then," I said, "show me where to sign." Though I likely couldn't draw a straight line in my current state, I would damned well try.

"Ha! Sign. There's more to it than that." He wiped his mouth with his sleeve and held up a finger to start a count. "Four things. You must have banns called three times in your home parish." He ticked off the next finger. "You must have a contract signed by a notary." Two more fingers, stuck together. "You must present the notarized contract to the town registrar so that the marriage can be recorded." He paused and squinted at his fingers. "That was four right there, wasn't it?"

I didn't argue. "Then this was all for nothing."

"So," Victoire said slowly, "if we do all of that, we will make the marriage legal?"

He blinked. "Well, I suppose so."

She turned to me, and said, soft and low, "This can work."

"But I'll be leaving."

"I will take care of it all. The banns, the contract, the registration. I can get it."

Until now, Victoire had seemed almost apathetic about the whole marriage thing. "You would do that?"

She hesitated, then nodded. "Two weeks, it will take. Two weeks for you to decide if you really want this or if it was a regrettable impulse."

I was a few hours and many glasses into the evening and didn't regret a thing. "You're giving me an out?"

"An out?"

"If it doesn't work, or if I . . . change my mind . . . well, you'll be no better off than you were this morning."

"*Oui*," she said. "But also no worse than this morning."

She held out her hand.

"And in that two weeks, you'll write to me?" I asked.

"Every day."

I took her hand.

But she didn't shake it right away. She stood for a moment, holding it.

"Will you promise me something?" she asked.

Her hand was warm. "Anything," I said.

She hesitated, her hand in mine. "Will you promise not to write in return?"

"Not?" Surely I didn't hear that right. "Wait, you don't want me to reply?"

"You said yours was a dangerous job. You said you didn't expect to come home." She licked her lower lip. "For me, the danger is losing my heart."

Something about her request made my face feel warm. I never thought my bumbling words could make a woman fall for me. Suddenly I wanted nothing more than to send her piles of letters.

But of course, I said, "Sure." I said, "Not a single reply." And she looked so relieved that I knew it was the right answer.

She shook my hand, more firmly than any handshake I'd ever received. I supposed, though, that this was the most important business contract I'd ever entered into. It deserved a serious hand-shake. My class ring—hers now—was cold against my palm.

I thought that would be it, the hearty handshake and a tipped hat in farewell. But halfway out the door, she suddenly spun on her heel and ran back to me. Pushing herself up on her tiptoes, she kissed me.

A guy isn't supposed to admit this, not when he's twenty-two years old and the brother of a confirmed playboy, but it was my very first kiss. I didn't know if they were supposed to be that quick or that weightless but I felt a little tight in my chest as she stepped back.

"Thank you," she said. My very new wife then walked out the door, leaving me with a pounding heart and the beginnings of a headache.

On the ride from Pruniers the next morning, my heart was still pounding. This time, though, with dawn breaking through the window of the train, it was due to planes and not girls.

I'd told Victoire that I was afraid, and I wasn't lying. We'd learned to rebuild Curtiss Jennys in Texas, S.E.5s in England, Sop-withs and SPADs in Scotland. We knew our way around engines and we knew how to rig a plane, but could count flying hours on our fingers. We were pilots, but pilots who spent more time under planes than in them. And even that time in the air, gliding over Texas deserts or the Firth of Clyde, I knew it wasn't the same. Not the same as here, where the sky lit up with shells, where smoke clung to everything, where ambulances bounced past, taking the dead and the living. To fly up over cannon fire with nothing much more than canvas and wood between me and two miles of air. Val hadn't lasted a month out here on the front. I had no reason to think I would last even that long.

The throbbing hangover I brought along from Pruniers didn't help, nor did the blushing recollection that I'd somehow managed to get married last night. Both Victoire and wine had let me forget, for an evening, that I was going to be, at last, a real live pilot. Emphasis, I hoped, on "live." My stomach lurched and I convinced myself that it was the lingering wine in my veins. Somewhere up there, Val was playing the lute and shaking his beautiful head at me.

I wanted to do nothing more than sleep for a week. As it was I got a jostled and icy cold nap on the train. My hangover didn't ease up, but I didn't mind. The longer the train ride, the better, in my opinion. I was probably the only one in my squadron who would've been happy as a hound dog to stay back tinkering with engines and unloading train cars rather than heading to the front. Of course I couldn't let any of them know. I cheered with the rest of the squadron and laced up my flying boots, all the while trying to not let anyone see how I was quaking in them.

I didn't know Victoire, yet I'd dragged her into the mess of my life. All she'd wanted was to cry in peace in the hallway outside of the medical department, but I couldn't leave well enough alone. A drunken priest and a desperate proposal later, and she was halfway married to a fraud. She thought I was a pilot. Little did she know I was only pretending. Good thing the padre gave her an out.

I'd begun to feel marginally better, until we rattled to a stop in Toul and climbed stiffly out of the train for the freezing walk to the aerodrome. As it loomed near and I saw the SPADs all lined up on the airfield, my heart started pounding again.

"You okay?" a guy asked. Big guy, Fitzhume, I thought his name was.

"I will be once I get warm," I tossed back.

He glanced up at the sky. "I hear it's colder up there."

I shivered involuntarily. "Don't remind me."

He gave me a look and I wished that I hadn't said anything.

We arrived in Toul to hear the same old refrain. *Not enough planes.* A thousand or so built out at Romorantin for the air service and there still weren't enough. They had some SPADs and DH-6s, but we'd never flown alone in either. A few were put aside for us to try out and get hours on, but, until more planes were delivered, we weren't going into combat. I tried not to look relieved.

The DH-6s, though, weren't anything to be relieved about. They were as slow and ponderous as hippos. The first time they put me in one, I taxied to the far end of the field, easing back on the stick. The Six merrily puttered along without so much as an inclination to go upward. It also wasn't much inclined to turn, and my first attempt ended with a series of curses and a line of unyielding trees.

"You've got to show the stick who's boss," Clarence Fitzhume advised. The bastard got it on the first try, making a graceful circuit of the airfield, before gliding down into a perfect landing. "It doesn't have an ounce of sensitivity."

On my second try, I tried his advice, yanking the stick back all the way to my belly button. The Six jumped to attention, swinging straight up, nose-first, into the sky. It didn't go very far before it stalled, but it managed to hang for a moment in midair, suspended from its sputtering propeller. I didn't know much about flying Sixes, but I did know I wasn't supposed to be parallel to the trees. As I clung, white-knuckled, to the feckless stick, the Six slid straight back down.

But my bruised ego was temporarily forgotten when, the next morning, I got my first letter from Victoire.

Truth be told, I didn't think I'd get a single one. Now that I was gone, there was nothing to stop her from disappearing. She had my name, if she wanted it, my ring, and the memory of a likely awful kiss. The rest was such a muddle that I wouldn't blame her if she didn't think it was worth sorting out. Someday she'd find someone else, maybe in Paris. Some dashing Frenchman with a mustache. Someone who didn't fly airplanes vertically or make questionable proposals in dark taverns.

And yet here was a letter in a cheap blue envelope, the "John Wesley Ward" written with dark ink. I opened it, knowing it wasn't from my mother, but hardly believing that the girl I'd half-married only days before had actually written to me.

29 October 1918

Dear Mr. Ward,

> *When I was learning English, I remember reading an old book called* The Polite Correspondent: Letters for All Occasions. *As thorough as the book was, it didn't have an example for this particular occasion. I'm not quite sure how one begins a letter to a husband she has known for exactly one day and eleven hours.*

> *Perhaps I should begin with the business at hand. Our business. I have written a letter to the old priest in my vil-*

lage, the one who watched me grow up, from baptism to confirmation. I wrote to him that very night and sent it off this morning, before the trains were out. If it reaches him this week, the first banns can be read on Sunday.

If I were being honest, that wasn't the only reason I wrote to him. Père Benoît, bless his stubborn soul, all but raised me. He taught me to read, taught me to pray, taught me to climb down from the plum tree when I got stuck too high. He's also the one who taught me English. He was a missionary when he was younger, traveling all over the world with nothing more than a spare pair of socks and a Bible. As his longest mission was tending to the savages of Arizona Territory, he comes by his English proficiency honestly.

He kept a globe in his office, shelves of books in English, and a Hopi pot filled with barley sugar candies. He never stood for excuses—his penances could make one weep— but also never stood for dishonesty in his parishioners. More than anything in the world, I loved Père Benoît.

So when I wrote to him last night, it was for the banns, but also for his approval, his blessing, or anything else he is willing to give. When the war crept close to Villers-Saint-Auguste, he sent me away to keep me safe, but also because he thought I needed to feel my way through the world without him. Well, I've made an awful mess of it so far, haven't I? I always worried that I'd grow up to be a disappointment to him. I hope I haven't.

Your wife,
Victoire Donadieu Ward

She was right about one thing: she had managed to make an awful mess of things. Pregnant, on the verge of losing her job, and now stuck with a nobody like me. Almost stuck, I reminded myself. At least she had that going for her.

For a moment, I forgot about her no-writing rule. I mentally started a response, to reassure her that it wasn't as bad as all that, that there was still a chance for her to find a mustachioed Frenchman to bring home to her Père, but then Clarence Fitzhume went into a stall and landed upside down between two goats and a hay bale. I folded Victoire's letter and stuffed it in my pocket. Fitzhume was the best we had in our squadron and he was being dragged out of the cockpit. Once fate had its say, Victoire would have all the out she needed.

I tried not to think about Fitzhume and his upside-down Six when my turn came up to try again. Today's attempt was somewhat more impressive than the last, if only because I got airborne. But, once up there, I couldn't get the beast to turn, not even a fraction. And so I sailed off across the trees, wondering how far I'd go before I could figure out how to land. It would be a long walk back to the aerodrome.

30 October 1918

Dear Mr. Ward,

You know, marriage is never this complicated in the movies. I think if Charlie Chaplin wanted a marriage in an instant, he would have a priest and two bridesmaids waiting in the wings, with the honeymoon cottage just a set away. No characters in the movies have to run around to secure banns and extraneous paperwork, unless their marriage satisfies the obscure whims of a will, a gambling debt, or an otherwise very necessary plot point. Some things sound easier over a cup of wine, no?

I've been told that you need an état civil, a certificate that proves your age and identity. The registrar very help-fully told me that an American birth certificate would suf-fice. Of course. He assured me all soldiers have such a thing tucked in their kit bags.

Could you wire your mother and ask for a copy of your birth certificate? I'm sure she has it on hand, probably framed and hanging next to your brother's medals. To hear you talk, vacating her womb was probably the last time you impressed her.

Your wife,
Victoire Donadieu Ward

Writing to my mother was always only slightly less painful than having a tooth pulled. I scribbled out six different versions of a telegram explaining that I'd married a pregnant French factory worker the other night, if only for the satisfying mental image of Mother fainting dead away upon reading. In the end I went with NEED BIRTH CERT PRONTO= ARMY STUFF= WES+ I left it to her to wonder at the vagaries of the military and its un-quenching demand for paperwork.

I took up another Six, sweating and arguing with the plane the whole way. I knew airplanes were supposed to go in more than one direction, I told it. I shouted and swore and insulted its airplane parents and progeny. Something must've worked, as the beast slowly, reluctantly turned. I realized, though, as I glided back to the airfield, that I'd have to land the thing in full sight of everyone lining outside the hangars. My last landing, in a far-off field piled with hay, had been furtive and somewhat soft. This one promised to be much more spectacular. The older pilots liked to hang around watching for this very reason.

I came in too fast, I knew. Men down on the ground were shouting at me, but I wasn't sure what they were saying. I zoomed past the field and had to turn around again for another try. Each pass was just as futile as the last, until I finally remembered to cut my motor, right over the same barnyard Fitzhume had used as landing pad. Those poor goats.

Envelopes arrived at the same time from both Mother and Victoire. Mother's was short and dismissive. WHAT KIND OF SON TELEGRAPHS HIS MOTHER= VAL WROTE THE NICEST LETTERS+ with no mention of the requested certificate. Victoire's was equally as short.

31 October 1918

Mr. Ward,

    With my last letter, I intended to show you nothing more than the famous French sarcasm. All apologies if it was read as anything but.
    Victoire Donadieu Ward

I hadn't been the least bit offended. By her stating the truth? I wouldn't be surprised if Mother did have my birth certificate framed. I was sure it had been, in her eyes, my one and only accomplishment.

More offensive was Clarence Fitzhume, who (thankfully or not) survived his pinwheel into the barnyard with nothing more than a terrific knock on the head, but came out of it a right bully. He cheerfully found an insult for each and every one of us, but was one of the best in a SPAD, so there wasn't much we could do.

I'd been sitting in the canteen, starting a reply to Victoire that I knew I wasn't allowed to send, when Fitzhume came by and swiped the pencil from my hand. "Hey, Jock Itch"—for that was his new, affectionate nickname for me—"writing to your boyfriend?"

"My wife."

He sat his oversize rear end on the table, right over top of my paper. "What inmate said yes to the likes of you?"

I wanted to say, "One nice enough to never say yes to the likes of *you*." But looking at him with his pig eyes and hammy forearms, I adjusted it to "One nice enough."

He cuffed me in the side of my head. My ears rang, but he seemed to be in a jovial mood. "Well, let's see a photo of her. I bet she looks like a goat. But does she have big knockers, at least?" He mimed a jostling bosom.

"Yes. No! I mean, really, Fitzhume. None of your business." Truth was, I had no idea. Something like that should be the *first* thing a guy would notice. But it wouldn't be very manly to admit that I'd been looking at her tears, at her back-straight stubbornness, at that one little smile she'd let slip. The way she licked the corner of her mouth when eating mussels. The way she unabashedly blew her nose. Fitzhume would've missed those little things. Even Val, for all his success with women, probably would've missed them. And yet those were the mental snapshots that always floated up when I was falling asleep at night (especially the nose-blowing, which was nothing short of glorious). Those were some of the things I remembered best about our few hours together.

With the image of Victoire and her handkerchief in my mind, I said, as politely as I could muster, "If you don't mind, I'd like to get back to my letter now."

He lifted the pencil right in front of my face and snapped it in half. "Without a pencil?" Fitzhume leaned closer, until his nose was inches from mine, and said in a completely awful voice, "I guess you'll have to use your own blood."

I left my broken pencil and paper behind and fled the canteen. The airfield was quiet, but I took a Six up to work off nervous energy. Of course, with no one around to watch, I made a somewhat decent flight.

Later that night, though, I practiced Fitzhume's glare in my shaving mirror. "I guess you'll have to use your own blood," I said, but I didn't sound chilling at all. A little squeaky, but not at all chilling. And my steely glare looked more cross-eyed than anything. I sighed and tucked the mirror back in my pocket. Try as I might, I'd never been able to be anyone other than plain old Wes. Poor Victoire.

1 November 1918
All Saints' Day

Dear Mr. Ward,

I haven't been sleeping much lately. I've been sick, all day and all night, so sick I can't lie down. Instead, each night after the lamps are out, I pace a circuit around my bed in the moonlight. Lines of French poetry run through my head until I'm too tired to think, then I just walk quietly until dawn. I'm so exhausted I'm hallucinating. The other night I swear I saw honeysuckle growing up the wallpaper of my bedroom. As I paced I had to keep stepping over the tendrils of stem and leaves that curled across the floor.

Today is All Saints' Day. Did you know I was originally named for one? Young St. Germaine, a woman of a thousand sorrows. As you can see, right from birth, I wasn't destined for great things. One day Père Benoît found me very seriously attempting to cry in the front pew of the church. I explained that I was trying to do St. Germaine justice. He gave me a stick of barley sugar, my first, right there in the church and told me that we weren't bound by our names. He said Victoire was a better name for me and so I changed it right then and there. Père Benoît has always thought I was bound for a victorious life.

If you had met me fifteen years ago, you'd have known a girl with dimpled knees who could always wheedle one more story out of the priest. If you'd met me twelve years ago, you'd have known a girl with too many freckles, too many "brothers," and too many stockings torn from tree climbing. Seven years ago, a girl on the edge of adulthood, still climbing trees to hide, but with novels and crossed-fingered wishes. Four years ago, a woman watching soldiers march across her country, knowing those wishes were gone. Six weeks ago, a woman blushing from a smile across a Pruniers tavern, on the verge of making either the very best or the very worst decision of her life.

Which Victoire would you have liked best? The story lover? The tree climber? The reader and dreamer? The taverngoer already tired of war?

Your wife,

Victoire Donadieu Ward

Maybe I was a dope, but I sort of liked all of them. I tried to picture the Victoire I'd met climbing trees or making herself cry over a long-dead saint. I thought of her unselfconscious nose-blowing and decided I could see her quite well with freckles and skinned knees. Why had she put "brothers" in quotation marks? Maybe there were so many that she lost track of them or accidentally included spare neighborhood kids in her count. I was certainly never in doubt about the existence of mine.

I had thought today's flight was going well. I took off nicely, made a few circuits, slowed, and leveled off as I came back in for my landing. But I didn't come down far enough. Nice and level, but too many feet in the air, I pancaked straight down onto the ground. The wheels came up right through the lower wings and I was escorted off the field by howling laughter.

I telegraphed Mother again. YOU FORGET I'M THE DIS-

APPOINTING SON= STILL NEED BIRTH CERTIFI-CATE+. She responded so quickly, the paper fairly crackled with anger as I unfolded it. I could just see her holding the delivery boy as she furiously wrote out a response, full rate and extra words be damned. SPEAKING OF DISAPPOINTING ARE YOU FLYING YET= VAL SHOT DOWN ENEMY AIRCRAFT AND STILL FOUND TIME TO WRITE HIS MOTHER ONCE A WEEK+.

I gave the telegram my best cross-eyed glare and informed it, "I'll reply in my own blood."

2 November 1918

Dear Mr. Ward,

The Romorantin doctor was despicable to begin with, but he suddenly found a streak of newfound morality and reported me and my condition. I'm surprised he waited this long. I've been dismissed on grounds of "inappropriate conduct." As though the other party to my condition was not just as inappropriate in his conduct.

The landlord (who must be an acquaintance of the good doctor) isn't much better. He heard tell of my dismissal and offered me an alternate way to "pay" my rent each month. Even though I didn't have a John Wesley Ward to sweep down the hallway to my rescue this time, I very firmly declined all on my own. I really wanted to kick him in a sensitive spot, by way of thanks for his generous offer. Instead I told him I'd be out of the apartment tomorrow.

So now, instead of working to send money home to Père Benoît (the roof of the sacristy has fallen in; he celebrates Mass in mittens and a stocking hat), I am left in my dismal little apartment, wondering how I'll even pay the rent on that.

I diligently searched the area before I found the job at Romorantin. There isn't any other work. If I want to find employment, I need to range farther afield. I need to use my imagination. Should I pack it all up and walk to Paris? I could dance at the Moulin Rouge, at least until I'm too big to see my toes. Should I find a job in another factory, building airships and submarines? Find my way to the seashore and repair nets torn by mermaids? Facing motherhood, women have few options.

Your wife,

Victoire

I WAS SUITING UP FOR YET ANOTHER ATTEMPT TO MAKE IT AIR-borne when I heard mail call. Along with Victoire's letter, I had an official reprimand for "conduct unbecoming." But she was right, it was just a slap on the wrist. (Along with the reprimand, I was assigned fatigue duty for a week and forbidden from flying. I was delighted.) But Victoire, losing her job, being sent from Romorantin. I'd never lost so much. Even with all my parents' disdain, I hadn't (yet) been cut out of the will.

After I changed, I dashed off another telegram to Mother. BIRTH CERTIFICATE PLEASE= ALSO SOME MONEY WIRED+. Her reply, read after I was off fatigue duty for the day, was just as prompt and lengthy as her last. VAL NEVER

ASKED ME FOR MONEY= I SUPPOSE IT IS TO SPEND ON STRONG DRINK AND IMMORAL WOMEN= YOU KNOW HOW I DISAPPROVE OF BOTH+.

I waited until I'd procured a hearty cup of the hooch that Private Hughely sold out of a tank in the engine shop before replying, WOULD YOU FEEL BETTER IF I SAID IT WAS FOR IMMORAL DRINK AND STRONG WOMEN=.

She didn't respond.

3 November 1918

Dear Mr. Ward,

> *I've been sorting through my few things, deciding what to pack up and what to sell. There isn't much here in my little apartment, you know. I have my coveralls and my one good dress. A hat and coat and pair of not-so-old boots. The crucifix that Père Benoît gave me when I left. A battered copy of The Wonderful Wizard of Oz. Three plain handkerchiefs plus one with a "JWW" embroidered very elegantly in the corner. They're all equally important to me, in different ways.*

> *What do you carry with you? What's important to John Wesley Ward? Is it the harmonica you played for me when you thought there'd been enough wine that no one would notice? The fancy wristwatch you checked no less than seven times as curfew approached? The handkerchief with your initials so lovingly embroidered? The ring you slipped off your finger and onto mine, gold and marked with "1918"?*

They might not be much, but maybe enough to hint at a life. A college boy, covertly musical yet overtly punctual, loved more than he thinks, but still more worried than he cares to admit about breaking the rules.

How close am I?

Have you written to your mother yet?

Your wife,

Victoire

Mother had embroidered me those handkerchiefs, a neat two dozen of them before I headed off to Yale. "I won't have a son of mine embarrass me by mistaking his sleeve for a handkerchief," she'd said as she handed over the stack. "Now don't disappoint me."

Don't disappoint me. I felt I'd been hearing that from my mother all of my life. From my early ventures out of the nursery to my entrance into the schoolroom, from my first day of college to the day I joined the air service. *Don't disappoint me.*

I never intended to. I toddled from the nursery straight behind Val. Even then, I idolized him. He always thought of the best games, built the tallest towers, drew the most terrifying pictures of dragons. I tried to keep up, tried to impress him, tried to practice his darling smile in the mirror when no one was looking. Mother would run a hand through his curls and call him her strong boy. When we grew and graduated, I was sent off to college. She kept Val, her favorite, near to her at home.

But even at Yale, no grades were high enough, no glowing reports from profs glowing enough. My father just harrumphed and my mother told me I could do better. I wondered if I'd ever be better enough.

DIDN'T MEAN IMMORAL DRINK BUT DID MEAN STRONG WOMEN= I wrote. HAVE MET SOMEONE= STUBBORN KIND AND DOESN'T MIND THE HAR-MONICA+.

She wrote back simply, MAYBE YOU ARE GROWING UP+.

4 November 1918

Dear Mr. John Wesley Ward,

I'm feeling somewhat more cheerful than I have been of late. I actually got a passable night's sleep, enough that I took a walk today out in the cold and crisp. Did you see the full moon out last night? The old women in Villers-Saint-Auguste always used to say that if you crossed your arms, spun three times, and wished on the full moon, you'd have your heart's desire. Père Benoît said that was nonsense and only prayer and a determined spirit could bring you your heart's desire.

I think prayers, determination, and crossed arms beneath a moon, well, all three just triple my chances. Don't you? I'd tell you what I wished for, but then it wouldn't come true. Let's just say it involves airplanes not plummeting through the clouds.

What do you desire above everything else?

Victoire

I think what I desired above everything else had changed in the past week. Increasingly it was blue envelopes, punctual as railroads, that made my heart pound the way it had that little moment she kissed me. Increasingly it was the thought of her face as I fell asleep, every night. Increasingly it was a hope that I'd make it through this okay so I could see her again. I had to. I didn't remember if her eyes were blue or green.

This time I really did take out a paper and pencil. Her rule not to reply, it was silly. I wrote it all down, all of those Victoire-inspired wants and dreams. I carried it in my pocket and the rest of the day, between unloading trucks, rigging planes, and repairing engines, I wrote until I'd filled up the whole sheet. I even got as far as procuring an envelope and addressing it.

But such declarations were probably ridiculous. All she'd said was that she hoped I didn't die. It wasn't exactly a prompt for an outpouring of sentiment. Married or not, we'd known each other for exactly twelve days. Stranger things happened in the movies, but in real life, people didn't fall in love so quickly.

I folded the envelope in quarters and pushed it into my pocket.

5 November 1918

Dear John Wesley Ward,

   With no work for me here and an apartment I won't be able to afford for very long, I've thought about leaving Pruniers. I was even thinking of going home, home, to Villers-Saint-Auguste and Père Benoît's saggy-roofed old *church. I could almost smell the pine trees and incense and woodsmoke that made up the little house in Saint-Auguste. I even secured a train timetable (as accurate as the things can be these days), so ready was I to go.*

But then a bedraggled letter arrived from him saying that the banns were set and that the first has already been called this past Sunday, on the 2nd. He wrote that he was proud of me for doing things the right way. I was a credit to my name.

Of course I feel now like I've been kicked in the chest by an ox. As a girl, I used to do everything for Père Benoît's approval. I wanted nothing less. But will I ever have it again? I lied to him, Wes. To a priest. That he doesn't know yet doesn't make it any better. What should I do? When he learns the truth, he'll have no reason to trust me.

Knowing what you do, how is it that you trust me?

Victoire

She may not have been honest with her fatherly French priest, but she'd been honest with me. She'd told me her troubles in that little tavern, the fears she had of being alone and not rising above expectations. I knew a thing or two about seeking approval. From my mostly absent father, from my teachers, from my mother. From Val.

Even my superior officers. When Fitzhume flew into a rage over a delayed repair and knocked me in the head with a wrench so hard my ears rang, I didn't say a word. He used to be a decent guy, before his crash. Though it pained me (literally), when the officer of the day asked me with raised eyebrow about the swelling lump on my head and the fuming Fitzhume still holding the wrench, I had to say, "It was an accident." The air service didn't want to hear about his misdeeds. They didn't want to lose him. He was a darned fine pilot. His ranking as a human being, though, well, that was up for differing opinions.

Anyway, who was I to judge Victoire and her misleading of Père Benoît? When I telegraphed Mother again about the birth certificate and money, she asked, ARE YOU IN TROUBLE= DID YOU GET A GIRL IN A FAMILY WAY+.

Technically I hadn't. But what reason would she have to believe me? *Really, Mother, I didn't get her in such a state. I'm just tidying up another guy's messes because I'm not a cad.* So I replied with a restrained, NO= JUST TRYING TO DO RIGHT BY SOME-ONE+. I wasn't any better than Victoire at revealing the truth.

6 November 1918

Dear Wes,

I've been sick again, so sick, I don't know why any woman would honestly look forward to this. I shouldn't worry too much about Père Benoît. I am already being punished by a much higher power.

But I'm also punished by the news I hear coming out of the Meuse-Argonne. So many lives lost, so many planes down. I pretended that last night's moon was full and hoped that you weren't among either.

Yours,

Victoire

Airplanes came down all the time and I knew my enforced week on the ground was almost up. Next, it could be me.

Fitzhume ended up in the barnyard again, a lot more cracked up than last time. I think the goats were just as surprised as he was. I was nearby, loading up bales, and ran with the others to help pull him out of the wreck. He looked dazed and didn't try to hit a single person on the way out of the splintered cockpit.

He was scratched up pretty good and his left hand was mangled something awful. As I got him into the truck, he said, "It was one of those headaches. It came on and, I think, I forgot where I was."

I climbed in the back with him. "It happens." Though he was quiet, I sat an arm's length away.

"It happens too much to me." He rubbed his head with his good hand and winced. "Ever since that stall a few weeks ago."

Before then he had been a little short-tempered, but no worse than most. But no matter how tough the guy, heads remained fragile things.

That's what they said about Val. One crash and one concussion too many and he'd become a different person. He started taking risks, more than he ever did before. Mother sent him letter after letter telling him to be careful, but Val seemed almost suicide-bent with the way he flew. After we got word that he died, Mother was inconsolable. She raged that she wished someone had tied him down and kept him from climbing in the plane that last time. She wished he'd listened to her. She wished he'd had someone watching out for him.

So when we pulled back up to the base and the lieut asked

whether the crash was really as bad as it all seemed—"Fitzhume is tougher than a SPAD"—I hesitated and thought of Val.

"Maybe more than a bandage this time," I said.

Someone had to watch out for him.

7 November 1918

Dear Wes,

> *I've received another letter from Père Benoît. He received the money I sent—my last paycheck—and, though it wasn't enough to repair the roof of the sacristy, it was enough to buy new shoes for the children.*

> *You assumed that my father taught me English, but it was Père Benoît. I never knew my real father, but the priest was père to me in both senses of the word. You see, in addition to tending to his parish, he also runs the Saint-Auguste orphanage. It's small and poor, but full of his love. I was the only girl there, trying to keep up with the boys and keep ahead of my legacy. I never met my mother, but she was a girl who "went wrong," as the villagers say. I was the result and she left me on the orphanage steps with no possessions but "Germaine" and the shadow of what she'd done hanging over me. Can you imagine what it was like to grow up beneath the weight of both?*

> *Anyway, that's why I couldn't return home pregnant and alone. It's what everyone expected. Odette's daughter, grown up to be a cocotte just like her. Everyone except Père*

Benoît, that is. He always had faith that I could grow up to be more. That I wasn't bound by my name or my mother's mistakes.

And maybe I already have broken free. My little one won't be left on the steps of an orphanage. Though I grew up surrounded by love, my little one will find it in my arms.

And, if you're still willing, in yours.

Yours,

Victoire

I fell asleep thinking of Victoire and the baby. Maybe it would be a little boy who drew dragons like Val or a stubborn little girl who climbed trees and read books. Somehow I found myself smiling still when I woke up.

I'd never thought of children before. I suppose most guys didn't. I'd made hash out of my life; I wouldn't want to do it to someone else's.

But Victoire had thought about it. Had thought about *me* with children. The thought made me feel suddenly warm, but then just-as-suddenly nervous. What if I screwed it up? What if I pushed away, like my parents, or walked away, like Victoire's? We couldn't all be saintly old priests.

For the hundredth time, I thought about ignoring the promise I'd made. I thought about writing and telling her about my dream. Maybe she'd tell me it wasn't ridiculous, that I might not be half-bad at taking care of a kid. Maybe she'd tell me again she hoped I didn't crash.

My musings were cut short with a summons. As of today,

my grounding was over. Tomorrow I'd be flying out with the squadron.

I telegraphed Mother. I WANTED TO LET YOU KNOW THAT I'M BEING SENT UP TOMORROW= WISH ME LUCK= I'LL BE FLYING INTO COMBAT+. Her response didn't come for hours, so long that I wondered if I should write again. When she did reply, it was with a terse IT'S ABOUT TIME+.

I couldn't leave it at that, not when I was flying out to dog-fights and miles of sky. My family knew too well how far a pilot could fall. YOU ALWAYS TOLD VAL TO BE CAREFUL= IN EVERY SINGLE LETTER YOU SENT= WHY HAVE YOU NEVER SAID THAT TO ME+.

She replied, BECAUSE YOU ARE THE ONE SMART ENOUGH TO SURVIVE+.

8 November 1918

Dear Wes,

After sending that last letter to you, I must have fallen asleep thinking of my own words, because I dreamt of the future. In it, we were in a snug house playing dominos by the fireplace, you and I and the little one (in my dream, a boy with round cheeks and serious brown eyes). In the rocking chair nearby, Père Benoît dozed. Though I thought I'd forgotten your face in all of its details, I could see it quite clearly there.

Life is full of decisions, some made in fear, some made

in loneliness, some made in a tavern over two mugs of wine. Even those that happen in an instant can last a lifetime. But they don't have to be wrong. Do not the best intentions sometimes reveal the best people?

I'm leaving for Villers-Saint-Auguste this afternoon. I'll tell Père Benoît, about the baby, about the dismissal. About you. Parents spend their lives protecting us, but at some point they have to cross their fingers and let us fly. I hope he'll forgive me for doing just that.

Perhaps I'll get there just in time to hear the second set of banns read. After that, only one more, and then it's official. Till death do us part. Business or not, we're stuck for the rest of our days. Ça alors, John Wesley Ward.

I shouldn't have made you promise not to write. I watch for the mail every day, on the chance that you forgot the promise or wrote despite it. I wish that I knew how you felt about all this. Because, as crazy as it is, as reckless as it sounds, I don't think I mind. I liked the dream I had last night. I wish you could've seen it.

Should I let the last banns be called? Or, Wes, should I stop them? Should I stop this? Though I don't want to, do you?

Victoire

Of course I didn't want them stopped. Two weeks ago, when I stood next to her in the tavern, making drunken promises, I might not have known that. But now, with that small stack of blue envelopes tucked in my inside pocket, I knew. I was heading up into the air, but I had something worth landing for.

November 11, 1918

Dear Father Benoît,

We have never met, but I hope I can convince you that I'm a good man. You see, Father, I am writing to respectfully ask for Victoire's hand in marriage.

I'm an American, so apologies for that, but I come from a good family. I went to college and studied far too many things. I didn't do half-bad at being a student, but things like that don't seem to matter as much these days. I've put my books away and have taken up a uniform. My brother flew with the Lafayette Flying Corps and I'm here in France to follow in his trail. I can't promise that I'll be as distinguished as him or that I'll fly as high, but know that I'm here, doing my best.

Before I met Victoire, I didn't know what that was. But I watched her strength, her honesty, her devotion to you and Villers-Saint-Auguste, and I wanted to be a part of it. She wrote to me and, through her words, I saw my own better. I saw my potential best.

I hope to meet you someday. I hope that you give your blessing and that you officiate at our wedding. I know, to Victoire, it won't be a marriage otherwise.

With all respect,
John Wesley Ward

Last night, I'd sent a late telegram to my mother. MOTHER ABOUT THE BIRTH CERTIFICATE= CAN YOU SEND+. As I posted Père Benoît's letter on my way to the airstrip, a reply

from the telegram waited. HAVE FAITH= I SENT IT THE
FIRST DAY YOU ASKED+.

I climbed into the plane, my heart already pounding. I thought
of the shattered engines we learned to repair, of Fitzhume's scrambled brains, of Val's bloodstained ID tags. It was awful. I shook
my head to clear it. From my pocket, the envelopes rustled. I sifted
through my wine-soaked memories of her. I needed to think of
something beautiful. As the ground crew got the propeller going
and the airplane roared the life, I suddenly remembered that Victoire's eyes were blue.

The guys were pulling out the chocks from beneath the wheels,
when Hughely ran out onto the field. "Ward, did you hear?"

I shook my head. I could hardly hear a thing as it was now.

"The rumor," he shouted. "They say it's over."

I leaned over the side. "What?"

He cupped his hands around his mouth. "Over!"

"What's over?"

Down the line, the other planes started. Propellers chopped
Hughely's sentences into pieces. " . . . Wilson . . ." he yelled. " . . .
Foch . . . railcar . . . Over!"

Before I could ask what he meant, the plane started moving
and the rest of his words were lost in the sound of a squadron of
engines.

I was still trying to piece it together as the plane lifted off. I
was too puzzled to worry about the takeoff. And it was perfect.
As smooth as any I made over Kelly Field. I sailed up in the right
of the formation and we were gliding across French countryside.

I could see the front before we reached it. The landscape became browner and more barren, the ground torn up by marching armies, the buildings charred ruins. It was November, but there was no harvest this year, not here. Old trenches snaked black across the countryside, even miles back. Along the horizon, puffs of smoke, distant and low, marked the frontline trenches. Lights from shells streaked the sky. Below, men surged.

The sky, though, was clear. Blue and cloudless and almost serene way above No Man's Land. No other planes waited. Looking straight ahead at the cerulean sky, it was easy to forget there was a war on below.

A row of cannons fired, all at once, a noise that shook the air with a line of light. I imagined I could hear it, even as far up as I was. And, as though an electric charge ran across the land beneath us, as though the war sparked and shorted out, everything stopped.

The shelling stopped. The cannon fire stopped. The wind blew away threads of smoke and gas to show men on both sides retreating.

The planes looped around, though I knew we were all watching below. And suddenly, rippling through the men in the trenches, the men still on the battlefield, so loud we could hear it above the planes and the wind, a cheer went up below. And I knew what Hughely was talking about. *Over*. The war was over.

I wasn't going to be shot down over a field of poppies. I wasn't going to die before those banns were called and before I could properly kiss Victoire. I wasn't going to have to worry about the little one growing up in a country wrung with war. All I had to worry about was his skinned knees and heartaches.

Years later, people would always ask, what were you doing the moment the war ended? Everyone had a story. Marching, recovering, pulling the pin from a grenade.

Me? I was composing a letter to my wife in my mind. I was telling her, for the first time, "I love you."

To Danielle,
who has always known when I need
a handkerchief and when I need a laugh

Hour of the Bells

Heather Webb

BEATRIX WHISKED AROUND THE SHOWROOM, FEATHER duster in hand. Not a speck of dirt could remain or Joseph would be disappointed. The hour struck noon. A chorus of clocks whirred, their birds popping out from hiding to announce midday. Maidens twirled in their frocks with braids down their backs, woodcutters clacked their axes against pine, and the odd sawmill wheel spun in tune to the melody of a nursery rhyme. Two dozen cuckoos warbled and dinged, each crafted with loving detail by the same pair of hands—those with thick fingers and a steady grip.

Beatrix paused in her cleaning. One clock chimed to its own rhythm, apart from the others.

She could turn them off—the tinkling melodies, the incessant clatter of pendulums, wheels, and cogs, with the levers located near the weights—just as their creator had done before bed each evening, but she could not bring herself to do the same. To silence their music was to silence *him*, her husband, Joseph. The Great War had already done that—ravaged his gentle nature, stolen his final breath, and silenced him forever.

In a rush, Beatrix scurried from one clock to the next, assessing which needed oiling. With the final stroke of twelve, she found the offending clock. Its walnut face, less ornate than the others, had been her favorite, always. A winter scene displayed a cluster of snow-topped evergreens; rabbits and fawns danced in the drifts when the music began, and a scarlet cardinal dipped its head and opened its beak to the beauty of the music. The animals' simplicity appealed to her now more than ever. With care, she removed the weights and pendulum, and unscrewed the back of the clock. She was grateful she had watched her husband tend to them so often. She could still see Joseph, blue eyes peering over his spectacles, focused on a figurine as he painted detailing on the linden wood. His patient hands had caressed the figures lovingly, as he had caressed her.

The memory of him sliced her open. She laid her head on the table as black pain stole over her body, pooling in every hidden pocket and filling her up until she could scarcely breathe.

"Give it time," her friend Adelaide had said, as she set a basket of jam and dried sausages on the table; treasures in these times of rations, yet meager condolence for what Beatrix had lost.

"Time?" Beatrix had laughed, a hollow sound, and moved to the window overlooking the grassy patch of yard. The Vosges mountains rose in the distance, lording over the line between France and Germany along the battlefront. Time's passage never escaped her—not for a moment. The clocks made sure of it. There weren't enough minutes, enough hours, to erase her loss.

As quickly as the grief came, it fled. Though always powerful, its timing perplexed her. Pain stole through the night, or erupted at unlikely moments, until she feared its onslaught the way others feared death. Death felt easier, somehow.

Beatrix raised her head and pushed herself up from the table to finish her task. Joseph would not want her to mourn, after two long years. He would want to see her strength, her resilience, especially for their son. She pretended Adrien was away at school, though he had enlisted, too. His enlistment had been her fault. A vision of her son cutting barbed wire, sleeping in trenches, and pointing a gun at another man reignited the pain and it began to pool again. She suppressed the horrid thoughts quickly, and locked them away in a corner of her mind.

With a light touch she cleaned the clock's bellows and dials, and anointed its oil bath with a few glistening drops. Once satisfied with her work, she hung the clock in its rightful place above the phonograph, where a disk waited patiently on the spool. She spun the disk once and watched the printed words on its center blur. Adrien had played "Quand Madelon" over and over, belting out the patriotic lyrics in time with the music. To him, it was a show of his support for his country. To Beatrix it had been a siren, a warning that her only son would soon join the fight. His father's death was the final push he had needed. The lure of *patrimoine*, of country, throbbed inside him as it did in other men. They talked of war as women spoke of tea sets and linens, yearned for it as women yearned for children. Now the war had seduced her Adrien. She stopped the spinning disk and plucked it from its wheel, the urge to destroy it pulsing in her hands.

She must try to be more optimistic. Surely God would not take all she had left.

A knock echoed through the foyer.

Beatrix's pulse stuttered. She did not expect visitors. In wartime, unannounced guests meant one of two things—soldiers at her door, or someone had died. Her hand flew to the pendant she wore at her throat, stamped with Adrien's initials.

Perhaps her son had written, she tried to convince herself.

The pounding at the door persisted.

Dread filled her limbs, leaden in its weight, and her legs refused to carry her to the door.

"Madame Joubert!" The postman's voice was muffled by the barrier of solid oak and the whipping of a brisk fall breeze. "Please, open the door. I know you're home. I can see the lights in your window. It's urgent."

Beatrix's heart pounded an erratic beat. She grasped the edge of the sofa for support.

"It's posted from Jean Largot." He paused. "Madame? I am going to leave it in your letter box."

A letter from Adrien's closest friend and fellow soldier. Beatrix clutched the duster in her hand, knuckles white. Inhaling, she reminded herself there was no need to be emotional. It would not help her now. She stalked to the spirit cabinet and poured herself a splash of the little remaining brandy. With two quick gulps the liquid disappeared. Whatever the letter contained, she would need courage to face it. She unlatched the front door and retrieved the dreaded missive. Once inside, she poured another brandy and sat on the sofa. She cradled the envelope in her lap, toying with its edges a long while.

At last, Beatrix slit open the envelope and smoothed Jean's letter. The page was slightly crinkled and the ink bled across the page from sweat—or tears? She read the letter once, and again, and then a third time. Hand shaking, she finished her brandy. A battle had raged near the Selle River. Though the Allies had won, the Germans had made their mark. When the ambulances arrived to tend the wounded, Adrien, along with many others blown to bits, had not been among the survivors.

An emotion swept over her, terrible in its force. In place of pain, hot venom surged through her, burning her core. In place of fear and aching, determination swirled, settled, and congealed, turning her heart to stone. They couldn't take him. She shook her head, refusing to believe it—refusing to believe her baby boy was gone. They had destroyed everything, the Germans. She glanced at the mirror on the wall opposite her. A roaring howled inside her, yet her features reflected no panic, no tears welled in her eyes. Only the clench of jaw indicated something was amiss.

Somehow, she would make them pay.

Soft spring light flooded through the window of the salon. Beatrix removed a screaming teakettle from the burner and poured water over tea leaves. She glanced up at the sound of footsteps on the front path.

Adrien slammed the door behind him in a huff. His tall frame was hunched, his hands balled into fists. "They hate me."

"No one hates you," she said, stirring the brew in her cup. He could be so dramatic.

"The kids at school called me a *boche*." A tear slid down his cheek. Embarrassed, he wiped it away angrily. "The *boches* murdered Papa, and now they're accusing me of being one?" He slammed his fist down on the countertop.

She cringed at the anti-German slur. She was born a German citizen in a small town in the Black Forest, a couple of hours' travel from her current home in Belfort, France. She'd met Joseph during his apprenticeship as a clockmaker. He had won her over with quiet humor and romantic gestures, surprising her often with his unique brand of poetry. When he asked for her hand, she accepted his French heritage as her own. Now the Germans were her enemies. Her people had killed him, shattered her life, and destroyed the country she had grown to love.

She would never forgive them.

After a moment of tarrying over how to reply, she said, "Show them you are a worthy young man and they'll leave you be."

"I'll show them, all right. I'll show all of you." He glared at her with a ferocity she recognized in her own father, so many years ago. Adrien had inherited it, a fact she could never share, not now.

Her son's face rippled and faded as her eyes slowly opened.

Beatrix jolted awake. She squinted and looked around, disoriented. Lace curtains floated over a window slicked with rain. The faint odor of vinegar tinged the air. Frowning, she turned and saw only the phonograph, its record motionless beneath the gleaming brass of the Morning Glory horn. The memory of Adrien, of his self-hatred, his hatred of who she was, had come in a dream to punish her.

Reality crushed her lungs and she couldn't breathe. She had to get out, leave this house of memories—at the very least until she knew her next move. She pushed up from the sofa and walked at a measured clip to her bedroom. With exquisite care she groomed herself. After sleeping so little last night, she'd slept most of the day away, yet purple circles had deepened beneath her eyes.

"Everything must appear in order, even when it is not," she could still hear her mother say, as she powdered her face. Now Beatrix did just as she had been taught.

After slipping into a plain day dress, she creased the letter with careful, perfect folds. She walked through the doorway joining the house and the clock shop and placed the letter next to a stack of ledgers. She hesitated an instant, then flipped one open. Inside, she'd pressed two dried poppies; symbols of beauty and hope, Joseph had called them in one of his letters. She couldn't bring herself to discard them. She closed the ledger with a snap. Her job had been to keep meticulous records of Joseph's income and supplies, as well as the inheritance they had received when his parents had passed. Who would inherit her estate now? Despair bloomed inside her, coating her throat and tongue like oil. Get out! She had to get out.

Beatrix rushed outdoors to face the November chill and blanket of melancholy sky. Today she was thankful for the cold. Let it freeze her face and limbs, numb her from head to toe. She didn't want to feel. Yet hadn't that always been her way? When Adrien skinned his knee or a classmate hurt his feelings, she had squeezed his hand and sent him on his way. To show too much emotion did not aid one in this life—her German mother had taught her that long ago. Instinctively she rubbed the back of her hand where the lash of a leather belt once split her skin.

What she would give to squeeze Adrien's hand again, to hold him tightly.

She pushed against the wind, down the solitary road to a block of stucco homes topped with too-cheery orange roof tiles. After several minutes of brisk walking, she reached the *centre ville*. The space between buildings vanished. A long line of town homes and apartment buildings framed the city streets of Belfort, overlooking the open plaza. Self-important French soldiers, guns strapped to their backs, stood at the mouth of each street. Belfort was the farthest point in the Alsace region before the German border. A medieval fort had been converted to the army's stronghold and soldiers and military policemen were posted throughout town and along the river.

Beatrix approached two soldiers laughing and jostling one another. They looked barely older than Adrien, who had entered the war at the tender age of eighteen. One of them punched the other in the shoulder and laughed. How could they find amusement at such a time? She looked down as she passed. Their leather boots were scarred and the heels uneven from months of patrolling, marching over uneven terrain, and over corpses.

Slain like her family.

The roaring began again, and a river of venom raced through her veins. She hated the Germans, and this infernal war. She picked up the pace, leaving the soldiers—the reminder of her loss—behind. On the opposite end of the square, the bakery was packed, as always. Customers spilled down the street in a line, waiting for their ration of the day's bread. As she passed the shop, the scent of warm yeast billowed into the cold evening air. Not wanting to catch the eye of anyone she knew, she tilted her head to shield her face from view.

Too late.

"Beatrix?" A woman called from across the street. "*C'est toi?*"

She looked up to see Geraldine Bernat bounding toward her, cloche hat snug over her auburn locks and baguette wedged under her arm. The woman never knew when to close her mouth. Worse, she had once sought Joseph's affections before he had come to Furtwangen to learn clockmaking. The minute Beatrix's path crossed his, it was as if no other had existed before them. Luckily, Geraldine hadn't seemed to mind, her feelings were easily swayed, and she quickly took up with another eligible man.

Beatrix didn't bother with a greeting and instead forced a smooth expression and prepared to dash past the bakery. The woman was kind, but nosy.

"Oh, darling, how are you?" Geraldine held her hat to her head to prevent it from blowing away. Her round cheeks were stained pink with cold.

"*Bonjour*, Geraldine." She avoided the question.

Sympathy filled the woman's eyes. "How are you holding up?" She adjusted the baguette that slipped from her grip. "What will you do with Joseph's little shop?"

"I . . . I don't know." Beatrix pressed her lips together to hold it all in—the terrible things she envisioned, the knot of emotion throbbing inside her.

Geraldine's eyes lit up, as if she'd happened on a remembered gem of gossip. "Have you considered returning home? Your family would be a comfort to you, I'm sure. Though traveling to Germany at such a time must be difficult. Well, in fact, being *German* must be difficult."

Several heads whipped around at the mention of that most hated place—the cause of their country's destruction and their lives.

"My home is here." Beatrix glanced at the line of customers. They had forgotten their fresh loaves and the mouths they needed to feed. Did a traitor lurk in their midst?

"A German?" a man asked, stepping from the line into the street.

"Who?" Another friend joined him.

Beatrix held her breath. To be counted among their enemies made her insides spoil like mold on bread. The same as Adrien had felt.

She locked gazes with Geraldine. "Nothing to be alarmed about, gentlemen. We are just being women, gossiping."

Geraldine's lips quivered as if holding back something she longed to say. It seemed to pain her to guard any secret.

Beatrix clenched her teeth, waiting for the woman to spill her secret.

"Madame?" The man read Geraldine's hesitation all too well.

With a wave of her hand, Geraldine dismissed him. "Just harmless gossip, as Madame Joubert said. Please, go about your business, gentlemen." Her lips curved into a smile.

Beatrix exhaled. A close call—entirely too close. It hadn't occurred to her that being widowed exposed her, but of course it did. Should she draw attention to her nationality, she could be run out of town, or at the very least, shunned.

"Thank you," she said. "For keeping my business private."

"You are as much a citizen as I," Geraldine said, patting her shoulder. "You're well regarded in Belfort, so you have nothing to worry about. We will all stand behind you should there be any issue. Though, I imagine it must be difficult for you to not feel . . . estranged."

Geraldine fished for a nugget of information—anything to share with the other ladies in their circle. Though Beatrix knew she was truly liked, war had a way of shifting one's opinions. Her need to keep her emotion sealed away became greater than ever.

"Thank you for your kind words, but I'm not feeling well," Beatrix said. "If you'll excuse me, I must be going."

She walked away quickly, past darkened shop windows, which peered at her with hollow eyes. Her own hollowness pulsed inside her, its edges turning sharp as knives to shred her insides. She fought to control the pain; its weight could drag her under if she let it. Breathless, she wound through several streets as fast as her feet could take her, desperate to outrun her agony, until the scent of the muddy Savoureuse River flooded her nostrils. Just one more turn and she would be there.

The river sprang into view, tamed only by the stone walls that channeled its tumult through town. She headed for the center of the bridge as if it held the answer. There, she leaned against the railing and stared down at the water churning beneath her feet. Heavy rains had filled the basin, fuller than she had seen it in a while. One could slip over the edge of the bridge and catch a current downstream, be gone in an instant. A few hopeless souls had done just that—ended it all—these last years of wartime. Beatrix closed her eyes, envisioning the rush of cold water under her skirts, swirling over her head and seeping into her lungs. She felt the burn of it, of bubbles escaping her lips and clambering to the surface while she sank into oblivion. How quiet and swift death would be—unlike the deaths of her men. But that wasn't just. She couldn't slip away quietly.

Adrien's face, contorted in pain, flashed behind her eyes. Beatrix cried out and clutched the railing to support her weight. She couldn't bear it. God, she couldn't bear it.

That spring day a year ago rushed back again.

"You can't go," she had said, voice firm. "I won't lose you both."

Adrien buttoned his jacket. "You can't stop me, Maman. I'm eighteen years old." He put on his derby hat. "I need to do this. For Papa, for my country."

"You would serve your father's memory better by being alive, taking care of your mother and his shop."

"So the men in this town can ridicule me? Remind me I'm not one of them every day? I'm a Frenchman!" He had stalked to the door and paused to stare at her a moment, disgust twisting his lips. Though he hadn't said the words, she could read his thoughts: it was her fault. Her blood ran through his veins.

A young woman approached her on the bridge, tugging her young son's hand. Though the little boy's cap was askew, his tidy trousers and miniature boots, polished to a shine, reflected his mother's care. "Madame, are you all right?" she asked.

Had Beatrix shown him—her little Adrien—how much she loved him? Had she held him enough, encouraged him? Did he know how she cherished every moment with him?

"I'm . . . I am . . ." Beatrix stopped, unable to finish the sentence. She tucked her arms around herself.

"May I escort you somewhere?" the woman asked. Concern filled her kind eyes.

"*Merci, non.*" She strained against the emotion flooding her throat. She didn't know how to do this, to endure such anguish.

The woman nodded and pulled her son forward. Beatrix watched as they waited at the edge of the bridge for a motorcar to pass. The mother fixed her son's cap and bent to tie an unruly lace on his shoe. Before standing once more, she kissed his cheek and embraced him. He squirmed in her grip. The mother laughed and stood again, leading him across the street and into town.

Beatrix balled her hands into fists. Her manners, the way she withheld her emotion, was expected. It was her way. When her feelings refused to dissipate, she funneled them into a logical plan. Joseph had teased her about her "Germanic strength and logic." Looking back, it seemed a polite way of labeling her reserve, her inaccessibility. Only in the privacy of their bedroom by candlelight, or in the odd moment with her son, had she let down her guard and shown her tender side. If she could have just one more day, one more hour . . .

Beatrix scarcely noticed the cold ground, the hum of street noise, the people going on about their day. She would never speak to her child again.

Adrien was gone.

Her stomach curdled and a fog enveloped her, obscuring her vision, distorting passersby on the adjacent street. She felt as if separated from her surroundings; the bridge floated beneath her. She sank to the ground and darkness swept her away.

"Madame, are you all right? Madame?" a voice said.

A horn split the air and Beatrix opened her eyes. A young man kneeled beside her, and motorcars and bicycles passed over the bridge. She rubbed her cold-stiffened neck. How long had she been here? Her breath had come in spasms and the nausea . . . she had panicked.

"I am fine."

He helped her to her feet. "Can I help you home?"

"No, that won't be necessary, thank you." She reddened. What a spectacle she had made of herself.

"Very well. Good evening to you." He tipped his hat and went on his way.

As she watched him bound across the street and out of sight, reality crashed around her once again. She had to prove to her son how much she loved him, to show him her regret. She would find them—the men who killed him—and make them pay for the wrongs they'd done, the lives they had destroyed. The image of dynamite flitted through her mind. A grand gesture of vengeance . . . this would prove where her loyalties lay, and her love, even if she might snuff out her own light.

She had nothing left to lose.

She wrenched her shoulders back, smoothed an errant lock of hair whipping in the wind, and headed back to town. If she wanted to find the regiment that murdered Adrien, she would need information, and she knew just the place to get it: Chez Louis, the tavern on the outskirts of town. She walked by it each time she traveled to town for bread and provisions. Soldiers, military policemen, and the women who sought their attention frequented the place, along with those seeking the latest information from the front. Soldiers went to relax for the day. Their bellies warm with wine, they would spill all they had seen—at least she hoped so.

Beatrix slinked inside the tavern. The odors of smoke and wine greeted her at the door. She shook off the discomfort of being out of place, a woman in a tavern at night. With any luck, she wouldn't be mistaken for a prostitute. She slipped off her overcoat and slid onto a stool at the far end of the bar.

The barkeep raised an eyebrow. "Madame Joubert, what brings you in tonight?"

She had forgotten Martin worked here. He had purchased more than one of their clocks for his home. She remembered his admiration for Joseph's handiwork.

"A brandy," she said.

Surprise registered on his features. "Are you sure you don't prefer a *vin rouge?* We've got very little brandy on hand, anyway. I'd have to charge you double."

"Wine it is." She clutched her hands in her lap. She was out of place, out of time, out of her mind. What was she doing here? She pictured her home with its three bedrooms, all empty, the shop and its cuckoos that heralded their master, the silent phonograph. The silence around her, yet the roaring within. *That* was why she had come.

Martin placed the glass before her without a word. He didn't need to say anything. How many widows had he seen? How many drinks had he poured for those in need of consolation, in search of some meaning in the cruel caprice of this life? Those who set foot in his establishment came to forget, and his job was to help them do it.

The front door swung open and a boisterous squad of soldiers tripped inside. A draft from the street sneaked in behind them and lifted Beatrix's hair. She shivered at its stealth, and the cold seeped into her bones. The men removed their hats and took their places at the bar, adjacent to Beatrix.

"*Trois vins rouges*, Martin," one said, settling onto his stool.

Once their glasses were in front of them, none said a word. Their day's work and the news over the wire sobered all well enough.

After several minutes more, the youngest of the bunch said, "You hear? The Allies pushed them back. Broke through the Hindenburg Line. Our biggest victory yet."

"At the Selle?" another of the men asked.

The young soldier nodded. "This could end the whole thing."

"I'll believe it when I see it," the man replied. "Every time we think we have the bastards, they rear up again and plow us with something new."

"They took down a lot of men I knew," the young man said, drinking deeply from his glass. "Defontaine and Poirier. Some captured in combat as well."

"Do you know who was captured?"

"Salazar and others. A few unaccounted for as well. You know the drill."

The bearded soldier nearest Beatrix said nothing during their conversation. Hunched over the bar, he didn't appear to be in a talkative mood. He turned his glass between thumb and middle finger over and over, lost in thought.

If she wanted information, she'd have to ask. She leaned closer to the silent soldier. "Where did the German troops flee, after the battle at the Selle? Do you think they might still be nearby?"

When the soldier looked up, she startled. Beneath the beard was a face she knew well—Laurent, Adrien's former classmate and friend.

"Laurent?"

"Madame Joubert?" His eyes filled with recognition, then surprise. "What are you doing here?"

"Looking for information," she said quietly.

He stared at her a moment without answering. Finally he said, "I'm so sorry to hear about—"

"Please, can we not discuss it . . . him?" She drank another sip of wine.

"Of course."

"So this regiment, do you think they're nearby still?"

"Doubtful. Most of them probably ran like hell. I suspect they took refuge in Strasbourg. It's their stronghold, and with talk of the war ending soon, I'm guessing much of the army has fled east."

She cast her eyes down. "I see."

Laurent seemed to read her thoughts. "It's dangerous, madame, even if the German army is gone. There may still be troops lingering near the Selle. The line shifts constantly. Towns have changed hands many times."

"But I can still travel near there?"

"You could, yes, though I would advise against it. Do you mean to . . ."—he paused—"to lay him to rest?" he asked gently. "I'm not sure if . . ." His words trailed off. He couldn't seem to voice what neither of them wanted to say—it was likely there was no body to bury.

"I'd like to pay my respects," she said, her lips stiff. Only they weren't the respects of which Laurent was thinking. Her mind raced. Did it matter if she found the exact regiment? She wanted them all dead. All the Germans. Any regiment would do. If she traveled to Strasbourg, she would need to know the lay of the land. She'd need a map . . . The one at the train station might be of use, but it wouldn't be enough to view it once. She would need a copy to track her course. She curled her fingers around her glass.

The surveyor, Pascal Thibaut! He would have all the maps

she'd need. He lived only a few streets away, but had been called to the front. His house had been locked up since his departure. She gauged Laurent's trustworthiness, his honesty. He had always been a good friend to Adrien. Would he help her? There was only one way to know for sure.

"And if I'd like to travel east?" she asked. "I assume the train would be too . . . direct?"

He shook his head. "Too dangerous."

"But"—how to put this?—"I speak German, remember."

"Oh, yes. I'd forgotten. You're German." He studied her expression for a long moment. "You could get yourself killed," he said, voice soft once more.

She swigged from her glass and set it down with a thud. "That's the least of my concerns, Laurent. How do I get over the border if I can't take the train?"

"I know someone who might take you, but you'd have to pay him a hefty sum."

"Money isn't an issue."

"It will take me a couple of days to reach him. He's not the kind of fellow who hangs around town too long, if you know what I mean."

"A couple of days is fine." She pushed a franc across the bar top to pay for her wine, and stood. "Here is my address—"

He shook his head. "That won't be necessary. Look, if he'll do it, he'll meet you here. Outside at three in the morning on Sunday. That's his routine. He'll want to be inconspicuous, you understand. He drives a black Alva."

With gas rationed so strictly, she wondered how this man obtained it. She didn't care, she reminded herself. She needed a ride.

"Thank you, Laurent." The beginnings of a plan fell into place, but she needed to go home to think.

He helped her with her coat.

"You don't know what this means to me."

"We are all desperate in war, madame. I know exactly what this means to you. Godspeed."

Without pause, she bolted for the door. As she passed the other men, they stared at her, one of them winking. The other soldiers thought she had arranged an understanding with the sergeant. She supposed she had. She stepped into the street, and night enveloped her.

AFTER SEVERAL HOURS IN THE DARK, BEATRIX LIT A DESK LAMP in the clock shop. A tent of golden light illuminated the paper beneath it. She ran a hand down the blank page and chose a fountain pen from her drawer. She would do this logically, the way she did everything—make a list of things she needed to do, complete each in an efficient fashion, and execute the plan with precision. There was no room for fault or fluster. Her feelings would be known in time. She would avenge her son's death—and show them all—the power of a mother's love. Silently, she made a list.

1. *Pack ammunition*
2. *Gather money*
3. *Write letter*
4. *Obtain maps*
5. *Plot course*
6. *Journey*
7. *Target enemy*

She rested the end of the pen against her bottom lip. The cuckoo clocks stirred around her and the room filled once more with their music. If peace were on the horizon like the sergeant said, there wasn't much time. She glanced at the window where morning light crept along its pane. Before long, the town would shake off its slumber like a great, stretching cat and come roaring to life. She must move quickly.

Beatrix walked to her bedroom, flung open the cedar chest at the foot of the bed, and withdrew a small valise, perfect for a two-day trip—or several sticks of dynamite. After closing the chest's lid, she ran a hand over the fine handiwork on its top. Joseph's love of woodworking graced every room in the house. Quickly, she locked the chest and her memories away with it. Being sentimental would only delay her.

Beatrix pulled on her coat and walked with measured steps to the shed on the farthest reach of the property. A stream, a thread of the Savoureuse, wound through the woods behind her house. Joseph had enjoyed leading Adrien through the thick of trees to the nook where the beavers built their dam. Year after year, the furry nuisances would dam up the stream, making it impossible to water their vegetable garden. Joseph would jam sticks of dynamite among the gathered branches and blast the creatures' abode sky-high. The music of Adrien's voice, full of glee at the spectacle, flooded her ears and she stumbled.

"Focus on the plan," she whispered aloud while regaining her footing.

When she opened the shed door, dank air puffed from the release of pressure. She stepped inside the dim room, wishing she had brought a lamp. Garden tools and watering cans sat in neat rows against the walls, and half-empty paint cans lined the shelves. Against the far wall, a series of crates and boxes were stacked from floor to ceiling. She looked for the telltale sign of danger painted across the crate's front. Near the bottom of the stack, two eye sockets and a crudely smiling mouth taunted her. There it was! She set the valise on the floor and shoved the boxes aside until she reached the one she had come for. The lid was nailed shut. She grabbed a shovel and knelt next to the box, careful not to drag her dress across the dusty ground.

"If you can't be beautiful, be tidy," her mother used to say. That was the day she had learned what her mother thought of her.

Angling the shovel along the edge of the lid, she pushed down on it with all her weight. The wood splintered just enough for her to wedge the shovel in deeper. Once more, she leaned on the tool. A great cracking rent the air and the lid split open. Inside lay a dozen sticks of dynamite.

Gingerly, she removed each stick and lowered them into her bag. When she reached the few remaining in the bottom of the crate, a viscous liquid pooled around them. She pulled her hand back. That couldn't be a good sign. Dynamite was unstable as it was. It would be best to leave those behind. She wanted to choose when to detonate the sticks, not have them surprise her. She peered into her bag, now filled with explosives. None were oozing, thankfully, though she wondered if they would detonate properly. She would just have to risk it. She picked up the bag. All she lacked were matches.

After locking the shed, she gathered the remaining items she needed indoors, and stashed her bag behind the bushes out front. If the sticks oozed after all, at least it would be outside.

"Beatrix?" a woman's voice called, startling her. "Did you lose something in the bushes?"

Adelaide. Beatrix looked up and saw her closest friend, a basket swinging from her arm.

"What?" she asked. Sweat beaded on her brow. "No, I thought I saw a rabbit and set a trap. I've had so much trouble with them the last few years." It was the truth, in part. She'd trapped more than a dozen rabbits who had pillaged her garden last spring. They'd made for good stew.

Adelaide moved closer, within eyeshot of the bushes.

Beatrix's pulse thumped an erratic beat.

"Are you all right? You seem . . . anxious this morning."

Beatrix swallowed hard, then bit her tongue to keep the truth from slipping out. "I didn't sleep well last night."

Adelaide's expression shifted to one of knowing concern. Her friend's warmth radiated around her, a trait in which Beatrix had taken comfort over the years.

"Would you like to join me for breakfast? I've just come from the bakery." Adelaide presented her basket, a smile upon her face.

Beatrix forced a smile in return, a foreign sensation after so many months. "*Merci, non.* I'm going to try to rest."

"I'll let you to it, then." Adelaide approached to embrace her.

Beatrix hustled down the path and into her friend's arms.

Adelaide rubbed her back and said, "Why don't you pop over later?"

"Thank you. I may, if I'm feeling better."

"Of course. See you soon." She turned to go, waving as she walked down the drive.

Beatrix watched her retreating form. It was the last time she would see her friend; she hadn't thought of that, of the good she would leave behind. There was so little of it, she had forgotten. Emotion surged up her throat once more and she dashed inside, afraid she might lose her nerve. She waited twenty minutes for Adelaide to make her way down the street. Once her friend disappeared from sight, she set off to enact the next phase of her plan.

BEATRIX ROSE FROM THE COUCH THAT EVENING AS THE CUCK-oos dinged five times. She stood over her list once more. With a steady hand she crossed off several tasks. She had written a letter to her sister-in-law, leaving the entire estate to her, though she lived abroad in America—there was no one else. She fingered the sack filled with francs to pay the driver. Though the driver knew the area, she didn't want to leave any detail to chance. She'd be traveling with dynamite, after all. Which meant one thing. Still, she needed Pascal's maps and she'd have to break into his house to get them. Beatrix inhaled a deep breath. No need to worry. No one would suspect her, a poor widow and . . . and childless mother. The strength of her will gripped her and she balled her hands into fists. She would raid Pascal's map collection, and hide until it was time to go to the tavern. But first, she had one more thing to do.

One by one, she took the clocks from the shop window and turned them off. They would not go on—she would not go on— and it was time to lay them to rest. She couldn't bear the thought of them running down slowly and falling into disrepair. After, she snatched the letter opener from her desk and headed outside to retrieve her concealed bag. She slipped the money and a box of matches inside and resealed it. Once she'd buttoned her coat, she walked rapidly to the end of the street, heart thumping in her ears.

She was almost there. As she rounded the corner she stopped. A window glowed in a house at the end of the street. Pascal's neighbor was at home; she would need to exercise extreme caution. She turned up her collar to protect her exposed neck against the wind and continued forward.

The shroud of night descended, and lights began to flicker on inside the homes. She would need to go quickly before the last of the light was gone. With each thwack of heel on pavement, her shoulders tensed. Just two more houses. She picked up her pace, praying no one would see her. The point of the letter opener poked the tender flesh of her forearm. She hoped the tool would do the trick.

When Beatrix reached the drive at the end of the cul-de-sac, her heart crashed against her ribs. She ducked beneath an archway festooned with dead vines, and headed down the gravel drive lined with clusters of dormant trees. Once the house came into view, she diverted from the path. Dew clung to her boots as she waded through the unkempt lawn behind the house. A deep breath steadied her nerves.

No thinking, only doing.

She leapt up the steps leading to a door. She palmed the letter opener and shimmied it into the keyhole. Though narrow, the letter opener did not bend enough to work. She bit her lip in frustration. Perhaps a hairpin? She pulled one from her chignon and jiggled it in the lock. It wasn't strong enough to dislodge the bolt.

Beatrix descended the steps and walked around to the side of the house. A stack of bricks had been thrown haphazardly in a pile, perhaps to repair a fire pit or adorn a garden. She pushed one over with her foot, contemplating her next move. She could use a brick to break a window on the first floor. It was risky; she might draw the neighbor's attention, but she had no other choice.

She grabbed a brick and retreated several paces. With a grunt, she hurled it at the center of the lowest pane. The glass shattered with a horrible crash. She cringed and looked about, praying no one had heard it. After a lengthy pause, still nothing stirred. She stared at the opening she'd created. Jagged shards jutted from the window frame. She needed a bigger hole if she was going to crawl through it. Silently, she built makeshift stairs with the bricks, save one. With the last brick, she smashed the remaining shards until the frame looked safe to pass through.

Somewhere a door slammed.

With a lunge, Beatrix hauled herself through the opening. She hit the floor with a thud on top of a pile of glass. Groaning, she peered down at her palms. Blood gushed from a wound on her left hand. She'd need to bandage it, or she'd lose a lot of blood. She scrambled to her feet and looked about the kitchen. An old apron hung on the pantry door. That would have to do. She ripped several pieces of the cloth and tied them across her palm. Once satisfied with her work, she set off to find the maps.

Pascal's house reeked of mold and dust. For an instant, she wondered if he would ever return; a dangerous thought. It dredged up more than she cared to think about. She pushed the thought from her mind and shuffled through each room, in search of his study. When she found it, she exhaled a relieved breath. Pascal's desk was covered with maps, tools, and volumes of cartography. A compass and lead pencils lay on top of stacks of notes. Another sheet listed the battles with coordinates. He had been tracking the German troops and the various French brigades.

Perfect.

Somewhere in the house a clock dinged six o'clock. She had minutes before the house went dark completely. With trembling hands she rifled through the maps until she came upon the one that looked most helpful—the outline of the Hindenburg Line and the frontiers of Alsace. Without hesitating, she folded the map in quarters and made her way back through the house. She slipped through the back door and started down the front drive, counseling herself not to run. Doing so would attract attention.

"*Excusez-moi?*"

She froze.

"Can I help you?" A woman stood in her front yard in her nightdress and shawl, her husband's boots on her feet. Her poodle tugged at the end of a leash, eager to track the invisible footprints of some small animal.

She must act rational, calm. "I beg your pardon? I'm just out for a walk."

"What were you doing on Pascal's property? He isn't here—" The woman stopped and her eyes widened. "I heard a noise. Something breaking." She glanced down at the map in Beatrix's hands, spotted with blood. "You're a spy!" she hissed.

"That's absurd." She kept her tone cool in spite of her racing pulse. "Your imagination has gotten the best of you. I wasn't on his property."

"I saw you! Just stepping off his lawn. What are you holding? If you have nothing to hide, show me," the woman demanded, placing her hands on her hips.

Beatrix remained glued to the spot. "I don't owe you an explanation. It's none of your business."

"Very well. Have it your way. I'm going to the police!" The woman turned on her heel, stumbling in her overly large shoes. In her clumsiness, she dropped the leash and the poodle bolted toward the line of trees behind the house. "Léo, you come back here this instant!" She waddled across the lawn as fast as her boots allowed.

Beatrix darted down the street at full speed. She didn't care if she looked guilty. She had to get out of there—now. Even if the military police didn't arrest her for breaking into Pascal's home, they might detain her for being German, should they discover the truth. Oh, Joseph, she pleaded. Rescue me from this life.

She ran to the beat of her heart.

FOR TWO HOURS BEATRIX HAD SHIVERED IN THE DARK, ducking behind buildings downtown, hiding from policemen, until her toes and fingers grew numb. When she could take it no longer, she slipped inside a church to warm herself. At half-past two in the morning, she walked to the tavern, toting her bag. Her heart thumped in her ears as she tucked herself against the building. When a shiny black Alva chugged down the street, she breathed a sigh of relief. He came. She climbed into the mysterious man's car and silently handed over the packet of bills.

"We can't take a direct route, you understand," he said. "There are MPs crawling all over the place."

"MPs?" She stared at the back of his black fedora.

"Military police."

"Do what you must," she said, gingerly placing her bag next to her on the seat. "Just get me to Strasbourg."

The car trundled over moonlit country roads. No one dared break curfew, and certainly no one else was foolish enough to drive along the front line. With each bump she glanced at her bag. Though she could not see the dynamite, she felt its power pulsing in the air around her.

If the driver only knew . . .

The next instant, the man slammed on his brakes. "*Merde.*" He swore under his breath.

Beatrix leaned forward. "What is it?"

"A checkpoint ahead."

The car beams poured over a pack of soldiers spread out in a fan, guns poised.

The driver hit the steering wheel with his hand. "I knew I should have gone the other way. *Merde!*" This time he yelled it. "If we get through this, we'll veer east of St. Die and slip through the border that way. If not, it's been nice knowing you."

Her stomach sank to her toes. If they searched her bag, they were both finished. She had to think fast.

He peered over his shoulder at her. "Relax and don't say anything. I'll try to talk us out of this."

Blood raced in her veins. She had made it this far, and she wasn't about to let some criminal mess this up for her. She clasped her hands in her lap and her spine went rigid. *Think, Beatrix.*

The car pulled to a stop and two soldiers flanked the car. One tapped the driver's window.

The driver cranked it open. "*Bonsoir.* What can I do for you, fellows?"

The soldier smirked. "You're in violation of curfew. Why are you on the road?"

Beatrix blurted, "We apologize, monsieur, but my sister is dying. If she doesn't sign the proper documents in time, our estate will be lost."

As in Germany, nothing mattered more to the French than carrying on the family name and securing inheritance for the next generation.

She dabbed at her eyes as if to stop tears from flowing. "Please, she has only hours left. We're racing the clock."

"Where are you headed?" the solider growled, unconvinced.

"St. Die," she said quickly. The last French town before Strasbourg. "She lives in an apartment there, alone."

The soldier leaned his head in the car window to check for suspicious items. His eyes fell on her bag.

Beatrix's stomach knotted.

He paused as if to ponder the bag's contents, then his eyes passed on, dismissive of its lumpy smallness.

"Traveling near the front line for the sake of your heirs, eh? That's noble of you, lady. Stupid, but noble."

She bristled at the soldier's retort. Her heirs that did not exist.

The soldier huffed and straightened. Cupping his mouth with his hands, he shouted to the others waiting for instruction. "Family property. Someone is dying. Headed to St. Die. Let them through." He stepped away from the car.

She leaned against the seat and exhaled.

The driver rolled up his window and drove on, past the barricade. "I told you to keep quiet," he said, words laced with anger.

"I saved us."

He nodded. "That you did."

They rode on in silence. Though the sun rose, clouds crowded the sky and light rain pattered against the windows. Fitting, as she would go out in fire and the rain could wash it all away. Another hour gone, and the Alva pulled to a stop on the side of the road. Beatrix awakened from a sleepy haze. A patch of trees framed a field running parallel to the deserted road. No houses loomed, no church spire or rooftops. Where were they?

"This is as far as I'll go, lady," the driver said. "Any closer and we'll be too near the Germans for my liking. If you head east through the trees, you'll be able to walk along the road. After about ten kilometers, you'll reach Strasbourg."

"Thank you," she said, opening her car door.

He turned to look at her. "*Bonne chance*. You're going to need it."

"I have nothing left to lose," she said, voice hoarse.

He took one look at her face and removed his derby hat, pressed it to his chest. "It's a devil of a war."

She met his gaze evenly. "It's a devil of a life."

The pity that bloomed on his face, on his sensitive mouth, was more than she could bear. She could hold it all together if she could just not talk about it, not be confronted with others' pity. Yet here it was, the sorrow again, and the roaring inside.

"It will work out in the end." Her words fell like stones, hard and cold, lifeless.

"You sure you want to go all that way on foot?" Concern etched lines around his eyes. He looked down at her boots, then assessed her overcoat and gloves.

She forced a tight smile. "I've survived far worse."

"You might find yourself in trouble," he insisted.

"I certainly hope so."

Without waiting for his reply, she stepped from the car, clutching her cargo, and headed down the sloping embankment toward the woods. The final leg of her journey, at last. With quick strides across the field, she reached the woods in minutes. When she stepped into its shade, a deep quiet blanketed her. A brisk wind whipped through the trees; the only sound came from the crack of spindly pine boughs knocking together. She watched the ground, intent on each root and rock's edge peeking above the soil. Should she trip and fall, the unstable dynamite could detonate on impact. Then all would be in vain. All three of their deaths would mean nothing; just a tick on the timeline of history.

She trudged forward for half an hour, hoping she was headed in the right direction. The tongue of her right boot slipped sideways and bunched near the arch of her foot for the third time, and the soul of her shoe rubbed her heel. A blister rose on her toe, growing more painful with each step. She leaned against a tree. Her head throbbed, and her bones ached with fatigue, the sort that could pull her under should she stop for too long. Besides, she might lose her nerve. A wave of self-loathing engulfed her. She couldn't give up now. What would she be left with? The beginnings of hysteria addled her thinking and wound through her weary body. She was tired, so tired.

A branch snapped.

Beatrix looked up. Who was there? She swiveled around to locate the source; surely a rabbit, or a lost cat from town?

A flash of green uniform and boots ducked behind a nearby bush.

A chill ran over her skin. It was no animal, but a man. She had to go now!

Terrified, she dashed as fast as her legs could carry her. If the enemy captured her, especially a rogue soldier in the woods . . . She closed her eyes against the series of hideous images flickering behind her eyes. She had to get there, to town. The dynamite clunked inside the bag as she ran. The roaring rumbled in her ears.

"You there!" a male voice called.

She wasn't going to make it. She stumbled forward, catching herself at the last minute. The explosives would blow and take her with them.

"Stop!" the man shouted.

Panic constricted her lungs and she choked on the swell of emotion she could no longer keep at bay. A clearing came into view beyond the trees. The road was just ahead! She willed her legs to go faster. In an instant she was in the open and racing along the road. She could see the fringes of town ahead. Strasbourg loomed. Too afraid to look behind her, she pushed forward, despite the burning in her legs, the rising ache inside. Soon it would all be over. She would never have to feel again.

At last, she reached the streets on the outskirts of town. The footsteps behind her had faded. She threw a look over her shoulder. The soldier stood at the edge of the road, half a kilometer behind her. He avoided the city? He was a deserter then, hiding until he knew his next move, or the war's advancement. She slowed as she entered town and leaned against the side of a building, panting. After a few minutes, she gathered her courage and continued on.

Strasbourg was eerie in its silence. No soldiers or police marched about; few locals walked the streets. The town held its

breath, waiting for something. Beatrix grimaced. She would en-
liven things shortly.

Ragged with cold and damp, bleary-eyed from exhaustion and
longing, she staggered toward a church and collapsed on its steps.
She could rest a little while, then make her good-byes and blow
the first German camp she saw to bits. Sacrifice herself for her
love—for the cause Adrien had held so dear. A crippling wave of
grief swept up from her toes and burst like stars of white-hot pain.
The sobs she had held at bay erupted in her throat and ripped her
open. Tears flooded her cheeks, and the sound of screams filled her
ears. Was that her? Her body curled around the sorrow. Her sweet
Adrien, her little boy. She screamed until her throat felt bloodied,
and her lungs groaned under the exertion.

A priest dashed from the church and crouched beside her.
"What is it, my child? Let me help you."

She studied his face, lined with his own suffering. "I-I'm sorry.
I am fine." She wiped her face with her sleeve. "I don't need your
help."

For a moment he stared at her, then stood. "I will be just inside,
should you change your mind. I'll have hot soup and a blanket by
the fire, waiting."

She nodded, and he smiled faintly before returning indoors.

Cold drizzle fell from the sky, wetting the stone around her.
She pitched her body backward and lay across the church steps
like a fallen bird—a cuckoo popped from its tower, broken and in
need of repair.

Oh, Joseph. She was so alone.

She peered up at the spires of the church, reaching toward
heaven. No matter what she did, she couldn't get them back.

All at once the pulleys in the bell tower whirred and the faint click of cogs and wheels sounded behind its walls. She could envision the hammer, poised in its place inside the tower. The iron bell gonged.

It was time. Time to be heard.

The clock gonged again and again, eleven times in all.

Beatrix pushed to her swollen feet. As the bells silenced, a crowd of soldiers flooded from a building at the end of the street and clapped each other on the back. Confused, she walked toward them, her limbs numb with cold, her insides hollow. Had the Germans decimated another French village?

"What's happened?" she asked a soldier.

"The war, *madame*. It's over! Armistice has been called. Today marks a new"—he choked on his emotion—"a new beginning." He wiped his eyes with his filthy hand.

Her head began to spin. She'd never repay the Germans for all they took from her. For her mother's coldness. Her breath grew ragged again.

"It's all right," the soldier said, seeing the look on her face. "We've survived. It's all over."

Her loss would never be over, but *she* must be. The bag of dynamite grew heavier, a reminder of her mission.

More and more soldiers filled the street. Some looked worse than others: bandaged, crippled limbs, or filthy and starving. Others looked fresh from the bath. She frowned, trying to make sense of it all. It didn't need to make sense, she reminded herself. She needed to get even, to end her misery. She looked around her. Why did she need to go farther? She could end it all here.

She opened her bag, fumbled with the box of matches, and re-trieved one.

"Is this a barracks?" she asked. Tears rushed down her face.

"A prison, madame. We've all just been released."

It was then she noticed their uniforms, the language they were speaking. They weren't Germans; they were French and Allied sol-diers. Her eyes flickered from one face to the next. Some appeared bewildered. Others whooped in joy and relief. These men would go home to their wives and children, their lovers, their mothers. The match pressed against the flesh of her palm. She would never share their joy.

Her legs collapsed beneath her and she dropped her bag. Sticks of dynamite rolled in every direction.

"Where are they?" she shouted. "The murderers who killed my son! My husband!"

Soldiers gaped at her, their eyes traveling over the sticks of dy-namite strewn at her feet. Many scattered out of the way.

"Madame, steady now." One brave soldier crept toward her. "Let me help you with that."

"I don't need your help. Stand back!" She held the match to the strip on its box.

The soldier's voice turned soothing. "But it's over." He inched closer. "There will never be another war like this."

"But I can't get my son back," she sobbed, allowing her emotion to overtake her at long last. "He didn't know how much I loved him. I can't . . . I must . . ."

"Let me help you." The soldier coaxed her.

Another soldier pushed his way through the gathered crowd. A bandage stained with rust-colored patches of dried blood wrapped his head and covered half of his face. He hobbled with the help of a cane.

"Let me through," he insisted, voice muffled by the confusion around them.

"Don't come any closer!" she shouted. With a stroke of tip against box, the match burst to life. If she couldn't have revenge, she would end her days, the pain.

The soldier paused a few yards away and tilted his head to the side to peer at her through his good eye.

Beatrix dropped the match.

"*Maman?*" Adrien's voice rang out like church bells.

That single, astonished word silenced the roaring in her ears. Hope brightened the edges of her vision and flooded her heart—a golden, beautiful thing—dissolving her anger, draining the bitterness. She clutched her chest at its intensity. Could it be true? She struggled to her feet.

"Adrien?"

He staggered toward her. "*Maman!*"

With a strangled cry, Beatrix gathered her son in her arms.

To those left behind in wartime,
may there always be hope.
Also, to the man I love.

An American Airman in Paris

Beatriz Williams

Paris. Mid-April 1920

H<small>E CAME TO</small> H<small>ARRY'S TO DRINK, NOT TO FIND A WOMAN, BUT</small> sometimes the one just naturally leads to the other, doesn't it? Sometimes you haven't got a choice.

Besides, you're in Paris! You're in Paris, in a smoky establishment not far from the Opéra, surrounded by souls in a similar state of reckless desperation, and who can resist that fug of inevitability? Sex hangs in the air, thick and musky, and it tastes like Scotch whisky. Nearly irresistible.

Octavian lights another cigarette, gestures for another drink, and considers the array of bottles on the wall before him, for example. Plenty of choice *there*, right? Except that there isn't. It's all an illusion. A fellow's got to drink something, or he'll die. You can choose *what* to drink, but you can't choose *whether* to drink.

All right. Maybe you can, if you try hard enough. If you *care* hard enough. Octavian has always believed in choice. Hasn't self-control been the guiding principle of his life? Until this moment, on this particular night, he's resisted that barbaric impulse to copulate, in the manner of his broken-down compatriots, with whatever lady happens to look fairest in the hazy glow of a quarter liter of decent Scotch whisky and a half dozen smokes. In fact, Octavian's abstinence has made him a legend. A religious idol, almost, except for that inconvenient absence of outward religion. J.C., his friends started calling him, way back in the middle of a Paris leave two years ago, and it stuck.

"Now, J.C.," says Jack Marmot, plopping sloppily on the stool next door, "just tell me what you think of that bird over there, talking to Dashwood. A real doll, ain't she?"

Octavian squints between the bodies until he finds Dashwood, and then the woman furled up next to him, lush and sleek-skinned, holding a slender Gauloises in one hand and a highball in the other. Her lips are dark, her hair is short and curling. Underneath a sheer black dress, her breasts are enchantingly visible.

He returns his attention to his drink and tips it back between his lips. "Sure. A real doll."

Jack leans close. "Do me a favor, J.C. I want to see this before I die. Why don't you just drag your handsome mug over there and relieve Dashwood of his responsibilities? He don't deserve a doll like that."

"He's welcome to her."

"Aw, what is it with you, J.C.? You don't like girls?"

"I like girls, all right. Just not that kind of girl."

"You gotta girl back home, J.C.?"

"Nope."

Jack finishes his drink and signals the bartender. "On account of I got to talking to an old buddy of yours, name of Peterson—"

"He's not a buddy of mine."

"Says he knows you, though."

Octavian pulls out the packet of cigarettes from his jacket pocket and fiddles the dwindling contents. "I guess we know each other."

"Anyway, Peterson says you got a girl back home, pretty girl. You kept her picture in your wallet. In your pocket, every time you went up on patrol."

"He said that, did he?"

"Yep. True or false?"

"I guess that's true."

The bartender arrives. Refills the glasses, without a word. Jack waits in drunken patience, mesmerized by the delicate flow of whisky against the black waistcoat of its source. When every drop is safely delivered, and Jack has clinked the careful edge of his glass with the edge of Octavian's glass, he returns to the subject of the photograph in Octavian's wallet. Because who doesn't want to hear more about someone's girl back home?

"So? What's the story? What happened to her?"

"Nothing happened to her, that I know of."

"All right. So what happened to *you*, J.C.?"

Octavian doesn't reply to that. What a question!—*What happened to you?*—as if it's not obvious what's happened to him. What's happened to all of them. Why it's impossible to return to an unspoiled America, to an unspoiled girl. Why they are smoking and drinking and fornicating in Paris, instead of returning home to nice clean lives and nice clean wives.

He shrugs instead. Shrugs and lifts his drink, examining the bottom of the glass, as if expecting to find some kind of message.

The cigarette burns implacably between the first two fingers of his right hand.

But Jack, it seems, will not be denied. "You still got that snap?" he asks, reaching in his pocket for his own identically smashed packet of pungent French cigarettes.

This time, Octavian decides to answer him. Why not? The existence of that photograph doesn't make a difference anymore. But at some point between the instant of opening his mouth and the instant of making voice, the smoke parts to his left and a woman inserts herself in the crack, very close, smelling of perfume and muscular Turkish tobacco, the scent of Paris. And gin. And something else, beneath it all: something salty and perspiring that sends the hot blood rushing where it shouldn't. She places a hand on the back of his neck—an interesting choice, and more pleasurable than Octavian expects—and bends right next to his ear to tell him she'd like to suck his *bite*. Octavian glances to the side, and without even trying he spies the tips of her enchanting breasts, puckering the material of her sheer black dress like a pair of large, textured polka dots.

"As a matter of fact," he tells Jack, not looking away, "I don't."

Which isn't the reason he finds himself in a taxi an hour later, trundling along the wet streets of Montparnasse while la belle Hélène (not her real name, but who gives a darn about that?) traces a few interesting fingers along the outside of his trousers. Still, it's *part* of the reason—the loss of that photograph—and anyway he's not thinking about *why* he's there, is he? My God. He's just *there*. Choiceless. He's closing his eyes and listening to the rapid crump of his heart in his ears. Savoring the movement of Hélène's finger along his *bite*. Wondering if he's really going to do it, holy God, really going to *do it* this time: fornicate with a woman he's just met: a lush, smoky, drunken, enchanting woman from Harry's New York Bar in Paris, who doesn't even seem to want to kiss him first. Who doesn't even seem to expect payment, other than the pleasure of his company.

Well, why shouldn't he? No law against it, is there? No human law, anyway. How many times has he watched his pals climb into similar taxis, in the company of similar women, since he started this whole business by walking into a U.S. Army recruiting station on the day after his eighteenth birthday, all chock full of shiny ideals, startling everybody in the room by announcing he knew how to fly an airplane? How many times has he watched his compatriots climb flights of sordid stairs, or line up outside sordid establishments, or—*faute de mieux*—simply fornicate in sordid corners, trying to reclaim a minute of joy from God's dispassionate clock?

So maybe it's time he gave in. Maybe the vinous, musky scent of this woman is what he really needs, after all. Maybe there's no point in keeping himself whole; maybe he's too late for that. Who knows? Maybe *this* is the way to make himself whole again—maybe this has been the way to salvation, all along—and Hélène's nimble fingers and unencumbered breasts are a symbol from God Himself. Or maybe not. Either way—and here la belle Hélène finds the topmost button of his trousers, just as the taxi swerves around a corner, the corner of the boulevard St.-Michel, where he keeps a room on the attic floor of a decrepit Second Empire hotel—either way, he lost that photograph of Sophie Faninal on the day of the Armistice itself, and you can't get more symbolic than that.

But that's another story, and isn't that the point of all this? The point of Paris, the point of Harry's, the point of Hélène. To forget that story. To forget the other stories. To forget . . . well, pretty much everything that came before.

Rembercourt Airfield, France. November 11, 1918

EARLY ON, YOU LEARNED NOT TO MAKE FRIENDS WITH THE other pilots. In the first place, you didn't have much time—five, six weeks—before your plane crashed or his plane crashed, and even in the intense atmosphere of a U.S. Army Air Service squadron, in which life took place at several times its ordinary speed, you couldn't learn much about a fellow in six weeks. In the second place, why would you bother? Either he died or you died. End of friendship.

Oh, sure, you got along with the others. You made a few buddies—fellows you could drink with on leave, fellows who'd loan you a franc or two when you were short. And there was the incontestable fact that you might (willingly, without a second thought) sacrifice your own life for your mate's life, should the opportunity arise, say, out of a clear blue sky.

But the trick was not to care too much. To care just enough.

Because, by the time a cold, gray October passed into a colder, grayer November, the man who had given Octavian his nickname (to take just one example) was long gone. Shot down a couple of weeks after that legendary Paris leave, and a few days later a Fokker flew past the base, very low, fluttering a white banner, and dropped a note in halting, courteous English: *Lieutenant Morris is killed and body buried with full military honor. Fondest respect.* The men who carried on calling him J.C. were likewise mostly dead, or taken prisoner (if lucky), or else too badly injured to fly. Not a single man remained who'd witnessed Octavian's improbable feat of abstinence that weekend, and the three pilots who accompanied him to the airfield through that bleak, drizzling midmorning of November 11 were all replacements of replacements, eighteen years old, white-cheeked. Octavian, who'd just turned nineteen, felt like a statesman.

"Right, boys," he said as the biplanes took shape before them, pale and spectral, "no one does anything stupid. We're making a simple patrol, northeast sector, Trier airfield, not trying to finish off the whole Boche army single-handed, do you hear me?"

"Yes, sir," said Johnson, a little cocky.

Yes, sir, the other boys said, more meek.

"Follow me, stay in formation, nice and tight. I don't want any idiot getting lost in the clouds. And watch out for any darned Fokkers hiding around. And for Pete's sake, don't get shot down. Christmas is around the corner. You don't want to ruin Christmas for your folks."

(Another reason for the sobriquet: Octavian didn't swear.)

Yes, sir.

The planes were waiting outside the hangar, noses tilted expectantly to the sky. A couple of sleepy mechanics milled about like ghosts in the spaces between them. Later, Octavian remembered thinking—as he strode toward the familiar rakish shape of his French-built SPAD in much the same way a knight might have approached his charger a few hundred years ago—*This is it, the last time I'm going up. My number's up this time.* But he always thought that before a patrol. Bad luck to imagine you were actually coming back.

Aloft, he was glad for his leather jacket, lined in sheepskin, and for his leather cap and his long woolen scarf and his goggles. For his cumbersome sheepskin gloves. The fog streamed past, cold and viscous. They climbed steadily, blindly through the frozen clouds: climbed on nothing but faith. Octavian could just see the biplanes at his flanks, holding tight, Matthews and Peterson and cocky Johnson, the best pilot among them, intuitive and reckless. Said he was eighteen but that was pure invention, Octavian knew. The kid was no more than seventeen. Farm boy from Missouri or Mississippi or someplace. Lost his virginity last week in Amiens—lost it twice, according to a grinning Peterson, who'd arranged the escapade—and had probably clapped himself in the process.

Octavian glanced at Johnson's airplane, twenty yards to the right, at the extreme edge of visibility, climbing without fear. *Idiot*, he thought affectionately. Everyone knew you stayed away from the war widows and stuck to the whores. Even virtuous J.C., who didn't avail himself of either.

The break came suddenly. One instant they were trapped in the dense, infinite vapor, and in the next instant they were free. Ice-blue sky above, gray fleece below. To the east, the risen sun, new and brilliant above the horizon.

Octavian climbed higher and leveled out. Eleven thousand five hundred feet, a decent altitude. Air thin and winter-sharp. The other airplanes tucked into place around him, so marvelously clear he could see the shape of Johnson's nose against the sky. He held the stick between his knees and reached into his pocket for Sophie's photograph.

Yes. About that photograph. The other fellows thought she must be his girl, this image in a picture that no one—not even Peterson—had ever actually seen. He kept it in his wallet when he wasn't flying, and in his pocket when he was. And when he reached altitude, and was flying toward his fate, he always took her picture out and fixed it between the windshield and the edge of the cockpit, so they were face-to-face, the two of them. Guardian angel, mortal man.

Sophie Faninal. He'd never actually met her. The photograph wasn't even that: it was a clipping from a newspaper, which he'd fixed on a piece of cardboard long ago and coated in clear wax. The girl in the picture was pretty enough—light hair and light eyes, returning your smile with hers—but it was her expression that did him in, every time he beheld her. Her delight. The way her gaze emerged from two dimensions to connect with him, as if she *knew* he was there, all along. The curious slant to her eyebrows, as if she knew the secret to happiness, as if she were (simultaneously, and not uncoincidentally) plotting some kind of mischief. Probably she was. At the time the snap was taken, Sophie was about three years old.

Octavian touched the corner of the photograph. Smoothed the edge of her springy light hair and told her not to worry. The tide was turning. Rumor and hope (if you could call this state of cynical expectancy *hope*) abounded. The war had to end sometime, didn't it? Before everybody ran out of men altogether. Men and SPADs and everything else.

Just hurry back, safe and sound, she replied.

All right, so maybe he was crazy, talking like that to a little girl he'd never met. But he wasn't completely nuts. No, ma'am. At the same time he was holding this imaginary conversation, he was also watching the speedometer, the compass; checking his watch, calculating the distance they'd traveled. When you couldn't see the ground, you had to rely on dead reckoning to figure out where the devil you existed atop the map of Europe, and Octavian prided himself on his navigation. All those sharp, precise numbers gave you something to think about, got your mind off what lay ahead. If you did it right, you found a rhythm that kept your heartbeat even, your breathing steady. Kept your mind clean, orderly, so that you noticed everything around you in simultaneous and infinite clarity, like God Himself: the line of the horizon, the faint undulation of the air, the angle of the sun. Those specks in the sky nearby, that might or might not be a squadron of enemy airplanes.

And Johnson's nose. So all right, maybe Octavian was breaking his own rule of late, allowing a bit of warmth to color his regard for a fellow human being. But how could you not take a shine to Johnson? The darn fool kept getting himself into scrapes, like an adventurous puppy, and getting out of them again with an audacity that might just keep him alive, if it didn't kill him first. Why, only last night, he'd had the nerve to break in on Octavian while he was reading—something every other pilot in the entire ever-loving United States Army Air Service knew better than to attempt— and kept asking his dumb, brilliant questions until, Lord above, the pair of them were actually conducting a genuine conversation. Johnson thought he was in love with the widow from last week. *She's a beaut, J.C., a real beaut. Tits like this*—here he made round, caressing movements with his two hands, like he was changing the oil on a Model T—*and so soft inside, good Lord Almighty, I was fixing to die. Came so fast the first time, I figured she'd laugh me right off the mattress.* Did she? Octavian couldn't help asking, and Johnson replied cheerfully, *Why, no, she didn't, bless her sweet heart. Kept on moving her hips like this* [he demonstrated] *and making these noises like a starving she-cat. So I thought,* Hell yes, *and I kept on going, and dammit if I didn't come again like the Southern Pacific, ten minutes later. Begged her to marry me, right then and there.* Octavian couldn't help asking whether she said yes, and Johnson said *Aw, of course she did, she ain't stupid,* and Octavian called him a dumb hayseed and a sucker, to cover the fact that he was actually, in the corner of his soul, a little bit jealous. Yes, jealous of Johnson and his widow of easy virtue, because at least Johnson wasn't going to die a virgin. Johnson knew what it was like to come inside a woman instead of an old shirt. Johnson—

And that was the second, that instant of fragile inattention at twenty-seven seconds past 11:13 on the morning of November 11, when the first Fokker blew free from the clouds below and angled straight toward him.

By two seconds past 11:18, his plane was diving toward the ground, engine smoking and undercarriage destroyed, following Johnson, who had already gone down defending him.

For a minute or two—or maybe more, who was counting?—Octavian remained still, not quite comprehending the fact that he was still alive. That the airplane had borne the insult without actually killing him.

But crashes were always like that. The first few seconds were the best ones, and it all went downhill from there. The pain kicked in, or rather the recognition of pain: in his chest, hard and stiff, so that he had to find a new way to breathe; in his right arm, near the elbow, possibly fracture; in his right leg, near the ankle, definite fracture. And he was in Germany by now. They had been angling daringly toward Trier, looking for enemy patrols, and should have crossed the border a short while ago. He was behind enemy lines, and the local gendarmerie would be racing to the scene any minute, if some bedraggled fraction of the German army didn't beat them to it.

But he was alive. That was something. Broken bones would knit. And the airplane, miraculously, wasn't on fire, though he could smell a faint acrid smoke in the air, somewhere. He moved his head on his stiff neck, and saw nothing but broken trees and turned earth, a wet and war-scarred landscape.

He placed his left hand on the side of the airplane and hoisted himself out of his seat. The pain in his chest made him gag. Beneath his jacket, his shirt was wet. A rib, probably, splintering through his skin. Better skin than the organs inside, though.

Getting himself out of the cockpit proved easier than he imagined—the airplane had come to rest at a convenient angle—but the drop to the ground nearly did him in. He lay on his back and stared at the stunted tips of the trees. You could still smell autumn in the air, just faintly: that syrupy flavor of wet, fallen leaves. But the smoke was growing stronger now, overpowering nature, and Octavian thought of Johnson, careering to the earth, trailing a slender, vaporous line from his engine, like a rope.

He rolled on his side—the left side, the one that seemed to have gotten out of this in better shape than the right—and braced himself on the fuselage. He was surprised to discover that he could stand, if he didn't try to put any weight on his right foot. There was a thick, knobbled stick on the leaves nearby, struck off a trunk by the driving nose of the airplane, or else an artillery shell from some recent bombardment, the evidence of which lay everywhere. Broken trees, craters of fresh earth. Ground that had escaped largely unscathed through four years of war was finally getting its due. In some places, the front lines were now no more than a few miles from the German border.

Octavian reached for the stick and set it upright on the leaves. The wood held his weight bravely. He looked up at the sky, and there it was: the faint smudge of charcoal against the drizzly gloom of the clouds beyond. In his lungs, he felt the sulfurous sting of burning fuel, all too familiar.

He took a single, excruciating step, and then another, and he was about to take a third when he remembered something important.

He staggered back to the cockpit, reached across the empty seat with his left hand, and pulled the photograph of Sophie Faninal from the edge of the airspeed dial.

JOHNSON WAS CLOSER THAN HE THOUGHT; OR RATHER, JOHNson's airplane was closer, only a few hundred agonizing yards away, wings and fuselage crumpled, billowing smoke from the nose. Of Johnson himself, there was no sign, until Octavian heard the faintest possible groan above the ominous whisper of the gathering fire, and he looked over the edge of the cockpit, between the struts connecting the two wings, and saw Johnson's cocky face, smashed beyond recognition and beginning to swell.

The air rumbled, and a lick of flame spurted from between the bent blades of the propeller.

Octavian leaned on his stick and unbuttoned his jacket, as fast as his stiff fingers could manipulate the fastenings. Another flame licked free, and then a roaring whoosh moved the air against his eardrums, and the engine exploded.

Somewhere inside the din, he heard Johnson cry out. He staggered forward, dragging his right foot, and the heat of the fire seared his skin beneath his shirt as he slipped the leather jacket from his shoulders and threw it over Johnson.

"Come on, kid!" he shouted. "Lift your arms!"

But Johnson didn't move. His airplane had wrecked on a little rise, and the open cockpit tilted to the side, away from Octavian. He sheltered his mouth with his shirt and stumbled around the tail, until Johnson returned in view, slumped over the controls, while the smoke and flame billowed from the nose and crept over the fuselage.

Octavian swore.

The heat was like hell itself, singeing his skin, singeing the tiny shaved bristles of his beard. It struck him with physical force, and he pushed himself through the way he might batter down a wall. The skin of the airplane was hot to the touch. He stuck his left arm in the cockpit—no good—he threw aside the stick and tried again, opposing the suffocation in his chest, opposing the pain that had gone so deep, he almost didn't feel it anymore. His left arm found the gap beneath Johnson's shoulder and wedged into place, and he just closed his eyes and heaved, heaved, until Johnson screamed and his body slid free, like a baby from the womb, sending them both into the ground just as the flames overtook the cockpit.

THEY LAY THERE ON THE WET LEAVES WHILE THE PLANE BURNED a dozen yards away. It was as far as Octavian could drag them both before the last of his strength gave way. The soles of his boots grew hot against his feet, until he wanted—irrationally—to take them off. Instead he pulled the leather jacket over both their heads. The smoke wasn't so bad on the ground, but his lungs were already raw. As for Johnson, Octavian couldn't even say if the kid was dead or alive. He didn't make a sound. Octavian listened for his breath, and thought he could hear a faint and irregular scratch. Or maybe that was just himself, Octavian, starved of oxygen. Stripped from the inside out.

The roar of the fire began to subside, but the plane still smoldered. Octavian lifted away the jacket and raised his head, just enough to see the blackened pile, resting in a hollow that he now realized was a shell crater. Or a bomb, dropped blindly from an Allied airplane at some point in the autumn push.

"Johnson?" he said. "You alive?"

There was a small movement in the dirt beside him.

"No."

"That's what I thought."

"Baftard," Johnson said, like he'd lost a few teeth, or couldn't move his jaw.

Octavian's chest started to shudder, but the pain of laughing cut short the laugh itself. "Still the same old Johnson," he said, and he didn't recognize the smoky rasp of his throat.

Johnson spit messily. "We fucked, J.C.?" The C was more like *fee. Jayfee.*

"Looks like it."

"Forry."

"*C'est la guerre*, kid."

Johnson didn't reply. Octavian reached out his left hand—the right arm, by now, was utterly immobile—and gave the boy a shove to the shoulder, not gentle at all. "You wake up, Johnson, all right? You gotta stay awake."

"Fuck you."

"That's better. Come on. I'll tell you a story."

"Fuck. You."

"I'll tell you something no one else knows, all right? I'll tell you about my photograph. The big secret."

Johnson's voice was packed with effort. "Fulla *thit*, Jayfee."

"No, listen. Just shut your mouth and listen, you cocky son of a gun. You maroon trying to be a hero."

Johnson grunted. Disgust, from the tone of it. Good. Octavian would take disgust over despair any day.

"All right, then," he said. "This girl, the girl in the photograph? The one you think is my sweetheart? I don't even know her."

Another grunt. Surprise?

Octavian continued, as if they were sitting at a bar, nursing a pair of beers. Or whisky. What he wouldn't give for a brown, neat whisky at Harry's Bar near the Opéra, where they knew how to make a solid American drink. A double. His fingers found a leaf and rubbed the two sides between his thumb and forefinger. "Well, maybe that's not true. I've never met her, not in person, but I know her like I know myself."

"Aw, thit, Jayfee."

"No, you're gonna listen, kid. You *need* to hear this. You see, this girl—Sophie's her name, Sophie Faninal—"

"The fuck?"

"*Faninal*, kid. Fan-in-al. See, she's a stranger, maybe, but I guess I've known her most of my life. She used to live in the house where I grew up. Greenwich. That's a town in Connecticut, right by the shore, about thirty miles from New York City. It's the first town you run into, once you cross the border into New England. Pretty town, full of rich people, horses, summer houses. A lot of stockbrokers. My pops, he was a stockbroker, and when we bought this house, you see, no one had lived in it for two years. It was a year after the panic, though, so we figured that's why it was such a bargain, because all the stockbrokers had lost their shirts, except Pops, I guess. Pops got lucky. Made out all right."

"Gotta point, Jayfee?" The voice was a little clearer now, like Johnson was actually paying attention. Rallying a bit.

"Yeah, I got a point. Anyway, one day, not too long after we moved in, I got to talking to the neighbor kid, and that's when I learned about Sophie. She was three years old when they moved out, and she slept in my exact bedroom, the best room in the house. Overlooked Long Island Sound from a turret window. Loved that room."

The leaf fell apart in Octavian's hand, done to death by the force of his callused fingers. He turned his hand over and allowed the pieces to shiver back into the ground.

"And?" said Johnson.

"And then, one fine September morning, like I said, two years before we moved in, some lunatic takes a kitchen knife and cuts open her mother's throat, ear to ear, right downstairs when Sophie's taking a nap."

"Holy thit."

Octavian picked up another leaf and started again. "So, the

story goes, little Sophie wanders in on her fat little legs and finds the body. The maid hears her crying and comes downstairs, and there's Sophie, tugging on her mama's limp arm, trying to wake her up, and—"

"The *fuck.*"

"Yeah, well. They thought the father did it, old Faninal, but before they could arrest him, he split. Split and took the family with him—Sophie had a sister, see, nine or ten years old—and nobody heard from 'em since."

Johnson spat out a little more blood.

"And that's that, I guess," Octavian said.

Another grunt, full of gurgling derision. "Point?"

"The *point*, Johnson, you bonehead hick kid, you numbskull hayseed, is that she's out there somewhere. This little girl who lived in my room and lost her mama. And the reason I keep her photograph, the reason I keep her with me—"

"'Cause—go back home—*shave* 'er? Huh, Jayfee?"

"Maybe. If I can find her, that is. Only I was kind of thinking . . .'" He closed his eyes, because the sight of the back of Johnson's head, matted with blood and hair and torn skin, was beginning to sway in front of him. "I was kind of thinking we might save each other."

"Full—*thit*—Jayfee. You—too—damn—a shave."

"Yeah," he said, inhaling the leafy rot, the poisonous smoke. Trying not to open his mouth too much. To draw too much oxygen across the surface of his excoriated lungs. "Too damned to save. I guess you might be right. Still—"

"*Hier ist es. Mein Gott! Was für ein Durcheinander!*"

Octavian slid his hand to the small of Johnson's back. Not that he needed to. Johnson knew darned well not to move, even if he could.

The voices grew in size, heavy and male. Two men, maybe three. Octavian knew a few words of German, not enough to understand them. He didn't dare lift his head and look. Underneath the leather jacket, he moved his hand to the pistol at his waist, a weapon he'd hardly ever fired. What was the point, up in the sky? You already had two nice efficient Lewis machine guns strapped to your wings, one on each side, ready to rain hell on somebody. Still. He remembered how. Octavian, he remembered everything. A curse, sometimes, but at this particular moment, in this particular copse of skeletal German trees, it was a blessing.

A cool customer. That's what his friends at Andover used to call him, and it wasn't just that he played hockey so well. There was something in his blood, something that chilled and slowed when danger approached, like the thickening of sea ice in the middle of January. The higher the stakes, the more everything slowed, the clearer his mind became: an extreme economy of thought and motion, as if he were a machine directing his own actions. As the Germans picked their way around the smoldering wreckage—soldiers? deserters? gendarmerie?—he held himself perfectly still, while his brain mapped out each possibility. The trajectory of his imprecise left arm, the direction of his attention, should the footsteps form such a pattern that Octavian, lying under the brown leather coat against the brown leaves, would have to defend himself by force.

"Jayfee?" whispered Johnson.

Octavian hardly heard him. The voices, muffled by the remains of the fuselage between them, were beginning to sharpen. But there was no pause in the complicated German consonants, no sign that the men had spotted them. Two men, he was now certain. He slid his pistol from its holster.

A soft, ominous rattle emerged from Johnson's throat.

The voices stilled.

Oh, Christ. Don't die, Johnson.

The body twitched next to him, and the action—involuntary—caused Johnson to make a noise of agony, stifled in his throat, as if he were choking on his own pain.

"*Dort gibt es,*" whispered one of the men, more loudly than your ordinary whisper.

Octavian's hand rounded around the butt of the pistol. His thumb found the safety latch, pushing it upward in the faintest possible click, just as a similar sound nicked the air a few yards away.

Johnson's throat made that gurgling sound again, a death rattle. One leg flinched, hitting Octavian's injured shin.

"*Achtung!*" someone called out.

Johnson was going to die. He was going to choke on his own blood, while Octavian hovered between the risk of surrender, and the risk of attack. Surrender: would these Germans accept it? Or would they shoot the two of them dead, without a witness in this dank and cheerless copse, in revenge for a brother or a son or a friend?

On the day after Morris went down in a spectacular ball of fire—Morris, the fellow who gave Octavian his nickname—they had caught a German soldier hiding out in a barn. The second

German advance had started a couple of weeks before (this was why Morris and Octavian had rushed back from Paris, cutting short their leave by a day) and everything was in chaos: frontiers crossed, lines retreating. The German was wounded in the shoulder and the gut, and he had fashioned himself a dirty bandage from a rag. The barn was attached to a small farm in which Octavian was billeted with a few of his squadron mates, and he and one of the other pilots found the German after following a trail of his blood through the new spring grass. Octavian volunteered to run back to the airfield for a medic and an MP, while the other man stood guard.

"Why the fuck?" said his mate, and he lifted his pistol and shot the German through the forehead, bang splat. "That's for Morris," he added, turning away, putting his pistol back in its holster, and Octavian—stunned, horrified—realized also that he was glad. That in some brutal, primitive corner of his heart, he had rejoiced in the act of retribution. Later, of course, such acts became impossible: not because they didn't encounter more Germans, but because they lost so many pilots. How could you seek revenge for the life of a man you'd only met a few days before? How could you seek revenge for an act—shooting down an enemy airplane—of which you yourself were guilty, a dozen times over?

But now, it seemed, God had arranged his own atonement. A life for a life, wasn't that right, since they were all God's children, and equal in His eyes? But it was a shame that poor young Johnson was now forced to pay Octavian's indemnity. Johnson wasn't present on that verdant May afternoon in the French barn. Hardly fair that he should die for it.

Octavian shut his eyes. Tested his left arm, tested his fingers wrapped around the pistol. The muscles of his abdomen, contracting in agony against his broken rib.

The leaves stuck to his wet cheek. He licked his lips and tasted blood, and he realized he'd been tasting it all along: that the bright, metallic flavor in his mouth was his own human blood.

"*Zeig dich!*" a man called out. "*Zeig dich! Oder ich scheisse!*"

Octavian fastened on the word *scheisse*. He knew what that meant.

Shoot.

He snarled his lips, flung off the leather jacket, lifted his left arm, and fired.

The first man, struck in the chest at a range of perhaps five yards, yelled a strangled "*Ach!*" as he flew backward and hit the soft, leaf-strewn ground.

The second man fired his own frantic pistol—once, twice—and Octavian, feeling nothing, coolly adjusted his aim and fired again.

The pistol jammed.

"*Halt! Halt!*"

Octavian sat with his arm outstretched, holding the pistol, hoping the man opposite didn't realize what had just happened. That Octavian was impotent.

"Stop!" This time in English. A female voice. "Please stop!"

"*Gertrude! Zurückbekommen!*" said the German, his pistol trained on Octavian.

He was old, Octavian realized in shock. Not a soldier at all. Just an old man in a threadbare wool suit, his face white and grizzled, his arm quivering. Both shots had missed—at least, Octavian hadn't noticed the impact—and the gun he held in his hand must have been at least as old and rusted as the man himself.

The girl. Gertrude. Octavian couldn't see her, but her voice had come from the right, young and frightened. She made a noise like a sob, and her footsteps squished against the ground.

"*Nein, Gertrude!*" cried the old man.

"Papa," she said, in a broken voice, and she came into view, bundled in a worn brown coat, her head covered by her hood. She bent over the fallen man and cried out. "*Mein Vater! Mein Vater!*" she said, gripping the man by his shoulders.

"*Ist er tot?*" demanded the old man.

"*Ich weisse nicht, Ich weisse nicht!*"

The old man's lips curled around his teeth, and Octavian knew he was going to shoot. He was going to shoot Octavian, and that was perfectly fair, wasn't it, perfectly fair and just, because Octavian had just killed Gertrude's father. Octavian had killed this poor old German man, lying among the rotting leaves; moreover, he'd pursued and shot down at least eleven additional Germans (possibly more) and a couple of observation balloons besides; he'd stood by in the springtime and allowed a German prisoner to be shot like a dog, and he hadn't once objected to any of this slaughter. So these particular Germans had every right to shoot him, just like he'd had every right to shoot them. Around and around it went, forever and ever, until nobody was left alive. *C'est la guerre.*

He dropped the pistol into the earth.

The old man's eyes narrowed into an angry squint, taking aim.

"*Nein!*" the girl cried. "*Onkel! Nein!*"

"*Er sollte sterben, den Hund!*"

"*Nein! Der Krieg ist vorbei! Es is genung! Bitte!*" She was sobbing now, rising up, grasping the old man's arm. "*Es is genung! Haben Sie nicht genung Männer starb? Der Krieg ist vorbei!*"

Octavian's hand went to his pocket, where he kept Sophie's photograph.

"Just kill me," he muttered. "Go ahead."

The girl turned to him. She tossed the old man's pistol onto the ground, next to Octavian's. Her hood had fallen back from her head, exposing a long flaxen braid to the damp air. Octavian thought she was perhaps fifteen or sixteen, for while her cheeks were concave and incurably hungry, the skin that covered them was still tender. Her eyes were flat and hopeless, the color of November. "No, soldier," she said, in English. "You did not know? The war is over."

She turned back to her father, loosening his clothes, and Octavian slumped forward. Then he remembered Johnson, and he looked back to see if the kid was still breathing, or whether he'd choked to death during the course of that little incomprehensible exchange. *The war is over.* What did she mean by that?

The crisis now past, his brain was beginning to lose its moorings and drift. There were now two Johnsons lying on the ground before him, and each of them had a new wound, a fresh piece of skull missing from the top of his head, a small mound of pink matter oozing forth from within, and Octavian thought, *So the old bastard didn't miss, after all.*

The war is over. Well, she was right about that. The war was over for him and Johnson, anyway. Johnson was dead, and Octavian was a prisoner. Lucky to be alive, maybe, and even luckier if he didn't die in a prison hospital. All of Germany was living on rats and acorns, people said, and an American prisoner would be fed last of all. His war was over. Everything was over.

He touched his pocket again with his stiff hand, but when his fingers slipped inside, seeking reassurance or maybe absolution, they found nothing.

The photograph was gone.

Paris. Mid-April 1920, just after midnight

OCTAVIAN FOUND HIS PAIR OF ROOMS IN THE MONTPARNASSE attic a little over a year ago, not because he wanted to write or paint or compose music or any darned thing, but because a few of his buddies lived there, and it was cheap.

By then his bones had knit back together, and so had the skin on his arms that had burned in the fire, though he hadn't noticed at the time. His face remained strangely unscathed, like a baby's, so you wouldn't know how many scars he bore underneath his clothes. The doctors all said he was lucky, fabulously lucky.

He thinks about this now, as the taxi nears the crumbling Second Empire building where he lives, No. 33. Not about luck, but about his scars, and whether they will charm or repel la belle Hélène, or whether she's too drunk to notice. (Is it taking advantage of a girl, if you're a virgin and she is surely not, if you're both drunk and she's the one who first suggested a liaison? He's not sure. The lines are all so blurry, in this bright modern age.) He thinks about poor old Johnson and his widow, a subject to which his mind turns with sordid frequency. *Tits like this*—he glances at Hélène's chest, and he realizes that he's well within his rights, for the first time in his life, to touch a woman's breasts. He lifts his stiff right hand, plunges it inside her dress, and does just that, like he's changing the oil of a Model T, and Hélène gasps obligingly and tilts her head back, and between that—the sight of Hélène's vulnerable dusky throat, the feel of her soft breast in his palm, the warmth of her hand on his crotch (so good, so *good*, *so good*)—and the whisky and the smoke and the darkness, he nearly disgraces himself, the same way that poor hayseed Johnson disgraced himself *his* first time. Except Johnson actually got his thing inside the widow first, according to his own account, and by God (here Octavian gulps for air, and the self-control that comes with oxygen), by God, a cool customer like J.C. can do as much. Can't he?

The taxi stops suddenly, throwing them apart in the nick of time. Hélène makes a panting little heap on the seat, her bobbed hair just shading her eyes, her dark lips smiling dreamily, while Octavian reaches in his pocket for the fare. The driver accepts his money without expression. Octavian opens the door and reaches for Hélène's hand; she lifts her head and asks him if he's got a cigarette.

"I guess so," he says. He pulls her forth from the taxi and sets her upright. She slings one arm around his neck while he hunts for his cigarettes in various pockets. The rain's stopped, the sky's clearing. Springtime in Paris. The cool, damp air clears his head a little, so that he's able to enjoy his drunkenness from the outside, as it were: to savor the smell and feel of the woman pressed against his groin, the dirty, disrespectful knowledge of what he's about to do with her. To exult in his freedom from self-restraint. (He finds the cigarettes and pulls two of them from the lips of the crushed packet, sticking one inside Hélène's mouth and one inside his own.) Why, heck, it's about time he throws off the shackles! God only knows why he waited so long—why, for so many years, he allowed the specter of a girl he doesn't know to cast her disapproval over the perfectly natural urges of a perfectly virile red-blooded American ace pilot. (He finds a match and lights the end of Hélène's cigarette, and then his own.) Why, goddammit, he's a war hero, isn't he? He's got a right to screw a pretty girl. He's got a right to fornication, after all that hell and sacrifice. He made the world safe for democracy! He ended all wars! So he's got a right. To the victor go the spoils. Only the brave deserve the fair. See? You can't argue with the wisdom of proverbs.

Hélène blows out a paper-thin stream of smoke and says she's getting a little cold, down here on the pavement.

"All right," says Octavian, and he takes her hand and leads her to the door of the apartment building.

The lock is stiff and doesn't want to turn, but Octavian coaxes it open while Hélène fumbles from behind at the buttons of his shirt. The door opens to a small and tatty courtyard, pots overgrown with brown winter weeds. There's a tree in the middle that Octavian knows to be a linden, though you can't tell at the moment because the leaves have stubbornly refused to unfurl this spring. Underneath the tree is a wrought-iron bench of tremendous age and decoration, the kind of bench your Victorian parents might have sat on while conducting a perfectly respectable courtship, and for some reason Octavian thinks it's a splendid idea to lead Hélène to this bench and pull her down with him.

She makes a fevered little gasp and puts one hand at his nape, while the other plucks at his shirt. "Ah, my love," she says, kissing his neck and jaw, "ah, Claude!"

"Octavian," he mutters. "It's Octavian."

Either she doesn't hear him, or she doesn't care. She goes on calling him Claude as she tears at his buttons, and Octavian, trying to find a way to uncover her breasts again in the middle of all this frantic activity, figures it doesn't matter. Hélène and Claude, fine. He gives up on her breasts and finds the edge of her dress instead, which has ridden up her legs to expose the tops of her stockings, the elastic of her garters, the slippery skin of her thighs. *"Mon Dieu!"* she cries, tilting back her head again, taking a quick and hissing draft of her cigarette, *Claude, fuck me, please, now!* And it sounds so inviting in French, so sinful and yet naturally elegant, that Octavian thinks, *Fine, we'll do it right here, I'm going to screw a woman for the first time on a bench in a courtyard, why not,* and he says, in her ear, "How?"

She laughs. "However you like, Claude. You know how I like it."

"But I'm not Claude."

"Shh!" She lays the first two fingers of her right hand across his lips, and that's when he realizes that she hasn't actually kissed him yet: properly, on the lips, the way other lovers kiss.

He nibbles her fingers. It seems the right thing to do. "Who's Claude?"

"Mon amant." She sways a little, right there on his lap, atop the bulge in his trousers, and finishes her cigarette. *"Mon ciel sur la terre."*

Octavian sucks in his breath, holds it, counts to five. Exhales with great precision. *My heaven on earth.* "When did he die?"

"Verdun."

The word is a sob. That word is always a sob. Hélène's small French body, made of tiny angular bones and hollowness, sharp and frantic an instant ago, has begun to melt in sorrow against his clothes. He doesn't ask more about Claude. He doesn't need to. Verdun is a time and a place and a manner of death, all rolled into one. Poor Claude. Poor dumb sucker. At least he got to fuck his sweetheart before he left, to fuck his dear little bird, his Hélène. Does he mind that other men have taken over that duty? That Octavian is about to fuck his dear little bird? Or, when you are blasted into minute chunks of fresh-blackened flesh by the proximate explosion of a Krupps artillery shell, are you released from your enslavement to petty human jealousies? Is Claude hovering in the courtyard right this second, cheering them on in their mutual pursuit of relief? Offering a much-needed hint or two to that dumb virgin J.C.?

"Please," Hélène says, nudging her hips, tossing away the stub of her cigarette into the paving stones. The courtyard is unlit, except for the glow of a couple of windows somewhere above them, but Octavian has always been able to see well at night. Hélène's eyes are half-closed and enormous, and the kohl has smudged underneath the bottom lids, so that she looks frail and somewhat bruised as she undulates impatiently on his lap. Her neck is long and slender, quite smooth, and the transparent fabric of her dress has come askew over her breasts, exposing one—small, young, bearing a tiny dark nipple—and disguising the other. Octavian's hands are presently resting at her waist, underneath her dress, and she's not wearing a corset or camisole anything like that, obviously, so there's nothing but bare skin under his fingers, warm and springy, musky-sweet, or is that the smell of her privates? Making him dizzy. Her thighs squeeze his, one on each side. Her humid cigarette breath comes in bursts. Octavian is so aroused, he's afraid of himself. Afraid of what he might do to her. Afraid of what he might *not* do to her.

All right. All right. You can do this. It's just anatomy, right? Just a matter of getting the parts in the right place. The world is populated, it can't be that difficult. But how the hell does he unbutton his trousers, when she's squirming on his lap like that? He lifts her up by the waist, but it's not enough space, he's too hard, so he sort of hauls her off his lap to the bench and stands up to unfasten the damned trousers and get on with it, release himself to the open air and—God have mercy—Hélène's waiting body, and that's when he realizes there is someone else in the courtyard.

Octavian holds himself still, hands frozen at his waist. His senses, dulled by whisky and sexual arousal, sharpen back to their habitual points.

He hears the breathing first: soft, shallow, rapid. Trying not to make itself known, and yet so obvious that he cannot believe he didn't notice the sound before. And then the smell. Damp wool. Greenness, almost floral but not quite. The vibration of a startled heartbeat.

"Who's there?" he calls out, in French.

"What's the matter?" Hélène says.

"Someone's here."

She makes a derisive noise. "Claude. Come back here. I have such a fever."

He doesn't move. He listens for more sound, in between the beats of his heart, and then he hears it: a tiny rustle, like the movement of a squirrel in a tree. He turns his head to the right and sees her, huddled in the corner, a dark feminine shadow outlined against the stone.

Octavian's hands fall in shame from his trouser buttons.

"Can I help you?" he calls gently.

The figure shakes its head.

"Have you somewhere to go?"

A small voice replies, in hesitant words: *"Je ne parle pas français."*

"English?"

She darts from the corner.

"Wait!"

Octavian moves after her, but she's so quick, he only just manages to grasp her fingertips. But it's enough. She stills in his hand. His heart thuds in panic. His cheeks are hot. What now?

Behind him, Hélène calls out, "Claude! What are you doing? Who is she?"

Who is she.

He reaches for the girl's hood. Fingers shaking. Eyes blurry. Brain spilling from his head. He pulls back the hood—so tender, as if plucking a tiny bird from its nest—and whispers, "Sophie?"

A smooth head of hair slips free, and then a braid, long and flaxen. She ducks her head and reaches for the hood.

"No! I have make mistake."

"But I know you!"

"Not anymore."

She pulls away and breaks for the door, but the sticky latch confounds her, and Octavian catches her and turns her to the light from one of the windows. Her face is hungry and familiar and pink with humiliation.

"I'm sorry," he says.

"Let me go."

"It's Gertrude, isn't it?"

"I have make mistake. Please, let me go."

"Why are you here? You found me here. Don't be afraid."

"I am not afraid." She tilts her chin a little. "I am sorry."

"I'm sorry, too. I—this—it's not what—"

She turns away and reaches into her pocket. "I bring you something, see. That is all. Here. If you want."

All at once, Octavian is cold, so cold he can't move. There are footsteps behind him, Hélène rising from the bench and approaching them in curiosity, the heels of her shoes clicking uncertainly on the paving stones, but Octavian is powerless to turn his head, powerless to lift his hand and accept the small yellow envelope that Gertrude holds in the space between them.

"Here," she says again. She's stronger now, and defiant. Her eyes widen fearlessly. There's nothing like moral superiority, is there? When you have caught a man almost in the act of sin, and he stands before you, degraded, frozen in shame. "You wanted this very much once, yes? Your photograph that you lose."

"Yes. I wanted it very much."

"You say this over and over, in the hospital. I make you promise to find her. Here." She nudges his stomach with the edge of the envelope. "Take. She is yours, not mine."

"Claude." Hélène's head lands smack between his shoulder blades, her arms around his waist. "Is this a lover of yours? Shall we bring her upstairs with us?"

Octavian wants to crawl out of his own skin. He wants to climb from inside his own head. He wants to touch Gertrude's cheek, he wants to caress her hair, he wants to kneel on the stones and rend himself. He takes the envelope.

"There it is," she says. "Now good-bye."

"Wait! You can't go out there alone!"

"I cannot *stay*." Withering voice.

He tries to place his hand on the door, but she ducks beneath his elbow and forces the latch to lift.

"Gertrude, please."

She turns in the doorway. Her face is shadowed now. "May God bless you, Mr. Rofrano"—and then she's gone, and Octavian is just a solid pillar of flesh, holding an envelope, staring into nothing.

Hélène yawns and tugs his shirt. "A great pity. She is so pretty. A German girl, isn't she? How do you know her?"

Octavian waits until the footsteps merge into the traffic on the other side of the wall, until she's gone. Gone where? If only he could move. He says quietly, "She rescued me when I was shot down, on the last day of the war. She brought me to the hospital."

"Ah, did she nurse you back to health? It is so romantic."

"No. She wasn't a nurse. But she visited me, every day, until I was well enough to be moved to a French hospital. She read to me. English books, mostly. She wanted to improve her English, she said." Octavian hesitates. "I shot her father."

"*Mon Dieu!* You shot him, really? Did he die?"

"Yes."

"And then she saves *you?*" Hélène laughs. "She is a saint, I think."

A saint. Is that how you describe Gertrude? Only she hadn't

performed any miracles, really, unless you count an act of grace such as the one Gertrude performed on that November forest floor a miracle. A sign from God that it was possible to forgive another's sins, even when your own heart was steeped in grief. That you could actually purchase a human soul by the coin of mercy.

Octavian says, "She brought me the telegram about my mother. The news that my mother died of the influenza."

"*Mon Dieu*. And you did not marry her for this?"

"It wasn't like that."

Hélène snorts. "Not for *you*, maybe. Poor girl. What did she give you?"

"It's a photograph. A photograph I thought I'd lost."

"Your sweetheart?"

"Not exactly."

"May I see her?"

"No."

She laughs. "Poor Gertrude. She's a virgin, no?"

"Yes."

"Ah, well. Nobody is perfect." She sighs wetly against his shirt. "You, too, isn't it so?"

"No. I'm not perfect at all."

"No, I mean you are a virgin, yes? You are also a virgin."

Octavian looks down at the envelope, on which his name is printed in careful block letters. CAPTAIN O. N. ROFRANO, U.S.A.A.S. He slides his fingers across the ink and discovers the stiffness inside, the square edges of the photograph, rescued from the fallen leaves. Has she survived the damp and the rot? Is Sophie's face still intact, or is she now obscured?

"I thought so," Hélène says. "You can always tell. But come up-stairs."

"Wait. Just—a moment."

Her hand slides to his elbow. "Come. There is no shame, Captain. I will show you how it is done. You are going to be a great lover, another Casanova, and then maybe when you have learned all these important lessons, you will go back to your pretty German girl and give her much pleasure."

He wants to tell her that he's not ashamed, at least about *that*, and that he's an unlikely candidate for a second Casanova, or even a third. That he can't possibly face Gertrude again. But maybe she's right. Maybe, in the aftermath of apocalypse, the only shame that remains is innocence. Maybe Gertrude has come to Paris on a fool's errand. Maybe he's better off without this envelope in his hands; maybe he should toss what remains of Sophie Faninal in the nearest dustbin, like a piece of furniture that is no longer in fashion. Maybe Sophie doesn't even exist at all.

Octavian shoves the envelope in his pocket and gives in to the persistent tug of Hélène's hand at his elbow. The whisky is wearing off, and his head is painfully sharp. He opens the door to the stairwell and leads Hélène up the worn wooden steps, flight by flight, her bony little hand like a claw inside his closed palm. She stops for breath on the fourth-floor landing, and it's so dark—the bulb's been out for weeks—he can see only her outline against the smudged wall as she pants and laughs, holding her hand to her chest. He puts his arm around her waist and lifts her.

Once inside his attic room, she looks around in a sort of amazed contempt. "But it's so shabby! I didn't know you were so poor. You don't look poor."

"It's home." He hands her a cigarette and lights it, and then one for himself. She thanks him and smokes for a moment in silence, next to the window, one arm folded beneath the other, regarding him without blinking from beneath her thick black eyelashes, like a dare. She is smiling a little.

"You are like a statue, monsieur," she says at last. "Don't you want to know what happens next?"

He doesn't feel like a statue. His heart is smacking, his blood is running mad. His skin is hot. His mouth is full of smoke.

He nods his head yes.

She turns around and gestures with her cigarette to the fastenings of her dress. He steps forward and fumbles away, until the sleeves—such as they are—fall suddenly from from her shoulders and she wriggles free and kicks the dress aside. She takes his two hands in her two hands and draws them around her waist, up the ridge of her rib cage, until he's holding her breasts in his palms. They are soft, and a little heavier than he remembers from the taxi, warm and pliable and exciting, and he thinks, *God, so this is what it's like, to hold a girl's breasts in your two hands, thank you.* She makes a breathless noise, straining upward against his hands, and he closes his eyes and rests his mouth against Hélène's short, dark hair.

"Ah, Claude," she sobs. "It's so good. Claude, I need it."

Outside, the sky is a metropolitan purple, and the opposite rooftop catches a bit of empty silver moon, and it's like there are no more people in the world, everyone is dead, and just he and Hélène remain to populate the earth. Her flesh shudders under his hand, and he realizes she's crying.

"All right," he says in English. "Hush, now."

He reaches in his jacket pocket for a handkerchief and draws Hélène onto the threadbare sofa. For perhaps an hour he holds her in his lap, while her sharp bones dig into his stomach and his groin, and her chest quivers against his, settling eventually into a flaccid sleep. He watches the progress of the moon outside, and when he wakes up into the pink dawn, Hélène is gone, and there's no sign that she even existed there, or that the incident ever occurred, except for the stub of her cigarette, stained very faintly with lipstick, in the bottom of an empty glass on the table.

And the envelope, still sealed, which he tucks into the pocket of his suitcase just before he leaves Paris the next morning.

The Photograph

Kate Kerrigan

Dublin, 2016

BRIDIE WASN'T HAPPY.

Her London-based daughter, Sharon, had been back in Dublin for less than three hours and she and her brother were already fighting. Sharon was home for a commemoration ceremony for the 1916 Uprising, in which Bridie's grandfather, Seamus O'Hara, was being honored. The president was hosting the event in his palace in Dublin's Phoenix Park and Bridie would receive a special medal on her grandfather's behalf, along with her father's cousin, Liam Maheady, whose own father was also being honored. Their ancestors' glittering careers in the Irish Republican Army had defined the O'Hara family for generations.

The whole country was alive with talk of the event and tickets were like gold dust. All had been fine, until Sharon announced that she wanted to bring her new boyfriend to the event.

"It's a 1916 commemoration, Sharon," her brother Frank was saying, "a celebration of the end of eight hundred years of oppression from the English. Our great-grand-grandfather led the revolution. So no, you can't bring some bastard British soldier along as your date!"

"Are you going to let him talk to me like that? Anyway it's not up to you. It's up to Mam. Mam?"

At thirty and thirty-four they still needed their mammy to referee their fights.

She hated when the kids behaved like this. Tomorrow was an important day for her. A time for remembering the past, honoring her ancestors, and remembering how they had fought to free their country from English rule. Her great-uncle, Padraig, had been shot dead for the part he had played in the Easter Rising, and her grandfather, Seamus, his younger brother, had gone on to become an IRA captain. This was a time for remembering the great things her family had done. Why did the kids have to ruin everything with their squabbling? Why did they always have to make everything about them?

Her son, Frank, was such an angry young man. He channeled it into revolutionary, left-wing politics, but Bridie wondered if that was such a good idea. Frank had inherited a social conscience from his forebears and that was good, but it didn't seem to be getting him anywhere. Mostly he just went to demonstrations, where he got himself wound up into an angry state. His sister was quite the opposite; no thought of anything beyond looking gorgeous and having fun. This was so typical of Sharon, bringing a soldier boyfriend to this, of all things. Lord knows she'd dated half the men in London at this stage. She could have easily invited that nice real estate agent from Wembley that Bridie's sister had fixed her up with. But no. There had to be a drama.

Thank God Sharon at least had the sense to book them both into a hotel, where she had left this "Dave" so she could slug it out with her brother.

Bridie, trying to stay calm, reached across the kitchen table and adjusted the feathers on her elaborate fascinator. It was the same shade of violent green as the dress and cropped suit jacket she was wearing. The outfit had been a horrible mistake. She had wanted to wear green as a patriot, but the shade had looked much softer in the shop. It wasn't until she saw it under her own kitchen lights that she realized how garish it was. On top of that the style made her look ancient. It was a real-great-aunt-of-the-bride monstrosity. However, it had cost a fortune and it was too late to take it back now.

"Calm down, Frank. Your sister can bring who she likes although perhaps . . ."

"Perhaps what?" Sharon snapped.

"Well, this . . ."

"Dave."

"Yes—Dave might not feel comfortable there himself. So maybe it's not such a good idea . . ."

Frank let out a triumphant snort while Bridie continued.

"I mean, this is a family day and I know you like him . . ."

Sharon closed her eyes in disgust, then opened them and glared at her mother.

"He's not just 'someone I like,' Mam—he's my fiancé."

"What?" Frank shouted. "You can't marry a Brit."

"You're engaged?" Bridie said. She tried to sound interested but frankly, she wasn't surprised. Sharon had been engaged at least twice before, that she knew about.

"I love him, Mam," she said, and she really looked like she meant it. Bridie believed her, but then, she'd loved the other lads, too.

"Ah yeah, I forgot," Frank said meanly. "You're only after the ring, anyway—you'll never marry him."

"This time it's different." Sharon was looking at her mother now with a strange, pleading expression on her face.

"Of course it is, because you have stooped even lower than usual with a British bastard."

"No, actually," Sharon said before turning angrily to her brother and shouting into his face, "It's because I'm pregnant!"

Bridie jolted. Jesus.

She couldn't take it in. Pregnant? Was Sharon serious?

Behind her daughter's heavily made-up face she saw her little girl's expression crumble, and Bridie knew it was true.

This was too much. Really.

She raised her hands in surrender to her shock. Sharon turned to her and said, "I'm sorry, Mam. I was going to tell you later but . . ."

Bridie shook her head and left the room.

"I can't take this in . . ."

"You stupid bastard—see what you've done now!" Sharon hissed at her brother as Bridie went upstairs.

Bridie's bedroom was her sanctuary. She had grown up in this house in Dublin's north inner city, just around the corner from Collin's Barracks Museum. After her parents died, she and Jim bought the house from her siblings. Jim had overhauled the place, turning it into a city-pad palace for the two of them to enjoy after the kids were gone. There had been so much for them to look forward to, but soon after the building work was finished, Jim announced he was leaving her. He "wanted more out of life." Of course, he had met another woman. Somebody not much younger than them both, but single. A career woman; his new boss, actually. Lisa was "the opposite" of Bridie, Jim said. He had made it sound like that was a good thing.

Bridie sat on the edge of her bed and looked out the window. There were crowds of people going into the museum. *Life happening,* she thought. Too much life. A baby. Trying to center herself after the shocking news, she turned her attention back into the room. After Jim had left her Bridie realized that she had lost touch with "who she was." Marriage and motherhood had clouded her sense of identity, so with the kids grown up and Jim gone, Bridie set out on a quest to find out "who" she was. She started by investigating her own roots and family history, which was how she learned all about her grandfather's part in the revolution. She dug out all the old artifacts and pictures from her own family history and put them in her old marital bedroom. There was something certain in history, a dependable truth in knowing where you came from. It made her feel secure.

Up on the mantelpiece was her grandfather's IRA medals from the war of independence. They were displayed on velvet in a mahogany box frame. The brave soldier, the great war man— one hundred years later and his ideals and his desire for freedom from British colonial rule were still bearing down on her family. Bridie sometimes feared that her son might sign up for one of these criminal paramilitary spin-offs that were always springing up in a misguided attempt to replicate his family's republican heritage. On a softer note, on the dressing table in front of her was a framed photograph of her great-aunt Eileen. Eileen was her grandfather's sister, and the picture was of her as a glamorous young woman standing in her uniform outside the National Gallery of Ireland, where she had once worked as a coat-check girl. She was so beautiful and yet Eileen had died a "spinster." Living with her brother's family for much of her adult life, Eileen had been like a second mother to Bridie. As she held the ancient picture, Bridie said out loud, "Weren't you the wise woman never getting married," then, enjoying the feeling of talking to the spirit of her beloved aunt, she added, "This frame is in a terrible state, Eileen. I think you deserve a new one."

Just as she said those words the flimsy, ancient piece of cardboard backing came away from its rusted tacks and the frame fell apart in Bridie's hands.

As she rescued the picture from the glass, Bridie noticed there was another photograph behind the one of her grandmother.

As she pulled it out from the crumbling piece of black velveteen it was mounted on, Bridie was astonished to find the photograph was of a young man. More surprisingly still, he was a British soldier in full military uniform.

East London, April 1918

Nineteen-year-old soldier Clive Postlethwaite stood in front of the photographer's backdrop. It was a bucolic image of the English countryside; the sort of landscape he had only ever seen from a train. He shuffled awkwardly toward the spot marked X on the floor, then smoothed down his hair and placed his private's beret across his freshly cropped head.

Clive was home on a few days' leave before being sent over to Dublin where he was to play his part in quashing the Irish revolution. It had been his father's idea that he get the photograph taken. George Postlethwaite had a friend who worked at a studio in Marlebone who said he could get him a good price. He was proud of his son and wanted to record Clive's first big step into manhood. This studio was one of the biggest in London. They could turn the picture around in three days, plenty of time before his son headed off to war.

"Put your leg up on this," said the photographer, sliding a small wooden box across the floor, "and loop your thumb into your belt. It'll make you look more manly."

Clive felt stupid, standing there in front of a stranger, all dressed up like this. He vaguely remembered when he was seven and his mother had taken him to have his picture taken while they were on holiday in Blackpool. They had put him in a cowboy costume, but he had hated the feeling of being "somebody else." He had screamed and cried. It had taken them ages to calm him down enough to get the picture. In his army uniform, Clive felt like he was still in fancy dress. It wasn't just the outfit that was uncomfortable, it was the whole thing. Clive knew he had to play his part, he knew the freedom of the world was at stake. But all the same, being in the army just did not sit right with him.

"Don't move," the photographer said. "Look at the birdie, don't blink, hold your body really still."

Clive held his breath and did not let go until the flash went off and the man came out from behind his huge blanketed box.

"Good luck, son," he said, coming over to shake his hand. Before Clive was out the door, the next uniformed soldier was already getting into place.

"Money is no object," his father had said to the photographer's secretary, a plump young woman who was wearing thick spectacles and far too much rouge. "We'll have two prints, one for his mother to put on the mantel while he's gone and the other one for his sweetheart." Then he winked at the girl and said, "Although he's got more than one, I'm sure. We might need half a dozen to cover them all!"

Clive didn't know where to look. The secretary laughed and winked at him, but it was a hollow gesture. She didn't mean it; she was just being polite.

Clive didn't have a sweetheart but his father hadn't noticed that. He had just assumed his son had a girl tucked away somewhere. The same way he assumed that Clive wasn't afraid of going to war.

Three days later, his father went to collect the pictures, leaving Clive and his mother in the house. His train would leave from Victoria that afternoon, but when Margaret went up to her son's room to pack his things, she found his bed already made and his kit folded, ready to go in the bag. His boots were by the door, tongues pulled back, ready for him to step into. They were so shiny she could see the reflection of her sad, worried face in them. Four months ago her son had never made his own bed or known one end of an iron from the other. The army had stolen her son from her. Now, it also seemed, it was to deprive her of the pleasure and purpose she found in doing for him.

Clive came in and found her looking at his boots.

"I've nearly just finished packing, Mum. You go downstairs and I'll straighten up in here."

She smiled weakly and part of him wished he could turn the clock back a year. His mother had hoped the war would all be over before he turned eighteen. It was the first thing she had said when war was declared. He had not thought about it himself one way or another. He knew he would either go into the army or get a starter job in the civil service. Either way it was just the way things were. When the war didn't end Clive was conscripted on his eighteen birthday. His mother had tried to hide it but he knew she was unhappy about it. He pretended he wanted to fight but secretly Clive hoped they would keep him in the training barracks and give him a desk job, or put him in the kitchen like they did with some of the younger lads. But they decided to send him to Ireland instead.

"I'll make you a sandwich for the train."

"No need," he said. "There'll be a mess car. They feed us well anyway." Then, seeing his mother's devastated expression, he added, "Not as well as you though, Mum. Any of that delicious currant cake leftover from yesterday?"

Margaret was placated but when his father came home and presented her with the photograph, she got upset again.

It didn't help when George said, "Something to put on the mantelpiece. To help you remember what he looks like."

"You make it sound like he's going to die . . ."

"Don't be so stupid, woman," Jack said. "He's only going to Ireland."

George laughed as if the very idea of Clive dying was ridiculous. But his laugh was as shallow as the girl's in the photographer's studio.

Margaret couldn't hold it in any longer. "He's only a boy, George!" his mother cried out. "He's too young."

"I'll be fine," Clive said. "I can look after myself."

It was what you said to keep the women calm. It was what you tried to make them believe.

"You're being hysterical, woman," his father said, raising his eyes to heaven at his wife's foolishness, then nodding across at Clive. "Look at him. He's as much of a man as I am. Anyway, all he'll be doing is keeping a few Irish peasants in their place. Bloody lucky he's not over in France, although I'd say that's where he'd rather be, wouldn't you, Clive? Out in the trenches, fighting the real enemy instead of just popping it to a few Paddies?"

George Postlethwaite slapped his son hard on the back and Clive said, "Of course, Dad," and smiled brightly at them both. Nobody had asked him if this was what he wanted or what he felt about being a soldier. Everyone just assumed. He was a man now and men went to war. After three months of training, Clive had muscles on his arms and legs from fitness training twice a day. He knew how to march, how to form fours and about turn. He knew how to make his bed and clean his kit and shine boots and shoot a gun. But Clive didn't know how to kill a man, and from what he had heard from the other lads, the Paddies were as dangerous as the Germans. Sneaky, too, and fearless. They had snipers, picking off uniformed soldiers as they went about their daily business. There was nearly as much hatred toward the Irish among the soldiers as there was for the Germans. More, in fact, because while the German army comprised soldiers like them, the Irish were rebels who had chosen to rise up at a time when the British Army had been weakened by the Great War. Many Irishmen had signed up to fight in the British Army, and these soldiers had the respect of their peers. The ordinary Irish people were British, as much as the Scots and the Welsh were, anyway. But after the Uprising their lads had come down hard on the rebels, executing fifteen of the ringleaders in one go. It was only then that the Irish people had risen up in force.

Although it was not as bad as the trenches, Ireland was not an easy billet. The newspapers didn't always reflect what was going on, but word filtered back from the regiments to the training camps on the worst places to get sent. Ireland was among them. Not for the bloodshed or the conditions but for the hatred. In the trenches you mixed only with your own—you were altogether. Everyone was on the same side. Although it was hard, the enemy was across the field, bombing and shooting at you. It was honest warfare. In Ireland you were in another man's country and on another man's soil. You were living among them and yet you could never be quite certain who the enemy was.

George offered to take the bus with him to Victoria Station, but Clive said he would prefer to go alone.

"I'll be back before you know it," he said to his mother as they embraced at the door. "Just think like I've stepped out to the shops."

"You're a good boy," she said, holding back her tears and putting her hand to his face.

"Oh, I almost forgot," his father said, "the photograph for your sweetheart."

He pushed across a pocket-size print in a velveteen mount.

"He doesn't have a sweetheart, you stupid man!" Margaret snapped.

George looked crushed. When Clive saw the glimmer of sadness in his father's eyes, he wanted the bravado and the bad jokes back. Clive reached out and took it from him anyway.

"Thanks, Dad," he said, and, winking, added, "Just the one will have to do I suppose."

George turned to his wife and said, "See there, woman, that's why he won't let us go to the station with him. He's meeting his girl . . ."

Clive laughed, then clicked his beret at his parents and headed off in his best soldier's swagger down the street.

As he walked away from his parents' house the fear began to take him over. Clive felt the bile reach up from his stomach to his throat. He barely managed to make it around the corner, out of their sight, before retching his mother's tea and cake into the gutter.

Dublin, July 1918

FUCKING REBEL BASTARD. HE DESERVED IT."

Billy was mouthing off again.

"I gave it to him, right here"—he tapped his temple—"with the butt of my rifle. Went down like a lamb he did. Should have shot him, too—would have if Carter hadn't been such a fucking poof and stopped me."

Everyone was afraid of Billy Jones, except Clive. Billy was rough and a little crazy, but Clive knew how to handle him. He and Clive had been trained together. They were from the same part of the East End so they knew each other vaguely from school, although they were from very different families. Clive was an only child and George worked in an office. Billy was from a family of ten whose father spent more time drinking than working. They lived on the charity of neighbors and whatever Billy could steal.

The two boys had met on the train up to Slough and ended up bunking together in the training barracks. That first night was the first that Billy had slept in a bed on his own. He had fallen out of the top bunk and, still half-asleep, cried out for his mother. A couple of the lads had come over ready to put the boot in, but Clive had stopped them. He had been terrified himself standing up to the yobs, but regardless, Clive wouldn't stand by and see anyone get bullied. "Steady, lads," he said. "Give him a break, yeah? It's our first night. We're all allowed to miss home for one night, ain't we?" Clive had a calm, sure manner that deflected their male bravado and they had shrugged and gone back to bed. Billy was street tough but his family were close-knit and he missed them. He never forgot the kindness and called Clive "my army brother." No matter what nonsense Billy got up to, Clive knew that he always had his back. He did not particularly want "mad" Billy Jones as a brother. However, he was glad Billy was on his side and not against him.

Three months after arriving in Dublin, Clive had settled into life at the barracks. Almost straightaway Clive had been given a job in the post room—replacing somebody who had been struck down with tuberculosis. They were taken to a sanitarium in case they infected the whole barracks and Clive's name was picked out of the list of new recruits. Clive enjoyed the work, sorting and delivering letters to the five thousand men who occupied the biggest barracks in Dublin.

Although the Uprising itself seemed to have been settled with the execution of the rebel leaders, the war in Ireland had gone underground. The word was that the republicans were consolidating, putting together an army bigger and better than the last one. Only an idiot would believe the determined Irish would do otherwise.

As a result of this, British Army active duty was essentially patrolling the streets, making sure that the rebels could see who was boss. This was a task that Billy and his chums took up with some gusto. They said they were angry at the Irish for deflecting attention from the Great War but Clive could see they were angry because they believed that the soft job of babysitting the Paddys made them second-class soldiers. Sometimes they were given information about rebel houses, and they attacked them, dragging the owners out and interning them for questioning. Other times, keen to justify themselves, they simply wandered the streets in uniformed gangs attacking anyone they didn't like the look of.

Clive knew that his job as post boy meant that most of the other young men had him down as a shirker. Sometimes Clive pretended he would prefer the guns and the street squabbles, but in truth, he was not cut out for fighting and he knew it.

Patrol duties aside, the soldiers were encouraged to stay inside the confines of the barracks as much as possible. All their needs were provided for within its walls. There were extensive exercise yards, games rooms, canteens—they even showed movies in the mess hall on Saturday nights to encourage the soldiers to stay on site.

Generally, Clive was happy to do this. However, on this sunny summer day, with the prospect of another afternoon listening to Billy and his friends bragging about rifle-butting rebels, he decided to go out into the city. He wanted to clear his head—empty it of all the war talk. He wanted to see if he could feel "normal" again.

Clive waited until the others had gone down to the recreation hall, then he went back to his bunk. He put on a blue cotton shirt over his army trousers and stuffed a woolen peaked cap in his pocket in case of rain. He didn't wear his army coat.

After signing out at the front entrance, Clive followed the River Liffey until he reached the center of town. The sun was warming the back of his neck as he walked across along the busy streets. He noted how many of them were still decimated from all the bombing. On foot, Dublin seemed a lot like the East End, with street sellers with their goods piled high in strollers, on wheelbarrows, or on anything else they could transport them in. There were gangs of youths in flat caps smoking on every street corner, just like at home. However, although it looked the same, it felt different. Menacing.

Clive began to grow nervous. The people, the crowded noisy streets were the same as home yet he did not belong here. He was an intruder. He began to believe he was being followed. There was a man in a tweed Gatsby hat he had passed when he was leaving the barracks, and there he was now again, smoking on a street corner over to his left. Or was it the same man at all? Maybe he was being paranoid. Clive's nerves began to get the better of him. Any one of these ordinary-looking men could be following him, waiting to spike him with a knife or pull a gun on him. Clive kept walking quickly, careful not to make eye contact with anybody lest they guess from his face that he was a British soldier. Part of him wanted to turn and go back to the barracks but it was too late. In any case, he told himself, he was just being silly. The thought of being imprisoned for another single day with Billy and his cohorts drove him forward up a side road toward a pretty square of quiet parkland.

Away from all the people, Clive started to relax. The man in the hat was nowhere to be seen. He had been imagining it after all. This was a grand part of town, full of Georgian buildings. It felt affluent here, quiet. English, but in a posh way. Clive stopped outside the National Gallery. His mum had once took him on the tube down to the National Gallery in London. She liked to think she was a bit posh, his Mum. He had not liked it much, but he remembered it was quiet in there, peaceful, like a church. That had been boring to him as a child but today it seemed like the sort of place he'd like to be. There was an old woman selling apples from a baby carriage at the entrance gate and Clive reached into his pocket for a tuppence and bought one from her. "Ta, love," he said and she gave him a toothless grin.

This place was all right after all.

He headed toward the door of the gallery with a slight swagger to his step. As he entered the gallery Clive realized that, for the first time since he had been drafted into the army six months ago, he felt somewhat free.

EILEEN WAS LEAVING FOR WORK. SHE STRAIGHTENED HER HAT in the hall mirror, then cocked her ear toward the narrow stairs to listen for her brother. It was force of habit. More than a year later, she still expected Padraig to call down, "Don't forget to bring me home an apple, Eileen!"

Every day she had brought her brother home an apple from the lady with the baby carriage outside Merrion Square. Nobody else got one. Just him.

It had been over a year since he had been killed and she still could not believe her darling brother was dead. She kept thinking he was just in another room. Padraig had taken part in the attack on Mount Street during the Easter Rising. It was mostly English soldiers who had died that day. More than two hundred of them and only a few from their side. Padraig had been unlucky.

Padraig was her older brother, but only by nine months. They were called "Irish twins." They had slept curled up together in the same narrow bed until they were nine and ten. Even after that Padraig and Eileen were inseparable. When he joined the Republican Brotherhood it had seemed to his younger sister like a sort of a game. He was so excited, a boy playing at war. She believed he would be safe. How could she have possibly thought otherwise? Her parents were confident, too, that the older men would look after him. The organizers of the revolution were honorable men; poets, intellectuals, idealists. Two of the leaders had come to the house after he was killed. They held their caps in their laps and cried. "He died an honorable death," they said. "You should be proud." But honor and pride wouldn't bring him back. Dublin was being razed to the ground. Her brother was just another dead boy under the rubble.

Their younger brother, Seamus, who was seventeen, cried tears of confusion that quickly turned to rage. He had wanted to leave that night with the rebel leaders and join the cause, but they would not take him with them.

"They're decent men," her father said after they left. Her mother said nothing.

Later, Eileen had stood beside her mother at the kitchen table as they peeled potatoes. They cried quietly. Tears ran down their faces in streams as they sobbed silently. Together but apart, they scooped up the hems of their aprons to dry their faces.

If there was anger about Padraig's death it was buried deep. The rebel war had thrown a veil of quiet sadness over the O'Haras' home. The cause he fought and died for was bigger than any individual loss. They knew that.

Eileen called out good-bye to her parents and younger brother before walking out the door and then straight out onto the quays. Their house was in the city center, not far from the museum where she worked—less than half an hour at a ladies' pace across town. The inner city had been ruined by the war, and every time Eileen passed by Sackville Street, where the heaviest fighting took place, she thought of Padraig. Today, however, with the sun shining, Eileen felt a lightness come over her. For the first time since her brother died, she had the sense he might be watching over her. She stopped and checked herself briefly in a shop window and as a man passed behind her in the glass, she imagined it was Padraig's spirit.

Then she turned up the side street and walked the back route to Leinster Lawn and the National Gallery, where she worked.

The gallery was quiet that day. Eileen was in the cloakroom when she turned and saw the figure of a young man in the entrance hall with his back to her. She heard the crunch of an apple being bitten and her stomach lurched. *Padraig? No. Padraig is dead.*

The young man turned. He was about her age, large blue eyes and quite delicate features, almost like a girl. His hair was very short and dark. He looked lost. Not many young men came in here. Certainly not on their own. He was wearing ordinary clothes, not the expensive fashions worn by foreign art students.

"Can I help you?" she asked him.

He seemed nervous and for a moment she thought he might walk straight back out the door. Then he seemed to gather himself and smiled. He had a broad smile. Surprising.

"I dunno," he said. "Can you?"

Ah. English. Cockney? She couldn't quite tell.

"Not unless you want to check your coat," she said.

"I don't have a coat," he said, "although I suppose you could take my hat."

"Well, if you come over here," she said from behind her counter, "I might just do that."

He walked across, then handed it to her. She put it beneath the counter and handed him a tag.

"Thanks," he said, self-consciously patting his hair, "although I thought you might like to show me around the place as well?"

Cheeky. Eileen didn't mind that. She was capable of a bit of banter. She had worked in a teahouse on Sackville Street before it was destroyed during the Uprising. She had loved the gossip there, the repartee with the customers. There was always lots of fellas, too, making a fuss of her, telling her she was pretty. There had been none of that since Padraig died; no time for romance, for fun.

"Well then, sir, how on earth would you know what a nice Irish girl like me might like and what I wouldn't like?"

The young man's face fell. She had upset him.

"I'm only joking," she said. The English were so different, the way they talked and everything? Taking everything you said at face value. So serious. Eileen had met a lot of English among the tourists who came into the gallery. Her brothers and cousins, her whole family were fighting the war against them, but they had never met an Englishman. Not properly.

Eileen smiled, just to make the young man feel better, then realized that she meant it. He seemed so nice. "Look here," she said. "I'm on my break in half an hour. If you come back to me then, I'll show you around if you like."

"I'd like that very much," he said.

Eileen let out a little laugh as he stood there in front of her, just smiling that broad smile. She nodded to remind him to hurry along and let her get on with her work. As he scuttled off into another room, she found she could not stop smiling herself.

CLIVE DIDN'T USUALLY HAVE THE CONFIDENCE TO APPROACH girls out of the blue like that, especially not ones as pretty as this one. She had hair the color of hazelnuts that fell in neat waves to her shoulder, and a sweet face with huge slanted eyes that put him in mind of a kitten. Perhaps it was the fact that he was away from home that had given him his brazen edge or perhaps it was a soft look he saw in her green eyes. Whatever it was, he was glad he had approached her.

Eileen started to walk him through the gallery.

"I only have half an hour break," she said, "so we'd better be quick because there are a lot of paintings!"

"How many?" he said. He didn't care, but thought he should be polite.

"Over two hundred," she announced with a flourish of her arms, "or maybe three—or four perhaps? Now, pay attention!"

He thought she must be joking. He hoped she was joking.

"This first room is part of the Dargan Wing"—she gave a little curtsy—"and here we have a very fine picture of a very grand man in a blue coat. As you can see he is wearing red britches . . ."

"Yes, I can see that," Clive said, trying to keep up. "Very impressive."

"Isn't it, though? And here," she said, sliding her feet over to the next painting, "is a magnificent painting of a very tall man in a hat."

"Very grand indeed," Clive said. "Who is it by?"

"I have no idea," she said. "I am a coat-check girl, not a curator."

She was funny. More than that, Eileen had an open, familiar manner that made Clive feel as if she had known him for years. He had not thought he was lonely but now, in the company of this earthy young woman, Clive realized that he had been craving the gentleness of female company.

For the next half hour they teased each other through the gallery until it was time for her to go back to work.

Clive did not want to leave her, but he was afraid to ask about seeing her again. He had not told her he was a British soldier.

As he was going to leave, she held out her hand.

"By the way, my name is Eileen," she said.

"Clive Postlethwaite," he said, taking it. Her hand was tiny and soft. Her handshake was firm and warm and made him feel safe. He didn't want to let it go.

She let out a small laugh. "That's some name."

"It's dreadful," he said. "Blame my father."

"It's distinctive," she said.

"But *not* distinguished," he added—letting her know he was not illiterate.

"Well, Mr. Postlethwaite. I hope you enjoyed your tour of the National Gallery and might call in to see us again, when you are next in town." Then she paused and added; "I can tell you're not from around here. Are you staying in Dublin long?"

Was she hinting that she knew he was a soldier? Clive was afraid to push it one way or another, so he just said, "For a while anyway," then tipped his cap and backed out the door, still looking at her, smiling.

Clive dreamed of Eileen every night after that. When he closed his eyes before he went to sleep in his cold, hard bunk each night he conjured up her face and remembered some of the silly things she had said about the paintings. He held his own hands together under the thin, wool blanket and imagined one of them was hers. The comfort of her imagined touch helped him sleep.

On his next day off, Clive went back to the gallery.

"Hullo, stranger," she said. "Ooh, look at you. You have a coat on."

It was his army coat, the one he had traveled from London

wearing. Clive had pinned a small piece of fabric over his stripes to make it look less military. He had worn it so that she might guess what he was and make up her own mind. It also meant he could bring the photograph with him. In any case, this time he had been less nervous leaving the barracks, less worried about being followed. Perhaps that was because he knew where he was going. The roomy inside pocket of his coat meant he also had a place to carry his photograph.

On an impulse one night he had written on the back of it: *To Eileen O'Hara. Your sweetheart, Clive Postlethwaite.* It was a foolish fantasy, making her into his sweetheart like that, but it made him feel happy. He justified to himself that perhaps one day, if the opportunity ever arose and he wanted to present her with it, at least the picture would be ready.

In any case, Clive decided that today he would ask Eileen to step out with him. She would say yes. She liked him, he was certain of it. He would take her to the pictures, or for tea somewhere nice. He had money. He had plenty of money to treat a girl right. Why not? It didn't matter to him that she was Irish, and she knew that he was an Englishman all right. He didn't have to tell her he was a soldier. Not yet, at least, not until she asked. He would ask her out today.

"And a hat this time, too," he said, handing over his cap again. "It's cold out there today."

"You're too soft," she said.

She was teasing him but he didn't know what to say back. He smiled, and tried not to look as nervous as he was feeling. Perhaps he wouldn't ask her today. Perhaps it would be presumptuous of him to ask at all.

"Do you have a break again?" he said. "I thought we might tackle some of the upstairs rooms?"

As soon as he opened his mouth the words just came out easily. That was the way it was with her. As if they were old friends, even though they barely knew each other.

"Really?" she said. "You want to look at more dusty old portraits? I'm on a half day. We can go for coffee if you like? There is a place on Westmoreland Street, Bewley's. It's not far."

"I don't much care for coffee," he said. *Stupid! Stupid!* No wonder he had never had a sweetheart. Why was he such a fool? He would walk to the ends of the earth with her!

But Eileen was not so easily put off.

"Well, if you care for *me* you can sit and watch me drink it."

She knew that he cared for her! She knew and she still wanted to go along with him! He was in heaven! This is what heaven felt like!

"I can do one better and buy it for you."

"Well, Clive"—she remembered his name!—"you can buy me two. Seeing as how you don't care for it, I'll drink yours as well."

They walked back down toward the city center. How different it all looked with Eileen beside him. These were her streets. There was no danger, no menace—just sidewalks he was walking along with her. Just buildings looking down on them both. Just people passing them by. Eileen chatted away about her family. About a brother with a funny Paddy name who had been killed in the Uprising. About her parents and how quiet they both were since he had died, and her uncles, who were all republican rebels. Clive didn't care about any of that. He was only half-listening to what she was saying. He wanted to take her hand, but he didn't dare. With each step her words washed over him in a sweet, light, lilting voice as he contemplated what bliss it would be to feel her small hand balled up in his again. To feel connected to her, grounded by her. Clive felt as if he had been floating through a fog of his own fear ever since joining the army. When he was with Eileen, the fear melted away.

As they were about to cross the road to Bewley's, Eileen nudged him from his reverie by saying, "Clive, do you know that man?"

Instinctively, he looked around.

"Don't look directly," she said, her voice a nervous whisper. "He's just ahead of us, across the road. There on the corner. In the cap . . ."

Clive's stomach lurched as he saw the man he had thought was following him two weeks earlier. Smoking. He was watching them both. Waiting.

"I think he's been following us," Eileen said. "I know him. He's in the Brotherhood. Follow me."

She quickly led him up a side street. Out of the corner of his eye Clive saw the waiting man throw his cigarette to one side and start to move. From behind the man two others suddenly appeared and they began to march determinedly across the road, waving aside trams and traffic. Eileen grabbed Clive's hand and they ran. She pulled him up another long, thin street and into a network of side alleys until, at the side of a tenement, she pulled him into what was little more than a hole in the wall. She crushed in next to him and signaled not to say a word. Clive was terrified. Not so much of the men and what they would do to him, but of the danger he had put this young woman into.

He did not know how long they stood there in silence. Five minutes or twenty. Their bodies crushed up as close as bodies could be. He could feel her heartbeat pounding through his shirt. He could smell her breath. Sweet, like she had eaten an apple. He longed to kiss her, but he had no right. Less of a right than ever, now.

After a while they heard the men's voices, echoing in the alleyway, sounding closer than they were.

"It's impossible," one of them said. "It's a bloody maze down here. They could have gone anywhere."

"We'll get him again. He left the same time two weeks ago. He's worth watching out for anyway."

"What about the girl?"

"Leave well alone. She's Padraig O'Hara's younger sister. That family has had enough grief without our adding to it."

Then Clive and Eileen heard their boots crunch away back toward the main street.

After they were sure the men were gone, Clive started to breathe. He didn't know what to say, other than, "I suppose coffee is canceled now?" He was trying to be clever, light, to break the terrible tension, but then Eileen started to cry.

"I'm sorry," he said. "We can still go for coffee if you like . . ."

"No," she said. "Bloody bastard war . . ." Then she reached up to his neck and drew him down into a passionate kiss.

As she kissed him Eileen continued to cry. The salt of her tears washed through their lips and into his mouth. They ran down his throat and into his belly; her tears grounded him and made him feel brave. Brave enough to stop this before it got out of hand.

He rubbed his face against her soft cheek, then gently pulled away saying, "We can't do this."

"Please, Clive," she said. Putting her arms around his neck, she looked up at him and said, "I feel so alone."

He wanted to tell her that he felt the same way. To ask her to pledge that they could be there for each other so that they would never be lonely again.

But he didn't. Couldn't. They could not be together. Not now. Maybe in the future? Who knew what this war in Ireland and the bigger war would bring?

They parted at the corner of the alleyway with no good-byes. Just the hollow, disappointed silence of the almost loved.

On his way back to the barracks, it began to rain and Clive reached into the inside pocket of his coat for his hat. His hand felt upon the studio picture of himself in its velvet wallet.

He cursed himself for not having given it to Eileen. He wanted her to have it. Even if they could not be together, she was his sweetheart now. She was the woman who should have his photograph.

He was so angry with himself that he almost threw the wretched thing away, but then Clive thought of his father and how adamant he was that he pose for them. The photograph wasn't for his mother, or his fictitious sweetheart. It was for him. So that he would know that some part of him, even if it was just a picture, might survive the war intact. Clive put the photograph back in his coat pocket and trudged up the quays back toward the Royal Barracks.

November 11, 1918

W HEN NEWS OF THE ARMISTICE CAME THROUGH, THAT THE war was ended, it was like the Royal Barracks Dublin was set on fire with joy.

Clive's first thought was of Eileen. In the months that had passed since that day on Westmoreland Street, Clive had thought about her every day. The dream of seeing her again had kept him going through the grueling, repetitive everyday life of a soldier. When he heard about the armistice Clive's first thought was, *Perhaps now we can be together?* Immediately he remembered that it was the Great War that had ended, not "their war." The Irish war, the war they were all engaged in, was only beginning. In the past few months alone there had been ambushes of British soldiers all over the country, outbreaks of violence. He never left the confines of the barracks anymore. The hatred toward the English was escalating, becoming more apparent with each passing day. They had not quashed the rebellion. The Irish were more determined than ever to get their country back.

Nonetheless, the soldiers in Ireland were as happy to hear of the end to the Great War as were their counterparts across the world. So the roar of victory ran rampantly through the corridors and dormitories, mess halls and recreation rooms of the Royal Barracks. The noise was so loud, the shouts of joy so fierce that stable boys were worried the horses would bolt—although it seemed that even their frightened neighing was celebratory, too.

The people of Dublin flooded into the streets. They were ecstatic that the hundreds and thousands of Irishmen who were away fighting in British regiments were to be returned to them.

Peace! However, the officers in the Royal Barracks encouraged a more cautious approach. Predicting the effect of thousands of drunk triumphant soldiers on the streets of Dublin, they bought in kegs of beer and prompted the men to stay on site with their celebrations as much as possible. They couldn't lock them up, not on a night like this, but they could encourage them to stay inside the barracks walls.

Billy was wild with triumphant one-upmanship, screaming and punching the air while shouting, "We won! We beat the bastards!"

Explaining that the Armistice was more a decision for peace than a body-for-body count was pointless. He was displaying the same conquering relish as if he had personally beaten someone at arm-wrestling.

As the night went on the men got drunker and drunker and the celebratory spirit began to turn.

While Clive had not drunk as much as the others, he had had more than he was used to. He felt that he deserved better. The ending of this war had done little more than remind him that the war that was keeping him apart from Eileen, apart from his family, was still going on.

He had thought he was getting off lightly being sent here, but it turned out they had drawn the short straw. He could never say that to the others. They would not understand.

It was late and dark and the corner of the barracks that they occupied had quieted down. Clive found himself with Billy, Paul, and Jack—two of their buddies, standing under the grand cathedral-like arches near the front gates. They were smoking in the crisp night air, winding down from the party. They were about to turn in for the night when Billy cocked his ear to the clear November sky and said, "Wait—can you hear that?"

The others listened. It was surprisingly quiet. Some music was playing off in the distance somewhere. Nothing like the street cacophony of earlier.

"Paddy music," he said. Billy started to pace. He was getting himself worked up. "They're playing rebel music. That fucking diddly-yi shit . . ." Clive started to get nervous. Billy was a lunatic. What was he driving at?

"They're doing it deliberately," Billy said, getting lucid in his anger now, "disrespecting us, and deliberately trying to wind us up . . ." Billy started to walk toward the wall. "Can you hear it, men? Fucking fiddles and that! Irish music on a day like today? It's not right . . . I'm going to put a stop to it . . ."

Billy grabbed his rifle then started to run toward the gate. The other three followed, more out of fear of what the hell "Mad Billy" was going to do. The soldier at the gates was half-drunk himself and barely noticed the group rushing out onto the quays.

"This way men," Billy said, half-running, half-marching now in that frightening military bully-boy stance he had when he was leading one of his unofficial "Paddy attacks."

With unnatural instinct, Billy came to a small house. There was music flooding out through the open front door. Complex whistles and fiddle arrangement, an almost tribal drumbeat holding it all together. Whoops of laughter—there was a party going on. Just like everywhere else in the city.

Billy was hopping from foot to foot. He was itching for a fight. Clive got a really bad feeling.

"Now, men." Billy was addressing them like he was an officer, trying to make himself sound reasonable and sane. "This is a rebel house. We know that because they are playing rebel music . . ."

The other two were actually listening. They were as thick as Billy. Clive knew he had to try to reason with him.

"Billy, I don't think this is a good idea. It's just a party . . ."

"It's a rebel party, Clive. Look," Billy said, closing his eyes. "I know you don't like the action, Clive, and that's fair enough. But you've got to admit, this is proper unacceptable . . ."

"No," Clive said. "What is unacceptable, Billy, is just barging in on people in their homes like this. For all you know this family could be celebrating the end of the war, just like us. There are thousands of brave Irishmen fighting in the Great War, far more than there will ever be rebels, you know that . . ." Billy looked at him openmouthed; clearly he knew no such thing.

Clive was making sense. Crucially, he wasn't scared of Billy.

"Maybe he's right," Paul said. "Maybe we should just go back . . ." Jack half-turned, encouraging a retreat. "You are all fucking cowards," Billy said, but Clive could sense he might be thinking better of it. Then the music stopped and a lone man's voice started to sing. Strong and loud, it came threading out the front door, its lyrics clearer in song than if they had been spoken in an Irish brogue.

> At the Windmill hills, and at Enniscorthy,
> The British fencibles they ran like deers,
> But our ranks were scattered and sorely battered,
> For the want of Kyan and his Shelmaliers.

Billy raised his eyebrows briefly at Clive, as if vindicating himself entirely of any ensuing carnage, then he charged into the house with the other two close behind him. Clive stood for a second, shocked. Aside from their drunk, violent stupidity, if this was a rebel house the occupants might all have guns, and only Billy was armed. If it wasn't, the consequences could be equally catastrophic. Although they were half-witted idiots, Clive could not leave his fellow soldiers behind to their own reckless fate.

In the sixty seconds it took him to follow them in, Billy's impetuous move had already created an ugly scene. There were at least thirty, maybe forty people crammed into the small room. Cowering up against the edges of the room were the women and children. At the center, sitting on low stools, were six or seven musicians, one of them little more than a child, another an old man, but three of them were big men. The one with the accordion was sitting directly in front of Billy. He looked hefty enough to fell any man with a flick of his finger, except that he had a gun pointed to his head. Gathered in all corners were at least five other men. Billy was way out of his depth and he knew it. He started screaming at the top of his voice, "GET DOWN! GET DOWN ON THE GROUND YOU REBEL BASTARDS!" Paul and Jack were standing next to him, their hands resting on their waists, reaching for the bayonet knives they had left in their lockers the night before when they were cleaning out their weapons after drill. Their faces were pasted with fear. A drunk, panicking Billy was just about as bad as it got. The idiot would shoot somebody, anybody, then the Paddys would overpower them and rip them to shreds.

"I WILL FUCKING SHOOT THE LOT OF YOU. I SAID PUT YOUR HANDS BEHIND YOUR HEAD AND GET DOWN ON THE GROUND!"

The women started gathering themselves into hunched balls on the stone floor over the children.

The room was so small there wouldn't be enough space for them all on the floor. Clive decided he could use that to reason with Billy.

"That won't work, mate," Clive said, looking across at him. The quivering crazy fear in his eyes gave way slightly. He was relieved somebody else was talking. His mate Clive was on his side.

"Look," Clive said, "there isn't enough space for them all on the ground." Billy let out a snort and hoisted his gun up a few inches, tightening his grip. "We won't be able to move about," Clive added. "Why don't you let the women and children go? Then there'll just be us and the men."

Billy shifted his feet, nearly stepping on a child's hand. He nodded and looked across at Clive. The other two soldiers were just standing there with their mouths open.

"Yeah, Clive. You're right . . ." Then, as if it were his idea, he said, "We're not savages, are we? We're soldiers."

"That's right, Billy," Clive said. "We're soldiers."

Billy took a deep breath, then nodded at the one woman still standing and said, "Go on then, get out. BUT NO FUNNY BUSINESS!" he roared, prodding the accordion player's cheek with the end of his rifle. The big man flinched. His eyes were dead with a blocked rage. If the gun went off by accident, which given Billy's shaking hands was more than possible, all hell would break loose. The women quickly gathered themselves up from the floor, some of the men reaching down to help them. "GET YOUR HANDS WHERE I CAN SEE THEM!" There was some slight shoving and chaos as the women tried to find their way out of the room, past the men who were crowded around the narrow doorway. Billy's nerves were really getting the better of him. "OI! WAKE UP, CLIVE—HELP ME OUT HERE, MATE, WILL YOU?" Clive didn't want to take his eyes off Billy for a second. As long as he was looking at him, Clive felt he could control him. There was sweat pouring down Billy's face; his eyes were blinking with the heat of the crowded room. If he became distracted for a minute, even just to wipe his face, Clive might be able to reach across and take the gun off him. Billy might even give it to him to hold. He looked across at Billy's open jacket and saw that Billy's bayonet was still in its holder.

Billy nodded at Clive to help get some of the women out. It was important to let him think he was still in charge, so he turned his attention to the figure standing next to him, who seemed stubbornly not to be leaving with the others.

It was Eileen.

Clive felt the whole room gather in around him, as if suddenly he might melt into the floor. She didn't say anything, just looked at him. It was Eileen, but not like he had seen her before. She was a version of herself: hard, angry, determined. She was the last woman there.

"Get rid of that bitch, Clive, will you?"

Clive didn't know what to do. He was starting to panic himself now. Whatever awful thing was about to happen, he didn't want Eileen hurt, so he looked at her and said, "Please leave the house, ma'am."

"I will not," she said. "I most certainly will not kowtow to any ignorant English bastard who comes walking into my house . . ."

She was angry, but it was the Eileen he knew, all right. Feisty. Unafraid.

"Are you going to let her talk to you like that?" Billy said. His arm was getting tired holding the gun. He wanted to get out of there now. He didn't even want to shoot anyone anymore. He had a headache. He wanted to go to bed. He wanted his mother.

"Jesus, Clive—you are some poofter, mate. Lift her up, she's only a woman! Just get her out . . ."

"Please," Clive pleaded with her.

"Or WHAT?" she said. She spat the word out at him. Cruel but beautiful. Why was this happening? Eileen had been right in the alleyway. War spoiled everything. There was no bravery, no nobility. Only ugliness and confusion.

"Or I will shoot your fucking friend here, you stupid bitch!" In the entertainment of watching Clive unable to get a small woman out of the room, Billy had dropped his guarded stance. The accordion player seized the opportunity, and in a flash turned and reached over to Billy's waistband and pulled the bayonet clean out of its sheath. Clive immediately, instinctively ran across and grabbed the gun. So now Clive was holding the gun and the huge accordion player had Billy across his lap with his own huge knife trained on his throat.

"SHOOT HIM—FUCKING SHOOT THE BASTARD, CLIVE—I DON'T CARE IF I DIE . . ."

The big man gave Billy a swift slap to the side of the head, which rendered him immediately unconscious.

Clive cocked the rifle, then opened it, removed the bullets, and handed them to Eileen, who put them in her apron pocket. She then took the gun from him.

"Thank you," she said. "We'll hang on to that. It will come in handy in the times to come, no doubt."

"What happens next?" Clive asked. He was trying hard not to address her directly. They could not be seen to know each other, although he felt certain one of the men was the one who had followed them to Bewley's.

"What happens next," said the accordion player, addressing him with cool determination, "is that we slit each of you from gullet to gut." Paul collapsed to his knees. Jack started to cry and plead. "Then we throw your bodies in the Liffey, invite the ladies back, and continue with the party. What do you say to that, lads?"

The rest of the men did not reply to him but their intention was clear. They stared across at Clive and the two pleading young soldiers, none of them moving or saying a word. The Irishmen's hatred was palpable. Clive felt sick with fear for his life, but he was not surprised by their reaction and he could not argue against it. The Irishmen's disgust was justified. The soldiers' fate was set.

"You will do no such thing, Kieran Maheady," Eileen said, in a voice as casual as if she were reprimanding a child. "I know everyone in this room by name and reputation. You are, every one of you, honorable men, not marauding murderers. These"—she looked at the pitiful figures of the two crying soldiers and Billy, still unconscious in the big man's lap—"fools, you could barely call them soldiers, aren't worth the bloodshed. Especially not tonight, of all nights . . ."

"They attacked our home!" one man called out.

"They can't just come in here and terrorize our women and children whenever they like!"

"We've had enough!" another called out. "The English bastards came looking for us. I say we send a message back to them!"

"No," Eileen said, her tone even more determined and certain than before.

"Padraig," she addressed the first man who had spoken, "haven't you a cousin fighting over in France?" He coughed awkwardly in reply. "You can all be as shifty about it as you like, but the truth is half our number are away fighting in the army alongside the British while we're fighting against them. I know at least five men here have family members fighting in the British Army whose mothers and sisters are celebrating tonight. We have our war for independence from the British, and we will surely fight it, but not tonight and not in this house."

Then she turned to Clive.

"Will you give me your guarantee that this"—she nodded over at Billy—"ignorant savage will be adequately punished when you get back to the barracks?"

Clive immediately took the bait.

"He'll be going back without his weapon, miss. The army looks very poorly on missing weaponry. He will probably be court-martialed and executed."

A couple of the Irishmen raised their eyebrows in approval. It was a lie. Billy would tell his officer that he had been overwhelmed by rebels and that they had stolen his rifle from him. It was happening all over the city every day.

Kieran looked behind at the others.

"What do ye say, lads? Will we let them go and get back to the party?"

The men looked across at Eileen and thought of their wives and mothers outside in the cold waiting, then gave him the nod.

Kieran rolled Billy off his lap and picked up his accordion.

By the time Paul and Jack were dragging Billy by the shoulders out the door, the music had already started again. The women and children were standing on the street.

"Was he shot?" one of the women said about Billy. "I didn't hear a gun."

"No, Mammy," Eileen said. "Don't be worrying now. It's all over." She had a younger man standing with her. The other brother Eileen had spoken about? He had that same hazel hair and her eyes. "Uncle Kieran only gave him a cuff."

"Thanks be to God you're all safe," she said, patting her hand on her heart. "I was afraid for my life."

Clive held back, hoping to speak with Eileen. "English bastard!" the boy shouted at him.

"Now Seamus," Eileen said, "no need for poor language. Go back inside."

"I'm not leaving you here with him."

"Go back in, I'm telling you, and see that Mammy and Daddy are all right."

He glowered at Clive and went back into the house.

Eileen looked at the ground. He did not know if she was angry or sad. If she wanted him to stay or go. She had given so much of herself, so easily to him before. Her humor, her friendship—now that was all gone. All that was left was the pain of what might have been. Of lost hope.

"I'm sorry," he said.

She just shook her head, keeping her face to the ground, hidden.

Clive put his hand in his pocket and pulled out the photograph. Her small hands were clenched tightly together in front of her chest. Her body was set rigid. Afraid at even the suggestion he might want to touch her, Clive carefully slid the picture into her apron pocket, on top of the bullets.

Still, she didn't look up.

"I love you, Eileen O'Hara," he said. Then he walked away before she started to cry.

LATER THAT NIGHT, EILEEN'S YOUNGER BROTHER SEAMUS picked up Clive's gun and said he would not put it down until Ireland was free from British rule.

Dublin 2017

To Eileen O'Hara.
Your sweetheart, Clive Postlethwaite.
September 1917

Bridie sat with the picture in her hand, astonished. Auntie Eileen in love with a British soldier? That couldn't be right! She was an activist in her day. She had fought alongside her brother Seamus. Although she rarely spoke about it herself, Eileen's name had always been closely associated with the Cause.

The pregnancy was temporarily swept to one side in the magnitude of this revelation. As Bridie tried to puzzle it out, the germ of a memory came into her head. She picked up her phone and rang her father's second cousin, Liam Maheady. He was in his eighties now, but his mind was as sharp as it had ever been. Liam's father, Kieran, had been an active member of the IRA and an oracle about the war. He was long since dead, but everything he knew was passed onto his son. Including his brilliant accordion skills.

Liam was surprised to hear from her, as they would be seeing each other the following day at the 1916 event in the presidential palace.

"Everything all right, Bridie? Are you still all set for the big day?"

She got straight to the point.

"You know that night? When the British soldiers broke into our house?"

"Ah yes. Armistice night."

"Did Eileen know any of the men?"

"How do you mean?"

"Was she friendly with any of them?"

"Jesus, Bridie, I doubt it. They came marauding into the house, brandishing guns and attacking the women and children . . ."

"No, I mean—when we talked about it before, I remembered you saying that Eileen managed to reason with one of the soldiers."

"Ah yes, when she talked them down. There was one that was more intelligent than the others . . ."

"Was he called Clive?"

"Bridie, what are you talking about?"

"The soldier she was talking to that night, the one who gave her the gun that Seamus carried with him, was he called Clive?"

"Jesus, Bridie, do you know something, I think he was? What on earth made you remember that?"

"Nothing," she said. "I'll see you tomorrow."

Bridie took the picture of the young man and laid it down on the dressing table next to the picture of her grand-aunt. They were the same age in the picture. A dashing young soldier and a beautiful young girl.

Eileen had kept his picture all those years. She must have loved him. Perhaps that was why she never married? Eileen was outspoken so her family had always assumed she was not the marrying kind. Maybe, instead, she had loved and lost, like so many war widows. On both sides.

Bridie put both pictures in her pocket. On her way back down the stairs she thought. *Why do the kids have to make everything about them?* She smiled. Because everything *was* about them. This was the present, not so different from the past, after all. A young British soldier was going to be the father of her first grandchild.

Sharon was standing at the sink, washing the dishes. As she lifted her dry wrist up to her eyes, Bridie could see she had been crying. Frank was smoking a cigarette at the back door. Fuming.

"Ring David and tell him he is very welcome to come along with us tomorrow."

"Do you mean it, Mam?"

"Well, if he's going to be the father of my first grandchild, we'd better make him feel welcome."

"B-but it's an insult to our heritage," Frank sputtered, turning rather red in the face.

"Love is love," Bridie said. "It didn't matter then and it doesn't matter now. Tell him he can wear his uniform if he likes," she added, putting on her coat and walking out the door.

"How can you even *say* that?" Frank shouted after her.

She didn't bother answering him. He was young and idealistic. Time would teach her son, as it had taught her, that none of us ever fully knows the rights or wrongs of anything. Especially not where love is concerned.

"Your republican auntie Eileen was in love with a British soldier," she said.

"What?"

"That's right. Dave is the second British soldier in the family." Not strictly true, perhaps, but it left him speechless which was no harm.

Then Bridie walked down to the high street to buy the best double frame she could find.

Hush

Hazel Gaynor

Monday, November 11, 1918
10:58 A.M.

ANNIE RAWLINS STOOPS OVER THE PALE, LIFELESS FORM AT the foot of the bed, her back turned to the narrow lattice window of the station master's cottage. She checks the small watch pinned to her apron and notes the time. Time is everything now. Time is what the infant doesn't have; what none of them have had since the war started. Too often, Annie has seen how everything can change in an instant: a gas attack, a sniper's bullet, a shell explosion, the dreaded telegram from the War Office: *The King commands me to assure you of the true sympathy of His Majesty and the Queen in your sorrow.* Another son, lost. Another mother's heart, shattered. Moments that arrive in a sudden second and roar endlessly on, forever affecting the remaining fragments of a broken life.

She looks at the helpless infant. A child, much longed for. A life, slipping silently away. She takes a deep breath, gathers her thoughts, and draws on all her years of experience.

"Come along now," she urges, working quickly to clear the mouth and nose. "*Breathe*, won't you. You must breathe."

The weak winter sun flickers against the rain-speckled glass at the window, hesitant to come inside. If only it would. Annie is certain that everything would be all right then. "*Everything feels better with the sun on your face. Don't you think, Mam?*" She sees her boys standing by the back door. Jack, the eldest, has his eyes closed. A carefree smile at his lips as the autumn sun bathes his face in a soft buttery glow. So handsome in his uniform. And there's Will, kicking at the dirt, his eyes red with angry tears because he is too young to go. "*It's not fair. I always miss out on the fun.*" She wraps her arms around him, hugging him tight to her, nuzzling her nose into his thick black hair. She is glad of his tears; glad he cannot go. "*It'll all be over by Christmas,*" Jack had said as he'd kissed her good-bye on the station platform.

It'll all be over by Christmas.

For Jack, it was. His war was over before most men had even arrived to fight. She sees his face and hears his voice as clearly as if he were standing beside her now. But he isn't. Never will be. There's only Will now. Out there. *Somewhere in France*. That's what his letters say. How her arms ache to hold him. She would fight for him if she could, would become his bones, his skin, his very breath, if only he could come home safe to her.

Sensing the long shadows cast by her boys' absence and Annie's fear for the infant, the sun creeps quietly away from the station master's cottage. It ducks behind a cloud, drawing the pale yellow light from the room. The fragile life in front of Annie fades with it.

She struggles on. "Come along now," she urges. "You've got to fight. You have to. You must breathe. *Breathe.*"

The infant's appalling silence fills the room like an autumn mist rolling down the valley, drifting away from the tiny form to settle uncomfortably against the framed pictures of stern-looking men and women on the oak chest, against the rose-patterned ewer on the night stand, against the faded hearth rug and the splintered floorboards, against the distempered walls and the blackened grate of the smoldering fire; the simple possessions of a hardworking, loving family. The simple possessions of a man who valued life too much to fight. Annie knows the names they call him. *Conchie. Feather Boy.* She has watched this family's suffering and wishes them no ill. Death doesn't belong here. Not today.

The silence is disturbed momentarily by the mother's soft moans. "My child. Where's my baby? Why doesn't it cry?" Her words drift through the fog of laudanum that clouds her mind, her questions a broken strand of slivered web, searching for an answer to attach themselves to as Annie stares at the limp creature on the bedsheets. The lavender hue of his skin is unbearable.

She looks up. "You have a son, Mrs. Miller." Her voice is firm and calm. "A beautiful baby boy. He is here."

Yet he is not.

His silence is suffocating. Annie pulls roughly at the buttons on her high collar, struggling for breath as she wills the infant to find his. "Come along now," she whispers, her fingers working as firmly as she dare, massaging the paper-thin skin at the place where she knows the smallest of hearts lies idle beneath. "You've got to fight. You have to. You must breathe."

The mute response chills her.

She checks her watch, the relentless sweep of the second hand paying no heed to the drama unfolding in the little room.

Time, and silence, march on.

ACROSS THE NEAT TAPESTRY OF ENGLAND'S HARVESTED FIELDS and berry-rich hedgerows, above the soaring church steeples that pierce the sky, through the quiet countryside, over the white-tipped rushing waves of the English Channel and on, beyond unfamiliar French villages with hopelessly romantic names, the silence reaches out.

Above the scarred fields of Les Gros Faux, a barn owl swoops low over the trenches and dugouts that segment the landscape like broken wickerwork. Only the keenest of ears can detect the rush of air against his ghostly wings. He settles on a single fence post, guarding the torn earth like a sentry.

Beneath him, Private Will Rawlins cannot breathe. Engulfed in a dark hell, his lungs burn with the desperate urge to take a breath. But it will not come.

He remembers the scream of the shell, his officer shouting at him to take cover. "Get down, man! Get down!" Air, rushing past. The dull thud and thump of earth, men, life raining down on him. Now, only silence.

His arms are pinned tight against him. He kicks out with his feet, sending an incomprehensible pain shooting up his right leg. He tries to scream, but something blocks his mouth, his nose. Realizing he is buried, smothered by the ground he had walked on not a moment earlier, he wriggles and writhes in desperation, his frenzied movements unfamiliar to him. He frees a hand, scrabbling at the stinking damp earth on his face, clawing and scratching to get it away, to break out of his tomb, but the earth is heavy and he is weak. Panic and terror take over, dispossessing him of conscious thought as he slips away from this hideous place and drifts toward a dream of autumn mornings knocking conkers from the great horse chestnut tree at the end of the lane. He balances on Jack's broad shoulders, laughing as they both tumble to the ground. He kicks a stone along the neatly furrowed earth, freshly plowed. He tastes the sharp tang of juice from the just-picked blackberries. He catches a minnow in a jar, and marvels at the shimmer and sheen of its scales in the sunlight. He kicks a football. Watches his grandfather light his pipe, the tobacco, mellow and warm. Simple things. A simple life.

And then he hears her. "Come along now." His mother's voice, her breath warm against his cheek. "You've got to fight. You have to. You must breathe. *Breathe*, won't you."

He drifts toward her. "They said it was over. Take me home, Mam. I want to go home."

The church bells were striking the hour of seven when Annie arrived at the Millers' cottage the previous evening. A tall candle burned on the windowsill. Everything was progressing smoothly. "Your baby will be here before that candle burns down, Mrs. Miller," she'd said. But he wasn't. The flame guttered and died. Dawn crept reluctantly into the room. Time marched carelessly on and still the child wouldn't come, not through the endless rise and fall of the laboring woman's pains, not through all the pails of steaming water or the bundles of towels and rags that the young girl had brought when Annie had asked her to; towels and rags that lie scattered about the bed covers now, speckled and spotted with crimson. They remind Annie of the words in Jack's letter. *The poppies are so pretty, Mam. They seem to grow in every field here.* It was the only letter he ever wrote to her. She shivers. Where is the girl with the coal for the fire? It, too, is cold and lifeless.

Behind Annie, beyond the narrow window, village life carries on, the familiar rhythms and patterns, sights and sounds of a Monday morning in Brimsworth: the children skipping and singing their rhymes in the school yard, the clang and clatter from the forge as the great shire horses are fitted with new shoes, the rumble of the wagons, the trill of a bicycle bell. But Annie hears none of this. She hears only the dreadful silence in the small room, and she wants to scream and shout at the injustice of it all. She has delivered a dozen blue babies in her time, but this one is different somehow. This one chills her. This one seems to hold all of their lives in its miniature frozen hands.

She glances over her shoulder as she hears the click of the latch at the door. The girl is back with the coal. She places the bucket down on the hearth and walks toward the bed, her boots heavy against the boards that creak and groan in sympathy with the melancholy she senses in the room. Her face pales. She clasps her hand to her mouth as she watches the midwife at work. Her manner is businesslike, efficient. The girl cannot take her eyes from the lifeless shape on the bed. Like the puddle of wax on the windowsill he is gray and still and stiff.

She glances at her mother and lowers her voice. "Is he dead, Mrs. Rawlins?"

Annie wipes the sweat from her forehead. "No, Beth. He isn't. He just hasn't worked out how to live yet. Go and fetch your father. Tell him to come straightaway." Her words are clipped and insistent. "Quickly."

Beth turns, and runs from the room.

The silence follows, leaving the small bedroom, creeping beyond the open door, tiptoeing quietly through the simply furnished cottage. It stops for a moment to consider a photograph of a young man on the sideboard, fresh-faced and smiling, proud to be in uniform and on his way at last. The much-loved twin brother who had just become an uncle again, and didn't even know it. It moves on, seeping out of the back door, wending its way along the dirt track roads of the village, past the grocer's shop, the pub, the post office, the public baths, the blacksmiths and the coal merchants. The people of Brimsworth go about their business, chatting in doorways, bundling distracted children along the narrow pathways, hanging the Monday wash on sagging lines. They are unaware of the tragedy unfolding in the little cottage on the corner. They are unaware of the great change that is about to fall upon them all.

The silence passes by, touching them with a cool breath. They feel it only as a stiffening in the breeze, pulling their hats over their ears, wrapping scarves and shawls closer about their shoulders. They hurry to be indoors, beside the fire. Only Bill Lacy looks up as he rolls a heavy barrel of ale from the drayman's cart into the deep bowels of the cellar. Only he senses the change on the wind. He stops for a moment and thinks about his son in France. He feels so very far away. He sighs, pushes up his shirtsleeves, and continues with his work. Keeping busy is the only thing he knows how to do. The only way he knows how to help. *Keep the home fires burning.* That's what the song says and that's what he'll do.

The silence pushes on, wandering through the cemetery, slipping easily between the spaces where the fallen fathers and sons of the village will never be laid to rest. It glides toward the church door, peers inside, and pauses to look around.

There he is. The praying man.

It meanders on, settling in the pew beside him, absorbing his muttered words. "Let them live, Lord. Please, let them live."

He repeats his prayer, over and over, until he can speak no more and falls into a wretched silence. He is being punished. He is certain of it. The life of his wife and child being taken in exchange for his because he refused to take up arms.

"Coward," they call him. "Conchie. Feather Boy." Their taunting jeers follow him everywhere. When it had snowed last winter, he didn't see snowflakes, only hundreds of white feathers, tumbling down, smothering him until he couldn't bear to look anymore.

As the village station master, Tom Miller had always been well regarded. His was a position of respect and authority. Now he is ignored. People pass him in the street. Even the young lads who used to ask if they could blow the whistle don't stop to say hello. The men who returned on leave or had been sent home, their bodies shattered and their minds broken beyond repair, men who had seen the very worst of all the horrors, still thought it was better to have done your bit than to have taken a moral stance like Tom and the other conscientious objectors.

"Tom?" A broad hand rests on his shoulder. "Would you not go home? See how she's doing? It might all be over. You might have a baby to welcome into the world."

Tom wipes his nose on the back of his coat sleeve and looks up at the vicar. Such kind eyes. He doesn't judge. He only prays for them all.

"I'm too afraid, Vicar. It'll be my fault if they die. My fault."

The vicar sits down in the pew beside Tom and places his hand on his. It is dry, like paper. Tom flinches under the man's compassionate touch. He wants to pull his hand away, wants to be alone with his fear and his guilt as he has become accustomed. But the vicar pays no heed. He wraps his fingers tight around Tom's and begins to pray. Tom settles onto his knees beside him, closes his eyes, and recites the Lord's Prayer.

After the "Amen," the church falls silent. Even the solitary bird flitting between the rafters high above finds a perch and is still. The figures in the stained glass, the hideous gargoyles, the organ pipes, the crows on the roof outside—they all hold their breath in the desperate hope that the dying infant will find his.

WILL WAS IN THE RESERVE TRENCH WHEN THEY WERE TOLD. They were due to rotate that morning, Eleventh Battalion's turn at the front, and the boys were nervous.

Nobody had slept that night. Shivering in his greatcoat, Will had thought about how anxious he had been to sign up; how keen they had all been to do their bit, to see some action. Bored with the long, cold nights in the reserve and communications trenches, they couldn't wait to get their orders to march to the front line. What fools they were. One of Lord Kitchener's Pals Battalions, formed from the entire village enlisting together, except for Tommy Miller and his misplaced morals. They weren't trained soldiers. Not one of them. They were just naïve boys looking for adventure. Naïve boys who were soon lost and afraid in the reality of war. Over his years of service, Will had seen unimaginable things: awful, agonizing deaths; the rotting corpses of the horses; the metal helmet all that remained of a dear friend. He'd seen men crack under the strain, throw down their rifles, and run from their posts, knowing they would be shot. Anything to prevent the torture of the front. Deserters were shot dead, an example to them all. The battlefield was no place for cowardice. That's what the officers told them. Lacking Moral Fiber. Not Yet Diagnosed, Nervous. Absent Without Official Leave. Missing in Action—there was a label for them all, yet nobody had a label for the simple truth: Afraid.

Will was sharing a smoke and drinking the weak trench tea with Privates Henderson and Walsh. They used to share a pint in the Blacksmith's Arms. Now they shared their smokes and their fears. They'd become like brothers to him. They alone were the reason he came back from leave, to give the next in line his turn back home with his loved ones.

Davey Walsh was teasing Will about a letter he had received from home. "Another letter from Martha Lacy? Trust you to fall for the publican's daughter. Always after a free pint you are, Rawlins. Never knew anyone for missing their round as much as you."

"Bugger off, Walsh. I haven't fallen for her. She keeps sending me socks, that's all. It's not like I'm going to marry her or anything."

"She seems to think you are. Our Mary says she's going around telling everyone you'll ask her when you get home."

Will laughed. "I'll ask her to pull me a pint. That's about all I'll be asking her. Anyway, you're only jealous 'cause nobody writes to you." He took a long drag of his smoke.

"Who needs letters? Had more than my share of French girls at the billets in town. Partial to a bit of English sausage, they are."

Will threw his packet of matches at Walsh's head. "French tarts, the lot of 'em. You want to watch it, Walsh. You'll be riddled with the clap."

"Might get me out of this shithole for a while. I'd be glad of a dose of the clap for a week if it would get me out of here and into a field hospital." He stubbed his cigarette out against his helmet. "Maybe I'll start writing to Martha Lacy. If I'm friendly enough maybe she'll pull more than my pint when I get home."

Will was about to punch Walsh in the stomach when a signal corps officer entered the dugout and handed the lieutenant a message. Will sensed something shift in the atmosphere, a change on the wind. "Shh," he hissed to the others. "Something's happening. Listen."

They huddled together, sipping their tea, listening to the muffled voices.

Will took a long drag on his Woodbine as Lieutenant Cavendish ducked beneath the wooden struts and leant against the sandbags. He scrutinized the man's usually emotionless face. His cheeks were pale, his eyes glistened, the muscles in his face contracted, his jaw tightening and relaxing, tightening and relaxing, stirred by whatever was written on the piece of paper he held in his hand. He cleared his throat. "Gather round, men. I have important news."

All the joking and larking around was instantly forgotten. This was serious. There was a shuffling and rearranging of crates and personnel as the men gathered around, glad of the extra body heat as they squashed together in the cramped space. The lieutenant cleared his throat again, stiffened his back, held his head up high. He straightened the piece of paper and started to read. The tremble in his voice was audible to them all.

"Official Radio from Paris—6:01 A.M., November 11, 1918. Marshal Foch to the Commander in Chief. 1. Hostilities will be stopped on the entire front beginning at 11 o'clock, November 11th. 2. The Allied troops will not go beyond the line reached at that hour on that date until further orders. It is signed by Marshal Foch at 5:45 A.M. this morning." He paused to let the words settle around them all. "That's it men. *La guerre est fini.* The war is over."

Will heard the words over and over again. *Hostilities will be stopped . . . The war is over.* He wanted to say something, but nothing would come, nothing seemed right. He looked around. All the men were frozen, mouths open. Henderson threw up. Parker laughed, quietly at first, then hysterically, uncontrollably.

Walsh stood up. "Well, fuck me, lads." He turned to the lieutenant. "We're really going home?"

The lieutenant nodded, his thick mustache concealing a smile. "Yes, Walsh. We are bloody well going home!" Will couldn't take his eyes off the piece of paper in the lieutenant's hands. He watched, mesmerized, as this imposing man folded the paper with astonishing care and put it in the pocket of his greatcoat, placed his hands behind his back, closed his eyes, and raised his head to the sky. "It is over."

At that, a gradual cheer filtered along the lines of men, growing louder, rippling along the trenches like a great wave of relief. Some lit a smoke, some laughed, some hugged each other as tight as their own mothers would and some crept quietly away to their beds and wept.

It was 0900 hours. Two hours to go. They were still due to relieve the men on the front at 1000 hours.

Will looked at his friends. "Well, I don't know about the rest of you, but I've always liked the idea of a houseboat in the south of France. When will we leave, sir?"

The lieutenant looked serious. "This is just an armistice, Rawlins. A laying down of arms. There's still a long way to go before any treaties are signed, but hopefully you'll be home for Christmas."

Henderson kicked his tin helmet across the ground, knocking over a mug and sending a shower of hot tea over everyone. "Bollocks to that. They said that four years ago, sir." He punched at the sandbags before falling to his knees and sobbing like a child.

There was little else said. They all had their private thoughts as they hunkered down and awaited their orders.

Will picked absentmindedly at the lice in his hair. "I didn't think it would be like this, Archie. Did you?"

"Like what?"

"Like this. The end. I didn't think it would be so quiet. I've thought about it so often, about hearing those words: 'It's over.' I always imagined we would run around naked and kiss each other, but I don't feel like doing any of that. I don't feel like celebrating at all."

"Yeah. I know what you mean. I just feel . . . I don't know . . . empty, I suppose."

Will lit them both a cigarette. "If the war is over, what does that make us now? I've been a soldier for so long I don't think I know how to be anything else. And what about all the men we've lost?" He thought of his brother, Jack. "They're not celebrating, are they, poor bastards. They're not going home."

A short march away, on the banks of the Meuse River, the shelling at the front was still heavy. As news of the Armistice spread, the men agreed to give it one last push, to burn up their guns, to give all they had left. To fight to the very end. A farewell to arms.

At 1000 hours, Eleventh Battalion was moved up to the front line. Shortly afterward, the orders were given to go over the top. As he scrambled over the muddy bank, Will heard the lieutenant's words. "It's over." But it wasn't. He was still running, his rifle cold and heavy in his outstretched arms. The shells still roared overhead. The men still fell around him, dropping like sacks into the filthy French mud, begging for their mothers as death crept too slowly upon them. Nothing had changed. Nothing was over. Christmas would never come around.

Trapped in his dark prison, Will feels his mother's arms wrapped around him, so warm and soft. He hears her, urging him to survive. "Breathe. Come along now. You have to breathe. You have to live."

"BREATHE. COME ALONG NOW. YOU HAVE TO BREATHE. YOU have to live."

Her words are all that disturb the silence in the small cottage bedroom. The clouds have darkened, the gray November day struggling to find its way through the narrow window so that everything seems awash with despair. Annie wants to scream. She wants to put her face to the child's and roar and shout until it roars back at her in outraged defiance. She draws on every aspect of her training and experience, working quickly and efficiently: massaging the chest to stimulate the circulation, breathing for him—short breaths, count to five, massage again. She sees charts and drawings in textbooks. The circulatory system. A diagram of a heart, valves, and arteries. Why won't it start? Why won't he breathe for her? While she works, time seems to pause around her.

She remembers her boys when they were born. Jack, so slight and fair and quiet. Will, all eleven pounds of pink, bawling mass of him, with a shock of hair so black her mother said you could have hidden currants in there and never found them. Jack was always the quiet one, always the first to get the coughs and colds. Will had always thrived. He was a boisterous, noisy boy and brought out the best in his older brother. Annie loved nothing more than to listen to them playing with their cousins in the fields at the back of the house. "Boys will be boys," her mother said whenever they appeared at the back step snotty-nosed and bloody-kneed.

Boys will be boys.

Jack couldn't get to the front soon enough. Teddy, the eldest cousin and a reserve soldier, had gone off first. The other cousins, and Jack, had followed as soon as the call came for volunteers, with Will having to wait until his nineteenth birthday. Annie had never dreaded a birthday so much. He was gone before the last slice of fruitcake was eaten.

It was sometimes too hard to bear, their absence. More than anything, it was the silence and order they had left behind in the rooms of her home that Annie found so unsettling. Beds not slept in. Doors not slammed. Songs not whistled over the breakfast table. She'd had to stop the pendulum on the grandfather clock; the ticking had become so loud it drove her to distraction.

"Make the bloody thing stop, will you, Arthur? Tick, tick, tick all bloody day. It's enough to drive a person daft."

It was unlike Annie to curse. Her husband did the necessary. It was stopped at one minute past eleven. She'd often wondered if that was significant, or if it was as inconsequential as the patch of carpet the clock stood upon. Either way, that clock haunted her. It stood in the corner of the front room, waiting; a constant reminder of the pause they had all felt since the boys left.

"We'll start it up when he's back, love." That's what Arthur said when he saw her looking at it out of the corner of her eye. "When he's back. Then we can all start moving on again."

He'd been saying that for three years. The silence of the clock had become as unbearable as the noise it had once made. Annie couldn't even bring herself to dust it, although her mother tutted when she saw the state of it.

"For all I care, it can be eaten by woodworm and covered in spiderwebs," Annie said. "I'd be happy to never see that bloody clock again."

Still, she wouldn't let Arthur take it away. It had become something of a memorial to the war and as much as she had grown to hate it and all it represented, she was afraid of what might happen if it wasn't there. So it stood in the corner of the room as it always had. A frozen relic to all that had once been and all that might be once again. Time, suspended.

AT THE FRONT OF THE CHURCH, TOM MILLER REPEATS HIS prayers. His hand feels warmer beneath the vicar's gentle touch. His heart beats a little steadier.

"The baby shouldn't have come, Vicar. Not until the end of December. What day is it today?"

"The eleventh of November, Thomas. The eleventh day of the eleventh month." There is a pleasant symmetry about the date that pleases the vicar. The church bells will soon chime the eleventh hour.

"'Not yet, little one,' that's what she said when it started. 'Not yet. You're coming to us too soon. Please, not yet.'" A tear slips down Tom's cheek as his wife's words sink through his bones. He shivers as he sits in silent hope. "'The child is in distress.' That's what the midwife said. Told me there was nothing more I could do to help. Told me to come here, to pray. To pray for us all."

"And it was the right thing to do, Thomas. We all need to pray at times like this. It can give us great comfort, and your wife wouldn't want you worrying at home. She's a good woman, Annie Rawlins. Delivered many a baby in this village. Your wife couldn't be in better hands."

Tom nods. Annie Rawlins *is* a good woman. He wouldn't have left his wife and his unborn child with anyone but her.

He opens his eyes and looks around the church. He feels safe within the cool interior of the centuries-old walls. There is nothing here to harm him. Nobody to point at him or cross the street to show their disregard. It isn't their words or the names they call him that pain him so, it is the disgust on their faces, the manner in which their words are said: spiteful, venomous, and cruel. They want to hurt him with their scathing remarks as much as the snipers' bullets might have hurt him had he gone to fight. The women he used to call friend and neighbor he now avoids. The church is his sanctuary, his prayers for forgiveness his salvation.

There is a movement behind him, the softest of shuffles. He turns to see Jim Allinson, the village blacksmith and church bell ringer. Tom doesn't want to be seen. He closes his eyes to make himself invisible and hears Jim shuffle past. The sound of his limp—an old war wound from the Boer—taunts Tom's conscience. Another reminder of his own cowardice. Sometimes he finds himself incapable of walking, crippled by the steady rhythm of his unaltered gait as the soldiers on crutches struggle past.

The door to the belfry opens with a reluctant creak as Tom resumes his prayers. "Please save the child. Please, Lord. I beg you. Can you hear me?" His whispered words echo off the stone pillars, wending their way into the rafters above him. The bird flits from one beam to another. Does he stay by choice, or is he trapped?

Tom allows his tears to fall as his daughter steps through the great oak door and walks along the cold flagstones toward him. She places his coat around his shoulders.

"Come quickly, Daddy. You have to come home."

OUTSIDE THE VILLAGE POST OFFICE, HARRY PARKER, THE POST-master, clips his trouser legs neatly above each ankle and cycles away. He hopes for a puncture or for his chain to come off. He hopes that somehow the terrible burden of news he carries in his mailbag will disappear; that something will happen to change the awful truth of its contents.

Everybody sees him coming. They avoid eye contact. *Not my house*, they pray. *Please, not my house. Not today.*

Annie has lost count of the number of times Harry has cycled past her kitchen window as she washes the breakfast dishes. She's forgotten how many times her hands have stilled in the soapy water as her heart quickened. *Please don't stop. Please don't.* Since the news of Jack's death, she cannot say how often she has willed him to keep going, urging the pedals to keep moving and the wheels to keep turning. Anything but the sound of the latch on the gate. Anything but the sight of the King's telegram again.

So far, her prayers have been answered.

It is always some other poor woman who has sunk to her knees on the scullery floor as the dreaded news from the War Office is passed to her with a deep apology and the sympathies of the King and Kitchener. But Annie is not at her kitchen window today. She doesn't see Harry rest his bicycle against the wall of her house and walk slowly up the narrow pathway. She doesn't hear him bid Ada Mullins good morning as she scurries past. She doesn't hear the joyful song of the blackbird in the beech hedge or the cruel click of the latch on the gate.

But her husband, Arthur, does.

He is buttering a slice of toast when he hears the latch. He looks at the clock on the wall, makes a note of the time. Somehow, that matters. He is glad Annie isn't here. The cat stretches on her cushion in front of the Aga, blissfully unaware of the dark cloud they all live under, every morning the same dread and fear.

Arthur places the knife carefully on the plate, stands up, steadies himself for a moment against the wooden table, and walks to the door. The blackbird in the hedge sings on. Arthur thinks about dying. Thinks that when it is his own time to go, he would be content if the last thing he heard was a blackbird singing. He wonders if they have blackbirds in France. He wonders if the birds ever sing for Will and the boys.

Harry takes something from his bag as he walks up the narrow garden path; the flower beds that hug the pathway are bare brown earth. They'll be bright with snowdrops in a few months, and then daffodils and crocuses and carnations in the summer. The Rawlinses always take great care of their garden. "They'll be home before the daffodils are out, Annie." He has said it to her every year, but the yellow flowers dance in the stiff spring breeze and still the boys don't come home. It is a cruel reminder of the passing of the seasons, of the passing of time; of life. On days like today, Harry wishes he could hide away for the winter. That he, too, could hide with the daffodils.

10:59 A.M.

BENEATH THE MUDDLED EARTH, PRIVATE RAWLINS SEES A light emerging. He is being pulled, dragged. His mother is tugging at his arms, wrenching them free from the dirt. She is brushing the mud from his face, breathing for him. He chokes and gasps, gulping in desperate mouthfuls of the crisp November air. It rushes to his lungs, cold and wonderful. Again and again he gasps and breathes, gasps and breathes. Then he is being carried, lifted onto a stretcher, jostled around like a rag doll. He wants them to stop. Wants to be still. The pain is too much. The men beside him yell and shout, issuing instructions and orders. He sees their mouths move, their faces contorted with urgency, yet they don't make a sound. Just a rush of air against his face. A gentle hush. He watches the blur of blue sky above him and imagines he is floating on his canal boat, his mother beside him. She tells him he has to go home, back to Brimsworth. He wonders if Jack and the rest of the boys might come out to play—kick a ball, collect conkers, catch a minnow. He closes his eyes and lets the silence wash over him like a sigh.

On the fence post, the barn owl watches for a moment until he is certain. Only then does he take flight, his vigil complete. A single white feather drifts to the ground behind him. The only sign that he was ever there.

THE INFANT'S MOTHER SLIPS IN AND OUT OF A FEVERED CON-
sciousness, her mouth too dry to speak, her mind too confused to find the words she wants to say. She looks about the room, this humble space where all her babies have been born, where she and her brother were born, where her own mother was born—and died. So much life and loss.

She closes her eyes. Dreams of a white owl passing the window.

A feather drifts from its wing, flutters through a crack in the glass, and settles on her heart. She hears the taunting words of the women who will no longer sit beside her in church; the women who cross the street to express their disdain for the man who refused to fight, and for the wife who failed in her duty to encourage him to go. She wants to shout at them. But she can't. Never has. "It's best to remain silent, Vera. What good would it do to stand in the street and have a great row? They have their opinions and we have ours. Don't give them the satisfaction of seeing how their words upset you. Walk tall. Bid them good morning. Smile. When this is all over, we will all sit together in church again. You'll see."

Dear Tom. Such a gentle giant of a man. She wants her son to grow up to be just like him: principled and kind-hearted.

Her son. Where is he?

She opens her eyes a fraction, sees the woman in the room, the white peak of her cap, the stiff starch of her apron. Why is she still here? So much time has passed. It must be a week, maybe more. The woman is hunched over something, talking to someone. And then she is lifting something impossibly small and still. Vera grips the bedsheets as she tries to clamber away from the searing cramps in her womb. Something is wrong. She can sense it. She lifts her head. "The baby?" The words are all she can manage. Her head feels like a lump of slate. She lets it fall back against the sodden pillow and listens to the crunch of gravel on the path outside the house. The click of the latch on the gate. Time slows and stills.

"WHAT DO YOU HAVE FOR ME TODAY THEN, HARRY?" ARTHUR likes to confront things head-on. He believes that if you fear the worst, the worst will happen. He will not give in to his fear. "Did I win the pools? Can I buy Buckingham Palace?"

Harry Parker smiles. "Ah, there's Arthur Rawlins. Never without a smile on your face. Don't know how you do it, Arthur. I really don't." Arthur holds out his hand and prays for the familiar handwriting of his son and not the typed formality of the War Office. "A letter today, Arthur. All the way from France."

Arthur grips the door handle and takes a breath. "Well, isn't that a thing. Annie will be pleased when she gets back."

"Another delivery, is it?" They've all noticed the increase in births since the war. Nine months after the men come home on leave, the babies arrive.

"Been out all night. At the Millers'."

Harry's face falls. "Ah. I'm heading there next."

"If you see Annie, tell her she's a letter from Will waiting for her. Lord knows what's keeping her this time. Some women would have had three babies by now."

"Will do."

The postmaster tips his cap and walks back down the garden path, his heart heavy with the burden he carries in his bag. He wishes Arthur had invited him in for tea. Wishes he could stall time.

Arthur waits for Harry to cycle off before he closes the back door. He rests his forehead against it, breathing a deep sigh of relief. The envelope shakes in his hand.

He returns to his buttered toast and says a silent prayer of thanks as he sits at the kitchen table and reads his son's words.

Somewhere in France. October 30th, '18.

Dear Mother,

I hope this finds you well. Not much to tell this time. I just wanted to wish you a happy birthday for next week. I hope the bonfires will be burning for Guy Fawkes. I'll be seeing a different sort of fireworks, of that you can be certain. There is talk of an agreement with Fritz. They say there'll be an Armistice before the year is out. I can hardly let myself believe it, so we fight on.

Thank you for the OXO cubes—they really do make the soup taste so much better. And if you could see your way to a packet of smokes next time you write, that would be good of you. I am collecting the little cards in the packets. It is cricketers this time. I only need two more for the set.

I hope Father is well and that the influenza is not affecting the village too badly.

I remain your loving son,
Will

The cat stands, stretches, and meows to be let out. Simple, ordinary things that punctuate the hour, the day, a year, a life.

Time moves on.

11:00 A.M.

As the church bells chime the first stroke of the hour of eleven, Annie flinches. Two minutes have passed. Two minutes is too long. Each chime sends a chill to her heart. Still the infant struggles to breathe; to be.

The echo of the eleventh chime passes. All is silent for a heartbeat and then the bells begin to peal, crying out their news, sending the message rushing over rooftops and barns, through open windows and down chimney pots. The villagers of Brimsworth stop to listen. Like a wildfire sweeping the land, England hears. Parish after parish, city after city, town after town, village after village learns the news they have all been waiting to hear for so very long.

"It is over!" they cry, falling into the arms of friends and neighbors, grasping the hands of strangers and lovers as they absorb the news. "It is over."

After four long, dreadful years, it is over. Their boys, their husbands, their brothers and fathers can come home. The tears fall with a thousand thanks and sorrows. In quiet corners of dimly lit homes, mothers and wives sink to their knees, lamenting the loss of their husbands and sons more keenly than ever before. It is over, and yet the ringing of the bells seems to mock them. It feels as though their struggle has only just begun.

At the public baths, young Agnes Robson rushes in to tell the women. "Did you hear? The war—it's over? They're coming home. Our boys are coming home!"

Of the five women she tells, only one has any cause to celebrate.

She puts her head in her hands and sobs silently. The others have lost everyone: sons and husbands. Gone.

They look at young Agnes, absorb the news for a moment, and continue to scrub their weather-beaten skin.

"That's as may be, Agnes," one of them remarks. "That's as may be. But I've still a week of grime to shift."

"But . . . aren't you pleased? We can all get back to normal now. It's over!"

The woman stops her scrubbing and looks at the young girl. "Nothing will ever get back to normal, Agnes. Nothing is over for the likes of me. Nothing can bring them back. Not even the end of the war means the war is over. It will never be over for some of us." She picks up the soap and scrubs with renewed vigor at her arms. "Not all the water or soap in the country can wash away our suffering." Her tears slide down her ruddy cheeks. "What was it for, eh? What the bloody hell was it all for?"

Tom and Beth Miller are at their cottage gate when Bill Lacy comes running toward them, his arms flailing in great circles like the sails on the flour mill.

"Did you hear? Did you hear? It's over, lad. It's over!"

Tom nods. "I did, Bill. I did." He takes his daughter's hand and they rush inside.

THE WHITE CAP IS THE FIRST THING WILL SEES WHEN HE STIRS. A white cap, standing in a stiff peak, like the Alps when they have snow on them. He will go there, someday.

She has her back to him, standing perfectly still, gazing out of the small gap at the side of the field tent. She is bathed in a soft peach light. It is a peculiarly pretty light. Will wishes he had his brushes and oils. He would paint her. Right here. He tries to lift his hands to frame her between his fingers, but winces with pain as he tenses his muscles. His fingers brush the cool of the sheets. His arms lie idle at his sides. A light breeze tugs at her skirt, moving it around her ankles like seaweed beneath the waves. She takes small sips from a mug—tea, he presumes—or perhaps she prefers coffee. He would like to know. He would like to know so much more about her.

He turns his head carefully the other way, looking around, trying to remember. Slowly, it comes back to him: the explosion, the smothering earth. He starts to panic, the bile rising in his throat. The bedsheets are pulled so tight across him that he cannot move his arms or legs. He tries to cry out but he cannot hear. He cries again, louder. She rushes to him, her mouth moving, but he cannot hear her. For an awful moment, he is back in his earthen tomb. Her mouth keeps moving as she looks at him, her eyes fixed on his so that there is nothing and nobody else in the world.

She has the prettiest eyes. Her hand, in his, so soft like velvet. She loosens the blankets, shakes his pillow, helps him to raise his head, gives him something to drink, and lays him gently back down. She stays with him, sits on the side of the bed, holds his hand. He grips it tight in return.

His breathing slows. His heart beats softer within his chest.

"You're very pretty." His words the softest whisper.

Her cheeks flush a beautiful shade of pink, just like the carnations in his mam's garden.

The nurse straightens the edge of her starched white apron and moves on to the next bed, but she looks back over toward him and in that very moment, he feels alive.

He says a prayer of thanks as he thinks of his mother and the words that brought him back from the earth. "Thank you, Mam," he whispers. "Thank you."

He closes his eyes and drifts into a peaceful sleep, visions of pink carnations dancing in the breeze in the garden.

THE COLOR SPREADS OUTWARD FROM THE CENTER OF THE IN-fant's chest, like paint in water. It moves over him, blotting out the blue and turning it a beautiful glowing pink.

Annie gasps. "Oh, Lord. That's it, little one. That's it."

The color floods his body with life. It is so astonishing it is like watching him being born all over again. His tiny fingers flex and scrunch into the tightest of balls. His toes and legs jerk and while the church bells ring out, Annie hears the most wonderful sound, as the child lets out the biggest cry. It is the greatest affirmation of life that Annie has ever heard. She swaddles him quickly, hugging him tight to her chest. She can feel his tiny little sparrow's heart fluttering against her breast.

"There, there, now," she whispers, laughing through her tears of relief. "There, there, now. That's the boy. You let it all out. You tell us all about it."

Tom and Beth rush into the room.

"You have a mighty fine son here, Mr. Miller. A mighty fine son indeed."

She carries him toward the narrow window, where the sun is

just peeping out from behind a cloud. The light dances into the room, brightening everything. "He's a real beauty, Mr. Miller. A real beauty. Gave us a bit of a fright there for a minute or two, but everything seems to be quite all right now."

With the sound of her child's cry, Vera Miller stirs from her dreaming. She takes the tiny bundle from Annie and lets the child suckle hungrily and noisily at her breast.

As the Miller family huddles together on the bed watching their tiny miracle learn how to be alive, Annie busies herself, tidying away the soiled rags and towels and bedsheets. She sets coal on the fire until it catches and the flames lick and spit with life. She leaves the small room then, sets the kettle on the range, and makes everyone a good strong cup of tea.

Only when she is leaving does she ask Tom what the church bells were pealing for.

"It's over, Annie. The war. It's over."

Her fingers fall still as she buttons her coat to the collar. "Well, well. Isn't that wonderful news. The news we've all been waiting for." She puts out a hand to steady herself against the dresser as she snaps her medical bag closed. Her knees are weak beneath her skirt. Her hands tremble.

"You get home now to Arthur and wait for your Will to come home. How about that then, Annie. We'll never forget this day, will we?"

"We certainly will not, Tom." She instinctively offers her hand for him to shake. It is a gesture. An olive branch on behalf of all the women in the village. "I'll be back a little later to check how everything is. A good feed and some rest should see him right."

As she opens the door to leave, the postmaster props his bicycle against the low stone wall at the front of the house. His cheeks are pinched; his face is drawn. Annie notices a telegram in his hand.

"Morning, Annie."

"Morning, Harry." She keeps her head down, pulls her shawl around her shoulders as she passes through the gate.

Harry places a hand on her arm. "Arthur says to hurry on home. Letter from Will."

She stalls; looks up at him. She wants to drop to her knees and weep but she is too proud. "Thank you." Her voice is a whisper on the breeze. "Thank you, Harry." She glances at the piece of paper in his hand, looks back toward the door to the little cottage. He shakes his head. "And God bless you, Harry. God bless us all."

She puts her head down and makes for home, the knock on the Millers' door behind her a sickening punch to her stomach. There is nothing more she can do here; whatever words are contained in that telegram, they will have to face it without her.

She walks briskly through the village, along the rutted lanes and roughshod roads, autumn leaves skittering along beside her. She enjoys the sun at her back now that it has won the battle with the clouds. The breeze tugs at her cap and hair. It feels urgent, blowing her along. She feels alert; alive. She can't wait to get home and begins to run.

Arthur is waiting for her, standing in the sunshine on the back step. She runs to him, throws her bag down onto the shale path, and throws her arms around him.

"It is true, Arthur? Is it true it's over?"

He looks at her, takes her face in his hands. He nods. "It's over, love."

They look into each other's eyes and understand as they hold each other, weeping for the son they have lost and for the son who will return to them and for everything that has passed in the years between.

IN THE STATION MASTER'S COTTAGE, TOM MILLER PUTS THE SLIM piece of paper onto the table and walks over to the sideboard. He picks up the photograph and runs his fingers over the glass to brush away the dust that has settled there. Such a proud lad in his uniform. So like her. It seems especially cruel that they should learn of his death on this day, of all days. Killed five days ago.

"They took you five days too soon, Danny," he whispers to the face in the photograph. "Just five days."

From the bedroom, Vera hears the muffled exchanges at the back door. She watches the postmaster cycle away. Head down. The baby lies at her breast. Pink and warm and content.

Her daughter sits at her side, watching. "What will we call him, Mam?"

"I don't know, love. What do you think?"

Tom walks into the room. He is tired-looking. He has something in his hand.

Vera flinches. "What did Harry bring?" She looks at her husband and all the years collapse in on her so that everything becomes this one small moment. A second, to change everything.

He hangs his head.

She looks down at her sleeping child. "Is it our Danny?"

"Yes. Yes, love. It is."

She steadies herself. "When did it happen?"

"Five." He can barely say it. "Five days ago."

"How?"

"Sniper. Wouldn't have known a thing. Quick and clean."

They have learned to do this over the years, to pray that when the time comes it will be quick and clean. Not a gas attack. Not lying for hours, dying in a filthy field. Not panicked and afraid and alone and in pain. "Quick and clean?"

"Yes, love."

She closes her eyes. Sees her twin brother. Young, smiling, fresh-faced, ready for whatever might come. He was brave. He had nearly made it. She rubs the top of her child's downy hair. "We'll call him Danny, after his uncle who gave his life so that our son could have his."

The child opens his eyes and looks at his mother. He understands. The smallest sigh escapes his rosebud lips. It drifts around the room, collecting all the worry and sadness, pushing it out of the open window, setting it free to play with the clouds.

It is dark when he wakes again. She is still there, beside him. The candlelight casts a shadow across her face.

"What day is it?"

"November eleventh."

His hearing is still affected. Her words are muffled and far away, yet he hears her. He knows that date. "Still?"

She smiles. Nods. "Still."

"The day the war ended."

"That's right. The day the war ended. Or so they tell us." She turns her head, looking around the rows and rows of stretchers and makeshift beds. "Not that you'd know much about that when you look around this place."

"Where am I?"

"A clearing station." She stands up, smooths the creases in the sheets. "You're going to be all right, you know, Private Rawlins. You're one of the lucky ones."

"What happened?"

She busies herself with a jug of water and a towel. "A shell." She sees the muscles tighten at his jaw. The tremble in his hand. "But you mustn't think about it. You're here now. Safe."

"My mam came to me," he whispers. "She told me I had to live." The nurse smiles and checks his temperature. "Is it over then?" he asks. "Like they say?"

"They've agreed an Armistice, yes. The fighting has stopped." She pauses for a moment. "Listen."

Will strains to hear. The only sounds are muffled coughs and moans from the beds around him. "I can't hear very well."

"You can. It's just so quiet. No explosions. No guns. It's so strange. I've forgotten what that sort of silence sounds like."

Will thinks about this for a moment. She is right. "It really is over, isn't it?"

She nods. "It just came too late for some." Her eyes fill with tears that break Will's heart. "Oh, it's silly of me to be crying when we should all be celebrating, but I can't stop thinking about the men who died yesterday—and this morning, and a few minutes ago. After all this time, all these years. What a dreadful, dreadful waste." She takes a handkerchief from her pocket and dabs her cheeks before smoothing her skirt and apron and adjusting a pin against her cap. "Anyway, you don't need me making you all maudlin, Private Rawlins. You've to get better so we can ship you out of here and get you home to your mother." She makes a note of something on a small pad of paper. "And your wife."

"I'm not married."

"Well, to your sweetheart then."

He looks at her. He has never seen anyone more beautiful. "And what if my sweetheart were already here. Right here, beside me. What then?"

She smiles, her cheeks as pink as rosebuds.

Somewhere in France. November, '18

Dearest Mother,

I am sure you will all have heard the news that the hostilities are at an end and the war is over. I know how much this will bring such happiness and relief to everyone in Brimsworth. We cannot quite believe it ourselves. It will be some time before we are demobilized and can finally come home, but for now please know that I am alive and well!

I am under the care of the nurses at a field hospital. I was involved in a shelling bombardment on the day hostilities ceased but am recovering well under the care of a very kind young nurse—from Tadcaster would you believe! Her name is Rosemary Bright and you really couldn't wish to meet a lovelier lass. I hope she might come for tea when we are home. I have told her all about your famous apple pie so I hope the trees have been generous this autumn and that the larder is full.

Please know that I think about Jack often. We have all spoken of those who fell. We think about them more now that it is at an end than at any other time.

There is not much more to say so I will sign off. How strange to think this will be the last letter I will write from here. So many words have been written, but so much remains unsaid. And perhaps that is how it should be. I never want to talk of this war again. I want to forget I was ever here. I want to walk along the stream barefoot and feel the slippery stones. I want to watch the tadpoles in the pond. I want to sit in the chair in the front room when the sun slips through the window and listen to the blackbird singing in the hedge outside. I want to lie in bed at night and watch the stars and hear nothing other than the church bells and the hoot of an owl. So much has changed, but I also know that much has stayed the same. It is that which we must cherish.

I remain your loving son,
Will

P.S. I saw a single red poppy in a field as we left the clearing station for the field hospital. I asked the ambulance driver to stop and pick it for me. I have enclosed it in this letter. It is for Jack and for all those who fell among those fields where the poppies once grew.

OF ALL THE LETTERS SHE RECEIVED DURING THE WAR, ANNIE Rawlins kept just two. The only letter Jack had ever written, telling her of the poppies in the fields, and the letter Will had written soon after the Armistice was declared, a single red poppy pressed between the pages.

Life, and time, marched on as the soldiers marched home that spring. The daffodils danced in the breeze in Annie's garden, and the poppies grew once more in the fields of France.

For Dad and Grandpa Tom.
With love.

About the Authors

Jessica Brockmole is the author of the internationally bestselling *Letters from Skye*, which was named one of *Publishers Weekly*'s Best Books of 2013.

Hazel Gaynor is the *New York Times* and *USA Today* bestselling author of *The Girl Who Came Home* and *A Memory of Violets*. *The Girl Who Came Home* won the RNA Historical Romantic Novel of the Year, 2015. Born in Yorkshire, England, Hazel now lives in Ireland with her husband and two children.

Evangeline Holland was raised on both coasts and straight down the middle of America, where the differing landscapes and cultures inspired her love of history. She is the founder of Edwardian Promenade, an acclaimed blog for Edwardian/World War I history, and has written for various history magazines. Her fiction includes *An Ideal Duchess* and its sequel. She currently lives in Southern California, with a possessive and territorial cat, a perpetually disastrous kitchen, and rooms full of books.

Marci Jefferson spent years writing procedure manuals as a nursing administrator before she realized such writing lacked the sweeping adventure she longed for. Her royal novels *Girl on the Golden Coin* and *Enchantress of Paris* received high acclaim, including a *Publishers Weekly* starred review and coverage by local and national media. Marci is pursuing her nurse practitioner's license while plotting her next novel.

Kate Kerrigan is the *New York Times* bestselling author of the Ellis Island Trilogy. Other novels include *Recipes for a Perfect Marriage* and *The Dress*. She lives in Ireland, where she writes a weekly newspaper column in the *Irish Mail*.

Jennifer Robson is the *USA Today* and international bestselling author of *Somewhere in France*, *After the War Is Over*, and *Moonlight Over Paris*. She holds a doctorate in modern history from the University of Oxford. Jennifer lives in Toronto with her husband and young children.

Heather Webb is an author, freelance editor, and blogger at award-winning writing sites WriterUnboxed.com and Writers in the Storm. Her works have been translated into three languages and have received national starred reviews. Heather is a member of the Historical Novel Society and the Women's Fiction Writers Association, and she may also be found teaching craft-based courses at a local college.

Beatriz Williams is the *New York Times, USA Today,* and international bestselling author of *The Secret Life of Violet Grant, A Hundred Summers,* and *Tiny Little Thing.* An honors graduate of Stanford University and with an MBA in finance from Columbia University, Beatriz spent several years as a corporate strategy consultant in New York and London before turning to historical fiction. She now lives with her husband and four children near the Connecticut shore, where she divides her time between writing and laundry.

Lauren Willig is the *New York Times* bestselling author of sixteen works of historical fiction. Her books have been translated into more than a dozen languages, awarded the RITA, Booksellers Best, and Golden Leaf awards, and chosen for the American Library Association's annual list of the best genre fiction. A graduate of Yale, Lauren has a graduate degree in history from Harvard and a JD from Harvard Law. She lives in New York City, where she now writes full-time.

BOOKS BY THE AUTHORS FEATURED IN
FALL OF POPPIES

AVAILABLE NOW

A DUCHESS'S HEART
BY EVANGELINE HOLLAND

ENCHANTRESS OF PARIS
BY MARCI JEFFERSON

LAND OF DREAMS
BY KATE KERRIGAN

MOONLIGHT OVER PARIS
BY JENNIFER ROBSON

RODIN'S LOVER
BY HEATHER WEBB

THE OTHER DAUGHTER
BY LAUREN WILLIG

AT THE EDGE OF SUMMER
BY JESSICA BROCKMOLE
ON SALE MAY 2016

THE GIRL FROM THE SAVOY
BY HAZEL GAYNOR
ON SALE JUNE 2016

A CERTAIN AGE
BY BEATRIZ WILLIAMS
ON SALE JUNE 2016